ALSO BY LAURA HENDRIE

Stygo

Remember Me

Remember Me

A NOVEL

LAURA HENDRIE

Henry Holt and Company
New York

Henry Holt and Company, LLC
Publishers since 1866
115 West 18th Street
New York, New York 10011

Henry Holt® is a registered trademark of
Henry Holt and Company, LLC

Published in Canada by Fitzhenry & Whiteside Ltd.
195 Allstate Parkway, Markham, Ontario L3R 4T8.

Library of Congress Cataloging-in-Publication Data
Hendrie, Laura, 1954–
Remember me : a novel / Laura Hendrie.
        p.   cm.
    ISBN 0-8050-6218-1 (hb : alk. paper)
              I. Title.
PS3558.E49523R46   1999   99-13302
813'.54—dc21   CIP

Henry Holt books are available for special promotions and
premiums. For details contact: *Director, Special Markets.*

First Edition 1999

Designed by Lucy Albanese

Printed in the United States of America
All first editions are printed on acid-free paper. ∞

1   3   5   7   9   10   8   6   4   2

THIS BOOK IS FOR

NIP, DON, AND ANDRE.

Acknowledgments

This book was made possible with the support of the Ucross Foundation, the Yaddo Foundation, and the Richard and Hinda Rosenthal Foundation via the American Academy of Arts and Letters.

I thank Sally Spillane for her embroidery books and Seymour Solomon, M.D., for his medical expertise.

Grateful appreciation goes to the committee, formed by various Societies of the Colonial Dames of America, who helped collect and record hundreds of historical samplers for their 1921 publication, *American Samplers,* from which this novel draws much of its inspiration as well as numerous direct quotes.

The advice, encouragement, support, and faith of many people helped make this story better. Thank you, Fred Ramey, Greg Michalson, Kent Haruf, Richard Giles, Kelly Wolpert, Karen Lound, Bob Shacochis and Catfish Petersen, Nat Sobel, Ray Roberts, Jan Wolosin, Ellen Hendrie, Jane Hendrie, and my neighbor Vickie Deane.

Most of all and always, thank you, Mark.

Part I

1

*No other care than this I knew
But perseverance brought me through.*

—from an American sampler, 1824

It starts on a gray afternoon in October with me standing at the edge of the highway, smoking a last cigarette and trying to believe that somebody would be along any minute. Ruben Johnson, for instance. He was supposed to plow the roads after storms. Or somebody on their way back from Madrillas. Somebody just out for a drive. It could happen. I wrapped the scarf Harmon Waters had bought for my birthday around my head and under my chin, squinting against the light. On days like this when the wind wasn't blowing yet and the fields so smooth and quiet, you could hear the plow coming miles away. You could hear anything miles away. But there was nothing yet, nothing except snow for every direction and a half-buried fence post and the smoke of my breath. I had four miles to walk—two and a half straight across the flats to the foothills, then one mile of curves through Holt Canyon to the bridge at the edge of town, and then a final half mile across town to the motel—four miles, and the road nothing more than a braid of tire tracks. Maybe three cars had traveled it since the storm. Maybe less. Because it was a Sunday, maybe nobody would come.

On the other hand, at least I'd caught a ride over the pass. Whether or not I had to walk the rest of the way didn't matter. I'd still be home before dark. I thought about my landlord, and how he'd be waiting for me, how he'd have coffee going, and some brandy, maybe dinner on the stove. He'd have to blow off steam at me first, bang around his office and kick the wastebasket, yell at me for screwing up my career and leaving him in the lurch, for being so young and selfish and stupid. You damn little fool, he'd shout. And I *had* been a fool. As long as he didn't try to rub it in, I could admit that. I was just glad to be back.

I picked up the bag of supplies I'd bought in Madrillas and tucked my hands in my coat sleeves. It would be a long walk—longer if the wind came up before I'd reached the protection of the trees—but at least I was finally heading in the right direction. I checked the highway one last time to see if I was going to get a ride or not, and then, without looking back to see if the dog was still there, I crossed the highway and stepped into one of the tire tracks that aimed toward Queduro.

I was an embroiderer by trade. Most people in Queduro were. It was a sheepherder's tradition that became popular sometime after the mining boom ended, when our town was left with nothing more than a few dozen Spanish, Indian, and Irish families who knew each other too well—also three bicycles, one tractor, five horses, no church, no school, no paved roads, a lot of boarded-up buildings that would never be used again, and a handful of untended sheep that ran in and out of houses at will, causing feuds between neighbors and sometimes shoot-outs at the bar. Those were the days when the road through Holt Canyon was so bad that a snowstorm in October could mean no one would be leaving the valley until spring. That's why needlework was so important. I'm sure, as a town it changed us: the way we saw things, the way we looked and talked to each other, the way we got along, the way we lived. Maybe even the way we got old. Any work does if you do it long enough. But for more than a century, nobody in Queduro took needlework seriously. Nobody considered it a career. It was just a sensible way to pass the time every winter when there was no money to be made.

But that, of course, was before the tourists. Nobody knew how they found us or when we realized we had something they wanted, but by the time I was born in 1969, embroidery meant money. Real money. If you knew your stitches and sewed hard all winter and had a clean inventory ready for spring when the tourists started showing up, embroidery was a way to get rich.

Or so said the inheritance embroiderers. They were the top earners, the ones who'd spent their lives on the needle, who could brag that they'd known how to sew an alphabet before they'd learned how to read one. They owned the creatorship rights to historical patterns that had been handed down through their families for generations, silk-on-silk work that could go for as much as fifteen, even twenty grand a pop. Work that could end up in books about historical embroidery, magazines about folk art, or even museums in New York. That kind of work.

Then there were the trade embroiderers like me, who didn't have a family's reputation to lean on or a set of inherited patterns. We were the ones who'd started late in life and couldn't brag about museums. Magpies, they called us, because in summer, when the season started, we had to use every trick in the book just to get the customers' attention and draw them down the line past every other trade embroiderer who was trying the same thing. That's why getting the right sales booth was so important.

I hunched down in my parka and glared at them as I walked by: thirty-five booths, all closed and locked for winter now, lined up out there in the snowy field like a row of wide-spaced teeth. Ever since I'd started calling myself an embroiderer, the Committee had been assigning me the lousiest booth they had: thirty-three. Thirty-three was way at the end of the line, about as far away from the heart of the sales area as I could get without being mistaken for a Porta Potti. Every time I asked for a better location, they voted me down. Dick Sweeny said I hadn't been a professional long enough. "Look at it from our side, Rose," he'd said. "How would you like it if you'd given twenty years to the tradition and then someone with only half that starts demanding an equal share of the crowd? Maybe next year we'll figure out how to move you in a little closer to the action—but for now you just keep at it."

As if I hadn't. I'd buckled down and learned my stitches, hadn't I? I'd learned them without any help from Dick Sweeny and his Commerce Committee. Considering the fact that I'd been given such a lousy booth every summer, I'd done damn well. Kept my head above water anyway. Maybe I had to paddle a little harder than most and maybe I didn't always get the price I wanted, but as long as I used a few of the traditional stitches in every piece, glued a Queduro Authentic tag on the back, and had my signs up promising a bargain, I was usually sold out by August. That's what the Committee didn't like. Even without their help, I could still survive.

The wind pushed the snow in little breaths across the fields ahead of me. I tucked my chin into my collar and walked harder. The real reason I hadn't gotten a better booth was because I wasn't willing to spout the Committee's version of Queduran history. Last spring I'd agreed to try— I'd even memorized some of the brochure they hand out to the tourists— but when I tried to say it out loud, I just couldn't. It was all slop and goo: how Queduran embroidery was not a hobby but the only known antidote to our long, dreary New Mexican winters when the roads were blocked by snow; how our sheep ranchers and apple farmers had depended on it to keep their minds off poverty, disease, death; how our miners had used it to keep from killing each other or themselves when the ground was too frozen to dig, and how those who survived the miners had done it because there was nothing else to do; how personal loss, starvation, and despair lay behind each stitch of the tradition but how, in spite of all that, many of the original motifs and poems had survived, passed down through the memories of all the hardy survivors to the present day, and so on. All of which was true, but I thought it sounded pathetic, especially when the men did it. I'd watch them hanging portraits of their Irish, Indian, and Spanish descendants out in front of their booths, hawking their hardships, trotting out the tragedies of dead parents and grandparents and great-grandparents for tourists who didn't even care. Why preach suffering like it's something holy? I shivered into my coat. I needed to make money next summer even more than I had last summer, but I couldn't see making it that way. When the tourists asked me why we all did embroidery, I'd just say it was a local tradition and leave it at that. Same as always. As long as they knew they were getting a good deal on a tradition, they didn't have to hear all the reasons why.

But that was summer. Now it was October, the tourists were gone, and instead of settling down and getting started on my work for next spring, I'd wasted a whole month with Harmon Waters. I was way behind schedule. I hadn't even drawn up my patterns. While I walked, I tried not to think about it. Worry wrecks the nerves, and nerves in embroidery are everything. At least I'd gotten my supplies in. All I had to do now was move into my cabin at the motel, set up my work, and get going. Five months to catch up, six if the winter was a long one. As soon as I'm up to speed, I kept thinking. But every time I looked up and saw how far I still had to walk, all I could think was how all the other embroiderers were already up to speed, already set up and busy with their needles. They weren't worried about whether or not Ruben plowed the roads. For all they cared, he could wait until spring. They were already snugged in for winter and stitching away at their inventories, right on schedule. How many times had they warned me about men like Harmon? How many times had they told me to stay focused on the work? In all that quiet out there, I could almost hear them gloating about it, *Too bad, Rose, too bad*.

I shook it off and walked harder. I'd been behind before and come out ahead. I'd been through plenty worse than this. This was nothing. So what if I'd gone off with a Texan and then decided to come back? So what? Who hadn't cut the wrong thread now and then? If they wanted to talk about me, fine. I'd lived in Queduro all my life and I was used to talk. After all, I'd had a father who'd run off when I was ten. I'd been raised by an uncle who'd been all but pecked to death by local gossip for trying to thumb his nose at embroidery. I'd heard it all, at least once. What difference did it make if they wanted to talk? As soon as I was settled in and back at work again, they'd find someone else to talk about.

I looked back over my shoulder. The dog was still following. He was a skinny black-and-white thing no bigger than a cat and wary enough to keep his distance, but he was still coming. When he saw me watching, he slowed down and sniffed at the snow, trying to look helpful. I growled and kept walking. I'd tried everything. I'd yelled at him, I'd chased him, I'd ignored him, and in Clovis, when I realized he was the reason I wasn't getting rides, I'd thrown gravel at him until he realized I meant it and ran off with his tail tucked, redeeming my faith in his intelligence. But as soon as a car stopped for me, he came running and hopped in as if he'd called for it himself. I didn't want a dog and couldn't afford to keep one, and if he was stupid enough to follow me anyway, that was his problem. He could've gone with Harmon and ended up in Texas with a back yard and steaks every night. Harmon would have been glad to offer a dog a new lease on life. Harmon with his big, cheerful, lonesome, sloppy Texan heart. It was pure relief to be on my own again.

Then I let that go and started thinking about the bathtub, an old iron claw tub that Birdie had picked up at a flea market and installed in my cabin at the Ten Tribes, the kind that takes gallons and gallons to fill and then steams away like a pot on a hot stove. The tub was one of the best things about living at the motel in winter. So wonderful it hurt to get in, water so hot I looked as if I was wearing red socks. But after I could bear it enough to sit down and then lie back in it and let it take me over, I could hardly think. What else is there in the world besides a bath? I'd have my things put away and the bed made up and my coffeepot perking out in the front room, but I'd forget all that and just slide down until my head was all the way under. I'd blow sounds and listen to my heart. I'd rub soap between my toes and along my hips and up under my breasts. I'd feel myself all over like my hands were a man in love. I hadn't had much interest in sex with Harmon, and I'd wondered about that, but it was still there; as soon as I saw myself stretching out in that bath, I could feel it stirring inside, like a little squirrel that had given up on the outside world and slowed down its heartbeat for winter.

I stopped walking to press my right elbow to my ribs, closed my eyes, and saw the mystery bruise there, yellow-brown, I imagined, and sore to the touch. But it would heal. It would all heal. I opened my eyes and then started walking again. I had to hand it to Harmon, he'd almost talked me into the mistake of a lifetime—and yet here I was, plugging my way back to town again. A little worn out, maybe a little ashamed of myself and a month behind schedule, but nowhere near to calling it quits. It's an amazing thing, how one minute you can be so sure you've made all the wrong decisions, that your life never worked right and probably never will and what's the use of going on with it, and not twenty-four hours later, there you are, thinking about a hot bath and seeing everything differently. It made me want to laugh out loud. Another breath of wind blew over the top of the snow, bitter cold, but when I looked up I was nearly to the cottonwoods at the mouth of Holt Canyon. Less than a mile and I'd be standing in the middle of town. I leaned over, scooped a handful of snow, packed it into a ball, and threw it straight up. Winter was coming and I was going to be fine.

2

Remember well & bear in mind
A faithful friend is hard to find.

—from an American sampler, 1730

But a mile is a long way in snow, and when I finally crossed the bridge my hands and feet were frozen. Of the three main streets in Queduro, Hemming would be the quickest, but it followed the bottom of the valley next to the river, in full view of the tar-paper and mud-brick and trailers perched to either side of it and, above there, stacked along the hillsides like a crowd of flat-faced sightseers, the rows of old clapboard homes, waiting for something to look at, their front picture windows flashing down toward the heart of the valley like binoculars. No, Hemming was not the route to take, and since I needed to go check on my car anyway, I went halfway up Filoselle Road instead and took the back alleys across town.

I still owned the blue '79 Plymouth station wagon that had belonged to my family—not much to look at anymore and the heater was broken, but she still moved once in a while and the locks still worked. I got out my keys, fumbled opened the lock, and got behind the wheel, the vinyl crack-ing with cold. In the back, everything I owned was frozen solid, my clothes, sheets, shoes, my Indian-head work lamp, my pots and pans, my embroidery bag, all my life before Harmon piled and freeze-dried for shipping. I pulled my parka sleeves over my knuckles, slapped the gas pedal to the floor twice, and tried the key.

The engine not only sputtered, it sounded like it might start. I held my breath for luck and tried again. It coughed, caught, coughed, and then built itself into a roar and stayed on, even when I lifted my foot off the gas. I felt better then. Not that a live engine made much difference, since I wouldn't be driving anywhere until the streets were plowed, but at least I didn't have to worry about finding someone to give me a jump.

While I waited for the car to warm up, I craned up to the rearview. Lately I'd been feeling a lot older than twenty-nine, but I still looked all right. A good strong mouth and pale freckles, the same blue eyes and proud jaw as my mother. Maybe a little bitten down from the cold, a little hollowed out from lack of sleep, but not bad. Not such a change for the worse that Birdie wouldn't know who I was. It's funny, though, how sometimes when you're outside and looking at a mirror, you can hardly recognize yourself. It's like all the details you expected to find have been glued onto a face you don't quite believe is yours. But however different I thought I looked, I'd probably look the same to him. I revved the engine and then shut it down and got out, locked the door, and pushed the key back in my pocket. At least everything was still safe.

The dog was next to the Dumpster, no doubt waiting for my next move and hoping it included food. I looked around the alley. The black brick walls against the whiteness of snow, the black telephone wires criss-crossing overhead, the windows above the drugstore with dust-colored shades—I didn't see anybody, but I knew I'd been noticed. In a town like Queduro where everybody knows everybody's business, you don't just leave for good and then show up a week later without being noticed. Everybody knew I was back. If they weren't watching out their windows by now, it was probably because they were already on the phone, spread-ing the word.

I started walking, stiff with cold. Of all the people who might decide to drive by right now, the one I wouldn't mind seeing was Frank Doby. A month ago, I'd been mad as hell at him, but it would be all right now. We'd be fine. Frank and I, we'd grown up together, and if we'd learned anything, we'd learned how to let things pass. I could picture him, the way he'd break into a full-out grin when he saw me. He wouldn't ask about Harmon, either. He'd always been that way, ever since we were kids, the kind of understanding I never had to ask for, the kind of loyalty I never had to pay back. I half expected to see his squad car pulling into the alley behind me.

It was Sunday, though, his day off. He'd be over in Madrillas, taking his wife, Angela, shopping, or to the movies. Maybe taking her down to Albuquerque to visit her folks. If the squad car came by now, it would have his new deputy, Silas K. Farrell, at the wheel. Silas K. was one of Frank's mistakes, a real loss to the taxpayers. I didn't need to deal with that.

Toes curling in and out as I walked, trying to feel them. It was probably just as well that Frank wasn't around. I needed to get settled before I saw him again, get my life back to normal. He was too much of a worrier, that was his problem. We couldn't even talk like friends anymore. Every time we tried, we just ended up back at my problems and how to fix them. It pissed me off. Maybe that hero act had earned him a Silver Star in the army, but there wasn't any need for it now. Not with me. Besides, he had his own problems. He had a whole town to answer to, a reputation to keep up, a deputy he'd never be able to trust, and a mortgage he had to pay. He had his new and, from what I'd heard, his very crazy wife, Angela, that's who he had to worry about. My problems were nothing compared to his. All I had to do was get to the Ten Tribes.

But when I got there, falling once on Flax Hill and getting soaked through to the bone, the office was locked. The neon Indian was off, there were no footprints around the door, the curtains were pulled, and when I yelled Birdie didn't answer. I tried again, and then I felt all the heat come up in me and I kicked the door hard. He was in there. Crabbiness was the only reason he wasn't letting me in, crabbiness and self-pity and the vanities of growing old. Just so I'd get spooked into thinking something had happened to him, just so I'd panic and fall all over myself with gratitude when he finally decided to open up. Birdie's tricks were too obvious, that's why they never worked. Not on me. I told that to the door and went around to the courtyard in back.

All ten cabins were locked up for winter, dark as log caves under the snow, rows of icicles hanging off the eaves like teeth. The one I always stayed in, the Ute, was at the far end. I glared at it and then cut through the snow to the back window of his office. The curtain there was pulled too, but I could hear the far-off sound of screaming and gunshots inside. I pulled my sleeve over my knuckles and knocked on the glass.

"I know you're in there," I called. "I can hear your TV."

The sound of his TV went away. I looked up at the cottonwoods arched overhead, branches bare as iron, and then back at the window, breath coming out like smoke.

"It's me, Rose. I had to walk in all the way from the highway. Ruben hasn't plowed the streets yet. Plus I fell on your damn hill."

"We're closed!" he cried. "Go away."

I studied my reflection and then put down the bag, unwrapped the scarf, flexed my fingers to get them moving, and tried to flatten my hair with both hands. My uncle, Bob Devonic, used to call it the kind of hair with its own temper, and since I hadn't cut it, it had gotten worse, but Birdie liked it anyway because it was the same dark red as my mother's. He'd never admit it, but he'd been a goner for my mother. Everybody said so and I knew it was true, because I sometimes caught him staring at me when he thought I wasn't watching. Not like a pervert, just like someone trapped underwater, like a body floating there, wondering why. If my mother hadn't died young, he'd probably have worked up the nerve to propose to her.

"Bird," I yelled, "I'm still out here!"

Wormy blue-white fingers crept around the edge of the curtain and he peered out, suspicious and old, pale eyes rimmed with pink and blinking against the light.

"What do you want?"

"What do you think I want?"

When he started to drop the curtain, I put my hand on the glass to stop him, the cold burning my fingers. "Hey, I got a dog. Look." When he did, I added, "And this week was my birthday. Remember?"

He squinted out at me. "What?"

"I just turned twenty-nine." I picked up the bag, my face so cold I was having a hard time working the muscles of it. "Let me in, okay?"

The curtain dropped and I saw myself in the window, breath spouting out before me. I heard him muttering on the other side of the curtain: *No way. Not this time. Good-for-nothing. Pissant.* I stared at myself.

"Since when did I become a pissant?"

"Since you were born. Go away."

I looked around at the cabin I was supposed to be in by now, turned back to the window and hit it with my bare knuckles, a sound as cold as all winter. "I'm going around to that door *now*, Bird. Do you hear me? I'll give you three minutes."

I went around to the front, but the door was still locked. I sagged against it. He just wanted me to know how pissed he was about my going away with Harmon. That's why he'd locked himself in and turned off his Indian. He wanted me to know he didn't need me anymore, that he could get through the winter just fine by himself. I could practically hear him screaming it at me through the window. I followed my tracks back out to the street, staring down the hill through the trees as if I might be thinking of trying someplace else. If there'd been any other place to try, I might have.

Tambour, Hemming, and Soutache ran straight as the tines of a fork along the length of the valley and then connected at the other end just before the bridge. All the buildings and houses along them snow-packed and empty, the whole valley shut down and deserted for the night, all except for Hermes, who stood at the bottom of the hill in the middle of the intersection under Queduro's blinking light, his tail wagging slow and steady as a pendulum. Hermes was a big black bony dog who'd gone blind from brain tumors. In summer when the town was full of tourists and traffic and noise, he might end up anywhere when he got lost; but in winter, all he had to do was listen for the click of the blinking light and follow it across town until he was fairly sure he was standing under it and then wait there for someone to pick him up. His owner, Teresa, would probably be too lazy to come herself. She'd call Frank. She'd remind him that retrieving her blind dog was just as important as anything else he was hired to do as sheriff, and whether or not he agreed, Frank would pull on his coat and gloves and go do it. That was Frank, always ready for duty, always first to the rescue. I was surprised he wasn't down there already.

I settled deeper into my parka. As soon as he heard I was back, he'd go check on my car for me, I could picture him doing it now, seeing how it was blocked in with snow and my footprints in the alley, knowing they were mine, taking off his cap to rub at his black hair, the way he always did when he was thinking, his jaw muscle tight, his dark eyes following my trail, wondering if he should follow it to see if I needed any help. It would be easier on both of us if he didn't.

I looked over at the dog. He was sitting a few yards away, facing the town. "If you want to take off, this is probably the time to do it, you know."

He looked at me and then back at the view. When I saw him cock forward as if he could hear someone coming, I turned and listened too. But there was nothing out there yet, just a dripping sound and the soft *womp* of snow falling off the trees over the street. I was freezing. I wiped my nose on my sleeve and then squared my shoulders and high-stepped back through the snow to Birdie's office. "I'm at the door," I yelled, "and this time it better be open! You hear me?"

It was.

Ever since the highway accident that had claimed my family and Birdie's sister in one fell swoop, I'd been spending winters at his motel.

The cabins weren't much more than glorified walk-ins and in winter just about as dark, but I could have done worse. At least they were warm and quiet and came with enough furniture to feel comfortable. I never stayed there in summer when the place was swarming with tourists, but in winter after the snows shut down the traffic, months could pass with nobody on the property but the two of us. The old man liked to pretend he was a tightwad year round, but as long as I didn't show up until after Labor Day, we could work out a deal on the rent. Most of the time he didn't even care about rent. All he wanted was somebody who could argue with him and adjust his TV antenna and fix his meals and handle the front desk when he started his drinking and then make sure he was sober if his older sister, Alice, decided to show up from Phoenix. And since all I wanted was a quiet place to stay in winter and didn't mind doing any of that, it worked out fine. It had worked out for twelve winters in a row. It was the kind of trust that unless I screwed up and did something to scare him, neither one of us needed to discuss.

The blue walls, the blue shag carpet, the blue couch and drapes, the red leather chairs, the wagon-wheel chandelier over the front desk, and all of it smelled like Pine-Sol. Birdie was nuts about Pine-Sol. Every year before he gave in to his winter thirst, he'd spray it on everything he owned. When Birdie was nervous, he sprayed Pine-Sol like a cat in heat.

"You trying to choke to death? At least crack a window or something." I looked down, fumbling for the zipper of my parka. My fingers couldn't feel anything and I couldn't see yet. "Jesus," I said, groping the wall for the light switch and nearly dropping my bag on the dog's head as he slipped in behind. "I'm frozen through."

Bird was behind the desk, gripping the edge of it as if to steady himself and staring at me bug-eyed. He had his bow tie on straight and his shirt tucked in, but his white hair was grizzling out over his ears like onion roots and he was shaking all over. I could see that he was spoiling for a fight and that he planned to give me one just as soon as he figured out how, but he hadn't shaved in preparation for it and something about him looked brittle and old. It spooked me how old he looked. I laughed.

"I thought you'd be halfway into your first bottle by now."

"I can't give you a cabin!" he cried. "Don't even ask."

"Okay." I dug around in my pocket for a Kleenex. "Just let me get my bearings."

"No!"

"You're not going to let me get my bearings?"

"You heard me! We're closed!"

I stood there dripping. "But I always stay here in winter." I stared at him. "The Ten Tribes is my home, Birdie. You know that."

"Not this winter, it isn't. By God, I'm closed for the season. Do you hear me?" When I opened my mouth, he jabbed his finger. "And don't you start, missy. I'll bet you don't have a week's worth of rent, do you? You never do. Twelve winters you've stayed here without paying full rent. Most of the time no rent at all. What do you think I am, a horn of plenty?"

I looked around the office and back at him. "So I walk four miles through snow to get here, and this is what I get."

"That's right." He was gripping the desk and trembling all over. "This is what you get."

I pushed the Kleenex in my pocket. "If you're going to act like this, I'll leave."

"Fine."

I got as far as the door. "I've spent two days hitchhiking," I said. "You understand that? I haven't had a meal since yesterday, I'm cold as hell, these boots I'm wearing feel like buckets of ice. Now, can we do this later? Just let me get settled into my cabin first."

"And which cabin is that?"

I stopped then, all the cold coming back into me at once. "What do you mean, which cabin? The cabin I've been staying in every winter for the last goddamn twelve winters."

He drew his mouth into a hard pucker and sucked air, then wiped his hand in a desperate sort of way across it. "You can't stay there."

A coldness was running like a line straight up the backs of my legs, like a fingernail scratching the blackboard. I looked around the room and back at him. "Why?"

"Because of my sister Alice. That's why."

"Ah. So that's why you're still sober." I felt the cold relax a little. "The old nag's been on your case again, huh."

"How dare you!" he sputtered. "You can't talk about her that way."

"Bird, I don't even know the woman. I learned it from you." I stepped around to the back of his recliner and lifted the curtain on the window. Alice's house stood across the street, the only other building on the hill, an old-fashioned two-and-a-half-story white Victorian that glowed like a face against the dark woods all around it. It was one of the nicer houses in town, fully furnished, with a view of the valley from her porch, but she hardly lived there because she had a condo in Phoenix she liked better.

Alice could live anywhere she wanted. Her younger sister, Florie—the one who died in the accident with my family—had left her a life insurance policy worth $200,000 back in 1985. Alice had cashed it in, bought her brother the motel as a consolation prize, and left town, though she still called at least once a week to make sure he was still grateful. Whenever she decided he wasn't, she showed up in a tan Eldorado. She was two years older than Birdie, though she didn't look it, a tall, skinny, shrivel-faced seventy-year-old with gray hair cut like a motorcycle helmet, ice-blue eyes, and cheekbones sharp as biblical commandments. Birdie always looked shrunken and weak compared to her. He said to stay away whenever she visited, and I did. I didn't like Alice. Not because she'd cashed in on the accident—if anyone in my family had taken out a life insurance policy, I'd have done the same thing—but I didn't like the way she refused to let her brother have his own life. She'd bought it for him and that meant she could show up any time. He couldn't peep a complaint. He couldn't even clear his throat. And as for his love of boozing, out of the question. Not *her* brother. According to her, he had never even enjoyed the taste. That's why I didn't mind stepping out of the picture when she was in town, because I couldn't stand watching Bird trying to be somebody else.

But looking out at the street, it seemed to me that Alice wasn't over there. Her porch was still banked with snow, and there were no tire tracks leading up the driveway to her garage. I looked back at Birdie. His hair was furred up in the back like a rabbit's tail and he was trying to unwrap a sour ball he'd picked from a dish of candy on his desk. Sobriety ruined his nerves, especially when it came unexpectedly. I looked around and saw bowls of wrapped candies on every flat surface in his office. I turned back to the window.

"I don't see anyone over there. Her chimney's not smoking. If she was in there, wouldn't she at least have a fire going?"

"I said she was coming. I didn't say she was here."

Under the light, his face looked as if it were shrinking in under the bone, leaving behind a pair of ears that were too big, his eyes a wide, helpless, red-shot blue. When he couldn't get the candy unwrapped, he slapped it against the desk and marched over to the coffee table to leer at the curtain, as if he could see right through it to her house. "She's going to sell my motel," he said. "She called this morning to tell me. She says if she sells the motel"—he stopped to steady his voice—"we can take a trip together. That's why she's coming back. To sell it."

"Why would she want to go on a trip with you?"

He glared at me. "You think a woman like that needs a reason for what she does?"

I looked down. The dog was sniffing the recliner, and I nudged him hard with my boot. For all I knew he wasn't housebroken.

"I don't understand why you let her get away with this, Bird. You never let anyone else push you around."

"Stupid, stupid—" He turned and shook his finger at me in real anger. "She's my sister, all right? She's seventy years old, and I'm the only family she has left. Not to mention that every penny in this place is hers. What was I supposed to do, hang up on her?"

He looked down at the carpet as if he'd dropped something and then grabbed another candy from the dish on the coffee table and began to work at it, arms shuddering. "These goddumb wrappers. You can't even get the things open."

"Well, this is shit." I yanked off my coat and dropped it on the floor. "Just because she hates me, I'm supposed to go sleep in my car? It's October, you know. There's nothing decent to rent now until spring—and with the money I'd have to spend on . . ." But I trailed off. Birdie was anchored in the center of the room, his fists jammed on his hips, sucking so hard on the sour ball he looked ready to pop a hole in his cheek. His lower lids were pulled down pink from sucking.

"You want all the pity for yourself," he cried. "Is that it?"

"Screw you. I don't want your pity. I want a place to live."

"Well, I want pity," he bawled. "And you know why?" He leaned over to spit the sour ball in the wastebasket. "Because I'm her brother. Not you. You can leave. You're just like everybody else. Go on, why don't you leave?" He wiped his mouth on his sleeve so hard his whole face pulled sideways. "You want to know why I have all this candy around? Because I was *this* close to pouring my first drink when she called. I had the cap open, I had the glass ready, I had the door locked, my music on. And what does she do? She calls up and says she's selling my motel and bringing me a new book to read. *How to Have Fun After Fifty*." He marched over to the TV and then back to the coffee table, stopping in front of it as if he were going to try kicking it over. "If she gives me one more book on how to have fun, Rose, I'm going to croak."

"You will not. I hate when you talk like that."

"Like what?"

"If you want a drink, drink. Throw out the candy and drink. Just stop acting stupid."

"Can you imagine us on a trip together?" he went on. "Hopping buses and trains and planes and me sitting there with the guidebooks and candy: 'Yes, Alice, we will, Alice, you're right, Alice.' When I asked her where she wanted to go, do you know what she said?" He turned to me. "Uganda. So I say to her, 'Al, just where in Uganda?' And she says, 'Don't worry, I'll take care of it.' Do you know what that does to a man, Rose? Do you have any idea what that says about me?"

"It says you're a survivor. That's what it says."

But he wasn't listening. He looked at the *Let's Live* magazine on the table, looked at it as if he wanted to burn it to ashes, but instead he sat down on it and cupped his head. "I told her I couldn't sell the motel. I told her she should stay in Phoenix and forget this craziness. But no, she wouldn't listen, not Alice. She says I need some fun in my life."

For a moment I thought he was crying. I looked down at my clothes. They say the trick to staying warm is layers, but in all the years I'd tried it, it hadn't proved much more than a lot of extra weight to carry around and too much time to take off. I decided to at least get rid of the boots; they were Harmon's galoshes, size ten, and even with three pairs of socks, as soon as I pulled out the newspaper I'd stuffed in around the tops, I could step out of them without undoing the buckles. I set them in front of Birdie's space heater and sat. The dog gave a little sigh, turned three times, and curled against the door.

There was a photograph on the mantel of Birdie's sisters, one of those blown-up colorized photos from the forties with a velvet background. They'd shared the same light-colored eyes, sharp cheekbones, and long noses, but on Florie everything looked as if it fit together right. The pretty one, that's how Birdie always summed her up. Alice, on the other hand, sat stiffly for the camera in a complicated-looking hairdo and a shapeless dark dress, everything about her saying she was the older one, the steady one, the one who would last. And she *had* lasted, though not with much success. She'd tried nursing school, and after she got bored with that, she volunteered to go work in some clinic in Africa, where she spent three weeks having the time of her life lecturing black people on personal hygiene until she caught some tropical disease and got sent back to the States. Since then she'd lived in Phoenix and, according to Birdie, spent all kinds of money on medicines, doctors, spas, and anything else that promised her health and demanded her money. It was sad, really, what people like Alice could do with two hundred thousand bucks. I took off my socks. They were soaked through, and so was the pair underneath. I took off all three pairs and laid them in front of the heater. My toes were red as berries.

"Tell me what you want me to do, Birdie."

He sighed and dropped his hands. "Go see Frank Doby. He knows the people who built that summerhouse on the south side. Maybe they need a caretaker."

"They hired Pech Salazar last month to caretake."

"Well, go talk to Frank anyway. He'll find something. He always has before."

"I don't want Frank involved in my life right now." I bent over and held my toes. They were cold as stones. "He's got too many problems of his own."

"And you think I don't?" Bird was pressing his fists into his legs to keep from trembling. "You're the one who says anything's a possibility. Why can't you just go back to wherever you were staying before you decided to run off with that monkey?"

It was pressing in on me, pushing down hard like a thumb. *Look at the weather out there*, I wanted to shout. *What do you think I am, a polar bear?* But I didn't. Birdie had never pitied me for anything, and I was grateful for it. I pressed my knees against my cheeks. "Why can't you just keep the motel open until it sells?"

He sighed and sank deeper. "It is open."

"You mean it's just closed to me?"

"What can I say? Alice made it clear from the start that you weren't welcome here. If she found out you've been staying here every winter since, I'd never hear the last of it."

We were quiet. He was staring at the carpet, his wrinkles pale and unsettled. I nodded and squeezed my toes under. I was thinking about my Uncle Bob, how he used to say that Queduro held nothing but uninvented opportunities. He said it was like living beside a river full of salmon, and all we had to do was figure out how to reel them in. He liked to say he couldn't sleep at night for all the opportunities we were missing. Sometimes, as proof, he'd take me and my little brother over to the south end of town to see Edna Big Spear. Edna had been born with no fingers on her left hand, and every summer she wrapped herself in an old Indian blanket and sat beside the lithium springs next to the bridge, selling Dixie paper cups at fifty cents apiece. The lithium water was free and nobody had to buy a cup from Edna if they didn't want to, but tourists always did. She'd tell them that if they wanted to take a picture of her, they could give her a dollar more, and they did that too. Bob had called her a genius. "You see that? Now *that's* what I mean, kid. No overhead, no advertising, no competition, and she's made a place for herself out of nothing but some water and a few cups." He said all his best ideas came from watching Edna work. In my mind's eye, I could see her now, braids gone gray and thin, body wider than ever, bending slowly to straighten the little rows of white cups at her feet. Last summer, she'd all but admitted to me that she was glad my uncle wasn't around to admire her work anymore. "Damn man, always talking and talking," she said, tilting back to drink her beer. "He was pretty crazy even before that accident, you know. If your family had lived through it, he probably would have fucked you all up anyway."

I tucked my hands up in my armpits and shivered. I missed Bob like crazy sometimes, but it was just the next thing and the next, that's what life boiled down to. It was what lay ahead of you, not what you'd left behind. That's what Bob would have said.

"Okay," I said. "So what happens if you don't tell Alice I'm here?"

Birdie looked at me blankly.

"She can't see my cabin from her house. Your office blocks the view. I could tape a blanket over the window so she couldn't see my work light on. I could come and go by the bathroom window. Or I could just stay inside." As I said it, it seemed possible. "If you tell her the motel's empty, she won't need to check, will she? And there's snow. She hates snow. She'll probably just put up a For Sale sign on the bulletin board at Steelhead's Market and then sit in her house waiting for the phone to ring. Don't you think?"

The blue vein in the hollow at the side of his head was beginning to pump. He shivered away from me. "She'll know. Somebody will tell her you're here."

"Why should they? She hasn't had a friend in this town since she cashed in that life insurance check and turned up her nose at everybody. I'll bet she could stay all winter and not get a single phone call." I waited. "Bird, she just needs to be with you for a while. I'm sure of it. Maybe she just wants to make sure you're sober. Who know what she's thinking? It doesn't matter. Once she gets here and finds out there's nothing to keep her busy, she'll pack her bags and leave again."

"It's not that easy. You don't know her. It won't work."

"It's got to work." I rocked back, hugging myself tight. "All I'm asking for here is a few days to rest up until I can figure out where else to go. Just a few days until I can get organized. That's all."

He was shaking his head. "I'm no good at lying. If she asks where you are, I'm dead."

"Has she ever asked where I am? In all the years I've known you, has she ever bothered to ask anything about me?" When he didn't answer, I twisted around, took two sour balls out of the candy dish, and handed one to him. "Fine," I said. "Suppose you don't let me in. Suppose you kick me out like you're supposed to." I looked down at the sour ball, wishing I had a hamburger and fries to go with it, and then unwrapped it. It was lemon, acid sweet enough to make my eyes water. "Then what happens?" I asked. When he didn't answer, I leaned over to blow on the wisp of white hair over the top of his ear. "Forget *me*, Bird. What about *you?*"

His face crunched in on itself, but he knew I was right. He might get a few late-season hunters and one or two traveling salesmen, but as soon as the big snows closed in, that was it. Nobody to talk to but Alice, and as soon as she decided to leave, nobody. Nothing to listen to at night but his own heartbeat and the antenna out there on the roof with the wind crying through it, *nobody's here, nobody's here*. He could pretend that giving me a cabin was risky, but he knew as well as I did that facing winter alone in an empty motel was worse. He turned and glared as if it was all my fault and then wagged his candy at me.

"The minute she starts asking questions, you'll leave?"

"I'll be gone." I switched the sour ball to the other cheek. "She won't even know I was here."

"And you won't drive your car in and out?"

"As soon I get it unpacked, I'll hide it somewhere in town."

He stared down at the candy in his hand. "This is a bad idea."

"If she finds out, you can say I broke in. You say you don't know anything about it." I put my arm around him, felt how thin he'd gotten since last winter, his collarbone hard as a hat rack. "I won't let you down, B. I swear to God."

He shuddered me off. "And what about her?" he cried. "You don't ever think about that, do you?"

He was glaring down at his sour ball, his cheeks a waterfall of pale skin. I nudged him in the belt. "What do you mean? Is she sick or something?"

He was about to tell me, but then I could see him change his mind. "She's getting older," he snapped, "that's all." He started fiddling with the candy and then stopped. "I know she's never been very kind about you, but on the whole she's decent and generous and good-hearted. And, by God, when it comes to devotion, that woman . . ." He trailed off, looking seasick.

"Come on, Bird. At least give yourself a reason to live until she gets here. I don't want you to get sick." When he didn't answer, I stood. "So where is it? Behind the couch?"

"Oh, God *no*," he howled, his hands quivering up like birds. "The minute I pour a drink, she'll walk right through that door. I know it. That's the way she operates."

"It's up to you." I sat next to him again. "But you did wait all summer for a drink, don't forget. And you haven't celebrated my birthday yet." When he muttered something, I leaned in to hear. "What?"

"What do you know about self-discipline?" he shouted suddenly. "The way you live. You don't know the first thing about self-discipline."

"Bullshit. You're not talking self-discipline. You're talking torture. Look at you. Your blood pressure's up, you look like you don't even remember how to eat, and your hands are shaking like they're hooked to machines. You really think you can go on like this?"

"*I gave her my word!*" He jerked to his feet, face flaring. "I'm sixty-eight, and despite what you think, missy, a man's word has got to be good for something. I'm her brother, and if she thinks I don't drink, until I know she's gone back to Phoenix for good, I'm sober." He stopped suddenly, looked around the office as if he didn't even know where he was, and then swallowed hard and sat down with a thump. His hands were shaking clear up to his elbows. "And don't you try to stop me, either."

"All right. Just calm down."

"*Ha!*"

"I said all right. I promise. You want me to unwrap that candy for you?" I pried it out of his fingers. "But just in case you've forgotten," I added, leaning into him, "I'm not the one who makes you drink."

His mouth fell, trembling. "Why can't you just leave me alone?"

"Because you'd get too lonely." I pushed the candy into his mouth and stood. "Can I have my key?"

He narrowed his eyes to a squint, shut his mouth, waited for a tremor to pass, and then got up and went behind the desk. He lifted the key to the Ute off its hook, started to hand it over, and then snatched it back. "Stay on schedule, didn't I tell you that? Think like a professional, I said, build a reputation. And what do you do? You run off with a birdbrain from Texas. *Pfft.* I might as well have been spitting in my soup for all the good my advice has done you."

"Harmon wasn't a birdbrain. I don't know what happened. Something got into me, that's all." I thought a moment and added, "I screwed up and I learned my lesson, okay? Now give me the key."

But he wouldn't. "I poured years' worth of embroidery lessons into you, missy, I taught you everything you know about the needle, and I stood up for you when nobody believed you could do it. I even talked the Commerce Committee into giving you a booth. And this is how you pay me back? If your mother were alive right now, she'd probably throw you out. She'd probably never speak to you again."

I looked up at the ceiling—textured plasterboard so close I could have touched it—and closed my eyes. The tiredness was coming on, coming down hard this time. I felt as if someone had sewn lead weights around the hem of my sweater. I opened my eyes.

"My mother is dead. Bird, I *am* grateful for what you've done, and you won't be sorry for helping me out. Are you going to give me the key or not?"

"Where are your manners?"

"Please, Master of the Universe, oh please, may I now have my key, please?"

He slapped it down and I picked it up, but when I felt the warm familiarity of that little piece of metal in my hand, I forgot everything. I didn't mean to, but it came over me all at once so that I had to turn away, holding it back, blinking hard to stop, trying to find my pocket to put in the key. Sometimes you can get so used to being afraid, you don't even know what to do with yourself when it goes away. When I'd caught my breath, when I was sure I wouldn't make a scene we'd both hate, I turned around.

"Thanks, Bird. Can I borrow your broom?"

But he was already storming through the kitchen to his bedroom, slamming the door behind him. I zipped on my coat and stepped into the boots, and after I unwrapped a handful of candies and lined them along the edge of the desk where he'd be able to find them, I called good-bye and let the dog and myself out.

3

Teach us the hand of love divine
In evils to discern
'Tis the first lesson which we need
The latest which we learn.

—from an American sampler, 1817

Two hunters had lost control of their vehicle on Madrillas Pass and ended up in a snowbank, and by the time Frank got them straightened out and back on the road, he was in a good mood. There was always that pressure when he first came up on an unreported accident—an awful pressure under his ribs that made him want to do anything except stop to see what was wrong—but as long it was only a vehicle, as long as no one was injured or missing or worse, that rush of relief always followed, especially up on the pass, where the road could be so treacherous. And the camaraderie of a close call, there was something about that, too. The hunters were middle-aged, red-faced, and overweight, not really hunters, Frank realized after he'd met them, just two wealthy businessmen out for the day in a Jeep Cherokee with a thermos of spiked coffee, looking for something to shoot at. They were dressed for state-of-the-art survival in new camouflage parkas and gloves and insulated coveralls, rabbit-lined bomber caps, and with a twinge of envy, Frank noted the L. L. Bean Trekker boots, which at $195 a pop would have taken him half a year to pay off; but they must have been stuck long enough for the cold of the afternoon shadows and the stillness of the mountain to get to them, because when they spotted him coming up the mountain, they both stumbled from the snowbank out into the middle of the road, waving and yelling as if they feared he might miss them. He could tell from the skid marks that they'd taken the curve too fast, and when they leaned in his window he could smell brandy. He'd liked them anyway, liked them because they knew how foolish they'd been without having to be told, nodding in unison when he asked if they could use a shovel. Puffing from the cold, eager to help, scrambling around their Jeep to check the position of the wheels, down on their knees scooping wildly at the snow around the rear axle, which was not stuck, while he used his shovel on the front tires, which were. When the Jeep rocked free, they hurrahed and banged on the hood and slapped him on the back as he got out to hand them their key. It was obvious from the way they were already sucking on mints and grumbling about road conditions as they handed back his shovel that they were expecting a lecture from him and at the very least, a ticket. Instead, he'd walked to the edge of the road, stepped into the two-foot rut left in the snowbank by their front tire, and with them looking on, not sure what was happening, he'd used the handle of the shovel to punch a hole through the snowbank to the view on the other side. When he looked back, he could see in their round and redshot faces that he was right: they had assumed a steel guardrail there, and now they understood, as they looked down into the ravine several hundred feet below, just what this was all about and how close they'd come. Before they left, they both insisted on shaking hands with him and giving him their business cards. A solemn moment, three men grateful for the occasional existence of luck. Angela did not like him to talk about his work, but on days like this, when everything had turned out all right, he wanted to.

At the top of the pass, however, it began to snow, and as he started down the other side he felt his good mood leaving him behind. It was getting dark, and he hadn't heard anything from Silas about the streets in

Queduro. He waited until the trees thinned from lodgepole to ponderosa, then juniper and piñon, but as soon as he was off the mountain and rolling along the white sweep of open flats, he picked up the radio mike.

"I'm coming up on the Queduro exit now, Silas. Did Ruben get those streets in town plowed yet?"

"Negative."

Frank groaned. Why had anyone thought that just because Ruben Johnson ran a garage and owned a crane, he'd make a good plowman? He pushed in the button. "What'd he say when you called?"

He waited.

"You there, deputy?"

"I guess I forgot about calling him." The radio clicked twice. "You want me to do it now?"

Frank stretched his face wide before he answered. "Yeah. And Silas? Don't forget next time."

"Ten-four. You got some calls here, boss. You want them?"

Frank punched the lighter, reached along the dash for his cigarettes, lit one, and lifted the mike. "Go ahead."

"Your wife called to see if you remembered to pick up her prescription. I told her you had it on your list, but she sounded pretty worried. She wants you to go straight home when you get back in town."

In Silas's voice, Frank could hear the kind of conversation Angela had given him. She was not much at hiding her needs. He lifted the mike to his mouth. "Anything else?"

"Teresa Steelhead says her blind dog's gone AWOL again. I offered to go pick him up myself, but she says she's got something to talk to you about."

"I'll pick him up on my way home. You just get Ruben moving on that plow. Tell him I want every road and alley in town plowed before dark."

"Ten-four." There was a pause. "Maybe I should call your wife back, tell her you got her prescription so she won't worry?"

"Just call Ruben. If there's a problem, call me back."

He hung up the mike and rolled to a stop just before the exit ramp to Queduro, narrowing his eyes at the trail of broken snow leading across the flats. Ruben Johnson was paid good money to keep the roads clear, but his theory was that the first serious snowstorm never hit until November first. Any earlier and he ignored it. If you pressed him, he'd slide out from under his crane, point his wrench at the calendar, and then slide back under. Ruben was like a lot of people in Queduro, seeing life the way it should be instead of the way it was. Frank sighed, popped the trunk of his car, and got out to put on his chains.

When he finished adjusting the tighteners and stood up to knock the snow off his jeans, he noticed the footprints in one of the tire tracks leading to Queduro. The thought of Rose Devonic having to all but break a trail in from the highway, probably in lousy boots, made him mad at Ruben all over again. He got in, switched on the heat, and drove slowly along the last of the dry pavement, the clacking chains going silent as he turned onto snow and then that high singing sleigh-bell sound as he sped up. In the field off to his right were the sales booths, a long row of them that in spring would be covered in signs and lights and arrows and flags, their windows fluttering with Queduran embroideries, and three-fourths of the town out here trying to make a buck. Now they were shuttered and padlocked, anonymous as a row of white coffins propped on end out in the snow. The Commerce Committee had asked him to patrol the booths regularly in winter to prevent vandalism and theft, but he'd never seen anything out here after the first snowfall except his own footprints, and he did not bother to stop now.

He looked back at the road, rolling his neck and straightening his arms, pushing hard against the steering wheel. He should have called Ruben himself this morning, instead of leaving Silas to do it. Silas was eager to follow orders, but as soon as he was told what to do he went right off and forgot. Frank dropped his hands to the bottom of the wheel, squinting through the cigarette smoke at the road up ahead. Next time he'd leave a note on the desk of what he wanted Silas to do. If they were going to work together with any success, that would be the only way.

In the cottonwoods next to the mouth of Holt Canyon were three small signs: Eddie Walk's Cafe, the Ten Tribes Motel, and, just before the road curved into the canyon, the Magpie Bar. Frank tipped his cigarette to the window as he passed it and thought about Rose. Last night he'd dreamed of her in a dress he remembered from high school, a pale green dress with a blue satin sash. She was sitting with a crowd at the Magpie, and when she spotted him at the window, she rose off her stool to wave to him, her red hair wild and unbraided. Frank didn't take much stock in dreams, and this was more like a memory he'd forgotten than a dream, but he'd woken to the tick of snow falling against the window and felt absolutely certain that if he got in his truck and drove up the pass, he'd find her Plymouth station wagon parked halfway off a curve somewhere with the windows iced over and her locked inside.

He'd told himself to go back to sleep, that even if she decided to come back for that old car of hers, she'd never try to drive it out in a snowstorm. Especially at night. Rose had big problems driving the pass. She could do it during the day—it made her sweat bullets, but she could do it—but she'd never consider trying it at night. Not in a snowstorm. He'd lain in bed telling himself this with his eyes shut, listening to his wife's quiet breathing and willing himself to believe that, wherever Rose was, she was all right, she knew what she was doing, and she wouldn't want him worrying about her. And he'd been right. At nine that morning, on his way out the door, he got a call from Birdie Pinkston at the motel.

"You told me to call if I knew where she was," the old man snapped, "so I'm calling. She left a message on my machine saying she'll be back this afternoon, if the pass is still open and she gets a ride. Satisfied?" Frank thanked him and all but had his ear blown off. "Is that all you can say?" shouted the old man. "I've got a foot of snow up here, Frank. I'm stranded. Marooned. Where the hell's the plow anyway? If you and the rest of the town expect me to run a motel, how am I supposed to run it if the streets aren't plowed?"

Frank held the phone away from his ear until the old man began winding down and then reassured him that he'd see to the plow and not to worry about Rose.

"I'm not worried about *her*, jackass. I'm worried about me. I could starve to death up here and you people wouldn't even—wait a minute. I got a call on my other line. Don't get off. I haven't finished with you." But seconds later, when he came back on, his rage had gone flat, suddenly sunken in a tired monotone. "It's my sister, Alice, in Phoenix," he muttered. "I better talk to her. You know how she gets." And he'd hung up.

Frank had driven through Holt Canyon uncountable numbers of times, but there was always something fine about coming around that last bend and seeing the canyon walls up ahead falling away like two enormous stone hands opening from a clap to reveal just enough room along the river for a few fields, a few streets, and the town. He passed the cemetery and Swan's barn and went over the old railroad trestle bridge, sliding a little on the snowpack as he turned at the other side in front of Steelhead's Market and started down Hemming. Next to the market, surrounded by chain link fencing and set back from the street, was a cinder-block foundation surrounded by tarp-covered piles of lumber and adobes, which, if the funding didn't dry up again, would become a new high school. The old school over on Tambour had closed in '89 because of an electrical fire, and due to a chronic lack of students, as well as trained teachers, the town had been sending its kids ever since over the pass each fall to the boarding school in Madrillas. The boarding school was supposed to be decent, and since Frank didn't have kids he didn't really have to care if it wasn't, but when the idea of building a new school in Queduro came up, he'd been one of the first to vote yes. You could have a post office and a market and a church and a laundromat and a cafe and a line of thriving tourist businesses on every corner, but having a school meant a town that wouldn't blow away. A town with a sense of substance to itself, a town with a sense of history and hope, past and future. The sight of all those building materials waiting for spring pleased him. He turned his eyes back to the road.

Up at the far end of town, he saw Teresa's black dog waiting in the middle of the intersection. Hermes was about a hundred in dog years and getting worse about directions all the time. Frank passed Dick Sweeny's new brick house, then the three bald-faced look-alike tar-paper houses that Orlando Ramirez had been trying to sell for three times their worth, then the Texaco, where he bought his coffee each morning, the Mineral Building, and the drive-up window at the Magpie Bar, where he saw Astra and someone else looking out. Astra could not sell liquor on Sundays, but she stayed open so the regulars had someplace to get dinner. Up ahead, Hermes sat wagging his tail slowly, duck-footed and patient, staring down at the snow. Frank sometimes wished he had a dog. Angela said she was allergic.

Silas came on the radio. "Boss, I forgot to tell you something. If you're still there."

He thought about it before he picked up the mike. "Go."

"Rose Devonic's back. I saw her walking up Flax Hill a few hours ago."

At least the kid had eyesight, Frank had to hand him that. "Go ahead."

"She didn't move her car out of the alley. You think we ought to have it towed, or should I just leave her another ticket?"

Frank rolled to a stop in front of Hermes, staring at the mike before he raised it to his mouth.

"You gave her a ticket?"

"The sign says cars got to be moved within twelve hours of snowstorms. She's parked right under it, boss."

Frank took a fierce hit off his cigarette and stared out at the dog.

"You still there, boss?"

"She's still parked there, Silas, because she's stuck there. And she's stuck there because you forgot to remind Ruben to plow the streets."

A pause. "I just talked to him. He's on his way."

Frank stubbed out his cigarette, then lifted the mike. "Good. And since I haven't authorized you to use my ticket book, Silas, I want you to go get that ticket and tear it up. You copy?"

"But I—"

"Good. Roger and out."

He slammed the mike against the seat and got out, cursing himself for having agreed to hire a deputy. All that crap from the Committee about how hard he worked and how much they appreciated it but how obvious it was that he needed help, especially in summer when the tourists started coming and things got busy, and what better man to start training for the job, they'd declared, than young Silas K. Farrell? Frank had been a fool to listen. Silas K. Farrell didn't give a shit about the town. All he wanted was the right to wear a badge, act like an asshole, and get paid for it. His first reaction to the death of Eli Sanchez's retarded son, Willy, last summer had been *good riddance*. Not *when* or *why* or *how's Eli doing*. Just a shrug and *good riddance* before returning to his magazine. Frank could have throttled him for it. If Silas had his way, people who needed help would not just die or disappear, they would be busted for vagrancy on their way out. That was what Silas thought law enforcement meant: power. Otherwise, why bother? And the strangest part of it was that the Committee thought he was doing fine. They were talking about buying him a uniform next summer. It mystified Frank how they could not see that behind all his talk about wanting to serve and help modernize his community, Silas was a coward and a bully who did not care what happened to anyone but himself.

"Hey, Hermes, your butt getting cold?"

The dog hauled to his feet and danced in place, whining a little. Frank rubbed the black anvil-shaped head and looked around the street. It was getting dark early these days, winter coming on hard and everything on the street closed up for Sunday, the air so quiet he could almost hear the river gurgling under the snow a block away. Then the low murmur of Ruben's plow started up over on Soutache. He turned and stared at the footprints that led through the snow up the hill toward the motel, wondering if he should follow them. Birdie had turned off the neon sign the Committee had bought for him—the only neon in Queduro, a pink Indian who shot yellow arrows at the moon every night—but surely she'd gotten in all right by now. *I can take care of myself*, that was what she would say. Even if he'd only come for Teresa's dog, she'd be mad as hell to see him.

He walked to the car with Hermes feeling his way behind, bumping into the edge of the rear door before he found his way around it and then heaving his front half up on the seat. "Go on. Jump. You can do it." The dog moaned, his tail slowly whipping the door. Frank got behind him and hoisted his back half onto the seat. "Some day I'm going to buy you a pair of springs for those legs." Hermes folded himself into a sitting position and cocked his head, waiting for the sound of the door. Frank glanced once more up the hill. It was an incredible thing, how she could just disappear without saying good-bye. But wherever she'd gone with Harmon Waters, at least she was back safe. That was the important thing. He slammed the passenger door and got behind the wheel.

He made a U-turn and started down Hemming, but when he got to the town clock, he took his foot off the gas and coasted to a stop. He was thinking about his wife, about whether or not she'd seen him just now picking up the dog. Their house was perched at the north end of Tambour, and from their front window she'd have had a straight view down to the blinking light. She'd be expecting him to go home first. And Teresa Steelhead was a talker. Even if he tried to cut her short when he brought her the dog, it would take several minutes at least before he'd be able to get out of there. He could see Angela now, trying to hold herself in and watching the street for his car. If he did not show up within a few minutes, she might call Silas again. She might even decide to call Teresa. Angela did not understand about Queduro, about how quickly rumors started and what they could do to people.

He turned the squad car around and headed toward his house. As he came to Gobelin Hill Road, he noticed Hermes already leaning for the turn, his black shape in the rearview like a pilot in a World War II aviator's cap. "You know exactly where we are," Frank said. "The only reason you pretend you're lost is so you can ride around in a patrol car."

She was not at the front window. He parked in the driveway behind his truck, noting from the tracks that it had not been driven. He gathered the books, searched the bags of groceries until he found her prescription, and got out.

The house had belonged to his parents, a one-story adobe like most of the houses around it, with a narrow portico that ran the length of the house and some tall pines in the front yard. Nothing fancy or new, but it was comfortable. He regretted not having the time to keep it up as well as his parents had done. He'd painted the roof and *vigas* of the portico white a year ago, trying to spruce the place up for his marriage to Angela, but the paint had been cheap and there was already a yellow stain creeping up through it, made more obvious by the snow. Next spring, he thought; though he knew that once the tourist season started, he'd barely have time to look at the house, let alone paint it. He picked the newspaper out of the snow, slapped it off, and went up to the front door. It was locked. He looked at it a minute and then went back to the squad car for his keys.

Her need to lock doors was new, and it bothered him. She said it made her feel safer. "If you'd had a childhood like mine," she'd said, "you'd appreciate locks too." He'd nodded, paid the bill for the dead bolts, and made himself an extra set of keys, but every time he came home and found himself locked out again, something inside him tightened. He could not escape the idea that she was doing it not just because she was afraid of break-ins—though that was part of it—but because he had once told her that nobody in Queduro locked their doors at night. She had caught the note of pride in his voice, his smug small-town contentment about one small gift he had to offer, and now, with everything else falling apart, it seemed this was the new game she was playing, daring him to deny her, testing him, maybe even looking for a weakness she could use later.

When he opened the door she was not there waiting, and when he called she did not answer. Van Morrison was on the stereo in the living room, and though the door was closed, he could hear the TV in the bedroom. "Angie?" he called. "It's me." He stamped the snow off his boots, listened a moment, and then stepped into the living room. "Honey? I got Hermes with me. I need to take him home to Teresa."

The sound of the TV disappeared. "Did you get my medicine?"

"Yeah. I got you some books from the library, too. Some good ones."

He waited, staring at the books he had brought. She would never read them. Giving her books was like offering a piece of gum to someone pinned down in the middle of the street by gunfire. He laid them on the couch and realized he was holding his breath.

"Did you get out today, Ange?" He squeezed his eyes shut and opened them again. "Come on, honey. Will you at least answer me so I know you're okay?"

"Yes, Frank, everything is dandy. Go take care of your blind dog."

"I'll be back in a few minutes." He started for the door.

"Leave my medicine." Her voice was sharp.

He looked at the bag in his hand and then at the door to the bedroom. "These pills you're taking. We're going to have to talk about them."

"They're prescription pills, Frank, and I need them. You don't know anything about it."

"The pharmacist in Madrillas says he won't refill this prescription next time without talking to your doctor in Albuquerque first. According to him, it's pretty dangerous, having so many refills for this stuff." He waited. "You hear me in there?"

"I'll deal with it."

"Angela?"

When she did not answer, he took a deep breath and set the package on the edge of his father's rolltop desk.

Teresa Steelhead answered her door in a blue dress and yellow apron. Like nearly every other Queduran, she had a fairly even mix of Hispanic, Irish, and Indian blood in her veins, but physically she reminded Frank of an aging Iowan housewife, round and small and apple-cheeked with thin, pinkish hair, black eyes, and a high sparrowlike tremble in her voice. Arthritis had forced her into retirement from trade embroidery, but she still made a decent living off the food store her husband had started, Steelhead's.

"Aren't you nice to bring him home for me," she cried. "I tried to call him back, you know, but I'm afraid that tumor's starting to affect his hearing."

"I expect he's just being stubborn. He found his way down to the blinking light all right."

They stood back to let Hermes grope his way over the threshold. In the hallway, he made a cautious circle until he was facing the door and then sat, black toenails clicking the wooden floor. Teresa shook her finger at him.

"Bothering our handsome young sheriff," she cooed. "Shame on you, Hermes." She turned to Frank and patted his chest. "But honestly, I'm just so glad you've come. I've got terrible news."

He was not surprised. Teresa's husband, Louis, had died a year ago after a long bout with cancer, and in her loneliness Teresa hadn't yet figured out how to start a conversation without introducing it as terrible.

"I can't stay but a minute, Teresa. I've got groceries to get home." He motioned to the street where he'd left his car idling, but she shook her head impatiently, grabbing his sleeve to pull him inside.

"I had the strangest phone call. I wasn't sure what she was even talking about at first, she was so frantic, but apparently she had some sort of dream about her brother being dead and she wanted to know if it was true or not. My lord, you should have heard her, though. Absolutely beside herself."

"Who are we talking about here, Teresa?"

"Why, Alice Pinkston, of course. Haven't you heard? She's coming back."

Frank looked at her sharply. "What?"

"Isn't that incredible? Come into the kitchen where it's warm and I'll tell you all about it. Come on now, you must be freezing," and with a surprisingly strong grip, she pulled him by the sleeve down a dark hallway.

Her kitchen was low-ceilinged with yellow cupboards, yellow daisy wallpaper, a yellow-legged table with a glass top, and two yellow chairs. The air was heavy with the smell of cooked food. Frank did not want to stay. She steered him toward the nearest chair and pushed him into it, waving off his protests.

"Nonsense. You're getting too thin from all your rushing around, and pretty as your young wife is, she certainly doesn't cook enough for you. Besides, look what I made." She squeezed around his chair, grabbed a pair of pot holders, reached into the stove, and brought out a platter of fried chicken, kicking the oven door shut behind her. "You do like drumsticks, I hope."

"You're spoiling me, Teresa, and I can't stay to enjoy it."

Her face fell. "But I made it especially for you."

"I'm sorry. I can't. Angela's expecting me home, and I've still got groceries in the car."

"Well. If you don't want it." She sighed heavily and looked down at the plate. "I suppose I could try to sell it at the store tomorrow."

Frank felt bad for her, but he knew better than to give in. "When I come in the store tomorrow for coffee, I'll buy the whole plate off you. I never say no to a good cook except when I don't have time to eat."

She clucked at the flattery and turned to the stove, laying the plate down and reaching for the foil. Frank watched the little diamonds of soft flesh showing between the buttons at the back of her dress as she bent over. He looked around the kitchen and stopped himself just before he started drumming on the glass tabletop.

"So Alice Pinkston is coming. You know how soon?"

"Where is my head?" She turned to him. "I didn't tell you everything yet. She's coming back to sell the motel."

It took Frank a moment. "Sell the Ten Tribes?"

"Yes. I think that's what she meant." She took a yellow dish towel from the counter, wiped her hands, and then slid into the chair next to him. "She sounded so jumbled, Frank. One minute she's saying she thinks her brother's dead, and the next she's telling me I'm supposed to put up a sign in the store saying the motel is for sale and somebody named Mr. Max will handle inquiries. Do you know any Mr. Max?"

"Not offhand."

"I don't either. I think he must be a realtor. How someone clear out in Phoenix could sell a piece of land in the middle of New Mexico, I don't know. Anyway, just as I start to believe that's why she's calling, she bursts into tears and says she knows her brother's in some kind of terrible trouble, only nobody will tell her what it is, so she has to come make sure. I told her she was being silly and Birdie was just fine, but she says, 'That's just what I'd expect from someone like you,' in this terrible nasty tone. And then she tells me to have you call her right away. And when I told her I couldn't—she called about ten this morning and I'd just seen the squad car leaving the valley, that's how I knew you were gone—do you know what she said? 'Go get him!' Can you imagine? As if I even drive anymore. As if just because she has all that money, I'm supposed to be her servant."

"Did you get her number?"

Teresa brought a slip of paper out of her apron pocket and handed it to him. "You can use the phone on the wall behind you."

"Thanks, Teresa, but I think it's better if—"

"Oh no, Frank, please, I insist. You just go ahead. I know how important this is."

He turned reluctantly to the phone. If he asked her not to listen, she'd be all the more eager to discuss why with her friends down at the market tomorrow morning. As he unfolded the number and started dialing, he heard her sighing behind him.

"I only hope you'll be able to convince her to go see a doctor," she said. "Something's not right, a woman that age getting so upset over a bad dream. She should see a doctor. I tried to ask her if she had, but you know how Alice is. She all but hung up on me. Maybe she'll listen to you."

He nodded as the phone began to ring.

"To tell you the truth?" Teresa was leaning across the table, whispering now. "I wouldn't be at all surprised if that poor woman isn't having a breakdown. That's what it sounded like. And now she's planning to drive all the way out here by herself? We can only keep our fingers crossed. At least she's driving a car that won't fold up like a matchbox in an accident.

"And what's worse," she continued, touching his sleeve to keep his attention, "Rose Devonic showed up again. You heard about that, didn't you? I saw her trudging up Flax Hill this afternoon looking absolutely frozen, poor thing, and heading right for the motel. Apparently things didn't turn out so well for her with that Texas man she ran off with. Not that I'm surprised. Poor little Rose has never had the instincts for choosing the right man. She's her mother's child straight through. Anyway. You know how protective Alice gets of her brother. If she shows up now all upset and finds that young girl already settled in at the motel for winter, she might never recover."

Frank nodded and stopped listening. He had never been able to feel much sympathy for Alice. True, she'd suffered a hard life—few friends, no marriage, a brother who drank, a sister who died, and wealth from that death that freed her from Queduro only long enough for her to travel to the other side of the world, where she'd gotten some kind of tropical disease that made her hair fall out. Now she wore a wig that looked like a pewter bowl and lived for her brother and fretted about thieves and pickpockets and mashers and talked aloud to herself and chased away kids who snickered behind her back. All of which would have won his sympathy had she not been so shrill and self-centered about it. Every time he answered the phone at his office and heard her starting in, his heart sank. He couldn't imagine what it was like to be her brother.

There was no answer. He hung up and turned back. "You know when she's supposed to arrive, Teresa?"

"She said in a week, but I personally think it's going to be tomorrow. Especially if she's worried about her brother." Teresa was leaning forward, holding the dish towel under her throat. "The way she sounded on the phone, she was already packed and half out the door."

He nodded and got to his feet. Teresa held out both her hands as if to stop him.

"Maybe Birdie can tell you something. I tried calling him all day. I left messages, but he just refuses to call back. Maybe he'll talk to you."

"Okay. I'll give him a call tonight when I—"

"Don't be silly. Use my phone."

"I think I'll see if Alice has called my house first. Thanks anyway, though." He moved toward the door.

"Well"—she sighed—"you probably don't want an old lady like me trying to help anyway. I understand that." She began to smooth the table with the dish towel. "But if it was up to me, I'd go right up there and talk to that girl, Rose. She's always known something like this could happen, and if she leaves now, she'll be saving everyone a lot of grief. In fact, I'm surprised she hasn't figured that out already. After all, she's intelligent. She must know she can't just come back here and pick up again where she left off. And now—well, from what I've heard, nobody's going to take her in unless she pays some kind of rent. That's what I've heard."

Frank felt his face hardening. "Rose has probably heard it too, Teresa, but Queduro's her home. And it's Birdie's motel. If he wants her to stay there, she has every right. You know that."

"Yes, in the legal sense. It's just that"—she paused, puffing up for something—"I just think, when it comes to that girl, it wouldn't hurt if you tried to be a little realistic for once."

He ran his hands through his hair and turned back to her. "I thought you liked Rose."

"I do. I'm a practicing Christian, you know that. I've always tried to be kind to people like her. But I'm a widow now, and I have to think about myself too, don't I?" She turned to him. "How can I afford to let her charge food and supplies at my store this winter when I know she won't be able to pay me back? She won't, Frank. She may be calling herself a trade embroiderer these days, but I heard her work last summer was an embarrassment. That's what my son Tommy says. And the Committee's talking about it too, you know. Dick Sweeny says if she doesn't start meeting Queduran standards, he won't give her a sales booth next summer. Frank, don't you see? She made almost nothing this summer, and then she spent all last month making a fool of herself with that Texan. Even if she's able to buckle down now and start working, she's never going to catch up. And her debts are just going to double, or maybe even triple, if she has to leave the motel and go pay rent somewhere. And the worst of it is—"

"All right, Teresa." He held up his hands to stop her. "If she wants, I'll see if I can help her sort things out. But none of this has happened yet, so let's just slow down a little. She's always managed her debts before, hasn't she? Didn't she pay off her grocery bill last August by cleaning out the back of your store? I seem to remember you saying she worked damned hard, harder than you even asked for."

"That is not the point, Frank. I'm not saying she doesn't try. She does. The point is"—Teresa lifted her chin and drew herself up to it—"I simply can't afford to have someone like that loitering around my store. It's not good for business."

Frank felt the weight shift in his heart. "Teresa. Your store is the only place in the valley to buy groceries."

"And that means I have to support her all winter?"

He drew his hand across his eyes. "I guess you'll do what you think is right. I better be getting home."

"But, Frank, that's just what I was coming to." She followed him down the unlit hallway, chasing him, he felt, toward the door. "How can I possibly send that girl away empty-handed when I've known her since she was a child, when I know what she suffered through with that uncle of hers? Oh, I suppose I can let her in the door if I have to—there's no harm as long as she doesn't try to charge anything—but I wish you'd just explain to her how awkward it is to have someone like her in my store. That's all. You can see that, can't you? Of course you can. We all know what she went through as a child, and we're just as sorry about it as we can be, but the fact is, we've been trying for years now to help her get back on her feet and it's just not working. You probably heard that she still refuses to join the church, haven't you? So what are we to do? If she insists on sinking her own lifeboat, we're not to blame, are we? And if she calls herself a trade embroiderer when she's nothing more that a flat-stitch seamstress, isn't she simply dragging down the whole tradition? Wouldn't it be better if we could just somehow get her to start a new life somewhere else?"

She stopped suddenly as if to catch her breath and hold it there, but then she was off again.

"But you know all this, don't you. It must tear you up to see a sweet girl like her slipping further and further behind. I understand that. But don't you think the sympathy has gone on long enough? I heard she was living out of her car this summer. Nobody knows where she was parked or how she managed to keep it a secret, but that's what I heard. She was too proud to ask for help, and the truth is, even if she had, nobody in the valley would've listened. And they're not going to listen now, not after the way she threw herself at that Texan. That's how people are talking, anyway." She was panting for breath as they reached the front door. "And if you stop to think a minute, don't you see what that means?"

He felt as if the dark hallway had been filled with bees. He glanced down at Hermes, who was sitting in the same place, staring at the wall as if he expected it to feed him. "What, Teresa?"

She looked at him with exasperation. "Frank. You've done all you can for her, but you have your own life to live too. She'll just have to understand that."

"She's always understood that." He opened the door and stepped out. It was dark now, the air was fresh and clean, and when Teresa turned on the porch light, he saw it was snowing.

"Be careful of those steps on the front walk. It might be slippery."

Her voice was high and sad, like a little bird trapped up in the rafters, and he realized then that she had not meant half of what she said, she had simply been trying to keep him there longer. As if she knew what he was thinking, she called to him as he stepped off the porch.

"I don't want you to think I'm heartless, Frank. I just want what's best for everyone. Especially for you. You're a good-hearted man, just like your father. Rose was lucky to have a friend like you."

He turned, trying to keep his voice from shaking with anger. "She still has me for a friend, Teresa. Good night."

He had already turned down Filoselle before he remembered he was supposed to be going home. Since the hill was too icy to turn around in the alley, he went on, groping along the dash for cigarettes and throwing the empty pack at the windshield. What did Teresa expect him to say? He'd grown up with Rose. They'd been best friends. During his stint in the army, he'd written more letters to her than to his parents—that was how close he'd been to her. He could never deny that. And why should he? She wasn't breaking laws or trying to hurt anybody. She was just trying to fit in somewhere, like everyone else. What was so wrong about that? Did Teresa think that he was supposed to pay more attention to public opinion than to his own conscience? That he'd be willing to turn a friend he'd known for almost thirty years into a messy little public relations problem he was expected to clean up after, simply because she lacked money to buy herself decent clothing?

Her face came up in the dark at him then, her red hair flung back in its wildness and her blue eyes flashing, vivid with laughter. He'd done it once already, hadn't he. Last September when Dick Sweeny, the Committee's chairman, had marched in his office to announce that she was still out at the booths.

"And don't you tell me to calm down, young man," Dick had sputtered. "I specifically told that gal when we granted her a sales permit, as soon as the season was over she was to lock up her booth like everyone else and give back the key. She was told. We could lose our lease with the BLM if they find out someone's living out there."

Frank had told himself that he had no choice, that surely if Rose put in a little effort, she'd be able to come up with a better solution than camping out in her booth. But as soon as he'd pulled up and seen her sitting in the narrow doorway trying to draw up an embroidery pattern, her wonderfully clownish face creased gray with fatigue as she looked up and grinned and waved him out of his car, he'd realized what he'd known all along: if she had any better place to go, she'd have gone there by now, and no matter what he suggested, no matter how carefully he put it, she wouldn't be able to think of him as her friend but only as a cop. They'd both tried to ignore it—he'd brought a six-pack of beer and she'd opened a can of sardines and they leaned against his squad car with their backs to the NO TRESPASSING signs, watching the late-season truckers roar by on the highway and talking about nothing, the way friends do, for nearly an hour. But when he'd finally screwed up the nerve to tell her that the Committee had asked for her booth key, she'd looked straight at him as if all she could feel for him was pity.

"*Asked* you? I'll bet they threatened to take your balls. I'm surprised you're still walking." And since the only other solution he had to offer was money and the address of the welfare services in Madrillas, he'd only made it worse. In the end she'd gone back to the booth, slammed everything she owned into her car, shoved his money back in his pocket along with the key—"Save your charity, Frank"—and burned rubber out of there.

Nobody knew where she was staying after that, but every night she'd walked in the bar hanging onto the Texan's arm, being loud and happy with him, dancing with him and making him laugh, even drinking with him, which she was not much good at. From the little Frank knew,

Harmon Waters was all right. He'd told Frank he was on a golf vacation from his job as manager of a telephone company in Austin. "I'll tell you what," he boomed, pushing a beer in front of Frank, "I been widowed once, divorced twice, left for dead by just about every woman I ever wanted, and I still believe in love. How's that for stupid?"

Frank found him too loud and too cheerful and noted that he never went anywhere without his sports cap on and a flask in his hip pocket. But at least he'd been kind to Rose. His sudden keen interest in her and her sudden keen willingness to be with him had caused people to see her differently, almost as if they'd never before noticed how striking she was or the fact that she might be lonely. That part was good. But something had gone wrong with Harmon Waters, and whatever it was, Rose wouldn't be telling Frank about it. She probably wouldn't even want to talk to him now. And the worst of it was, he couldn't blame her. If he'd been in her shoes, he'd have done the same thing.

At the corner of Filoselle and Hemming, he spotted the flashing blue light of the plow coming down through the trees. At least she'd be able to move her car before morning. He turned left toward the bridge, too wound up to go home yet. He wanted to drive a little, clear his head—blow it out, as his father used to say. Now that Angela had what she needed, she wouldn't be waiting for him anymore.

He crossed the bridge at a crawl and came up on the cemetery, a scatter of crooked snow-capped stones and a wooden cross peering out at him at a slant from the other side of the barbed wire. Both his parents were there now, his mother from cancer in '93, his father a few years later from a stroke. Rose's family was up there too, mother, uncle, brother, all under one stone. Everyone who'd died and left someone in Queduro was up there, a whole town of Indian, Irish, and Hispanic ghosts, headstones like rows of miniature houses, the fancy ones with wrought-iron fences to keep out deer and livestock. He was only thirty-one, but unless Angela insisted on moving out of the valley, he'd end up with a piece of real estate there himself.

After the cemetery fence quit, the darkness off that side of the car was complete, snow diving hard for the headlights and the walls of the canyon echoing his chains on the snow. He slowed down. The truth was, he was not much of a sheriff. He wanted to be, and if for no other reason than that the town would probably let him keep his job. But times were changing. More and more locals were starting to think like Silas, that the job required the kind of action they'd seen on TV: shoot-outs and car chases, handcuffs, warrants, arrests. Frank had learned how to do all that as an MP at Fort Benning, but after he'd returned from his tour in Panama, his father had told him not to worry about most of it. Frank senior had gone twenty-five years as sheriff without even needing a weapon. A loose-limbed, easygoing man, the kind who just knew how to be with people, how to talk to them, and how to understand. His deeds as a cop were legendary. The Phillips incident, for instance, when Rufus Phillips decided to shoot his cow in the head and then hold his wife, Juana, and their child, Annie, at gunpoint inside Snow's barn at the south end of town. Frank senior had walked into that barn with no more protection than the wooden cane he used for his bad leg. Everybody thought he was pushing his luck—even Frank thought so—yet an hour later Juana and Annie had walked out of the barn as if they'd only gone in there to shear sheep, and a few minutes later Rufus Phillips had appeared, looking hollow-eyed and contrite. At Frank senior's urging, he'd apologized to the crowd gathered in his field before climbing into the back of the squad car. "When it comes to handling local situations, son," Frank senior had said afterward, "you'll find that peer pressure works just as well as handcuffs. Mostly better."

In the five years since Frank had taken over the job, he'd mostly agreed. With the exception of a few tourists who were too drunk or mixed up to listen to reason, most people belonged somewhere, or wanted to. All they needed from him was to be reminded of it at the right moment.

But it had not worked for Rose. The more he'd tried to help her, the more the town tried to push her out. A lot of the problem was the Commerce Committee, whose members seemed to think their new motto, LET'S CLEAN UP QUEDURO, meant more than just hauling in Porta Potties and putting out trash bins every spring. They were talking work standards and quality control. Now that real money was involved, they were turning the embroidery business from a community tradition into a pass-fail test. Of course, if they voted to take away her booth next summer, she could still sell her work out of the back of her car. But Teresa was right: if Rose didn't have the authority of a booth and a big inventory ready to sell, she wouldn't make enough to pay the price of thread.

Tomorrow then, he thought, he'd go see Dick Sweeny and the Committee about letting Rose keep her booth. He'd appeal to Dick as a family man, as a churchgoing man, as a responsible member of the community. If that didn't work, he'd offer to pay Rose's booth fee in advance. He'd offer to pay it anyway.

But as he came out of the canyon onto the flats, he shook his head. Trying to convince the Committee that Rose still deserved a booth would never work. It might even make things worse. People like Dick were polite enough not to mention it, especially now that Frank was married, but they all knew how he'd felt about Rose back in high school, or thought they did, which meant that anything he tried to say in her defense now was, in their eyes, only further proof that they didn't need to listen. *Okay, Frank,* they would say, *good idea*—rolling their eyes as soon as he turned away. Frank tilted his head one way and the other to crack loose the tension. His father would've known how to handle it, how to make people like Dick Sweeny and Teresa Steelhead listen. He felt an ache that he couldn't ask him now.

He'd planned to turn around at the mouth of the canyon, but instead he opened his window and kept driving. He was sorry it was snowing. He liked leaving the valley on clear nights, driving straight out under a sky full of stars and the land in all directions, feeling the wide-open loneliness of the flats and then, at the highway, turning back. A jackrabbit jumped into his headlights as if thrown, barely missing the wheels before skidding back off into the dark. On nights like this, he often found himself wishing he had an emergency to go to. Wishing the road were dry or that his tires were studded, wishing someone was out there waiting for help, wishing he could step on the gas and fly.

4

Behold and See
What My Parents
Has Don For me.

—from an American
sampler, 1808

When Eudora Devonic got pregnant, she was still living with her parents in Holopaw, Florida. Barely sixteen, and though she'd been warned about strangers since before she could ride a bike, about what they would want and what would happen if she gave it too easily, she apparently didn't listen. Or not enough. Maybe she thought an older stranger from another state didn't count, or maybe she was just being contrary. She lived for being contrary. After saying hello to a stranger twice her age one night at the state fair and allowing him to buy her a candied apple, she agreed to go for a ride in his car with him. That was that. Two months later, she found out she was pregnant, and after her parents finished yelling at her they said she would quit school, have the baby, and give it up for adoption. But Eudora had never given up anything she wanted to keep. It was in her blood not to give up anything. Instead, she packed her bags, stole forty-five dollars from her father's wallet, and ran off to find the father of her baby in New Mexico, where he lived, he'd told her, as a famous inheritance embroiderer.

That's the story of how my mother left home, how she gave up everything she'd ever known and loved by convincing herself she was giving up nothing. That was Eudora, so sure of the stitches she never thought out the pattern. In any case, that's how she ended up in Queduro with my father, Walter Bean.

Walter Bean was about as interesting as a can of soup. He had all kinds of possibilities—good looks, a place to live, an established career, and a new wife who'd do anything to help—but what he enjoyed most was griping. She tried to fall in love with him anyway, but by the time I was born she'd developed the habit of staring at her hands whenever he started in, which allowed him to imagine that she was quietly soaking up every word he said and her to imagine that she was banging him on the head with a frying pan. He was bored with embroidery, he wanted more money, he loved his dead mother, hated the neighbors, worried about taxes, ached in bad weather, and wanted to learn golf. That, along with an almost endless description of Cape Canaveral—the place he'd visited after stopping at the state fair to meet my mother—summed up his topics of conversation in our home for ten years. Ten years! Then one day he thought up a new topic, and after writing a twelve-page letter to my mother explaining, among other things, how the tax laws would benefit her more if she was single, he ran off with another inheritance embroiderer named Peggy Ramirez.

When my mother, who was eight months pregnant, first opened the letter, she started laughing. She laughed so hard she dropped my father's embroidery work on the floor and had to sit down. "Rose," she cried, when she at last began to catch her breath, "I was wrong. There *is* a God." She covered her face and shook her head without saying anything, almost as if she were praying into her hands, and then she jumped up and spent the rest of that night packing our bags for Florida and calling neighbors to say good-bye. If she was scared of anything, she was scared he might change his mind and come back. That's just how much of a tragedy losing Walter Bean was.

But the next day in Madrillas—right after she decided to stop in the courthouse to legally change our names back to her maiden name of Devonic—we went over to the bank to get the money and found he'd closed out the account. My mother turned from the teller's window, still smiling, and fainted, and two clerks had to carry her into the manager's office, where she lay on a green leather couch until the doctor came. He said there was nothing wrong with her, and her baby seemed fine too, but that was the end of her laughing. By the time we got back to Queduro, she'd even stopped talking. She said in a note that I shouldn't worry, it was just something she felt like doing, but a few days later she realized it wasn't her decision. She scribbled a note saying she couldn't talk. Then she thought she couldn't breathe. Then she took a carving knife out of the kitchen, and holding her swollen belly with one hand she tiptoed upstairs to her sewing room and sat in the brown chair by the window.

I don't remember how long, but it was longer than one day. I think it was more like two days, though it's hard to believe I actually lasted that long before I got scared enough to tell somebody. Since I understood she wouldn't want neighbors involved, I rode my bike down to the sheriff's office—Frank's father was the sheriff back then—and said that my mom needed him to come to our house. Without asking why, Mr. Doby put on his hat, put my bike in the trunk of his squad car, and drove me home. He didn't act shocked or talk down to her or try to joke her out of it, and he didn't bawl me out for not coming to him sooner. He just said she wasn't going to hurt anybody, she was just scared and it was normal, and then he sat on the ottoman in front of her and took the knife out of her hands and began to rub them until she finally turned from the window to look at him. He didn't ask her anything, he just let her cry and cry. Then he told me to run a bath for her, and when it was ready he lifted her out of the chair. Despite the size of her belly, she was hanging from her shoulders like they were the only solid part of her left. Frank's dad walked her to the bathroom door, and then he told me to help her and he went downstairs to make coffee and a big pan of scrambled eggs for us.

Back in those days, I knew Frank because he lived down the street from us and delivered our paper and we sometimes raced our bikes down Gobelin

Hill, but that was about it. I was in fifth when he was already in junior high, so I never wondered whether we'd be friends. He was just another kid. But from the very start I liked everything about his dad. After he took the knife away from my mother, he couldn't even turn around without finding me watching. I watched him go home at night and come to work in the morning. I watched the way he walked with his cane and how he leaned over his plate when he ate at the cafe, how he rubbed the back of his head when he thought something was funny. I was too shy to visit with him, but I'd walk by his office most days after school just to see if he'd wave. He always did.

Then my little brother Kyle came into the world. After my mother recovered, she had to find work. She wasn't much of an embroiderer, having only been at it a few years, but since that was the only work available, she became a subcontractor, working twelve- and fourteen-hour days to finish other people's embroideries. Doc Mutz warned her to slow down, but she just laughed in a tinny way. She was laughing at everything in a tinny way. I decided it would be easier on her if I went to stay with the Dobys. To make it easier for them to invite me, I showed up on my bike at sunset and rode around out in front of the house until they asked me in for dinner. Three nights of that, and they got the hint. Mrs. Doby gave me the couch at first and later cleared out the little half attic over the kitchen for a mattress, and Mr. Doby fixed up a wooden ladder so I could climb in and out of the hole. Of course I wanted to know how my mother was doing with my new baby brother, but mostly I stayed with the Dobys. I stayed over six months. They never asked why I was there, they never said I owed them anything, they never looked at me like it was time to leave. We were like a family. Mrs. Doby signed my report cards and took me shopping when I needed clothes; Mr. Doby taught me how to scrape a horse hoof, play chess, and whistle with two fingers.

As for Frank, I made it clear at the start that I was only there because of his dad, but pretty soon I liked him too. It was hard not to. He was funny and clever, he didn't brag or push me around unless I pushed him first, and he didn't mind sharing his dad. He had black hair that yearned in every direction, and because I had red hair that grew the same way, we could've been brother and sister. Sometimes I thought we were. It was because of Frank that I started liking school and making good grades. Everything he did—sports, homework, friends, chores, even sleep—it just all came so naturally to him, I felt I could do the same thing. Every Friday night the four of us had dinner on trays in the living room and watched *Tales from the Crypt*. Anyhow, that's how I first got to know Frank.

But then Bob Devonic arrived. He was my uncle on my mother's side. He said he'd come clear across the country to meet me; that he didn't mind hard work; that he'd realized he belonged out west while crossing the Mississippi; that he had at least a dozen ideas on how to get rich; and that, if we needed one, he'd found out from the neighbors where we could pick up a clothes washer for next to nothing. He was only a few inches taller than me, but built thick through, like a lumberjack, and red hair, like mine, only brighter, and a voice that carried even when he was trying to whisper. When Frank and I first rode up on our bikes, we didn't even get our kickstands down before Bob was explaining that the house would look better if we planted a garden, and he'd noticed a dent in the fender of my bike he could pound out with his mallet and a gutter at the side of the porch that needed to be reattached. He thought we should buy a car so we could take sightseeing trips on weekends. "Of course, it's up to your mother," he said to me, "but I personally believe that out of all the instinctual needs we humans have to put up with—sex, food, sleep, fresh air, water—the most important and least recognized need of all is beauty. It's what magnifies us into human beings. Wouldn't you say? Or not?"

I liked Bob right away. I didn't know where he'd come from—I'd never even heard of him before—but I thought he was the first sign of life in our house since my mother had thrown a dozen of my father's family plates out the window. Bob could fix anything, he didn't mind noise, he was strong as a bull, a better cook than my mother, and, best of all, his arrival meant that the house wasn't so quiet. Bob loved to talk and he loved me. He loved talking with me so much that he looked hurt when my mother came home from work and wanted some peace and quiet.

Not that he didn't love her too. He was figuring out a plan so she could quit embroidery. A new career for me and eventually for Kyle so we wouldn't have to depend on the needle. I was already a year into it, taking lessons twice a week from Birdie, but Bob was convinced that I could do better as soon as he figured out how. It was all he talked about. He'd gotten a degree in American history and he'd done a lot of different things in Florida—masonry, plumbing, swimming pool building, mill work, metal welding—but he didn't see any of that as being useful to us.

"There's two sides to this country," he'd say as he unlocked our garage, where he'd set up his workshop. "Out east you make other people's ideas. Out west you make your own." Bob was always working on ideas. "Your mom's been telling me to check out that teaching job at your school," he'd say, squinting through the cigarette at the corner of his mouth while he tightened down a two-by-four in his vise. "But I just can't see it. I mean, look at this town. It's incredible." He'd lift his cigarette from his bottom lip, eyeing the piece of wood as if it were Queduro, and then put his cigarette back in place and start sawing. "If a person wants to be worth anything to his family, he's got to do it his own way. He's got to take a good hard look at what's needed, and then he's got to provide. That's what the West is about: ideas. That's why a lot of people here don't make it. They keep thinking all they have to do is catch somebody else's treadmill and go for a ride. That's what everybody back east does, you know. That's about the only form of transportation around. Sweet Jesus. You should have seen me all those years." He'd look down at Kyle, asleep in his stroller, and then look at me. "That's why I'm holding out, Rose. I know your mom's worried sick, but I'm an idea man. That's what she needed me for, and that's why I'm here. In fact, I think everything's beginning to connect up now, even all those no-neck jobs I had in New Jersey. Even our man Kyle over there, off in his dream world right now while I blabber on like this, even he's part of it. Everything's joining up now, coming together, pointing us toward something, something big. It's just going to take us time to figure out what it is."

I nodded. I wasn't sure what he was trying to say, but it took away my breath to have an adult talking as if I did. My mother didn't talk like that. Even Frank's parents didn't talk like that—and Birdie, who was the only other adult I spent time alone with, didn't talk at all. He'd sit next to me in his kitchen with a smell coming off him like old wax, staring at my mother while I picked away at my alphabet sampler. If she looked up from her own embroidery, he'd blush from the throat up and hand me the scissors. I knew my future didn't interest him, and my mother knew it too, but he'd offered us free embroidery lessons and she didn't have the money to hire anyone. At night, she'd get out the Bag Balm and smooth it on my hands, telling me how proud she was of them and of what they were going to do for us when I grew up.

Meanwhile Bob was in the garage, talking his ideas out, thinking aloud the possibilities, shaping them with his hands. Most of them were miniature models for bigger ideas he thought tourists might like. His cowboy-hat Ferris wheel, for instance, or his western-style diner. His backyard fountain, seven feet tall and made of tin boots spilling water over spurs that would turn like miniature waterwheels and make something-he-hadn't-figured-out-yet in the center light up. He gave up ideas like these before they were finished, and sometimes he couldn't talk for an hour or two afterward. But he kept going. Sometimes he went back to work in his shop after we went to bed. He couldn't stand the thought of watching me and Kyle enter the embroidery tradition. He couldn't stand the thought of anyone doing it. From my bed at night, I could sometimes hear him lecturing to himself out in the garage while he worked: *I'm telling you people, you're on the right track but taking the wrong train. If you want to make real money and achieve freedom, you don't try to sell tradition at five cents a poke. You sell history. You sell legends. The glory of the Old West! Think big! Think bigger!*

A lot of what he said sounded crazy when I was listening to it from my room—and thinking about our neighbors listening in, too—but when I was out there in the garage, when I could watch him thinking out loud, see an idea as a fact and then right in front of us, making it with his bare hands, it was hard to believe he wasn't going to come up with something.

And he did. He wanted us to carve wooden Indians. He wanted us to carve the best wooden Indians ever seen out west. Not just cheesy-looking cigar-store Indians either, he told us as he waved to the driver of a truck carrying what would be the first of many loads of ponderosa logs to be dumped in our back yard. Life-size Indians or bigger. Indians with character and pride. Indians who had lived the life and been the heroes. Indian monuments. Indian memorials. Sculptures. Art.

My mother didn't want to hear it. She said Bob didn't have the vaguest idea of what he was doing, that he was an overgrown child without an ounce of common sense. She couldn't forgive him for having spent all his money to come live with us instead of sending us money so we could move out. When he tried to show her the carving tools he'd bought, each one wrapped in chamois like fine silver, she tightened her mouth, bowed over her hoop, and embroidered so ferociously the thread broke. She said she wanted a real life for Kyle and me, not a souvenir trading post. "You think I haven't seen enough souvenirs in my life?" She threw the tools against the food cupboard and started crying.

I was upstairs with Kyle, listening through the floor vent. Bob was apologizing for scaring her and telling her he understood exactly why she was worried. But I knew his mind was made up. So did she. When he promised not to spend any of her money, not to discuss his ideas with any of her friends, and not to let anybody from town into the back yard, she gave in. "Fine," she said. "Do what you want, then. But don't try to mix up Rose in this. A whole year she's been working with Birdie Pinkston. A whole year out of her life, and in another five, her hands will be ready to catch on to embroidery. You can't ask her to risk her future in this town now. I won't have it. Neither will she. You're not even her father."

I loved my mother. I didn't want to scare her. I wanted to please her in every way. I just couldn't see why she didn't understand how Bob and I felt. Who wants to spend their life bent over a needle and thread? Who? By the time she got home from work the next night, I'd already decided. Maybe I wouldn't get to learn a proper oellet from Birdie, maybe I wouldn't see as much of Frank and his parents as I wanted, but I wouldn't be poor little Rose Bean anymore either. I'd be Rose Devonic, and my uncle would teach me chisels and rifflers and how to mix paint.

And he did. He was serious about teaching me anything I wanted to know and learning more of it himself, sweating like a horse and chatting away as he squatted next to me. *Go ahead, partner,* he'd whisper, holding the chisel to the edge of the wood while I lifted the mallet. *If we're going to do this, we're in it together.* Within a week my hands looked like an embroiderer's joke, stiff as claws, bruised, blood-blistered, and calloused. I didn't care. I liked the smell of wood chips, epoxy, and lacquer. I liked the *tock* of the mallet and the feel of the wood curling under the blade. I felt the same way Bob did, that whatever we were up to, we were on our way to something big, something permanent, something the embroiderers of Queduro would never understand.

5

Here in this green and shady bower
Delicious fruits and fragrant flowers
Virtue shall dwell within this seat
Virtue alone can make it sweet.

—from an American sampler, 1799

The professionals say it isn't half so much talent as practice. Practice, they say, years and years of practice until you've forgotten what you're practicing for, until you're beyond judging it, beyond liking it or hating it or not wanting to do it or wanting to do it all the time. Nine, ten years of practice, and if you're lucky that's when the surrender comes, when your mind gives up being able to think about what it's doing and lets your hands take over. That's when you become a professional embroiderer, when you realize that no matter what the rest of you is doing, whether you're sleeping or arguing or doing laundry or walking down the street, even if you've told yourself you'll never embroider again, still there will be those hands, humming away like power tools with no off switch. That's how Birdie described it. His parents started him on the needle when he was six. By the time he was twenty, he had to sleep with his hands pinned under him. A lot of pros did. Any other position and their hands kept them awake. The only time Birdie didn't sleep that way was when he'd passed out from drinking, and then he'd drop like a load of kindling, sprawling all directions. But even then, even when he was four sheets to the wind, if you looked closely you could still see his fingers moving. He'd officially retired from embroidery the day Alice bought him the motel, but when he drank, it always came back to him. Sometimes I'd catch him staring at his hands, holding them up to the light and turning them back and forth at the ends of his wrists. "They're thinking," he'd whisper. "I can feel it." Then, unless he was able to drink himself blind first, he'd be trapped behind his desk for weeks, red-eyed as a rabbit, watching them stitch out their work until they were done and he could enter the world again.

But my hands were just hands. They knew how to do the work, but they were nowhere near to doing it on their own. They had already hardened by the time I was finally serious about learning embroidery and my mind too tangled up in its own thoughts for surrender. Sometimes when I worked long hours, if it was late at night and I was deep into the rhythm of one particular stitch, I could almost feel something coming, like a hum in the blood at the tips of my fingers. But as soon as I stopped, there was nothing. Birdie said not to worry, that one day I'd just look down and find them already at work. I wanted to believe him, but so far I hadn't seen anything of the kind. Embroidery was still just one stitch after another, and most of the time it felt even slower than that.

This year especially. For one thing, I'd never worked with a dog in my cabin. I kept expecting distractions. I tied him to the foot of the bed so he wouldn't sneak up on me. I put his bowl on a sweater so it wouldn't bang if he suddenly got it into his head to check for food. I washed his feet after his visits outdoors, and I put newspapers all around the bed. I watched him like a hawk, but none of it was necessary. His favorite thing besides food, which he liked to swallow fast and without chewing, was sleep. He could go from one meal to the next without even lifting his head. When I'd open the bathroom window and set him outside, he'd jump down off the trash can and go wagging into the woods behind the motel, but then he'd come right back for more sleep. He slept so much I figured he had worms, which was his problem, I kept telling him, because I didn't have any money for a vet.

But after a day or two I began to think he wasn't sick, he just knew we were hiding. How else to explain why I never saw him cross the courtyard out in front of the cabin where he might have been spotted? Also, he never scratched at the door or made noise. He did moan if I was slow to share my food, but it was only a little sound and faraway, the kind of sound you could mistake for wind blowing through a crack. When he wanted the bathroom window to open so he could get back in, he'd just sit out there waiting. Not a peep. I had to admire it. Whatever he'd been through before—getting smacked around or shut in somewhere or dumped off to starve—it had straightened him right out on priorities. Food, shelter, sleep. He didn't notice the rest of it.

The Ute cabin wasn't a bad place to work. The brown log walls made it dark, and with the blanket taped over the window it was black as night inside, but once I had the heat up and my Indian-head lamp throwing a circle of light on the table and some coffee going, there was a coziness to it. It was like being in a little burrow underground. I had a bed, a hot plate for cooking, a table and chair, and the couch when I was tired of work. I had a cupboard for my finished canvases and a closet for my clothes and a bathroom with a mirror, a toilet, and a tub. I had what I needed. All I had to do was set up my canvases, lay out my threads, maybe check the lock on the door again, and then sit down to work.

But every time, just as I was getting set to start sewing a pattern, some lousy little nothing of a thought would start threading its way into my head. Like what I'd done with my bra, for example. I could almost believe I'd left it with Harmon Waters in the motel room in Lubbock. I could remember standing in front of the mirror in the bathroom in it and wondering if he would notice how old it was and if he'd mind or not, and I could remember taking it off. I just couldn't remember throwing it away. So where was it? I didn't need it—who needs a bra?—I just needed to know. The only other place I could think of was in my car, maybe under the back seat; but then I'd start wondering if I'd mixed it in the pile of laundry I'd asked Birdie to wash, if maybe he'd accidentally dropped it on the floor next to his washer. So should I go over there and check? Or should I wait till he came to the cabin and then ask him to check for me? Not that his sister would come off a two-day road trip and make a beeline for his clothes washer—but what if she did? What if, say, she'd spilled something on her good shirt? It was possible. I'd think about this until I could see that wretched old bra just glowing like a piece of kryptonite on the floor next to his washer, until I was pacing back and forth, listening for her Eldorado to arrive and then her footsteps storming down the sidewalk for my cabin.

But then I'd think how ridiculous it was. So what if my bra was on the floor in Birdie's basement? So what. Does a bra have to mean something? Alice wouldn't have a clue. She might think he'd finally gotten himself a girlfriend, or, if that was too much of a stretch, she might think it was an old one of hers. Alice had so many clothes she probably never remembered what she owned. I should just stop thinking about it, let it go, and get my work done. But as soon as I'd sit down with a needle, I'd find myself wondering if I was starting to let *everything* go, if my mind was beginning to unravel without me knowing it. I'd get this feeling that I needed to crack loose the tension in my neck and move around, put my face to the bathroom window for some air or check on my car or brush my teeth—anything; that if I didn't, if I just stayed so perfectly, perfectly still and cut off my mind for the sake of finishing a few stitches, I'd come bouncing out of the cabin next spring barking like a dog. And the pathetic part was that Alice wasn't even in town yet. I couldn't imagine what I'd be like then.

So when Birdie finally banged on my door on the third day, whispering through the wood *she's back*, it was more of a relief than anything else. I got dressed and organized the cabin so I could leave fast and spent the afternoon with the lights off, watching the door. But she didn't come and didn't come, and eventually I checked to make sure the blanket was taped flat around the window and then turned on my light and started working. Really working. It was like all the knotted-up energy of the past three days had finally come untangled with one good yank. I worked without thinking about the need for it. I worked straight through until dawn and then let the dog out the back window, took a bath, let him back in, made us some sandwiches, and crawled into bed.

When I came awake, it looked like noon outside but I felt fresh for the first time in weeks. I did sit-ups, had some breakfast, a pot of coffee, and then rolled a cigarette and sat down to work again. I'd already finished half of one piece—nothing fancy, just a small Home Sweet Home sampler in satin stitch—but if Birdie could keep bringing my groceries, doing my laundry, and keeping my whereabouts a secret, I could picture myself with a whole pile of finished embroideries by spring. I could picture selling my car, paying off my debts, and renting a trailer on Gobelin Hill, one with a year's lease and space for a garden. No more moving, that's what I kept thinking. No more asking for favors. The idea that I could look Frank in the eye, tell him I had a place of my own, and mean it.

When I laid my hoop aside, it was past dark again. I made a cheese sandwich and more coffee, let the dog out the back window, turned off the light, and peeled back the blanket on the front window so I could see what was happening over at Bird's office. The neon Indian was still off, his lights were on, and his curtains were closed. I said it out loud: *This is our last winter together.*

But I don't know. Saying thoughts out loud can make them turn. One minute it's a great idea, and the next you have to wonder. I pulled up my work chair, threw the edge of the blanket behind my head, and ate dinner staring at his office, wondering what he was doing over there: if he'd told his sister he wasn't selling the motel, if he was still sober, if he'd remember to bring me my groceries. Finally, about nine, I duct-taped the blanket back down, pulled the dog in through the bathroom window, turned on my light again, and went back to work.

Avoiding Alice turned out to be easy. As soon as she settled in her house and got her utilities and phone working, she didn't come out again. A week went by: nothing. The only reason I knew she was still there was that Birdie said so. He said she wasn't feeling well. He said I could go get my car out of Eli Sanchez's barn and park it next to the Ute. I could take the blanket off the window, come and go as I pleased, and even use his office to make calls. "It doesn't matter whether you're here or not," he said. "Do what you like. If she sees you, tell her you're the maid."

I didn't. I didn't trust Birdie's judgment. Since Alice's arrival, the spark had gone out of him. He spent nearly every day with her, and then I'd see him afterward in his office, sitting with his back to the window, tapping his pencil end to end on the front desk. An hour, even two hours like that before he'd get up, turn on his TV, and go make himself dinner. One night when I slipped over to his office to ask whether or not he'd faced down Alice yet about selling the motel, he just looked at me like I was hopeless and told me to go away. It made me mad. It was like he'd given up, like he wanted her to win. All he did was sigh. "You think the world revolves around you?" he said. "She doesn't even know you exist."

But if he believed that, he was wrong. She'd seen me. It happened the first day he used the Eldorado for errands. I'd always assumed he wasn't allowed to even touch it, so the afternoon I heard it pulling out of her driveway in a squeal of power steering, I peeled back the tape at the edge of the blanket to see if he was over at his office, and there she was at the window, staring at my cabin with a face as blank as the moon. My heart about quit. I was so sure the game was up, I packed everything again, but that night when Birdie dropped by with my groceries, he didn't even mention it. I decided she knew I was there but hadn't decided what to do about it yet. Maybe she was thinking up some way of getting back at Birdie, a humiliation he'd never get over, a trap. When I spotted Frank's squad car parked in front of her house, I was sure of it. I'd never had to deal with Alice, but I knew from listening to Birdie's stories that she was the kind of old lady who believed in good and evil, the kind who could wage war against you as if she'd been assigned to it by God.

So I began to fret. Should I leave? Should I go ask Frank what she was up to? Should I ask him what to do? That seemed like a good idea. I took a five-dollar bill from my emergency stash in the bottom of my Indian-head lamp, pulled on my parka, dropped the dog out the window, and crawled after him. I was thinking I'd go down the hill the back way, through the trees, and offer to buy Frank a cup of coffee and some pie at the cafe. It would be like old times. I'd introduce him and the dog. Frank liked dogs. I was in a rush to find him.

But halfway down the hill, the scrubby twigs scratching my face and grabbing my coat and getting caught in my hair, I realized what I was doing and stopped. How could I think about sharing a coffee with Frank? I was hiding out in a motel that was supposed to be closed. For all I knew, Alice had already reported me and Frank was planning to nail me for trespassing. It was crazy to think we could go back to old times. So I stood looking down at the town through the trees, until I knew it was impossible, and then I called the dog and stumbled back up to the cabin to work.

One afternoon soon after that, I heard Birdie out in the courtyard shoveling snow. He scraped his way down the sidewalk, step by step, toward my cabin, stopping to shovel each cabin porch as he went along. After he'd shoveled my porch—from the sound of it, nearly taking the paint off the boards—he went quiet. When I put my ear to the door to listen, I could hear him breathing outside.

"I can't do this anymore," he whispered.

I opened the door, yanked him inside, and shut it behind him. His nose was swollen red with cold, but the rest of him was gray and shrunken, his hair standing up as if magnetized, glowing white. I tried to take the shovel from him but he wouldn't give it up.

"What can't you do, Bird? You mean stay sober?"

He shook his head.

"Has she got a buyer? Is that it? Should I get out of here?"

"What?"

"What'd she do? Did she do something?"

"No."

I waited for him to go on, but he was somewhere else. I wasn't even sure he knew I was there. I pried the shovel out of his hand, helped him off with his coat, and sat him on the bed. He kept staring at the door and blinking. "I want to be a good brother," he said. "I told her that." Then he started blinking and his hands were shaking worse than ever and I could see he was going to cry.

"You *are* a good brother," I said. "I think you're the greatest brother she could ask for."

"I don't." He was staring at the door, his chin shaking like yogurt. "Do you know what I was doing just now? I was trapped in her upstairs bathroom pretending to fix her plumbing because I didn't want to go downstairs and hear her crying. She's begging me to take her to Africa. She says she doesn't have any friends left. She says it's her one big dream before she dies. I don't know what's wrong with her. She even tried to get down on her knees. My own sister. Can you imagine?"

He put his hands over his face. I put my arms around him and rocked him until he gave in to it. Then I pulled his galoshes off, shooed the dog off the bed, swung Birdie's feet up, and spooned down behind him. I pulled my blankets over us and held on while he cried, petting his forehead. Maybe he was old enough to be my father, even older, but we'd never held our needs against each other. It was just a form of friendship. That's how people survive, not by charity or pity but by knowing who to trust without having to ask. We both knew that.

When he got through the worst of it, I reached over his shoulder and laced my fingers through his to keep them from raveling at the blankets. I was sure he was ready to give in to his thirst now, I could feel him moving toward it in his mind. Myself, I didn't care if he drank, I just didn't want him to kill himself trying not to.

He was quiet and then he cleared his throat, trying hard not to sound like his nose was full. "What's all this crap?"

I raised my head. He was pointing at the graffiti carved into the log wall beside the bed. "The tourists do it every summer."

"They do, do they?" He was quiet a moment. "How can you stand this filth first thing in the morning?"

"I sleep with my back to it. Besides, it's not all filth. Look." I pointed to a little heart with an arrow through it on one of the logs. *"M.S. loves L.H.,"* I read. "That's not filth, is it?"

"That's destruction of private property. That's what that is. Put them in a log cabin and they think they can carve anything. Look at that." He jerked free of my hand and pointed to the sketch of a prick. "They act like a bunch of beavers."

I pressed my face into the soft, clean whiteness of his hair and started giggling.

"Stop it," he snapped. "You're dirty-minded. Let me up."

He batted me away, and I knew then he was clearing the decks for a decision. He stood, adjusted his belt, stepped into his galoshes, and started to prowl the cabin. I watched him go to the cupboard and look in. He took out a jar of peanut butter, shaking his head in disgust.

"What's wrong?"

He slapped the cupboard shut. "I need to blow my nose. Where the hell are your tissues?"

"There's toilet paper in the bathroom."

He huffed. "I don't use toilet paper."

"Too bad. We don't carry tissues."

He marched over to the closet and stood before it with his hands on his hips, looking in. The dog was in the corner, curled up on a pile of folded clothes.

"And how long has this closet been missing its door?"

"I don't know," I said. "Long as I've been staying here."

"*Pfft*. Why I thought I'd want to run a motel for tourists." He turned, surveying the room like a captain at sea. "Look at the light in here. This cabin is no better than a bat cave. How can you see enough to work by?" He went to the wall and chopped at the light switch, leering over his shoulder. "Look at that. They even broke the damn light."

"It just needs another bulb."

"I thought I gave you another bulb."

"You did." I lay back on the pillow, wondering what he was coming to. "I use it for my work lamp."

"Well, don't think you can just walk off with it," he snapped. He marched to the couch, glaring down at my sketches. "Pathetic."

"You taught me everything I know."

"I taught you your stitches, missy. I'm not responsible for your ideas or lack of them. What's this supposed to be?" He pointed to one of the drawings, scowling.

"Magpies. Tourists are nuts about magpies and Zias. It's like instant cash."

He snorted. "Embroidery's gone right down the drain ever since people started figuring out ways to sell it."

"I have to sell it. Come on. How do you like the one at the end? The one in the sketchbook."

He stepped to the arm of the sofa, clapped his hands behind his back, and peered down. He grimaced at the overhead light and back again. *"Pfft."*

"Hold it under the light where you can see better." I watched him bring it to the table and hold it under my Indian-head lamp, leaning back at arm's length to focus. "It's a bird's-eye view of the Queduro valley," I coaxed. "I have to finish the smaller work first so I have enough inventory to fill my booth, but I want to do that piece afterward. At least start on it. I'm going to do it big, a three-by-six canvas, with the filoselle I bought in Madrillas. Real bright and everything. See Red Mountain and Holt Canyon on the left? And the Mineral Building down on the right?"

He sniffed. "What do you propose to do with all this sky area? Flat stitch?"

"That's the beauty of it." I went to my embroidery bag for the piece of silk. "I'm going to appliqué this silk onto the canvas. Look at the color. It's rich as gold. Watch." I unfolded it, like a piece of air in my hands, and smoothed it against the paper. "It's going to fit between the sides of the valley like this. It'll give the scale of things, you know. Like when you're up on the overlook watching a sunset, and you realize suddenly how big it is compared to the houses down in the valley."

"Scale, schmale," he growled. "It's going to look like you got too lazy to sew the top half of your canvas."

"No, it isn't. It's going to look like a big golden sky. A beautiful sunset." I glanced sideways at him and then back at the sketch. "Maybe I'll put in some magpies."

"Magpies will look like people flying past in tuxedos."

"At least they'll be dressed." I grabbed the pad from him. "Unlike some of the people I've seen you embroider. Which I am not supposed to mention, especially to your sister."

His face twitched as if I'd pinched his cheek. "Is that a threat?"

"If you don't quit ragging my ideas, it will be."

We glared each other down, and then he waved me off and sat on the chair, bending over to buckle his boots. I squinted at the sketch, but it was no use. Now that he'd said it, it was obvious. Even with a whole swarm of magpies flying across it, the silk would just be one big flat blob of yellow with a tangle of stitches along the bottom.

"Fuck."

He bucked back from his boots. "Don't you use that kind of language around me."

"I'll say fuck if I feel like it. And thanks to you, I feel like it now. This was supposed to be my big showpiece."

He looked at me and his mouth went hard. "Give me that." He stood, slapped the pad on top of my threads, and reached for a wax pencil. "If you want to use that piece of silk, you do this." He bent under the lamp, hair glowing like silver thread. He drew some lines and then slapped the pad against the table again. "You get rid of all that crap that's supposed to be landscape and you do one big scavenger bird in the middle of the silk, like that"—he hit the paper hard—"with a good solid satin stitch. That's what."

I bent over his shoulder to sneer, but then I saw what he'd done. His magpie was flaring up with its head cocked sideways, clever and sly, like it had spotted something interesting down below.

"Jesus. That's way better than any of my magpies."

"Of course it is." He pushed me out of his way and strode to the door. "I don't have time for this. I've got work to do."

I looked up from the pad. "Are you going over to your sister's?"

"Damn right I am. And you know why?" He swung the door wide. "Because I am going to tell her, missy. By God, I am going to tell her right now to her face."

He told her he was going to renovate the motel. The next morning he was out in the courtyard on his hands and knees patching the sidewalk with a kitchen spatula and a plastic bucket of mixed cement. Then he started repainting the tribe names on the doors of the cabins until it threatened to snow again, and then he nearly slid off the roof of the Apache fixing a leak. Then he borrowed Eli Sanchez's truck and came home with twenty aluminum gutters, two for each cabin. I sat by the window so I could keep an eye on him while I worked. Twice I saw him drop the hammer, stumble down the ladder, and bend over, holding on to his knees to catch his breath, hair blowing out all directions, his face a blotchy, dangerous pink. But I didn't try to stop him, not until the next afternoon, when I peeled back the blanket and saw him out there with a little electric Homelite chain saw, looking up at the cottonwoods. I slammed down my work and cracked the door of the Ute.

"What the hell are you doing now?"

"Getting rid of this tree."

"Where's your sister?"

"In bed."

"Is it safe to come out?"

"How should I know?"

I grabbed my parka, pulled on my boots, and stepped out.

"You don't know how to run a chain saw. Where'd you get that thing anyway?"

He ignored me. "Potential lawsuit in a windstorm. Every single one of those dead branches up there."

"They're not dead. They're just bare."

"They're dead. I noticed last summer." He bent to fiddle the starter button, his white hair shaking loose. "I ought to clean out all these old trees. One dies, they all start dying."

"You will not. Stop it, Bird. These trees were here before you. They're the best thing about this place." I paused. "What's your sister going to say if she comes over and finds you cutting down all your trees?"

He looked up at me and then started the saw. Alice was a complicated part of why he did and did not drink. I ran to the side of the office and peeked around the corner. The shades on the front of her house were down. I ran back.

"Birdie," I shouted over the saw, "you can't do this! You hear me? At least hire somebody. These trees are too big."

"Too big?" He shut off the Homelite and straightened up. "I've cut down trees twice as big as this one."

"And when was that? Fifty years ago?"

He snarled and walked back to the office without using his knees. When he came back, he was wearing a pair of protective goggles and yellow earplugs. He bent over and switched on the saw.

"Stand back, Rose!" he shouted. "I'm going to drop her between the Hopi and the Navajo, but we better play it safe." With goggles and earplugs, he looked like a bug. He hefted the saw to his thigh, snapping the extension cord behind him, and circled the tree, looking up. He held the blade edge at knee height, his neck folding pinkly over the edge of his parka, white hair blowing backward, and the air sang as the saw bit in, a wing of wood chips flying away. I stepped closer to him, making sure that his office was still between me and Alice's house. The tree was as big around as he was. It did look as if it was weighted to fall between the Hopi and the Navajo, but I was no more of an expert than Birdie. I ran to the Ute. The dog slapped his tail once on the bedclothes when he saw me open the door. You stay, I shouted, and slammed the door and ran back to Birdie. The saw was eating its way through the wood. Birdie's face was as red and twisted as a cedar knot. I yelled for him, but he didn't hear.

When he finished the undercut, he put the saw on the ground, staggered back, pushed up his goggles, and reached in his parka for his handkerchief. I stepped closer to him. He was shaking all over.

"You're a goddamn mule."

"Used to do this all the time. Cut down ponderosas plenty bigger than this one."

"Yeah, and you weren't sixty-eight then, either."

He said something I didn't catch.

"Bird, come on, quit. You don't look well."

"It's just a headache. I'm halfway through now."

"Why don't we call Eli? He can finish it for you. He cuts down trees all the time."

"Sanchez can't handle this. The cluck's a drunk."

"And you aren't? I happen to know a dry drunk when I see one." I was angry. "Why the hell can't you go to AA like a normal person? Why do you have to do this?"

He looked at me, his white hair shimmering with sawdust, and I thought he was going to give in. But then he looked at the cottonwood and his mouth hardened again. He pulled down the goggles, the rims pulling his lower lids to pink. He felt to make sure the earplugs were still tangled in the hair of his ears, and he bent over the saw. The shriek closed him off from me, forcing me backward. Drawing his lips wide, grinning against the sound, he laid the blade into the wood, angling down toward the first cut.

When the wedge finally popped free, he stepped back, reeling. I thought he'd have to stop then. He looked up at the tree and then revved the saw and stepped clumsily to the other side. I watched him gather himself and then set the saw to the bark again, his arms and legs quivering with the effort.

When the tree began to move, I shouted a warning, but he'd already seen. He stepped back, cutting the saw off, and in the fresh silence we both looked up.

There was nothing at first, and then a long, slow groan like something ancient, and the upper branches of the tree began to move away from the arms of the trees around it. I stepped behind Birdie and grabbed him by his parka belt, but he slapped away my hand. There was a slow-motion creaking noise as the tree began to twist sideways off its stump, a *woosh* noise I turned from, and a great smash and the fallout of branches clattering all around on the sidewalk. I turned back. The tree had made a three-point landing directly in front of the Ute. The dog was at the window, his front paws on the sill and the edge of the blanket hooked on one ear. He was peering out through the branches at me, not sure if he was in trouble yet. Birdie was standing with his back to me, looking down at the trunk, big around as a truck wheel and about six inches from his left foot. He dropped the saw as if his hands had forgotten. A magpie flew past, cawing once, and it was very still.

"Well," I said, "I hope you're satisfied. You all but took out my cabin *and* my dog. Are you all right?"

He lurched sideways and turned to me, trying to push off the goggles. His face was shining in sawdust and he was weeping. "Goddammit," he cried. "Did you see that, Rose? Goddamn, let's have a drink. Where's Alice?" And then he put his left hand to his cheek as if he had a toothache, dropped to his knees as if he were about to pray, and then onto one side, buckling like a little twig.

6

Children like tender osiers take the bow,
As they first are fashioned grow.

—from an American sampler, 1826

There was one doctor in the valley, D. G. Mutz. His office was in his house. He'd been practicing for forty years and he loved his work, but nobody went to him anymore unless they had to because he was so old and deaf and shaky. I had to shout into the office phone just to make him understand there was an emergency. When he finally got it, he said he'd be there in a few minutes. I hung up wishing I hadn't called at all. At the rate Mutz moved, a few minutes could take an hour. And then what? I looked over at Birdie. I'd gotten him on the couch and pulled off his boots, but he hadn't said anything yet and he was gray as a sidewalk, his eyeballs rolling around under his eyelids. Maybe it was just a bug, one of those twenty-four-hour flus or something. I held the phone, trying to decide who to call. I wanted to talk to Frank. I wanted to talk to him so badly I could taste it. I looked at Birdie again. One of his hands was twitching in a normal every-day sort of way, but the other one wasn't. Frank would say get him to the hospital in Madrillas. He'd say don't wait for Mutz. *Don't wait!* I dropped the phone, skipped over the coffee table, turned Birdie on his side so he wouldn't roll off the couch, and then bent to his ear, orange as a dried apricot against the silk white of his hair. "I'm going to get help, Birdie. You hear me? I'll be back."

And then not knowing if I was getting him help or not, I fled out the door and across the street.

I knew she kept her doors locked whether she was home or not, but I also knew from having helped Birdie install her smoke alarms that she always left a key under the mat by the kitchen door. I also knew the house was a typical Victorian: four rooms downstairs, four rooms up, and a wide polished wooden staircase in the center with dim pink lights on the ceiling and old-fashioned wallpaper. When I pushed open the door, the air felt warm and padded and I could hear a TV somewhere. I circled the kitchen, searching for keys. I ran to the living room, searched there, then into the hallway to check the coat closet, glanced in the dining room, and ran for the stairs. I stopped at the top. Behind the door to the left at the end of the hall, I could hear TV laughter, also a whirring sound. When I put my ear to the door, a voice called, "Birdie, is that you?" I pushed open the door.

I expected her to scream, maybe throw something. When she didn't, I thought I'd opened the wrong door. The room was dark, crammed with furniture: the whir of a humidifier, the smell of Pine-Sol. But as I was about to close the door and try the next one, I saw something move and it was her, lying on the other side of a lampshade and a line of high-backed easy chairs. She was propped on pillows on a high bed, peering forward to see me through a spout of fog coming from the humidifier.

"I have to borrow your car. Where are your keys?" I saw her brown pocketbook on a pile of magazines and sprang for it. "Birdie's sick. I need to get him to the hospital."

"What is the meaning of this? Who are you?"

"The hospital!" I shouted. "He needs a hospital, and that's fifty miles from here." I turned her pocketbook upside down and emptied it on the card table. Kleenex, comb, wallet, a plastic-covered photograph, a notebook, candy, pens, eyeglass case, a kitchen fork, keys. I shoved the keys in my pocket. "Doc Mutz is coming. He'll tell you. I'll call you from the hospital. And Alice, this wasn't my fault."

"Now I know who you are," she said slowly. "I know exactly who you are."

I closed the door behind me. "I'm a good driver," I yelled over my shoulder. "I'm sorry!" and I raced back down the stairs.

I'd never driven anything but my Plymouth, and when I put the Eldorado in reverse and touched the gas, the thing bolted out of the garage like a tiger. When I hit the brake in the middle of the street, I bucked to a stop that nearly took off my neck. Then another lurch to the office and I threw it into park, pushed on the heater, and ran inside.

Birdie couldn't have weighed more than a hundred pounds, but I had a time getting him into the back of the car. I pushed him in up to his waist, and then while he slid slowly out again, I ran to the other side, caught his shoulders, and dragged him in the rest of the way. He was drooling. I rolled him on his side so he wouldn't choke and then ran back through his office to his bedroom. I grabbed a quilt and pillow off his bed and his wallet off his dresser and ran out to get him tucked in, and I ran to my cabin for my license and my stash of emergency money. When I got back in the car and turned the key, I heard a grinding sound that made my throat close, but then I realized I was in a car with an engine so quiet I didn't even know it was on. When I noticed my breath coming out like smoke, I leaned to slap at the dashboard buttons trying to get some heat going, and there was a bang on the window next to my ear.

It was Alice, her mouth set like a splinter, her chin trembling, her rubbery white cheeks spiderwebbed with veins. It was her hair that scared me most: not the thick iron-gray I remembered—a wig, I realized suddenly— but wispy thin yellow-white hair, almost like shredded bits of filoselle silk stuck to her skull. Her eyes were bluer than I remembered, the same sky-dyed blue as Birdie's, but not like his at all. Blue like a chemical warehouse on fire. She was holding a large wooden box against the front of her black raincoat and her face was wet.

"Get out of my car, you monster. Get out."

I got out. She pushed me aside and leaned in to see Birdie. "Oh my *God*! How could this happen?" She straightened up, looking across at her house and then out at the valley, as if she was going to run for help.

"We need to get him to the hospital," I said. "If we take him to the emergency room in Madrillas and tell them—"

She turned so hard the belt of her raincoat snapped the car door. "*Don't* you tell me what to do. You think I don't know how to take care of him? I'm his sister. I've looked after him all my life. This is *your* fault. Get away from my car." I stepped back and she got in, thunking the door behind her. The engine shrieked against the ignition and I called through the window that it was already on. She lifted her chin as if she hadn't heard and backed up, running into the snowbank behind her. She turned the wheels, power steering squealing in protest. When she came around, she slowed and rolled down her window. I leaned to it.

"If you want, I can call the hospital and tell them—"

"You did this!" she cried. "Get off our property. I never want to see you again. Get off!"

Then her window closed and she took off, the rump of her car swerving on ice as she turned onto the street, white smoke pumping out the exhaust pipe. There was a red rusted-out Chevy Luv chugging its way up the hill and losing traction—that was Doc Mutz—but she roared by him and on through the blinking light without even slowing down. I watched through the trees until I spotted her at the far end of town, fishtailing in front of Steelhead's Market to get on the bridge, and then, a moment later, a quick flash by the cemetery and she was gone.

My ears were ringing. Mutz was backing up his Chevy Luv for another run at the hill. I turned to Birdie's office. I was sure I'd closed the door, but it was wide open. I went over to it and looked around and then stepped inside. It took me a moment to realize what was missing. She'd taken the box of motel keys off the wall.

7

All our gaiety is vain
All our laughter is but pain
Only lasting and divine
Is an innocence like thine.

—from an American sampler, 1809

Frank was waiting for his change at Eddie Walk's Cafe when he looked out the front window and saw the Eldorado coming. He took his toothpick out of his mouth as the big car bounced off Flax Hill and through the blinking light onto Hemming, and when he realized just how fast she was coming, he dropped his wallet on the counter, stepped around old Eufanio Johnson, and rammed open the door to wave the car down. It was Alice, all right, but she wasn't slowing up for him. He shouted as she passed and then heard a high, choked cry up the street behind him that made him turn to see Dick Sweeny standing on the sidewalk outside the Magpie Bar with a white look of confusion on his face. On the side-walk opposite Dick, carrying an embroidery bag strapped over his chest bandolier-style and bumping the weight of it sullenly from knee to knee as he stepped off the curb, was Dick's seven-year-old son, Billy. Billy was bundled in an oversized parka with a fur-lined hood that blinkered his view, so that instead of seeing the danger he trudged out to the middle of the street and stopped, wailing at his father, *But it's too heavy!* and trying to lift the strap of the bag over his head. Frank shouted and began to run. Billy's father shouted too and held up his hands, as if to push against a wall of air, and that's when the boy finally lifted his chin and turned to see the oncoming car, his furious little pout falling open in wonder.

It seemed to Frank that the moment snagged there like a photograph—he would always be running, Dick Sweeny would always be holding up his hands, and little Billy would always be peering out from underneath his hood to see the Eldorado bearing down on him—and then time started up again, the car swerved around the boy by inches, fishtailed to the end of the street for the turn, flew over the bridge, and vanished around the corner of Swan's barn.

Dick stumbled across the street and grabbed his son, shaking him hard and then pulling him tight to his chest. "For Jesus' sake, didn't you hear me?"

As Frank ran up, he saw the boy's mouth, open and soft and pink under the shadow of the hood.

Dick craned around wildly. "Did you see what she did?" he cried, his voice catching on itself. "She nearly hit him!"

"Hats and me saw it!" Tommy Steelhead was coming fast across the street from the bar, pulling his girlfriend, Hattie Rodriguez, by the wrist. Tommy was a tall excitable boy with long wrists who'd been having a hard time lately staying out of fights. "We saw it all from the window," he cried. "She was coming like a bat out of hell, Frank. She must have been doing fifty."

"Try goddamn sixty," cried Dick. "If she'd been doing fifty, my Billy would've had time to get out of the street. Jesus H." He turned to his son, pushing back his hood. "You all right, boy?"

Billy's eyes were as big as money. "I almost got runned over." He looked up at Frank. "You was running."

"I was, Bill." Frank squeezed Billy's shoulder. "I'm glad you're okay, though."

"Hey, Frank," called another voice. "Everybody in one piece?"

Frank turned to see Eli Sanchez shrugging on his coat as he crossed the street. Thickset and balding, shadows of blood under his eyes. Until a few years ago, when he'd crushed his hand in the revolving door at the county courthouse in Madrillas, he'd been one of the most talented embroiderers in Queduro. Now he worked at the hardware store and drank too much, and everyone knew his young wife, Maria, was running around with other men. But for all that, he was still good-natured and uncomplaining. He nodded to Dick as he came up and handed Frank his wallet.

"You're okay, Billy, aren't you?"

Dick jerked his son out of range. "He's lucky to be alive, that's how he is." He twisted the strap of his workbag roughly off Billy's head and threw it over his own shoulder. His face was very red. "Who in hell does she think she is, driving like that? She could have killed him. She could have mowed my boy down like a blade of grass." He turned to Tommy and Hattie, and his eyes narrowed. "What're you two looking at? Nobody's hurt, okay? Now get lost. Get."

Tommy's face dropped its grin. "Who the fuck are you?" he said. "We didn't do anything. We're just trying to help."

"Come on, Tommy," said Hattie, putting her hand on his arm. "I'm cold. Let's go back inside where it's warm." She was a thin-boned, pretty girl with a layer of makeup so thick it looked as if it came on and off in one piece. "Come on. Don't get mad. Let's just go, okay?"

"All right, Hats." Tommy threw one last hard look at Dick and started for the bar. At the curb, he turned and walked backward, calling, "But I don't see why the hell I'm the one always gets bitched at when all I did was try to help."

Frank put his hand on Dick's arm and stepped forward. "And you did help. Thanks, Tommy."

"Like hell," muttered Dick. "He was hoping to see blood. That's all he wanted." He turned to Frank. "What are you still standing around for, Doby? Aren't you supposed to be the sheriff?"

"I'll take care of it, Dick. You need to calm down."

"I don't need nothing. That was as close to a hit-and-run as I've seen." Dick stepped closer. "I don't care how rich she is, and I don't care how old she is, if you don't deal with her properly, I will, you understand? I will."

"All right, Dick."

"Don't you *all right, Dick* me. That old woman nearly killed my son. Now, come on, boy. And keep up this time." He took Billy roughly by the top of the hood and began to steer him across the street, the boy waving his small mittened hands like stars, trying to keep his balance.

"You might be interested to know," murmured Eli under his breath to Frank, "that old Dick has been over at the Magpie celebrating his divorce with vodka tonics since early this morning. Plus, when he saw that Cadillac flying down the street, he hopped to the other side. Didn't think to remember his son until he'd saved his own skin. That's a lot of why he's so upset now."

"I can't blame him. I'd be upset too."

"Yeah, well. If you decide not to execute old Miss Pinkston by firing squad, he'll probably survive. Mind if I walk with you?"

"Not if you don't mind walking fast."

They started quickly down the street toward the squad car, chins tucked against the cold.

"I haven't seen Rose since she got back from Texas," said Eli. "You?"

"I been pretty busy."

"Me too, yeah." Eli sighed. "And you know how she gets. Bites your head off if you interrupt her while she's working." He paused and added, "So you haven't seen her yet?"

"You trying to tell me something, Eli?"

"Goddammit, Frank, I guess I am." He took a noisy breath. "Rose's car is parked behind my barn with about half her stuff still inside it. She left a message on the windshield saying she didn't want to keep it up at the motel because Flax Hill gets too icy, but I don't believe that's the only reason. I think she's hiding out in one of those cabins. I think the old man's bringing her food and keeping her a secret. That's why we haven't seen her in town yet. I also think that's why he hasn't turned on the neon Indian. He's trying to convince his sister—and the Committee—that he hasn't got anyone staying up there."

"I know."

Eli stopped walking. "You do?"

"There's no real way *not* to know it, is there?"

They started walking again.

"So you think maybe Alice found out about Rose being there?" asked Eli. "You think that's why she roared out of town like that?"

"If I can catch her before she gets to Phoenix, I guess I'll find out." They were coming up on the squad car. "Can you do me a favor, though, Eli?"

"Name it."

"Can you go over to my office and check on Silas? I'm worried that Alice might have called him and told him to go arrest Rose."

"She'd do that?"

"I don't know. I hope not. But if she has, and Silas is ready for action, will you tell him I want him to stay where he is? I'd tell him myself on the radio, but it's better if he hears it in person. Tell him I mean it. Tell him he can call me on the radio if he has questions."

"I'll tell him he'll get his ass kicked if he moves from that desk."

"Thanks." Frank opened his door, got in, and started his engine. "How come I didn't hire you as a deputy?"

Eli laughed and lifted what was left of his hand in a salute. "Because I'm a coward and I drive like a grandmother. I prefer to keep my butt on the bar stool and leave the glory to you. Good luck."

As soon as he was safely out of the valley, Frank hit the accelerator, but he did not spot her car until he was out on the highway heading for Madrillas Pass. She was not only speeding but, as she roared up into the pass, she began crossing the yellow line back and forth with the curves. He followed hard on her, his mouth dry, switching on his alternating beams when there was no reaction to his bar light, his heart pumping and angry now. What the hell was she up to? She had to have noticed him in her rearview by now. But still she kept on, gliding out of view, one curve to the next. The weather had held for the last week and the road on the south side of the pass was dry pavement, but on the north side it twisted like a snake into the refrigerated winter-long shadows of the mountain, every curve steep, narrow, probably still icy. She had to know that; she'd driven it enough times—a guaranteed accident if she didn't slow down. He hit the siren in three short warning blasts and then switched it on full, shaking his head. If anything she seemed to speed up. At this rate there was no way he'd catch her in time. On the last wide curve before the summit, he lifted his foot off the accelerator with his teeth clenched and his hand already reaching for his mike, knowing he'd failed and that what would happen to Alice Pinkston in the next few seconds on the curve just past the summit would be very, very bad. She flew toward it as if eager, not a single flash of brakes.

But death never allows plans. As he topped the hill, he saw that she'd lost control on the first patch of ice and tried to brake there for the curve, going into a spin instead—but the spin had turned her car clockwise toward the mountain, instead of toward the edge, so that now she was parked in the middle of his lane, stopped there as if waiting to see if he'd be able to stop as quickly. The grade was steep, the ice bad, and he had to pump his brake carefully to keep in control as he moved into the left lane and past her car and slowed to a stop several yards below. As he backed up, his tires slipping sideways, he saw her sitting rigid at the wheel, looking like an electric shock had passed through her face. She was also not wearing her wig, her head with its bits of hair here and there vulnerable-looking as a child's. He unrolled his window.

"Miss Pinkston. Unroll your window there."

She was gripping the wheel as if she were still driving, staring up at the hill they had both just come over.

"You need to move your car off the road. Right now. This minute. You hear me?"

She looked over at him and then lowered her head, resting it against the steering wheel.

He checked his rearview and then rolled forward to park on the inside shoulder of the road. He got out and ran back, straining for the sound of another car coming. The pavement was a gray shine of ice. She was lucky she hadn't spun right off the mountain. When he opened her door, she held out her hand and he took it and helped her out. She was crying, her face wide open with it.

"Oh my God. What have I done?"

"You spun out, Miss Pinkston. You were driving way too fast—" He stopped. Her brother was lying in the back, wrapped to the chin in an embroidered quilt, the whites of his eyes showing, his face a mottled gray. Frank glanced at Alice—she was shaking her head, pressing her knuckles against her mouth—and then leaned over the seat and pulled down the quilt to check the old man's neck for a pulse. It was weak and rapid. He could not see any bleeding and did not smell alcohol. When he thumbed open the thin eyelids, one pupil was a large black dot, the other almost lost in its fierce blue iris. "Jesus." He backed out, wiped his mouth with the back of his hand, and then took Alice by the elbow and led her around to the passenger side. He helped her in, slammed her door, and then ran around and got behind the wheel. He turned the car around and pulled off the road behind his squad car.

"I'll be right back."

He jumped out, lost his footing on the ice and went down hard without feeling it, got up, and ran for his car, reaching in the window for his radio mike.

"Silas. Come in. Over." He stared at the view off the side of the mountain without seeing it, praying he was not in a dead spot, praying that Silas had not decided to leave the office. "Silas K. Over?"

"What's up, boss?"

"I got a medical emergency on the north side of Madrillas Pass. I need you to call the hospital in Madrillas, tell them to send an ambulance to meet me. I'll be driving a tan 1997 Eldorado, Arizona license plate"—he stopped and leaned sideways to see—"twenty-two eighteen. They'll probably see me coming down when they get about halfway up the mountain. You got that?"

"You mean Alice Pinkston's Eldorado?"

"I'll call you land line when I get to the hospital. Out." He grabbed his key out of the ignition, rolled the window shut, locked the door, and ran back to Alice's car. How many times had he told Silas not to use names over the radio in an emergency? He jumped in the Cadillac, glanced at Birdie, and told Alice to put on her seat belt. He pulled onto the road.

"There's an ambulance coming. We'll meet them halfway." He pulled off his knit cap, forcing himself to let up on the gas before the next bend. "Miss Pinkston? Can you tell me what happened?"

"I blame myself for this. If only I'd gotten us out of there. I shouldn't have listened to him. I knew I shouldn't, and now it's too late."

"Did he take something? Is that what happened? Do you know if he took medicine?" He looked at her. She was wearing a black raincoat as thin as paper. "Can you talk to me a little? Miss Pinkston?"

"Medicine?" Her voice was high-pitched and shaky.

"Yes. Maybe blood pressure pills? Heart pills? Anything like that?" He pressed the accelerator as the road turned to pavement again and almost immediately had to let up. He heard a sigh from the back and craned up to the rearview. Allergic reaction? Heart attack? Stroke? For all the times he'd studied his First Responder's book to prepare for emergencies, he'd focused almost entirely on chapters dealing with what he might find at an accident: internal and external injuries, broken bones, bleeding, hypothermia, heatstroke, heart failure, shock, gunshot wounds. Everything he'd learned about assessing the cause of illness flew past him in a chaos of symptoms.

"She poisoned him, didn't she?"

He glanced over at her.

"That girl. She poisoned him. That's what you're saying?"

Frank looked back to the road. "No, Miss Pinkston. I'm no doctor, but I don't think anybody poisoned him."

"Then why is he like *that*?" She gripped his arm as if to yank his hand off the wheel. "Don't treat me as if I'm a know-nothing. I'm his sister. What have you people done to him?"

Frank kept his eyes on the road. "You have to let go of my arm so I can get us down this mountain." He waited until she let go and then cleared his throat. "Miss Pinkston, alcohol isn't the problem this time. At least I don't think so. I can't smell it on him."

"Of course you can't. My brother hasn't had a drop of liquor in twenty years."

Frank widened his eyes at the road. Twenty years? He let it pass and went on. "I also want to say that Rose Devonic would never try to hurt your brother. I know this for a fact."

He felt her staring at him, building for it, and he was sorry he'd even tried.

"How can you say that?" she burst out. "She killed my little sister, didn't she?"

He looked at her sharply. "What?"

"Didn't she kill Florie?"

He blew air, shaking his head. "God bless it, Alice. You say the craziest damn things."

"I beg your pardon?"

"Rose didn't kill your sister. Your sister's death was an accident. Don't you remember?"

"Yes. Florie died, and there was that Rose girl standing there, still alive."

Shock, he thought. Possibly serious. Still, he could not keep his anger to himself. "I don't want to hear you say that again. That's as cruel and wrong as anything I've ever heard. You lost your sister in that accident, and I know that was hard, but Rose lost her mother, her uncle, and her little brother. She lost her home, everything. She suffered more than you or I can guess. Plus she was only sixteen. Do you hear me?"

After a moment, she sniffed huffily. "Well. I'm just trying to put two and two together." But as Frank breathed out the last of his anger, she burst out, "She was there when Florie died, and then today, when my brother got sick, there she was again. She's always there when people die."

"Miss Pinkston. I need you to stop."

"Why should I?"

"Because I asked you to."

There was a long silence. Then in an almost girlish voice she mewed, "I won't do anything unless you call me by my first name, Alice."

He looked at her and then back at the road. He hated her. "All right. Alice. Can you tell me about your brother? Was he taking any prescription drugs? Did he fall, maybe? Do you know how long he's been like this? The EMTs are going to need to know."

When he slowed for the curve, he saw that she was pressed against the door, a tear spilling off her little withered mushroom of a chin.

"Alice?"

"I think something's wrong with me," she whispered. "I can't remember what I just said. I'm trying my best, but I can't remember."

He nodded, and when the road began to level off a bit he took the next bend and the next, and then suddenly he was in another car on this same highway years ago, sitting next to his father while Rose sat in the back holding on to her uncle, the four of them hurtling down this very mountain with the accident behind them and their old lives gone, changed forever. Florie Pinkston was dead, Rose's mother and brother were dead, and Rose's uncle Bob was dying, everybody knew that, but he kept saying it over and over again: "It's nobody's fault, you guys. We tried our best. We have to remember that. We tried, right?" Frank wiped the back of his hand across his mouth. He'd been afraid to look at Rose. She'd needed him to look at her—not out the window, not at her dying uncle or at the blood in the back seat, not at the road or at his father, but at her, something to connect them together again, to bring her back, to make it all right even if it wasn't. He'd felt her eyes on the back of his head that whole drive, begging him to look, begging him to see she was at the very edge of her life, hanging there not for rescue—it was way too late by then for rescue— but only for him to tell her to go on, she could do it, she was strong enough, he believed in her. He hadn't, though. He looked over at Alice and forced himself to say her name. When she looked back at him, it was all right. Nothing was ever that bad if you just did it instead of thinking. He smiled for her and took her hand a moment, a hand as light and cool as parchment paper, before turning back to the road.

8

Teach me to feel anothers smart
And teach my tears to flow
Teach me to soothe the sorrowing heart
And give relief to woe.

—from an American sampler, 1801

When Mutz realized there was no emergency for him to look at, he gave me a bitter look, turned off his car, and plucked out his keys. When I tried to stop him, he waved me off. "I'm not getting any younger, young lady, and making house calls in cold weather for no reason doesn't help. I'd better fortify myself with some coffee."

I watched him go toward the office. He walked in slow motion with a bloated-looking back that was close to being a hump. The worst of him was his smell, like a used hospital bed wrapped in wet wool. When he finally got through the doorway, I squeezed past, went behind the desk, and tried Frank's office. The line was busy. I tried his home number. While it rang, Mutz hung his coat on the hook behind the door, studied the room with slow blinks, settled himself with a wheezy sigh into Birdie's recliner, and removed his wire-rim glasses. When he swayed forward to look back at me, his eyebrows raised in a now-where's-that-coffee look, I banged down the phone and went to the kitchen. I didn't want to wait on Mutz, didn't want to sit with him, didn't want to listen to him, but it was my fault he'd come. He patted his breast pocket and pulled out a handkerchief. "So what were his symptoms?" Mutz loved practicing medicine, but he loved even more having a whole afternoon to talk about it. I took a TV tray out of the cupboard and banged it on the stove.

"He just fainted and wouldn't come to."

"What's that?"

"I said, he fainted," I shouted.

"You young people." He sighed, wiping his glasses. "Mumbling your words so a doctor can't hardly hear you."

I filled the smallest mug Birdie had with coffee, put the milk pitcher and the sugar bowl on the tray with a spoon, and took it out to the other room, setting it down next to him and leaning to his ear. "HE JUST FELL DOWN."

"He did, did he? Where?"

I took his glasses, fixed them back on his ears for him, and pointed toward the window facing the courtyard. He nodded thoughtfully.

"Ice is a real problem for old people, you know. Why's that tree cut down out there, I wonder?"

I bent to his ear. "I HAVE TO LEAVE."

"No, thank you, sweetheart, I prefer to fix my own." He swayed sideways with a grunt to reach for the sugar. I went behind the desk to try the phone again.

"Rosie. Come sit down here and talk to me. What did he look like when you found him?"

I punched at the numbers. "What difference does it make?"

"Speak up, dear."

I leaned over the desk. "HE LOOKED SICK."

"Well, of course he looked sick. Concussions are tricky things, you know. You shouldn't have let him leave without me having a look first. A man can get up from a bad spill saying he's fine, looks fine, acts fine—but if you don't have the doctor check him out, he can walk out the door and keel over dead. He's not alone now, is he?"

"Alice took him." The line was still busy. When I saw Mutz still waiting for an answer, I went over to the mantelpiece and pointed hard at her photograph. "SHE TOOK HIM," I yelled. "SHE TOOK HIM. HER."

Mutz tilted his chin up to see through his glasses, and I went to the phone. "Ah, yes, the older sister," he said. "Well, she always wanted to be a nurse, you know. Shame, how she didn't go through with it. I could have used a nurse in this town, believe you me."

I switched the phone to the other ear, willing Frank to pick it up. Even Angela. It rang and rang. Mutz was still looking up at the photograph. "She's had several health complaints lately, but I'm not too worried," he said. "She's needs attention more than anything else. Most women her age do. Last time she called, I said, 'Alice, I wish I could make some money off you, but the fact is, from cholesterol to blood pressure, you're absolutely A-One. You're just getting older, that's all.' She was livid, of course." He chuckled under his breath, then lifted his coffee with both hands, his lips opening like a long, trembling, purple flower. "Do you think you might have a little something in your cupboards to snack on while we chat?"

"They aren't my cupboards and it isn't my food."

"Anything so long as it's low-fat. Have to watch my weight."

I slammed down the phone and went to the kitchen, yanking a box of Butterfingers out of the freezer. Twelve years ago, when I'd first come here to live and found so much chocolate in the freezer, I'd thought Birdie was buying it for me. I thought he was going to try to bribe me into being nice to him, into forgetting I'd lost my family. To see how long his pity would last, I'd eaten a box of them and then walked into his office and thrown up on the new carpet. That's how little I understood about Birdie. I didn't even know he drank back then. I took the box out to Mutz and slapped it on the TV tray.

His eyebrows knit together. "I have to watch my weight. Goodness, no. Chocolate isn't a good idea."

I shrugged and went to the couch. If he could be deaf so could I. I watched him open the box, select a chocolate bar, and place it in the pocket of his tweed jacket, his hand rattling under the lapel like a beating heart.

"Now, what was I saying?" he asked. "Oh, yes. People are far healthier these days than they used to be when I first came here—but that's the doctor's dilemma in a small town, you know. Our aim is to put ourselves out of business. For that reason, I sometimes wish I'd become an embroiderer. You always have work to keep you busy, eh?" He bent forward for another wary sip of coffee. "How's *your* embroidery coming along? Have you learned enough to make a living off it yet?"

I shrugged and ripped a cuticle down to blood.

"Well, don't you worry. You had a late start compared to most, but with any luck—you just keep working. Don't give up hope. Hard work for the soul and all that." He stirred in two more spoons of sugar and took another sip. "If you've got half the spunk your mother had, I expect you'll do fine. She was a quite a lady, that Eudora. I'll never forget when she was in labor with your brother—dead of winter, no heat in the house, no access to the hospital, and him coming breach. She and I had to work like dogs just to get that baby out in one piece. She was a fine patient, though. Some of these young gals nowadays, they'll scream and curse and claw, call you names. But that mother of yours, she was a real trooper."

I stared at my boots. Listening to Mutz's medical achievements was like being forced to stick your head inside a bee's nest.

"She was a handsome woman, too," he went on. "Tragic how she never remarried after your father left. I'm sure she had offers. Any idea why she never considered another husband?"

"Do you honestly think I'd tell you?"

"What's that?"

"NO."

"Well, I always thought it a pity, her being so stubborn. She was a fine-looking woman." He took another sip and put his coffee back on the tray, lacing his fingers over his belly. I whined and sucked at the edge of my finger, eyeing the clock behind Birdie's desk. It would take Alice another half hour to get to the hospital. I wanted to talk to Frank. I wanted to talk to Eli Sanchez, see if he could ask his brother-in-law who worked at the hospital to make sure Birdie got a decent doctor. I wanted to stand up and tell Mutz to get off his fat butt and go home.

"And what about you, Rosie? You're still an attractive, healthy-looking youngster. I certainly hope you're not thinking of throwing in the towel. Where are all your beaus?"

That did it. I dropped against the couch and held a pillow over my face. I couldn't believe he was doing this now.

"Oh, I know what you're thinking, but I've learned a thing or two in life. No matter how many losses we suffer, we still have to get on with it. Take that lady, for instance." When I lifted the pillow, he was waving toward Alice's picture. "I'm sure you heard how devoted she was to her sister, Florie?"

I put the pillow back over my face, but he went on anyway: how she'd fainted dead away at the news, how she'd thrown herself on the coffin, how she'd lived on tranquilizers, how she'd driven to the site every day after it happened to weep. I stopped listening. I'd heard it before, and none of it made sense. If Alice was so crazy about Florie, why didn't she offer any life insurance money to Florie's husband, Ben Snow? Everybody knew that's where the money was supposed to go—and would have, if Florie had remembered to change the policy when she'd gotten married. But no. All Alice had done was cash in, throw a big funeral party, and then shuck Florie's twin girls, Andy and Jessie, off to two different boarding schools back east. It made me ill just thinking about it. Two twelve-year-olds left with no one but their dad and each other, and Alice decided to split them up? That was devotion? That was plain old revenge, even Birdie'd said so.

When I realized Mutz wasn't talking anymore, I lifted the pillow to see if he'd gone, but he was just leaning forward, ready to make his point.

"Young lady, you may feel that tragedy gives you the right to wallow in self-pity, but I'm here to tell you that you need to enjoy the world, not curse it. Look at Alice. She packed up her losses after that accident, dried her eyes, and went traveling. She didn't give up and let herself go. We can rise above anything, Rose. That's the miracle of life. That's why God made your burdens so heavy, because He knows you're strong enough to carry them. Just look at yourself. Despite all you had to endure as a child, you still managed to grow into a fine young person. Isn't that the power of God's love at work? Oh, I know," he said, raising his hand to stop me from interrupting. "I'm an old man and I should stay out of it, right? Well, I try when I can, but the trick to being a good doctor is knowing what's going on, not just in the body but up here"—he tapped at the side of his head—"in the mind. Hurtful memories and such, Rosie, they're not worth keeping."

"What are you talking about?"

"So your uncle had a few crossed wires. So he made some mistakes and ended up causing a tragedy that could've been avoided. Is that any reason to hate the whole world? Of course not. Take a lesson from Alice Pinkston. Move on with your life. It's never too late to start fresh. And who knows? A beau may just change your whole outlook."

I stared at him. "What mistakes?"

"What?"

"WHAT MISTAKES?"

"There's no point in getting angry about it, child. I've known you since you were a toddler. I know what you've been through. Don't you think you've suffered enough for your uncle's delusions? He's dead and gone, Rosie. He's not able to return from the grave if you decide to get on with your own life for a change. In fact, I'll bet if you started working on your personal hygiene a little, you could come up with all kinds of young fellows."

"What are you talking about, my uncle's delusions. My uncle was brilliant."

"What?"

"You didn't even know him. You were such an asshole, you wouldn't even say good morning to him on the street. And another thing. Why do you think you know me? I never talk with you. Except for my birth and maybe a couple of flu shots, I've never even been in your office. You think you know me? You don't know shit."

"You'll have to speak up, sweetheart."

"I said, you are the smelliest, most ignorant old flap-footed fart I ever met."

He cocked his head. "My hearing isn't perfect, you know."

That's when I threw his coat at him, grabbed my own, and walked out.

9

Honor and renown
will the ingenious crown.

—from an American
sampler, 1786

The Magpie was the oldest working bar in town and the only place that served food on Sundays. The front room was high and narrow, with a line of black-and-white stools along a bar on one side, black-and-white vinyl booths along the other, a tangle of tables and chairs in the middle, and a pool table at the back. In summer the air was dark and cool, and the music on the jukebox wasn't half bad. But that was in summer. In winter, when customers brought their work to the bar, the Magpie was more of a sweatshop. The pool table was closed, work lights were installed over the booths, music was outlawed, and conversation discouraged—which sounds like a peaceful place for work, but with so many of the regulars jacked up on coffee in order to finish enough needlework to start drinking, it was anything but. Paul Martinez had threatened to stab Tommy Steel-head over nothing more important than who'd borrowed whose scissors. The owner, Astra Pisby, had been known to jab her number 14 needle in the groin of anyone getting in her light. Until the end of the day when the work was packed away so the drinking could start, even asking to borrow the phone could be ticklish. All the same, when I walked into that familiar smell of beer and linen and sweat and felt the leather door close behind me, I was glad I'd come.

Several booths had work lights on, but the bar stools were still empty. Astra was up at the end next to the cash register light. She glanced up from her needle, cracked her neck, and returned to her work. I stepped to the bar and waited. I could smell coffee brewing behind her, but I didn't ask. When Astra was working, it was better to let her start the conversation.

"Surprised to see you here, Rose. It's cash only, you know. And you're not drinking it in here until after eight P.M."

"I know. Can I use your phone to call Madrillas?"

She looked over her bifocals at me and then at the five-dollar bill I slid onto the bar. "Suit yourself. Just keep it down."

She was doing her inheritance piece, the one she'd gotten from her great-great-grandmother back in 1886:

> *The winter tree resembles me*
> *Whose sap lies in the root,*
> *The spring draws nigh; as it, so I*
> *Shall bud, I hope, and shoot.*

Walter Bean had left me an inheritance pattern, but my uncle had convinced my mother to sell the rights to it. It had gone:

> *When with the needle I'm employed*
> *Or whatsoever I pursue,*
> *Teach me O Thou Almighty Lord*
> *To keep my final end in view.*

A bad joke, since the only final end Walter Bean had in view was quitting. I'd never regretted Bob's decision to sell the rights to my legacy, any more than I'd regretted my mother's decision to change our last names back to Devonic. Who wants to grow up under the name of a quitter? Bob Devonic might have done some pretty crazy things, but at least he wasn't a quitter. Not like Walter Bean. As far as I was concerned, Bob was a hero. One of the most talented men to set foot in Queduro—and one of the best fathers anyone could ask for, save for maybe Frank's dad. I could have told Mutz that. I could have told him a lot of things. I didn't want to think about all I should have told him.

"That blue's nice, Astra."

"Rose." Astra pulled off her bifocals. "Do I look like I need to hear what you think of my work?" Her eyes were a pinched, painful-looking red, but that didn't mean anything. Everyone who did embroidery in winter had red eyes. She was just in one of her moods.

I crossed the room, nodding at the trade embroiderers who looked up empty-eyed from their work, and then pushing open the swinging door to the kitchen. Astra's father, Pete Pisby, was asleep on the couch under the phone, mouth wide and his magazine, *Politics at Home,* on his chest. Pete's mind was mostly gone, but he still spent summers out at the embroidery booths with his magazine, showing everyone willing to look that on page 137, where Dwight and Mamie Eisenhower are pictured reading the newspaper in their living room, a framed embroidery on the wall behind Dwight's left ear just happens to be the piece Pete once sold to a collector for a hundred dollars. When I sat down, he moaned in his sleep and the fingers of his right hand twiddled his fly.

I tried Frank's office again, but Silas answered so I hung up. It was too late for Frank to help now anyway. I thumbed through the phone book for the hospital in Madrillas and dialed that number. When it started ringing, I sat back. I was hungry; I could feel my stomach dropping with it. Astra hadn't cooked anything on the grill since last night, but it still smelled of bacon. I looked over at Pete, his mouth buckling in on itself from his snores. Even he smelled a little like bacon.

"May I help you?"

"I want to know about a patient. He just got there. His name is Birdie. Birdie Pinkston."

"Are you a relative?"

"I'm his cousin."

She asked me to spell Pinkston and then put me on hold. I bit the inside of my mouth. Maybe cousins weren't close enough. Maybe I should've said I was a sister. Why did they need to know who I was? Why weren't they getting back on the phone? It was like the nightmare where you're running as hard as you can and not going anywhere. The whole day had been like that. All I wanted was to hear that he was alive.

"Hello?"

I felt all the heat rush to my face. "Is that you, Frank?"

"I thought you'd be calling, Rose. I asked them to give me the message."

His voice was soft, too soft. I switched the phone to my other ear. "So?"

"The doctors are in with him now. It looks like he had a stroke."

I didn't know what to say. "They're sure?"

"I think so."

I opened my eyes, saw my face stretching sideways in the edge of the metal counter in front of me. "Isn't that what happened to your dad?"

"My dad was ten years older. He was ready to go. I don't think Bird is. He'll probably be fine."

That was the difference between Frank and me: he was always so sure everything would turn out. Frank thought nobody ever died until they were supposed to. There was a crackling between us, and for a moment I could hear someone's voice talking on another line far away. Then it faded and I could hear Frank breathing again.

"Frank? I was only trying to help. She got really ticked off when she saw me, but there's no reason for it. I swear."

"I know. I should call you back when we can talk. Are you at the motel—wait." I heard him cover the receiver, his voice murmuring something, and then suddenly, Alice was on the phone.

"I want you *out* by the time I get home, do you hear me? I don't care what Frank says. I don't care what anybody says. I know who you are and you don't belong there. *Out.*"

"Wait. Listen. I'm sorry about all this, but you need to listen."

"*Sorry?* Is that all you can say?"

"I'm just asking you to calm down and listen. Okay?" I took a deep breath. "Now, the thing is, it's winter out there. And your brother and I, we had a deal going that I could stay in one of his cabins——"

"Oh my God! Does she actually think she can talk to me this way?" I could hear Frank in the background, trying to coax the phone away from her. "Let me tell you something!" she cried. "My poor brother will be lucky if he lives through tomorrow, so he has nothing to say about deals anymore. And neither do I. And *you*." She panted. "You better be out of there before I get back because I am not without my sources. You understand?"

There was a clanking on the phone and I could hear her crying, and Frank and another man talking to her, and then the sound of them walking away. I gripped the phone hard, praying Frank to pick it up. He did.

"Rose? It's all right. She's just upset by the news. She'll calm down."

"Is she still there?"

"One of the nurses took her to the waiting room," he said. "But I need to get off the phone."

"Will you tell her I didn't want this to happen? I was only trying to help. Honest, Frank, you know how I feel about Bird——"

"As soon as she's calmed down, she'll be able to listen to reason."

I nodded, looked over at Pete, and pulled my knees up under my chin. "Can I ask you something, Frank?"

"What's that."

"If your brother had to go to the hospital, would your first reaction be to run into his office and grab his motel keys?"

"What?"

"She took his box of motel keys."

"You mean the one on the wall? Where he hangs all the cabin keys?"

"Yeah. She pulled the whole damn box off the wall."

He was quiet a moment. "Are you saying you can't get into your cabin to get your stuff?"

"No, I can get in all right. I just want to know if you think that's strange or not."

He paused. "People can get mixed up in emergencies," he said, "especially older people. She was probably pretty scared."

"I know. So was I. But a reaction like that—does it make sense?"

"No. Not really."

"Thank you. That's all I wanted to know."

Another pause.

"Birdie's doctor is Geraldo Thorn if you want to call back later. I'll tell him who you are."

"Thanks. Okay." I wanted Frank to talk to me, to *me*, but I could tell by his voice he was trying to balance too many thoughts at once. Maybe we both were. "I'll hang up now. Thanks for being there for Bird."

"Rose? Alice won't be coming back to Queduro for at least a couple days, maybe more. You can take your time about moving out."

"No, I'll go first thing in the morning. It's better that way. What's the pass like?"

"Just take it slow and you'll be fine." He hesitated. "If you don't feel like driving it by yourself, you can wait until I get back tomorrow. Eli and I can drive you and your stuff—"

"Jesus, Frank." I snorted. "When are you going to learn?"

"I don't mean it as charity," he said. "We could work out a trade."

"Yeah, right. I'll bet your wife would just love that."

"My wife—" he said, and stopped.

"I can look after myself, okay? All you ever do is make me feel worse. I'll be fine. I'll go to the women's shelter, get some food stamps and welfare, get my embroidery done on the side, be back in the valley next spring, right on schedule. No problem."

"I know."

"Damn you, Frank, stop sounding so worried. I'm fine, all right? I can do this." As I said it, I felt my throat closing. "Just believe in me, okay? Give me that much. Go take care of your own problems and do what you have to do. Besides, this isn't your fault. At least you're at the hospital with him. I didn't even make it out the driveway." I looked up then and saw Astra at the door, holding her embroidery hoop against her chest. "Got to go."

I hung up, but it was too late. Her eyes were wide.

"Did I hear you say somebody was in the hospital?"

I looked over at Pete and then back at her. "If I tell you, and then you go out to the front room and tell everybody else, I'm not going to be able to get out of here without talking to all of them. I don't want to do that right now. Please, Astra."

"Dear God." She let go of the kitchen door, put her embroidery on a tray, and began to pull off her cotton gloves. "I thought something was up when you came in. You look like death warmed over." She dipped back for the door and leaned around it. "Terry," she called, "watch the bar. And the rest of you just mind your business. I'm having a private conversation in here." She stepped back and let the door close behind her.

"You sure know how to thin out the crowd, Astra. Thanks a lot."

"If you want privacy, you should turn on the fan before you make your phone calls." She leaned on the counter in front of me. "So?"

"Birdie had a stroke."

"Oh, God. Come on here. Come on. What the world's coming to, I don't know." She waved me over to the door, winging me under her arm and out to the front room.

"Alice Pinkston's brother had a stroke," she announced to the room. She led me to the bar, left me next to a stool, and went around to the other side. "So how did it happen?" She set two cups on the bar and reached for the coffeepot. "Come on, hon. What happened?"

Everybody was listening. Sooner or later, they'd all find out anyway. I sat on the white stool. "He was doing some yard work."

"*Yard* work?" She clapped her hand to her heart. "Why in the world would he be doing yard work?"

"He's only sixty-eight. I've seen your father doing yard work, and he's got to be close to a hundred."

"Men." She poured two coffees and slid one over to me along with the cream and sugar. When Astra wasn't working, she was a whole different person. "So?"

"So he fell over and she took him to the hospital. That's all. He's alive. Frank says he's going to be okay."

"At what cost, though." She clucked and put the coffee back, shaking her head. "And that sister of his, she's a nervous wreck to begin with. She'll never be able to manage this."

"She's all right," I said. "Frank's with her."

"At least she can afford a nice nursing home like the one Dick Sweeny used for his dad—what was the name of it? Peaceful Glen. I've heard it's decent there. It's got to be better than the state hospital where we ended up putting my mother last year, after she had her breakdown. That I know."

"Bird's not going to a nursing home."

She cocked her head sideways at me. "I thought you said it was a stroke." When I didn't answer, she shrugged and lifted her coffee. "There's always hope, I guess. When we packed up my mom, her mind was already gone, which was a blessing. She never really knew what hit her."

"Most of them don't when they get that age," said someone behind me.

"Did you hear about the aneurysm my brother's wife in Cincinnati had?" Paul Two Trouts came up and nudged me in the waist. "Astra, you heard it, didn't you? Jesus Christ." He settled himself on the stool and leaned forward with a heavy sigh. "Painting her kitchen cabinets. Keeled right over and laid there in a pool of yellow paint. Still can't walk or talk. My brother's only forty-two, you know. His whole life still ahead of him. He's holding on now, but I'll bet you nine to one they end up divorced."

"You know that old woman at the cigarette store in Madrillas?" called Maria Sanchez. "That was a stroke. Eli said she used to be as normal as anybody, can you believe that? I'd die I ended up like that."

"I'd rather go that way than some," called Tommy Steelhead. "What about that spastic kid in Alamosa last summer? His mom takes him in a wheelchair to the country club, and while she's talking to somebody he rolls into the swimming pool. And his mom couldn't swim. Yee."

And so it went. Everybody who got the news about Birdie seemed to think it was their duty to tell me something worse. At first I thought they were trying to be polite, give me some elbow room by not asking questions, but then I realized that they didn't care what happened to Birdie, they just wanted the chance to tell what had happened to them. By nightfall nobody was working anymore, the jukebox was on, and the room charged with noise. I'd never heard of so many diseases and doctors and different ways to die. It scared me a little, the way everybody seemed so eager to get to the details, especially when they were talking about family, almost as if all love ever amounted to was a clear-cut case of suffering that you could brag about later. When Dick Sweeny came strolling in, already drunk and saying nobody had anything to tell *him* because he'd almost seen his son crushed like a melon out on Hemming Street that very afternoon, I got my coat off the hook and went for the door.

"You wait, Rose."

It was Astra, coming from behind the bar to press a five-dollar bill in my hand.

"What's this?"

Astra turned and glared at the room. "Can you people learn to mind your own business for just two minutes?" She waited until they turned away and then led me to the door. "It's your phone money. God knows, you'll need it now. Frank would want me to give you something. If I had more to spare, I would, but it's not exactly a flush time of year, what with everybody in here on credit until spring."

I looked at her, those flamed eyes and wisps of gray hair coming out from underneath her hair net. All my life Astra had tried to slip in a little charity and make me grateful. I handed the money back.

"I made a long distance call, Astra, and I want to pay for it. I pay my own way, just like anybody."

Her eyes bulged. "I am not taking your last five dollars, Rose."

"What makes you think it's my last five dollars?"

She jammed her fists against her hips, staring at the floor and then back at me, jutting her jaw hard and leaning in. "Has anybody in this bar suggested anywhere for you to move if you leave the motel? They haven't, have they? Not even the old-timers back there in the corner, who are always talking about getting laid. And you know why? Because they can't afford it. It's winter, Rose. Everybody's on a budget. Everybody's working or married to somebody who's working. If you don't get out of here before the snows close the pass, you'll be stuck until spring with no place to live. I don't want that on my conscience, all right? Now stop being such a damn fool. Take the money before I change my mind."

She turned away. Everybody was watching. "The thing is," I said slowly, "I happen to be a trade embroiderer now. I do the same stitches as you, I sell my work to the same tourists, I spend my money at the same store. Just because I don't have a permanent home like most of you, I don't understand why you think I'm so different." I looked around the room. "Seems to me, I deserve respect as much as anybody. Or is that something you have to buy these days?" I leaned over to the table next to the door. "Here, Dick," I said, handing him the money. "You probably need this more than I do."

Dick Sweeny looked over in confusion at Astra and then arched in his chair, trying to hand the fiver back. "I'm not going to take this. I'm the chairman of the Commerce Committee, for God's sake. I don't need money. Especially from you."

But I brushed his hand away and walked out.

Without the Committee's neon Indian shining over the Ten Tribes, that whole corner of the valley was black. Until you were on it, you couldn't even tell there was a street up Flax Hill, let alone a motel at the end. I parked my car in front of the office and got out. Overhead, the wind was rising in the dark, clacking the branches of the cottonwoods together. I shivered and went around to the courtyard. Even with snow on the ground, it was black. I was halfway across before I remembered the tree Birdie had cut down somewhere ahead of me. I closed my eyes and opened them and saw no difference. I backed up until my feet felt the edge of the sidewalk Birdie had shoveled clean and then followed it, hands out like the blind, until I got to the Ute.

The dog was fine. He was just glad I'd come back. I let him out and listened to him moving in the dark, sniffing at the tree, though I couldn't see it. I followed the sidewalk back to the office. To my relief, Mutz hadn't decided to lock up on his way out. I turned on the light, called the dog, and took off my parka.

I checked the fridge first. Milk, a loaf of bread, a bottle of Pepto-Bismol, a plate with a half-eaten pork chop, a saucepan with some kind of white soup. When Birdie was in need of a drink, he couldn't hardly eat at all. I unwrapped the chop, sniffed at it, changed my mind, and called the dog, who looked as if he was thinking about peeing on the yellow plastic trash can. He took the meat as if it were lined with razor blades, wagged once, and slid around the corner into the living room. He trusted me around food but he preferred to eat by himself.

I opened the freezer. Along with three cases of Butterfingers, it was stockpiled with TV dinners, Birdie's meal of choice when he was drinking. I helped myself to a couple of Butterfingers and then checked the cupboards.

After the cupboards, I checked the bathroom, the bedroom closet, the linen closet, behind the toilet, and under the tub. I went out to the front desk and checked through the drawers and then under the chairs, the sofa, the trash. I checked everywhere I could think of. Then I walked through the kitchen, and right on the table next to an ashtray full of candy wrappers that was sandwiched between the A-I sauce and the catsup on the lazy Susan, there it was: an unopened pint of Jack Daniel's.

I pulled up a chair, finished off the candy bar, and studied the bottle. He must have been inches from giving in. Less than inches. I unsealed it, opened it, and passed it under my nose. I didn't like hard liquor much, but Birdie did. Our first winter together, he'd been able to keep that fact from me for five months. I might never have found out if he hadn't started carping about my laziness. He said that vacuuming was the least I could do, since I was eating him out of house and home, and he might pay me an allowance if I started doing it on a regular basis, so after thinking it over I finally took out his Hoover one day and found a pint of Boodles tucked inside the bag. I took it back to my cabin and drank half of it as an experiment and threw up in the tub. When he burst in the cabin and saw his gin half gone, he called me a mistake of nature, I called him a stinking old fart, and we ended up in the kind of fight that sounds like two cats down a well. But that was the first time we said anything real to each other, and since then we'd gotten along fine. Now, twelve years later, watching my reflection in his kitchen window, I imagined my cabin out there in the dark, waiting for me on the other side of the fallen tree. Watching the window, I took a drink, my reflection a ghost pouring heat into my chest.

I couldn't blame Alice for throwing me out, not really. Birdie was her whole life, at least when she wasn't in Phoenix. She'd never forgive me for letting him have a stroke. She'd blame me for everything, even the tree in the courtyard. I'd be lucky if she let me near him again. In a way, it was Birdie's fault. He'd never once stood up to her, never once tried telling her to butt out. Every time she cruised into town, he simply curled up and played possum until she let him alone again.

I stared at the embroidered tablecloth, the matching curtains on the window, and the matching pot holders by the stove, all of them done by Alice back in high school. The roadrunner salt and pepper shakers were her idea, and so was the plastic air-freshener flower, the tatted doily under the toaster, the yellow happy-face stickers on the fridge, and the little sponges by the sink shaped like ducks. Why would a man live like this, smothered under tablecloths and duck sponges and happy faces? I lifted the bottle, knowing the answer. Alice was his sister. His like or dislike of her had nothing to do with it. Me, I was just somebody else. I closed my eyes and leaned back to drink.

When I lowered the bottle, I was staring at my reflection again. Despite what my life had come to in the last few years, I still had enough to make men want me—Harmon was evidence of that—but under the hanging lamp of Birdie's kitchen I saw a yellow corpse with black holes for eye sockets and hair like dried blood against my skull. It was almost thrilling how scary I looked. There was a ripple in the glass, and if I moved my head a little to the left, my chin disappeared completely. I turned, felt my reflection turning too, and looked through the door at the stool behind Birdie's desk. For thirty years, he'd sat there daily, whether he was open or not, whether he was alone or not, whether he was sober or drunk. I turned back to the window. *Here's to you, spook.* I leaned back and drank, hard this time, and when I came up for air I remembered his embroidery. I screwed on the cap, feeling better, and got a paper bag out from behind the trash can. I took the bourbon with me and went down in the basement.

Birdie was the only person in Queduro who could embroider and drink at the same time. Not that he bragged about it. Ever since he'd given up the needle to run the motel, he liked to say that embroidery was a vanity, a crutch, a seventeenth-century form of brainwashing. As long as he had his motel, Birdie would never again, as he put it, bow to the needle. But that was when he was sober. Soused, he was a master. He could sew anything. He didn't even use charts. It all came out of his head. I pushed away the luggage next to the dryer until I got to the trunk at the bottom. It was an old leather thing with brass rivets and handles at either end. I lugged it to the middle of the basement where the light was better and sat on the floor with it. One more hit of bourbon and I put the bottle away, wiped my hands on my pants, flipped up the latches of the trunk, and lifted the lid.

Inside, under a layer of long underwear, cotton gloves, and some bottles of fancy wine he was saving, was a whole series of silk-thread scenes he'd titled the Kama Sutra. The finest even-weave silk, and every square inch of it worked in Bella Donna and silk threads—stitching so fine, so tight, the figures moved under the weave as if they were alive. His women weren't square-cornered and stiff, they were real women, disorderly, sweating, agonized women. And as for the men—some winters when Birdie had shown them to me, I'd had to stand up and walk around his basement afterward, shaking and shaking my head. Bird liked to experiment with color, especially when he got into brandy or port, but whether the figures were olive green or sunset orange or sky blue, the tone was always true for what they were doing to each other. You could smell human flesh in those scenes, hear the groaning. Sometimes I'd go upstairs and look at Bird working behind his desk by the light of the window with his ruined face and his little potbelly and his sparrow's chest, his white hair fizzing out over his ears, and I'd wonder where in the world he'd learned that kind of passion. As far as I knew, he'd never had a real girlfriend, never cracked a racy magazine, never even thought of spying on his motel guests. Sober, he could hardly watch me straighten the front of my shirt without blushing. That's why he had to be drunk to do embroidery. Drunk, with a needle in his hand, he could let go, let it out. I took a deep breath, pulled on the cotton gloves, and began shuffling the pieces together and folding them into the paper bag. Maybe he was right to hide them from Alice, maybe his friends down at the bar who were cranking out flat-stitch I ♥ NEW MEXICO samplers wouldn't have appreciated his talent, but every time I saw what he did with a needle, I almost couldn't breathe.

By the time I got upstairs with the embroidery, I'd decided there was no point in waiting until morning. I was thinking how it would be in Madrillas, me and the dog at the women's shelter, with all those unlucky, beaten-up homeless women and babies watching us while I told them Birdie was dead. I knew it wouldn't happen that way—for one thing, they wouldn't allow the dog, and for another, Birdie wasn't dead—but I was drunk. I stuffed another paper bag with frozen dinners—Birdie could always buy more if he needed—and dumped in the bowls of candies from the front desk and *The Lost World of Sir Arthur Conan Doyle*, which had been mine once, a couple of pot holders, and all the duck sponges. I was slamming around by then, breaking things and crying, though I wasn't sure why. Maybe it was for Birdie getting sick, or maybe for Alice and the way she'd blame me for everything, or maybe for Frank and the way I'd yelled at him for making things worse when he was only trying to help. Or maybe it was all for me and how in hell I was going to survive in a town on the other side of the pass where no one even knew me. I don't know. When you're drunk, it's hard to tell.

10

When soon or late we reach that coast
O'er life's rough ocean driven
May we rejoice no wanderer lost
A Family in Heaven.

—from an American sampler, c.1808

By the time we finally came up with an Indian that my uncle thought was good enough to sell, a whole year had passed and my hands were hard as dog pads. The Indian was Tatanka-Iyotanka, better known as Sitting Bull: six and a half feet tall, four hundred pounds of ponderosa with the hard-spread mouth of a great leader, chaps, braids, a scar just below his mouth, a coup stick, and an eagle feather rising straight off the back of his head. Since Frank's dad had offered to lend us his old Chevy truck, we'd decided to haul the Indian out to the embroidery booths the night it was finished and set it up next to my mother's booth as a surprise.

But none of that happened. The day Bob finally sent me inside to phone Frank about the truck, no one answered. I let it ring and ring and then rode my bike over there. I knocked and waited and then tried the door. It was locked. Later I found out they were down in Albuquerque attending a sheriff's convention, but at the time, sitting on their front steps and looking out at the empty street, I felt as if they'd disappeared forever. I'd forgotten them, so they left. I'd let them go, so they went. By the time Bob realized I was missing and came looking for me, I couldn't even talk. He was holding Kyle, who was asleep on his shoulder, but he sat next to me and pulled me onto his lap to cry.

"Good God, Rose. What the hell have they done to you?"

So I told him. I told him how I'd been teased for being poor, for not having a father, for having a mother who subcontracted her work out to other embroiderers, and for ending up with an uncle like Bob who everybody said was crazy. I told him how miserable I was, how nobody in my school liked me, and how the only people who'd never laughed at me were the Dobys and now they were gone. I went on and on. I was shameless. When I ran out of real reasons to cry, I started making up reasons, but Bob didn't seem to notice. He went on holding my head against his chest, stroking my hair and not saying anything. Finally I pushed away from him. "Aren't you going to say *anything*?"

He looked surprised. "Like what?"

"I don't know. . . . Like, *stop bawling*. Or *don't worry*. Like, *it's going to be all right*. Can't you even say that?"

"But I don't know that it's going to be all right, Rose."

"Why can't you say it anyway? That's what most grown-ups would do."

"Let me ask you something." He looked out at the street. "What do you believe in? I mean, in the big sense. I mean, when you wake up scared in the dead of night and all you can think of is how you're going to die. What do you believe then?"

I had no idea. I never thought about dying when I was scared. I just thought about being alone. I wanted to tell him I believed in the Dobys, but somehow that wasn't good enough. The Dobys were just regular people, people who could leave, people who weren't even related to me. I thought again. The embroiderers were always saying I should believe in tradition. My mother was always saying I should believe in hard work. Doc Mutz was always saying I should believe in God. "I don't know," I said finally. "When I get scared, I guess I believe in God."

Bob nodded and sighed. "With me, it's been a progression," he said. "When I was a kid I believed in God. Then I believed everything they told me about God. Then I started believing everything they told me *not* to believe about God. And you know where I'm at now?"

He looked at me in a far-off way and then looked out at the view again.

"I'm down to meat and potatoes, Rose. I believe in myself. I believe in myself and in you and your mother and little Kyle, here. I believe that's all I've got, and the weird part is, I'm pretty sure that's all I need. Yep. That's what I believe." He scratched his chin in a thoughtful way and then turned suddenly, grabbed my hand, and smack-kissed it. "You know what I was thinking, Rose? I was thinking if I go talk to old Mr. Gonzalez over there, he might lend us his son's truck. You agree?"

So he went next door to see Mr. Gonzalez. Then he crossed over to Freda Medina's to see about her husband's truck. Then he told me to take Kyle home while he went down to talk to Mr. Steelhead at the store. He came home with a dark look, got his wallet, and went down to the Magpie.

But nobody wanted to lend us a truck. Nobody wanted to even come see what we'd done. All year the embroiderers had been talking about him and his new idea. They liked him well enough—it was hard not to like Bob—but his opinions about embroidery had hit everybody wrong. Even when he offered to pay for the use of a truck, they all had excuses. "My transmission's bad." "My tires are worn through." "I got to be here for a phone call." "I'm waiting for my wife." I stood at the door, watching his face get darker, his voice going quieter. When Ben Snow couldn't come up with an excuse, only shook his head and returned to his drink, Bob stared at him for a full minute and then smiled and held up his hands. "All right, everybody. I understand. No hard feelings, right?"

That's when Cal Peters turned around in his chair. "What you don't understand, Devonic, is that we're here to relax because we've been out all day earning a living at the booths. Unlike some, we've been working."

"Unlike some, Cal?" Bob was smiling ear to ear. "How can you say that? Aren't we all working here?"

Cal snarled and turned back to his drink. "Maybe it all depends on your definition of work."

"You think?" Bob was still smiling. "What's your definition, Cal?"

"I know the definition of *not* working," Cal answered. "*Not* working is when you're living off a woman who's got two kids to feed already."

"Oh, not for much longer, though, Cal," said Bob. "Haven't you heard? My niece and I have learned how to carve Indians. All we need now is someone with a truck who can haul our finished work out to the sales area so we can sell it. What about fifty bucks? I figure fifty bucks would cover the expenses for helping us haul a wooden sculpture four miles. Don't you think?"

Cal lifted his head slowly and looked in the mirror at Bob, who was holding up a fifty-dollar bill.

"Are you trying to bribe us into giving you a booth?"

"A *booth*?" Bob burst out in a clean, easy laugh. "We don't need a booth, Cal. Our Indian's going to sell long before we'll ever need a booth. No, we just need to get our work out there where the tourists are, like everybody else. But no, no booth, please. Just tell us where you want us to set him up, and we'll be fine."

There was a stillness in the room.

"We don't sell pipe dreams in Queduro. We sell embroidery. Traditional Queduran embroidery."

Bob grinned over at me, though I don't think he saw me, and then looked back at Cal. "Meaning?"

"Meaning, if you want to sell a bunch of wooden Indians, maybe you ought to go do it someplace else."

A murmur of approval went through the room.

"Well, Rose. You heard the man." Bob's voice was still cheerful as he tucked his money away and turned to me. "I guess we don't have to fuss with the sales area now. That's a relief." He hitched his pants, placed a half-dollar on the bar though he hadn't ordered anything, and asked if I was ready. I felt their eyes on me, the whole room looking at me. I nodded.

We went outside and around the corner and started up Gobelin Hill at a hard march, me running to keep up. Halfway up, he finally began to slow down, and at the top he was ready to stop. He put his hands on his hips and looked off at the houses and trailers below. "Can you believe that, Rose?

They don't want us in this town. They're not even going to let us show our work here." He didn't sound angry so much as surprised. He kept shaking his head, twisting his mouth back and forth. When I realized he wasn't going to start walking again unless I reminded him, I took his hand and we walked home, neither one of us talking.

But Bob was no quitter. The next morning the Indian stood in the garage wrapped head to toe in blankets and tied with rope. Bob was up in the rafters, rigging a pulley. "You ever hear of an endless chain, Rose? That's what we're going to do next time because it's safer, but since we don't have enough pulleys, we're going to have to start with the good old block and tackle." He tapped the pulley to make sure it swung free and then crawled back along the rafter toward the ladder and came down. His face was red and excited. "Now, I figure this one's about four hundred pounds, and with two ropes, every pull on the rope gives a mechanical advantage of two, which means all we've got to do is lift a hundred and fifty pounds. We can do that, can't we?"

I nodded.

"The main thing I'm worried about is that rafter. It'll hold this time, but after today we ought to plan on buying a couple of two-by-fours for bracing, don't you think?" He took the end of the rope and handed it to me. "You'll be behind me, and once we get him up high enough we'll go from there. Ready?"

As soon as we leaned against the rope, Sitting Bull tilted backward and like a magic trick began rising slowly up to the creaking rafter overhead. We hoisted him as far as he would go, and then Bob told me to wrap the end of the rope three times around the wooden beam behind me. The beam was old and creaked—it seemed as if the whole garage creaked— but when Bob let go, the Indian stayed up there, bobbing a little, turning slowly.

I watched Bob go out and start up the new Plymouth station wagon that my mother had recently bought in Madrillas. She had been dating the car salesman there in exchange for low interest payments. It was the first car she'd ever owned or driven, the car she hoped would eventually get us all back to Florida. Bob backed it into the garage, and then we took the rope and, bit by bit, the Indian drifted down. The luggage rack bent under him like pipe cleaners and the roof popped as he came to rest. But then it was all right. Bob undid the ropes and folded back the blankets so the Indian's head was in full view, lying there glaring at the garage's ceiling as if to burn a hole through it. We used the ropes to lash him to the roof of the car, and then Bob drove back out to the street and parked. "Don't you worry about this town, partner," he called, leaning over the windshield to check the ropes. "This town is nothing. First thing tomorrow, you, me, your mom, and Kyle, we're going to take this Indian on the road."

My mother came home from work early that night so she could practice her driving. She was carrying my baby brother, and Pete Pisby was carrying the bag of embroideries she was finishing for him and trying to keep up with her while they walked. She was looking straight ahead and, watching her come, I felt my belly go sour with fear. She had no interest in carving; she hadn't even bothered to peek inside the garage. Embroidery was her life and returning to Florida was her dream, and watching her from my hiding place behind the hedge as she thanked Pete, took her bag from him, and turned up our street, I couldn't see how that was ever going to change.

But it did. When she saw the Indian, everything changed. She stopped dead, and a flat, stupid look came over her face as if she couldn't think anything. She looked over at Bob, who was waiting on the porch with a unlit cigar in his mouth, and then she looked back at the Indian. She just stared at it. "Oh my *God*," she whispered, as I came up behind her. I had to take her embroidery bag before she dropped it.

I looked over my shoulder and saw Ilfonso Martinez coming up the middle of the street with his mouth open and, beyond him, at the corner, Teresa Steelhead with her hand over her mouth, then Mrs. Franklin and Mr. Rodriguez. Eli Sanchez and Vernal Sweeny and the Johnston girls. One by one they came up Gobelin Hill Road, their faces wide with shock. An hour later, when Frank and his parents pulled into town, they found three-fourths of the population standing out in front of our house.

Why? Because that first Indian was not just a pipe dream, not just a cheap little souvenir to make a fast buck from, not just a hunk of wood that would ruin the paint job on our new station wagon. That Indian was Sitting Bull, the greatest chief of the northern plains, maybe the greatest chief ever. And with everything about him so huge and powerful and dark, and his face so real and alive and glaring skyward, that Indian was *beautiful*.

Looking back, it was like a dream, the voices muffled and everything in slow motion and light. I remember my mother's face and Pete Pisby's froggy mouth clapping as he tried to speak and the low whistle of respect that Frank's father gave when he saw what we'd done and how Frank's eyes were so wide—until then, I hadn't shown him anything but the mistakes we'd chopped up for firewood—and I remember Bob's grin getting wider and wider around that cigar.

And then, in the middle of it all, Kyle began to scream. I don't know why. He'd seen the Indian before in the garage, he'd played in the sawdust and patted the wooden moccasins and sucked on the rifflers until his cheeks were red. But when he twisted around on my mother's shoulder and saw the Indian strapped to the roof of our car, his mouth pinched downward and he pushed his hands up under my mother's hair and started screaming. We all stopped and looked. Kyle never cried. Not at loud noises or big dogs or strangers who wanted to hold him. Not when he was hungry or left alone in his crib in the dark. So quiet my mother sometimes worried about him being normal. But when he saw the Indian on the top of our car, he screamed as if he'd been building for it since birth. My mother had to take him inside and walk around and around the table with him, cooing lullabies until he stopped. That was the end of it. The next time we showed him the Indian, all he did was look. None of the Indians we made over the next four and a half years scared him. It was just the first sight of that Indian on the car. Years later, I'd ask myself why. Did he see the future then and what would happen to us; it was there, right in front of him, there and then gone, with no chance for him to warn us later?

At the time, I forgot as soon as it was over. My mother was happy again, that's all I cared about. While Bob did the dishes, she put Kyle to bed and then she got out the map and asked Bob to show her all the places we were going to take our Indians. She was all lit up, laughing and talking.

Oh, she worried about whether she'd have the strength to use a mallet and who would look after the house while we were gone and if the Plymouth would hold up under the weight. But embroidery and poverty and never being good enough wasn't a part of it, not anymore. When Bob came out of the kitchen with a glass of beer for her and milk for me, she took it with a giggle and held it up. "Here's to my family," she said, and though the fingers of her right hand worried at the button of her sweater, her black eyes shone bright.

Bob stood between us and raised his own glass. "To the spirit of Geronimo," he said quietly. When he looked down at me, I stood and raised my glass. It was a solemn moment. *Geronimo!* we shouted, and the three of us drank.

11

There is a land of pleasure
Where streams of joy forever roll
Tis there i have my treasure
And there i hope to rest my soul.

—from an American sampler, 1814

I was listening to the wind through the branches of the cottonwoods and thinking about food. Breakfast, this time: eggs and bacon with a basket of warm tortillas in blue cloth, a bottle of milk, a tea loaf of warm pumpkin bread, a fresh glass of OJ and a side of half-dollar pancakes. The pancakes were especially nice, thin as gold lace, the way my uncle used to make them, dripping with butter on a blue plate on a white linen tablecloth, that good rich smell of pancakes rising to meet me. But as I turned to ask for syrup, I felt a pain in my shoulder, and then I remembered falling over the tree the night before on my way back to the cabin and losing my temper and batting my way through the branches, and that I was supposed to be gone.

I opened my eyes to the blackness up in the rafters. When I stood, the cabin walls swayed. I fumbled on my parka and pulled the blanket off the window. It looked late, maybe past noon, the sky a blank white and the branches of the cottonwoods black against it. The tree Bird had cut down was resting on its elbows over a pool of broken twigs out in the snow, and my purse was hanging by its strap on one of the branches. I went out to yank it loose and saw a ripped paper bag, and boxes of TV dinners everywhere in the snow under the branches, and all the other things I'd taken from his kitchen and dropped or thrown when I'd fallen into the tree. Luckily, I must have hung on like death itself to Birdie's embroidery, because that bag was still propped upright in the snow. The air was bitter cold. I looked around the courtyard and then gathered everything in my arms and went back in my cabin to pack.

Leaving a place you know as home is never easy. I needed to figure out who to leave the dog with, and that depressed the hell out of me. Though it was his fault for picking me in the first place, I couldn't even look at him without feeling guilty. Also, I was just finishing a good-sized embroidery and didn't see any point in losing my rhythm. And I wanted to pack right—not just throw everything in and drive, but careful, thoughtful, organized packing. When you have to move, it's like embroidery: you can't just jump around. You have to be methodical, make sure you finish tying up all your business in one place before you move to the next. If you don't, you can wind up not quite remembering where you are or where you stopped last, and then pretty soon it doesn't make any difference anyway. Let that go too far, and all of a sudden you don't care who you are anymore or where you belong, and you're curling up for a nap on somebody's doorstep. I'd seen it happen to perfectly good people. It nearly happened to me when I ran off to Texas with Harmon Waters. That's why I was hesitating.

It's also not so easy facing the idea of moving to a shelter. Living in a building full of homeless people. I was thinking I'd ask for a job when I got there, show newcomers around, maybe, or baby-sit the kids. Then it would be more of an even trade. But I kept wondering what it would be like, being there all winter. Except for the two weeks I'd stayed with my grandmother in Florida and the week I'd traveled to Texas with Harmon, I'd lived my whole life in Queduro. Now I was going to move to Madrillas? And then there was the drive itself. I was pretty sure my car would start—last time I'd gone to check on it, I'd found a note from Eli saying he'd cleaned the points for me, checked the timing, and disconnected the battery to store it in the heated part of his garage until I needed it—but I had lousy retreads. What if I had a blowout on the pass and couldn't use my spare? What if I hit a blizzard and skidded off the road? Blizzards were always blowing in out of nowhere on that mountain. Would anyone stop to help me? Would they understand how serious it was? I'd been stuck plenty of places, but I wasn't interested in being stuck on the pass at night. Not in the Plymouth. As soon as the sun went down, the road would be ice, temperatures life-or-death, and hardly any traffic. So I'd fall asleep in Birdie's bed, listening to the ten o'clock weather on his TV and telling myself I'd been screwing around long enough, that I had to start thinking about the future and be on the road early the next morning; and then in the morning I'd rush around trying to get things packed and ready and meanwhile listen to the weather and watch the sky and think about storms and breakdowns and my luck and Birdie and how short the days were now; and suddenly I'd realize it was once again too late in the day to start the trip. It was bad. I felt like I had a gun pressed to my head, as if any decision I tried to make was only going to pull the trigger faster.

A lot of it was Birdie's fault. I wanted to be sure he was all right before I left. Every day I checked the answering machine in the office and there was nothing, and neither one of Birdie's phones rang. Finally I called the hospital. I'd forgotten the name of the doctor, but I got hold of a nurse who knew Birdie. She said he was out of intensive care. "He's resting comfortably and we've started speech therapy," she said. But what did that mean? That he'd be coming home soon? That he'd know how to talk and walk and run a motel? That he'd want to see me? Would he remember me? I couldn't just leave, not knowing. So I stayed.

Four weeks later, I happened to look up from my embroidery as Alice's Eldorado rolled by the front window of the office. She'd been coming home every few days, always in a rush, hurrying inside and then back out to her car with paper bags, plastic bags, boxes, or clothing on hangers, most of the time not even glancing toward the motel. It was as if she'd forgotten it was hers—which meant that either Frank had convinced her to forget about it or she thought I was already gone or she didn't care anymore. All I had to do, besides making sure the outside lights were off, was narrow the crack between the front curtains until she left again. It wasn't usually much of a wait, an hour or two at most. Sometimes she was in such a rush to get back to Birdie, she left her car idling in the driveway. It got so I didn't even feel my heart jump when she showed up, but just sat there like anybody's neighbor and watched. Sometimes she looked so preoccupied I didn't even bother pulling the curtains.

But this time was different. She was in a rush, but when she got out of her car she hurried over to her garage instead of to her house. I moved back from the window. She wore a candy-pink calf-length quilted parka and pale purple rubbers, an expensive-looking yellow scarf covering her hair and tied under her chin, and a pair of owl-eyed sunglasses. It made me mad, the idea that she could buy herself winter clothes while her brother lay in the hospital with a stroke. She'd probably bought a whole new wardrobe to suit the occasion. Money was Alice's answer to everything. When she raised the garage door, fingers outstretched as if it might fall back on her, her parka sleeves slipped down her arms, showing gold bracelets on pale blue wrists thin as bone.

When she turned, I expected a reaction on her face, because the curtains were just wide enough apart that all she'd have to do to see me is glance up. I was ready for it, holding my breath and prepared, but, as usual, she didn't. She hurried down the driveway, baby steps so as not to slip, though there was no ice, and popped the trunk. She went around to it and leaned in. I bent closer to the window. At first I thought she'd bought herself a bicycle or an exercise machine, and then a sharpness like a needle went through me, and I knew it was a wheelchair.

She rolled it to the passenger side of her Eldorado and set the brakes. I watched her open the door, bend in, and slide Birdie out. He wasn't that much weight, but he wasn't helping, and she was seventy years old. I watched her struggling to get him in the chair and then I put away my embroidery and went in the bathroom for a shot of Listerine. I found a brush in the cabinet, brushed out my hair, and braided it. By the time I got back to the window, she'd shut her car in the garage and she was patting Birdie down, tucking a plaid blanket around him. I closed the curtain and picked up my coat. I had an idea. If it didn't work, if she wanted to throw me out anyway, fine. At least I'd be able to say good-bye to Birdie. I took a deep breath, lifted my chin, and opened the door.

But she wasn't there. He was wrapped like a plaid mummy in the wheelchair, facing the motel. Then I noticed that her kitchen door was propped open; she must have gone inside to get things ready for him. I closed the door to the office, crossed the street, and walked up her driveway.

"Hey there, Bird."

He looked as if he'd been baked down in a furnace, like a whitehaired little boy almost, his ears standing out from his skull, pink at the edges, his head tilted sideways as if his neck was giving way, and his mouth open in a who-the-hell look. I squatted next to him with my hand on his knee. "I know what you're thinking," I said, "but don't worry, I've got a plan."

"What are you doing there?"

The force of it threw me off balance so that I had to catch myself on the wheel rim. I straightened up to meet her as she came on, her long parka open and flapping against her like wings.

"Just thought I'd drop by to say hi." I meant to look her straight in the eye, but she was too much. I crouched on my heels again next to the wheelchair. "How goes it, Bird?"

"He can't talk." She spat the words.

I snorted at the idea, but he did look bad. The left half of his face was the Birdie I knew, all hard angles and bone with an eye that was snarling at me, bright as a blue crystal, but the right side was quiet as sleep. When I touched his right cheek, the skin felt runny, like a rubber mask melted on one side. I looked up at Alice. "Maybe he doesn't feel like talking."

"If you're quite done, we've had a very long day. He needs to go in the house and have dinner."

I couldn't see her eyes because of the sunglasses, but her face was twitching like she was crying. Her lips were chapped and I could see she still wasn't wearing her wig under her scarf. Not that I'd expected her to exactly breeze through Birdie's stay at the hospital, but it shook me how bad she looked. Her skin was the color of mayonnaise. I straightened up slowly, folded my arms, and looked down Flax Hill toward town.

"Miss Pinkston? I just want to remind you it wasn't my fault he had a stroke. Frank told you that at the hospital, right? Or the doctors? That it wasn't my fault he got sick?"

"Fine. And would you like it to be your fault if he catches his death from cold?" She was gripping the handles at the back of his wheelchair, bristling at me like a guard dog. She began to push at the chair, but the brake was on. When she leaned over to release it, I leaned over and slapped it back on.

"Couldn't you use some help, though, Miss Pinkston? I could do all kinds of things for you and Bird. I could make meals and do laundry. And are you going to be able to get him in and out of that wheelchair by your-self every day until he starts walking?"

"He's not going to walk."

I looked down at Birdie. "Why, I've never heard such crap in my life. Birdie's going to walk again."

"Are you saying I don't know what's wrong with my own brother?"

"No, but I—"

"I'm in charge of his affairs now. I'm the primary caretaker."

"I know, but don't you think—"

"Do you have extensive experience with illness?"

"Extensive? No, but—"

"I do. I went to nursing school. Plus, I worked in Africa. I may be a lay person to some, but it's not as if I'm an idiot."

I stopped. I couldn't smell booze, but that didn't mean anything. Maybe she was a secret drinker, like her brother. I squinted at the street and then at Bird and then back at her.

"All I want you to know is that I'm strong, I'm willing, and I'm easy to get along with. You could call on me day or night. Think about it." I waited, studying her face to see how she was taking it. "I could stay over there at the motel. That way, I'd be close but you'd still have your privacy. And if somebody showed up wanting a cabin, I could get them registered and settle them in. Or if you found a buyer for the place, I could show them around. I could be like a manager."

She looked over at the motel and then tucked her chin and peered over the tops of her dark glasses at me, her blue eyes yellow-rimmed and terrible. "Are you asking for a job?"

"Well, yeah."

"That is *exactly* what I thought." She bent over to release Birdie's brake. I kicked it back on.

"But you don't have to pay me. I don't care about the money. We've got this friendship, Miss Pinkston. It means something. Can't you understand that?"

"You? Friends with *my* brother?"

"Why's that so hard to believe?" I looked down at him. "Say something, damn it. Don't let her do this."

"I think it's time you went home. Come along, Birdie. We need to go inside before it gets dark."

It wasn't anywhere near dark. I watched while she began to push at his chair.

"The brake's on."

She gave me a hard-faced look. "I don't need help from you. I don't need help from anybody. I'm having a wheelchair lift installed in my house this afternoon, and Sheriff Doby and I have hired a professional nurse."

"A nurse." I felt slapped. "You and Frank hired a stranger for Bird? Somebody he doesn't even know?"

"For your information, she's a remarkable woman from the agency in Madrillas. She's worked with all kinds of stroke patients before. In fact, there she is now, right on schedule." She stepped past me and lifted her arm to wave. "Oo-hoo! Mrs. Fleet! We're up here!"

I turned. A woman carrying a pale blue suitcase was trudging up the hill, a grim thickset woman with a fur cap on a square haircut that matched her mouth, a navy blue parka, and legs as solid as tree trunks. I looked at Alice.

"You think *that's* going to make him feel better?"

She drew herself up, pursing her lips together. "I know who you are, you know. Frank seems to think I'll forget, but I won't. You were in the accident that killed my sister, Florie."

"So?"

She put her hand on her heart and shivered away from me, turning to look down the street. "That poor woman!" she whispered. "Hauling her suitcase up here all by herself from the bus station!" She hurried out into the street to greet the nurse.

The nurse shook Alice's outstretched hand briskly and then handed over her suitcase and stared up at the two-and-a-half-story clapboard. From the way her mouth stiffened, it was obvious she disapproved. I watched Alice heave the suitcase up the front walk, her face tight with excitement. The nurse tucked her purse under her arm like a quarterback with a football and headed for Birdie, her small black eyes taking me in and discarding me at the same time.

So there was nothing to do but bend down and give the old man a hug good-bye. I whispered that he shouldn't worry about Alice finding his embroidery and asked if he wanted anything before I left. He didn't answer, didn't move an eyebrow or even try to close his mouth, but as I stepped back and watched the nurse push him up the driveway to the back door, reverse him, tilt him backward, and bump him over the threshold, it seemed to me that he looked as if all he really wanted was a drink.

12

If I Am Right Oh Teach My Heart
Still In the Right to Stay
If I Am Wrong Thy Grace Impart
To Find the Better Way.

—from a sampler by Patty Coggeshall, c.1795

Every morning at exactly five-fifteen, Mrs. Fleet places her hands over her nightgowned heart and begins the silent mantra that will focus her thoughts for the day. She got it off a bronze plaque that her husband, the late Dr. Fleet, had in his office at the Peaceful Glen Nursing Home: DILIGENCE + CLEANLINESS = SERENITY. Diligence, cleanliness, serenity, she thinks to herself. She thinks it slowly, purposefully, matching it to the beat of her heart, like a sluggish car engine turning over: diligence, cleanliness, serenity (breathe); diligence, cleanliness, serenity (breathe); and when she's thought it several times, each time a little faster, then suddenly it's past her heart and the engine catches, starts, and she opens her eyes to the new day. Mrs. Fleet is sixty-five, but she doesn't feel a day of it. Even when the night has been a long one, she's always up before the birds.

Few people in this world enjoy their work, but Mrs. Fleet happens to be one of them. She's looked after more elderly patients than she can remember, but she's never complained. Hard work keeps her going, keeps her sleeping soundly and her thoughts in order. In her opinion, the late Dr. Fleet would have lasted far longer if he hadn't decided to retire. It was knowing that he didn't have anyone waiting for him in his office, that he didn't have to get dressed every morning in his lab coat and tie, that he could slip into lazy habits and no one would care. Three months of retirement, and *poof!* a lifetime of discipline blown out the window. Flabby, ill-humored, and sullen, refusing to speak civilly, eat right, or take his daily exercise. After he was diagnosed with Alzheimer's, even his best friend, Dr. Tulippes, couldn't handle the tantrums. But who could blame Dr. Fleet? A respected and hard-working doctor, a brilliant man forced toward the ultimate irony, to serve out his last years as a patient in the very facility he had designed and run almost single-handedly. It won't happen to her, not to Mrs. Fleet. Mrs. Fleet rides on. A discerning eye, a steady hand, a calm voice. She may be old enough to collect a pension, but she's as sharp as ever and still willing to work. That's what counts. That's what she told Mrs. Guynn at the Home Health Care agency in Madrillas. Willingness and know-how. In her twenty-seven years at the Peaceful Glen Home, she's seen it all—unscrupulous nurses, unsanitary practices, disrespectful doctors, unmanageable patients—and if she's learned anything, it's how to smooth away problems before they develop. She can certainly manage the Pinkston case. After all, it's an easy assignment, only one patient. Mrs. Fleet has managed entire wards of patients by herself. In many ways, she's at the top of her form. Diligence, cleanliness, serenity, she thinks as she smooths the front of her starched uniform in the mirror. She would not have it any other way.

She's pleased to note that her new employer has installed an electric chair lift for the stairway, but there is still much to be done. During the night, she's prepared a list: hospital bed, portable commode, bath seat, heat lamp, remote control for the television. Rocker knives, oversized spoons, nonslip rubber mats, two dinner plates with rims, and three sloped bowls. Also foods to maintain bowel movements, lotions to prevent bed sores, Velcro to replace buttons and zippers. When she hands the list to Miss Pinkston and sees the look of bewilderment—exactly the look Mrs. Fleet expected—she simply nods, takes back the list, and asks for the keys to the Eldorado.

Mrs. Fleet would prefer something smaller, easier to maneuver, and less pretentious than a Cadillac, but of course she can manage. She gets in the slow lane on the highway, drives the fifty miles to Madrillas well under the speed limit, and parks in an empty lot behind the mall so as not to get blocked in by cars. In one hour, she's ordered or bought everything Mr. Pinkston will need and is on her way home to Queduro again. She is already thinking of it as home, thinking of everything she will reorganize there. She presses the gas pedal with her dainty white shoe, and the big car accelerates for the top of the pass.

Mrs. Fleet was not expecting to be hired as a live-in. Most stroke patients need professional help only occasionally, three times a week at most after leaving the hospital, but in this case such an arrangement proved impossible. For one thing, though she was willing to relocate to be closer to her patient, she was unable to find suitable accommodations. The only available winter housing in the entire village of Queduro is a small, rather shabby-looking motel owned by Mr. Pinkston himself, which is, of course, closed now. On the other hand, Miss Pinkston has a very pleasant guest room upstairs and assumes Mrs. Fleet will be staying there. Mrs. Fleet is just as glad. She doesn't like the thought of living in an empty motel, especially one as primitive and secluded as that. She doesn't relish the thought of tramping up and down the steep stairs in Miss Pinkston's house twenty times a day either, but at least she won't have to face icy streets every morning and the possibility of falling and breaking a hip on the way to work.

Another reason for agreeing to be a live-in is that Mr. Pinkston needs work. Not only has he failed to recover the use of his right side, but according to his speech therapist he often displays a violent temper. Mrs. Fleet suspects that the doctors classified him as unretrainable. She herself believes no one is unretrainable. Her threefold solution: a positive attitude, a firm hand, and a professional demeanor that will encourage Mr. Pinkston to understand that he won't be allowed rudeness, especially toward his caretakers. Miss Pinkston has been the first to agree.

But the main reason Mrs. Fleet decided to take this job is that Miss Pinkston is becoming ill herself. Mrs. Fleet is quite sure of it. The tense facial muscles, the nervous hands, the defensiveness, the confusion, the restlessness, the inability to recall simple instructions. At their first interview, Miss Pinkston had interrupted Mrs. Fleet's analysis of Mr. Pinkston's treatment to say that she'd be taking him to Africa in the spring. Africa! Afterward, the Home Care supervisor, Mrs. Guynn, tried to suggest that Miss Pinkston was still distraught over her brother's illness, but to a professional like Mrs. Fleet, the truth is obvious. After all, she's a nurse. She's seen enough in her lifetime to know the warning signs. She watched her own husband die of it. No, she told Mrs. Guynn, Miss Pinkston might be able to give the impression that her thoughts are still in order, that she's only hiring a nurse for the sake of her brother, but the fact is, Miss Pinkston will soon be in need of a nurse herself.

When Mrs. Fleet turns into the drive, she sees her new employer standing at the kitchen window, half hidden by a curtain and holding herself rigidly at the throat. Agitated, thinks Mrs. Fleet. She glides by into the garage. When she lets herself into the kitchen, Miss Pinkston is hovering at the doorway.

"My lord." She laughs. "Do you know what I thought? For some reason, I thought you'd stolen my car."

Mrs. Fleet nods politely, not in the least surprised. "You don't have to worry, Miss Pinkston," she says, sliding the bags onto the counter. "You'll get used to my comings and goings."

"Oh, I know. I'm glad you're here. I went to nursing school too, you know. For almost a year. Before I went traveling."

Mrs. Fleet smiles. She's noticed that people in Miss Pinkston's condition often develop the rather unpleasant habit of crowing about their past so as to further obfuscate symptoms of mental deterioration. She folds her arms over her chest to show a polite lack of interest. "Perhaps you should go see if your brother is awake now." She says it in a professional, no-nonsense tone of voice and waits until Miss Pinkston cowers back and goes into the living room. Then she turns and puts away the groceries.

By Christmas, Mrs. Fleet has established a daily routine and all Miss Pinkston can do is coo with admiration and gratitude. At seven each morning, Mr. Pinkston is roused from bed, lifted to the potty, and then wheeled to the bathroom. After his bath, he is shaved, groomed, dressed, fed, and placed at the window while Mrs. Fleet washes the breakfast dishes. Miss Pinkston is eager to help, but she lacks confidence as well as skill, and it's easier on everyone if Mrs. Fleet does everything herself. At ten, physiotherapy, then a nap with the infrared lamp; at eleven, the second meal; at one, speech practice. She ignores the belligerence and the weeping. Stroke patients are often overemotional and self-pitying. Afterward she reads aloud from the Bible, and at two she moves him to his bedroom and turns on the TV for him while she straightens the house and runs errands in the Eldorado. At four, dinner; at five-thirty, a lotion massage to prevent bed sores and 2 milligrams of Valium to help him sleep; and at six she puts him down for the night. It's the same schedule she kept at the nursing home, and it works like clockwork in private practice too. Miss Pinkston is amazed.

"What a wonder you are," she cries when she comes downstairs to find the house cleaned, her brother asleep, and dinner waiting on the oven. "How did I ever manage without you?" She's still in the very early stages of the disease. When she's not fussing over her brother or admiring Mrs. Fleet's work, she's in her bedroom with the door closed, typing and faxing things and making phone calls to someone called Mr. Max, sometimes several times a day. Sometimes she sounds so happy and busy and self-assured in there that Mrs. Fleet, who often stops to listen at the door, has to wonder if her take on the situation is correct.

But her doubts never last. She'll be bringing Mr. Pinkston's lunch upstairs, for instance, and hear Miss Pinkston dart back across the hall to her bedroom, trying to close the door without letting the hinges squeak. Other times, she hears her wandering through the house talking nonsense.

Mrs. Fleet can't help but notice that the woman is also becoming paranoid about danger, especially at dusk. In medical terms, it's called Sundowner's Syndrome, and whether it's due to the shadows lengthening out in the front yard or the darkening of her own memory, or perhaps just a childish need for attention, whatever the cause she tends to start fretting about safety just as Mrs. Fleet starts to feed Mr. Pinkston his dinner.

"I'm sorry to bother you, Mrs. Fleet," she'll say timidly from the doorway, "but I just noticed someone in the trees outside. Do you think you could come look? Or should I just call the sheriff?"

Mr. Pinkston is not the easiest person to feed, and between trying to get enough food down him to call it a meal and Miss Pinkston's paranoia, Mrs. Fleet sometimes gets a headache. "I'm busy here, Miss Pinkston," she'll say in her coldest voice. Or, "Why don't you go watch the television now, Miss Pinkston?"

Sometimes it works, but not always. Miss Pinkston is a proud woman, and that makes everything more difficult. "I don't like you!" she'll cry. "And I'm richer than you are anyway." Those are her bad nights, when she ends up going from one window to the next for hours, whispering to herself and shaking her head.

Visitors are another problem. After two of them stop by for a chat, Mrs. Pinkston storms into the kitchen and says that from now on she expects Mrs. Fleet to send them away. "They're just coming here to snoop. They don't care about my brother. They just want something to talk about."

Mrs. Fleet smiles thinly, licks a finger, and turns the page in her Bible. She can understand why Miss Pinkston fears visitors, but to turn them away would be foolish. It would be like adding gasoline to fire. They would never stop snooping then. No, Miss Pinkston can hide upstairs if she wants, but Mrs. Fleet will let in anyone who comes to the door. She knows the dangers of denying visitors their right to snoop. Most of them only come once anyway, and they're harmless enough; she can hear them upstairs with Mr. Pinkston, telling him jokes and stories and sweating it out, trying not to notice his unintelligible grunts and groans, his paralyzed right side, his adult diapers, his portable commode. They leave quickly and noisily, their faces slack with relief, but there are always those who want to confer with her before she can close the door. She keeps her answers polite, positive, and brief, which is exactly what they're asking for. Then they start their good-byes, pumping her hand, thanking her for all her hard work. *We sure are glad you're here, Mrs. Fleet.* By the end of the month, it seems as if the entire village has tracked mud through her house at least once for a look-around, but after that the doorbell stays quiet, and for many days, there are no more interruptions.

Then one night she wakes from a deep sleep, turns on the light next to her bed and stares at the phone until it rings a second time, and then answers it.

"Mrs. Fleet? It's Frank Doby. You remember me? The sheriff?"

She squints at her alarm clock, and when she sees that it is past midnight her heart begins to pump. "Mr. Doby."

"Yeah. I'm wondering if you could help me. Alice is down here at the office, and I need to know what's going on."

"She's there now?"

"She's okay, of course"—he hesitates—"but she says someone broke into her house. She's pretty upset."

Mrs. Fleet stares at the ceiling. How could she not have heard Miss Pinkston leaving? She must have been out cold. "I see."

"Yeah." He pauses. "I'm assuming everything's okay, though. Am I right?"

"Yes." She clears her throat. "Would you like me to come down there?"

"No, no, it's snowing out and I probably woke you. I'll just give her a little time to calm down and then bring her home in the squad car. She can pick up her Eldorado in the morning. I just wanted to let you know where she was."

Mrs. Fleet tightens her hold on the blanket. "Thank you, officer. I . . . thank you."

"Good night, then. Sorry for disturbing you."

She puts the receiver on its hook and lies back in wonder. She can feel her heart thudding, feel how hot her cheeks are. Why was she so sure that he was going to fire her? He can't fire her. He can't even come in the house without her permission. He is not her employer, Miss Pinkston is—and

132 · Laura Hendrie

Miss Pinkston is not about to fire her. She's indispensable. If it weren't for
Mrs. Fleet, Miss Pinkston would be lost.

The truth is, Mrs. Fleet has been fired before. The worst day of her
life, "laid off " were the words they used, but it was the same as fired.
Fired. Twenty-seven years of patrolling the hallways at the Peaceful Glen
Home, the bright jingle of her keys and how her patients would call out
for her and she would be there—all that comfort she'd given, all those
years of personal sacrifice and professionalism—and she'd been fired.
And why? Because of a patient named Mr. Bevel, who decided to sneak
behind the nurse's desk one day to investigate her purse. He'd waited
until she was busy giving meds down the hall, and then he'd sneaked into
her purse and taken the little silver flask. Mr. Bevel, who could not control
his own bodily functions, gulping brandy like a sailor just as his son, the
one who never visited but once a year, decided to pull into the parking lot.
The son who should've been grateful he had anyone to take care of a
father like that, the son who probably never dared touch a diaper or a bed-
pan or cut yellow toenails himself. Seven in the morning and there he was,
dressed in his expensive three-piece pinstripe and dark glasses, tiptoeing
down the hall to his father's room to drop off a pair of sweatpants before
he ran off to his million-dollar job, and no doubt relieved when his father
wasn't there in the bed—oh, good, he could just leave the clothes and get
out fast—but instead he'd found his father in the closet with the silver
flask and the name Fleet engraved on it clear as day. She'd tried to explain,
but he'd pushed her aside as if she were some kind of beggar and roared
down the hall, banging doors behind him: *Fire her! Fire her!* And they had.
That was the worst shock of all. All those years of backbreaking work, all
those double shifts, all those extra hours she'd put in, training inexperi-
enced nurses and handling patients no one else could deal with—and in
the end, nobody even willing to listen to her side. All they could see was
that flask and the old man in the closet. That flask, she thinks, her little
eyes burning as if sand has blown in them. A keepsake, a memento, one
of the few things of her husband's that she had kept—and why not? On
the way home in the taxi sometimes, it was fine then, nobody had to know
and it did no harm, just a sip or two after work, settling back against

the leather seat and slipping her shoes off and rubbing her tired calves and that little cat's tongue caress of something sweet burning in her throat as the streets rolled by. But at work, never. Not so much as a drop. How could she, with her responsibilities? No, she rearranged the bulletin board, checked locks, organized meds, studied charts for mistakes. But never liquor. And those young nurses, their faces so smug and stupid, so relieved to see her getting fired, giddy with it. She despises the idea of nursing homes. The pettiness, the politics. The way they time you and watch you and wait for you to slip, the way they can fire you without even letting you defend yourself. She'll never go near that place again. She'll never be put in that kind of place, either. When she gets to the stage where she's unable to manage by herself, she'll take pills. She has a cache of Percodan stored up in a safe-deposit box in Madrillas, and she'll do it. She will. She's not afraid of dying.

She rolls on her side and looks at the wall. She may be a few years past her prime, she may even miss a beat now and then, but she's still going strong. Nobody's going to fire her from this job. She's in charge here, and Miss Pinkston is utterly grateful. She appreciates everything Mrs. Fleet does. "She's a saint," Miss Pinkston says over the phone to her friends. "I couldn't survive without her." And she's right. In another year or so, as her illness progresses and her forgetfulness worsens, she'll be even more right.

Mrs. Fleet narrows her eyes at the wall. In nursing school, they taught her to maintain a professional distance from her patients, and she sometimes wonders why. With Miss Pinkston, for instance. Her dementia has been progressing much more rapidly than even Mrs. Fleet would have predicted—in fact, at the rate things are going now, it may be only months before Miss Pinkston is fully incapacitated by her memory loss—and who will she turn to then? No children, no husband, no friends she can trust. No one except her brother, and he'll probably never fully recover. *Diligence*, Mrs. Fleet whispers at the wall. *Cleanliness. Patience.* She kicks her legs free of the blankets and sits up. Miss Pinkston needs a professional she can trust. Someone who can keep her from being shipped off to Peaceful Glen when her brother dies, or possibly even before that. That's what the town is waiting for. They're waiting for Miss Pinkston to do something unforgivable, something so peculiar they can push Mrs. Fleet out of their way and pack Miss Pinkston off to the nursing home right along with her brother. The way they gape at Miss Pinkston's things when they visit, as if they're already figuring out what to bid on at the estate auction, and that polite sympathy in their voices—*How you think she's holding up lately, Miz Fleet? Think she's still managing okay?*—why, they've probably already made the legal arrangements! All they need now is a good excuse. Mrs. Fleet stands, trembling all over, her hands clenched tight. She's not going to let the Pinkstons get thrown out of their home. That's why she was hired: because she's more than just an overpaid sitter, more than an illiterate, clock-watching, first-year nurse. Mrs. Fleet has twenty-seven years of experience under her belt, and she knows exactly how to keep the upper hand in situations like this. By the time she's done, they'll all know it. Starting with that sheriff whoever-he-is. She pulls on her bathrobe, and when she hears the squad car pull into the driveway, she hurries downstairs to keep him from inviting himself inside for coffee.

The next morning she concentrates on securing the house. She turns down the hot water heater, removes the knobs on the stove, and hides the downstairs phone. After making a mental tally of the doors and cupboards she'll want control over, she calls the hardware store. The man laughs outright when she orders twelve cylinder locks, and then, realizing she's serious, says that the locks he carries are key padlocks, "and most of them been sitting on the shelf since the dawn of man." His name is Eli Sanchez—he says they've met before, when he stopped in to visit Mr. Pinkston—and though she doesn't care for him or his humor, she agrees to let him bring the padlocks so he can figure out what type of hasps to order. He arrives in an old truck with whiskey on his breath, and after showing him the house, letting him speak with Mr. Pinkston a moment, and then escorting him out, she tests each lock and key to make sure it works properly. Not that she expects Miss Pinkston to wander away in the near future—since the sheriff brought her home, she's been hiding in the house as if she'll never leave again—but Mrs. Fleet must be prepared. Miss Pinkston can't admire her enough. She claps her hands to her breast with relief when she sees the locks. "What a mind reader you are, Mrs. Fleet. Locks are exactly what *I* was thinking."

On the fourth of January, Mrs. Fleet takes her reading glasses from their case, knocks on Miss Pinkston's bedroom, and tells her it's time to deal with finances.

"You don't mean to say I haven't paid you yet," cries Miss Pinkston.

Mrs. Fleet smiles politely but reassuringly and takes a seat at Miss Pinkston's desk. The top of it is surprisingly neat, with pencils arranged in descending length in the wooden box next to the blotter, but the inside of each drawer is a chaos of bills, most of which, just as she suspected, turn out to be overdue. Mrs. Fleet sorts them according to priority.

"But I don't understand what you're doing," says Miss Pinkston from the hallway. "I usually pay bills myself. I've done it for fifty years. I always pay the fees for my checks. I never bounced a check. Is that it? Did I bounce a check?"

Mrs. Fleet studies the account ledger, shaking her head in pity. Like so many wealthy senior citizens, Miss Pinkston has been the target of every charity, church, political movement, con artist, and junk mail advertiser in the country, and from the entries in her ledger, many have been rewarded lately for persistence. Ten dollars to UNICEF, twenty to the Red Cross, twenty-five to Feed the Children, a hundred and fifty to the local church. The list goes on. Mrs. Fleet purses her lips. She has nothing against charity, but it infuriates her to think that the innocent victim of a memory disorder could be taken advantage of so callously. She makes a mental note to sort the incoming mail before her employer has a chance to see it. How else to avoid such waste?

Then there is a stack of motel business envelopes squirreled away in the back of Miss Pinkston's middle drawer. The envelopes are addressed *To Alice*, and sealed inside each one is sixty dollars in cash. Eight hundred and forty dollars in all. Mrs. Fleet clucks her tongue in pity. Heaven knows what paranoid fantasies have caused the poor woman to prepare cash envelopes for herself. She's probably planning to hide them around the house for emergencies or give them away or bury them in the back yard. Mrs. Fleet has seen it before. One of her favorite war stories about Alzheimer's—though, as she well knows, certainly tragic—is that of a short fat southern banker named Mr. Wilson, who became so fearful of being robbed that shortly before his wife brought him out west and had him committed to the Peaceful Glen Nursing Home, he confessed that he had hidden all his money under the magnolias, causing his wife to spend several thousand dollars bulldozing their estate before she discovered that he had confused the word *magnolia* with *mattress*. Fortunately for Miss Pinkston, no money will be misplaced or lost, not with Mrs. Fleet at the helm. She puts all the money into one envelope and places it in her purse. Not that she would think of taking Miss Pinkston's money—not in a million years, not in a trillion lifetimes, stealing is against her very core of being—but she'll need to maintain control of the money from now on, and collecting these envelopes before they leave the house is one sure way to do it.

For the legitimate bills—electric, water, heat, and garbage—she places each check with its bill in its proper envelope and seals it. For others, she hesitates. An enormous bill from an orthodontist in upper New York State, for instance.

"Did you ever get your teeth fixed in New York, Miss Pinkston?"

Miss Pinkston looks astonished. "That's none of your business."

"Fine." Mrs. Fleet smiles tiredly. "Have you ever been to New York?"

"Of course not. Why?"

"That's what I thought." She turns back to the desk and throws the bill away. She throws several bills away. Then she gets out her calculator and balances Miss Pinkston's checkbook. Her numbers are neat, careful, accurate, her subtraction double-checked. Miss Pinkston has long forgotten what Mrs. Fleet is doing at her desk. She's at the window, chewing on her lower lip and shaking her head.

Next, Mrs. Fleet makes up a grocery list and calls Steelhead's Market to say that she and Miss Pinkston will be calling in their groceries from now on. When the woman says she doesn't have delivery service, Mrs. Fleet says she regrets that she and Miss Pinkston can't leave the house until Mr. Pinkston is well. She says this matter-of-factly, absolutely, and then she waits through an impudent silence until the woman at last offers her youngest grandson, Augie, as delivery boy. Mrs. Fleet places her order, asks that it be delivered to the back door, and hangs up.

"But I don't *want* someone I don't know coming here," cries Miss Pinkston. "I was trying to tell you that while you were talking. He'll have to come in, we'll have to feed him and sit with him and talk to him. That's the way this town is, that's what they expect when they visit somebody. Especially if they have to come all the way up the hill on foot."

Mrs. Fleet smiles. "You don't have to worry, Miss Pinkston. I know all about towns like this. If you wish, I'll take care of it myself."

And she does. Half an hour later, when a little black-haired boy with enormous eyes and a runny nose appears at the kitchen door tugging a red wagon full of groceries, Mrs. Fleet takes the handle from him, pulls the wagon over the threshold, and shuts the door. She unloads the groceries, and when she opens the door to hand the wagon back, she finds the boy standing there in tears.

"I thought you was keeping my wagon," he says.

She pays him from Miss Pinkston's wallet, gives him his wagon, and shuts the door.

When she goes into the living room, she sees Miss Pinkston peeking around the edge of the curtain at the south window, following the boy around the outside of the house. She's talking to herself about rights, about trespassing and ignorance, working herself into a fret. It's a delicate balance, being her friend and her employee while at the same time gently taking control of her affairs.

"You don't have to worry," says Mrs. Fleet soothingly. "That young man is our friend. He'll be delivering our groceries from now on."

"But he can't. Everybody's going to think I'm so lazy. They're going to talk and talk and talk about me. You don't know how they are. They're like magpies out there. *Yak, yak, yak.*"

Mrs. Fleet decides to change the subject. "I think it's time to clean silverware. Don't you?" She steps to the lowboy behind the sofa and starts removing pieces of silver. "Miss Pinkston?"

Miss Pinkston appears at her left side. "Why should I want to clean silver?"

"Then you don't have to," says Mrs. Fleet quietly.

Miss Pinkston frowns. "I wish you weren't here all the time. I wish you'd go away. I can look after my brother myself. I don't know why you're always here."

Mrs. Fleet is quiet. Then she says, "Perhaps there's something interesting on television. Would you like to go see?" she asks. "Alice?"

Miss Pinkston puffs like a startled bird. "You're not supposed to call me Alice. You're my employee."

Mrs. Fleet reddens. "Whatever you wish, Miss Pinkston."

"I wish you'd call the police, that's what I wish." She goes back to the window. "Nobody has a right to trespass," she says, "even if they're delivering groceries. Look at that. Like it's not even our property."

Mrs. Fleet gives up on the silver and goes over to her employer.

"Miss Pinkston. Look at me, please." She has a professional tone and she knows how to use it. When Miss Pinkston does as she's told, Mrs. Fleet smiles and drops her tone back to a comforting level. "Now, you have to understand. We asked that boy to come, and he'll be coming from now on. He brings us our groceries. . . ."

Her voice trails off. Out on the sidewalk, to one side of the pine tree in the front yard, is a young woman staring intently at Mr. Pinkston's bedroom window. She looks unkempt and in need of a hot meal—down in it, as the late Dr. Fleet might say—and though she's not exactly hiding behind the tree, she's not moving out from behind it either. She pulls something out of her pocket and bends over, her dark red hair wiring in all directions. A rolled cigarette, Mrs. Fleet notes, narrowing her eyes.

"Who is that, Miss Pinkston?"

"As if you didn't know."

Mrs. Fleet turns to her. "I don't know."

Miss Pinkston's mouth falls open. "You don't?"

"No."

Miss Pinkston shivers and turns to the window. "I don't care what Frank Doby says. He doesn't know everything. I know some things. She killed my sister. I don't have to like her at all." She turns, storming into the hall and up the stairway.

Mrs. Fleet turns back to the window. The young woman is still there, smoking drugs in broad daylight. Not only that, she's waving at Mr. Pinkston's window.

Sheriff, there's a young person outside the house. I'm not sure what she wants, but I'd like you to take care of it please."

She waits.

"Mr. Doby?"

"Is this a woman about twenty-nine? Dressed in a lumpy green parka? Dark red hair?"

"You know her?"

"I expect I do. How exactly is she bothering you?"

She hesitates, then says, "She's staring at Mr. Pinkston's bedroom window."

"She's not on the property though, is she?"

Mrs. Fleet tightens her grip on the receiver. "Mr. Doby. This person is smoking marijuana."

"Oh, I doubt that. Rose doesn't have the money for drugs. It's probably just tobacco."

Mrs. Fleet looks at the receiver and then puts it back to her ear. "I don't care what she's smoking or why. I'm calling you because handling vagrancy is your job."

"Rose isn't a vagrant. She's a friend of Birdie's. I didn't know she was still up there, but she's not going to hurt anybody. You don't have to worry."

"She's upsetting Miss Pinkston."

"I know. She always has."

"I beg your pardon?"

"There's a few things you should know, Mrs. Fleet. How about I come over after I get done with my paperwork here?"

She stiffens. Having the sheriff in the house will upset Miss Pinkston, will probably only make this day more complicated. "I'd rather you didn't," she says. "Miss Pinkston is upset enough as it is."

"Okay. How about I come over tonight, after Alice is asleep?"

"If you are referring to Miss Pinkston," says Mrs. Fleet, enunciating every word, "I'm afraid that's not possible. She doesn't normally go to bed until after nine P.M. And by then I'm usually asleep myself."

"How about eight then."

This time it is not a question. In an icy voice, she tells him to come at eight-thirty and hangs up. When she looks out the window, the red-haired person is gone. There is something off about the tone he's taken with her, Mrs. Fleet can feel it. She turns to the mirror. Disrespect, she thinks, that's what it was. Impudence. She puts one hand on her chest. She's breathing irregularly, shallowly, almost as if she's been running.

Sheriff Doby circles the living room, studying Miss Pinkston's shelves of glass figurines, his hands behind his back as if he's been taught to guard against his own clumsiness. Then he wedges himself carefully between the couch and the coffee table and sits, leaning forward with his elbows on his knees. He is tall and wide across the shoulders, the kind of big-boned handsome man who, Mrs. Fleet notes with satisfaction, understands just how far out of his element he is in a living room this dainty and clean. Instead of a badge and uniform, he's wearing jeans and a plaid shirt, and for all the charm he's trying to soften her up with as he makes small talk, she sees coldly that he has not even taken the time to comb his rather shaggy black hair. Mrs. Fleet, on the other hand, is dressed impeccably, her hair shaped perfectly, her nurse's uniform freshly laundered and starched, her chalk-white shoes placed side by side, flat on the carpet. Her hands are scrubbed pink and resting lightly on the arms of Miss Pinkston's Queen Anne chair. She places the sheriff's age at thirty-three, perhaps even younger. Nervous, she thinks, as she watches him make small talk, a people pleaser, insecure as a boy, possibly a bed wetter at one time. Ineffectual too, probably all his life. Finally he says, "We might as well get down to what I'm here about."

"If you wish, Mr. Doby."

"Let's see," he says with a sigh. "You been working here, what, a month now?"

"A month and one week."

He nods and looks at the ceiling, then lowers his voice. "She's upstairs, right?"

"I believe she's in her room. I'm sorry to have to tell you, Mr. Doby," she adds, "that whether or not my employer is asleep is none of my business."

"I'm not asking you to divide your loyalties, Mrs. Fleet. I just don't want her to hear what I'm about to tell you. You have enough to worry about."

"I do my job," she says, though she relents by lowering her voice. "And I do quite enjoy working for Miss Pinkston."

"Good. I know she appreciates it." He sighs again and runs his hands through his hair. "I guess you must know by now that she tends to get confused, though, right? That you can't always trust her judgment?"

Mrs. Fleet remains silent.

"The person you saw outside the house this afternoon—her name is Rose Devonic. I'll vouch for her straight through."

Mrs. Fleet stares at him. "Go on, Mr. Doby."

"The thing is, she was raised by an uncle who had this idea that he wanted her to learn something besides embroidery." He pauses and looks up. "You know much about the embroidery in this town, Mrs. Fleet?"

"I am afraid not. I rarely have time for hobbies."

"Oh. Well, embroidery is no hobby, believe me. Not in this valley. It's a tradition, a career like your nursing, and you need years of practice for it. It takes most of a lifetime to develop. And Rose didn't have that, you see, because when she was first starting out, her uncle got this idea to carve wooden Indians. He was a hell of a wood-carver. You've never seen what a piece of wood could be until you saw his work." The sheriff looks up, stumbles a little when he meets her eyes, and rushes on. "Anyhow, the embroiderers in this town didn't appreciate him, especially when they saw how serious he was about rocking the boat. He got laughed at something awful, and when he and his family started taking their work on the road and making real profits, they got blackballed. No matter how hard they worked or how much money they made, nobody who did embroidery wanted to listen, nobody wanted to be glad for them, and for four long years, whenever that family drove out of town to go sell another Indian, every embroiderer on their street wished them bad luck. You may not understand this, Mrs. Fleet, but in a town as small as ours, that kind of treatment is powerful stuff. It's like voodoo, or a disease: you might not feel it at first, you might not even notice, but then it starts to wear you down. Anyway, it wore down the Devonics. Bob, the uncle, he didn't feel it much because he'd never felt much about the community to begin with, but Rose basically dropped out of school. They stopped buying food from Steelhead's Market, stopped taking walks after dinner and doing their laundry at the laundromat and going to the cafe for breakfast on Sundays. And then one night, they were taking one of their Indians over the pass to deliver it to a customer in Santa Fe, and it fell off the roof of their car and caused an accident. A real bad one. Alice's younger sister was caught in it—I'm sure you've heard from Alice about Florie?—but so was Rose's uncle, her mother, and her little brother. All of them died. Rose was only sixteen. It was like all the bad luck that the embroiderers had ever wished on her and her family came true at once." The sheriff looks up, rubs his palms in exasperation, and plunges on. "The reason why I'm bothering you with all this is because Rose wouldn't have survived in this town if it wasn't for Bird. When she decided she needed to learn embroidery, he took her in and taught her. Nobody else was willing. Birdie was the only trade embroiderer who tried to help, Mrs. Fleet. Nobody else. Birdie was it."

"An interesting story, Mr. Doby," says Mrs. Fleet crisply, eyeing her watch. "And how does this affect me?"

"Well, the thing is, they've been friends a long time. In fact, I think if it wasn't for Rose, Birdie would have shot himself years ago. He's never been the happiest old coot in the world, even before his stroke. Rose always cheered him up. She's like a daughter to him. And that's why she's sticking around now. I think she's hoping to help him feel better. The only problem is, Alice is kind of mixed up about Rose. I guess she never quite forgave her for surviving the accident."

"Ah," says Mrs. Fleet coldly. "So you would like me to sneak this Rose person into the house behind Miss Pinkston's back. I see."

He looks up from under his dark brow, shaking his head. "I don't mean that at all, Mrs. Fleet. Rose would never come in here against Alice's wishes. I'm only trying to explain her position."

"Her position," says Mrs. Fleet, "does not concern me. My position does."

"That's why I'm telling you all this. You don't have to worry about Rose bothering you. She just wants to keep an eye on things. She understands the situation here with Alice and Birdie."

"And you are suggesting that I do not?" She places her hands on the arms of the chair and stands up.

"No, no, you probably know more than anyone else." He runs his hands through his hair. "If it'll make you feel any better, I'll go talk to Rose in the morning. I'll tell her you don't want her hanging around too much. I'll tell her it's scaring Alice. Maybe she'll listen. I just can't promise it. She's awful fond of the old man. He's all she's got."

He pauses as if he wants to say more and then reddens as if he's said too much. Then he looks sideways at the coffee table, cupping his mouth with his hand, and in that one gesture, that one pathetic flash of doubt, Mrs. Fleet sees the truth. Sheriff Doby has a weakness for this Rose person. He may even be in love with her.

"Well," he says, "it's late."

"Perhaps it is." She ignores the handshake he's offering and steps to the edge of the front hall.

"Yeah, I'll let you go now. Good night, then." He walks past her to the front hall and then stops, looks at the doorknob, and turns. "I was just wondering, though."

She waits, lacing her hands in front of her. What a fumbling, bumbling, pathetic young man he is. "Of course, Mr. Doby," she says with contempt. "What is it?"

"How come you needed to buy twelve padlocks the other day from Eli Sanchez?"

For a moment, she can only stare at him, shocked by his impudence. Then she motions him back into the center of the living room so their voices won't carry up the stairwell.

"Mr. Doby. I do not tell you how to do your job, and I would appreciate you not telling me how to do mine."

"Oh, I wouldn't do that," he says hurriedly. "You're the nurse, not me." But still he hesitates, scratching the back of his neck. "It's just all those locks. There's no need for them. Not in this town. Heck, I know how Alice is about break-ins, but in all the years my dad was sheriff here he had one robbery, and that turned out to be a joke Doc Mutz was playing on Louis Steelhead. And I haven't had any. Break-ins, I mean."

Mrs. Fleet nearly laughs out loud. She would like to tell him that there are two sides to every door. She would like to tell him why the acute care facility at the Peaceful Glen Nursing Home has a 24-hour lockup policy for every door, window, and closet in sight. *And it isn't to keep out intruders, Mr. Doby, believe me.* But of course she won't. He knows nothing about Alzheimer's. He doesn't even know the depths of Miss Pinkston's illness.

"Very well, Mr. Doby," she says. "I'll tell Miss Pinkston she doesn't need to worry about theft."

"I'd appreciate it. It might help calm her down a little. Good." He stretches, uncomfortable, wanting to leave, she thinks. "Well, I guess I'll be going."

"However," she adds, tucking her chin, "I am afraid that if Miss Pinkston insists on installing those locks, I'll be forced to obey her wishes. She *is* my employer, Mr. Doby."

He turns slowly and looks at her. "Well, yeah." But instead of leaving, he goes to the window, pulls aside the curtain, and looks out at the dark. "There's something you ought to know about that, though, Mrs. Fleet."

"It's late, Mr. Doby. It's extremely late, and if I am to keep to my schedule—"

"It wasn't Alice's idea to hire you," he says. "It was mostly mine. In fact, I kind of talked her into it. So I feel I have a responsibility to make sure you're doing things by the book."

Mrs. Fleet stands very still, staring at the back of his neck. She wants to stand absolutely still, to wait him out, to make him squirm and redden, to realize his rudeness, to fumble for an apology. But when he turns, his face is quiet, his dark eyes focused and watchful.

"I see," she says. She swallows the tremble in her voice, steps to the Queen Anne chair, and sits, her back to him. "And what can you possibly accuse me of?"

"Nothing. As long as Birdie's okay and Alice likes you, I have no complaints." He steps in front of her and sits on the edge of the coffee table, his focus suddenly as intense as a laser. "I know she isn't the easiest person to be with," he says quietly, "and I know that between her and her brother, you must feel pretty beat at the end of the day. But I don't want any funny business." He leans forward on his elbows, his hands out. "I don't want to hear about anybody getting locked up against their will. You understand?" He stops, looking down to rub his palms together. "I'm not the kind to hold a person's past against them," he says. "But I've got to tell you, the woman at the Home Health Care agency in Madrillas, she wasn't all that sure you could handle this job. I want you to prove her wrong. Will you do that for me?"

From a great distance, Mrs. Fleet hears herself say yes.

"Good. I'll be going then." He slaps his thighs and stands up, towering over her. "I know you need this job, Mrs. Fleet. I just need to be sure I've done the right thing by convincing Alice to hire you."

She sits in the Queen Anne chair, staring at the coffee table. She listens to the clock on the mantel ticking, and the ceiling overhead creaks. Probably Miss Pinkston, frightened by the sound of the front door closing. Mrs.

Fleet is thinking of some of the patients she's handled: Mrs. Walker, who hid spoons in her brassiere; Mr. Ausslander, who couldn't keep his hands to himself; Mrs. Carnegie, who mewed and spat on all fours like an animal; Mr. Powers, who scrubbed himself with an invisible sponge. The younger nurses had nicknames for the difficult cases, nicknames they used in front of the patients when Mrs. Fleet wasn't there to forbid it. Wheeze, Mary Mother of God, Queen Elizabeth, the Swimmer, the Italian Stallion, Mr. Snot. She thinks of Mr. Bevel, slouched over in the closet with her brandy flask. Popeye, he was called. Then she thinks of her late husband, Dr. Fleet. What a difficult patient he was, especially toward the end, yelling at her from his bed whenever she walked by, calling her pee-brain, lard-ass, the b-word, the c-word, sometimes worse. Filthy, filthy talk. Whenever Mrs. Fleet had to give him his meds, she was always careful to remind her nurses that abusive language was a symptom, that as the neurofibrillary tangles increase within the cortex of the brain, patients with presenile dementia of the Alzheimer's type often exhibit an unfortunate loss of control over their emotions as well as their speech; still, she'd regretted the hospital's decision to have him placed on her ward. His fondness for foul language whenever she stepped in the room had undermined her authority with the entire staff. As if he'd been yelling words like that ever since their first date back in 1956, as if she were worth nothing more than bedpans and soiled sheets, his voice going on and on. If she'd been less professional, she would have nicknamed him Shit Mouth. In a sort of dream, she turns out the lights, climbs the stairs, and goes into her bedroom, locking her door when she hears Miss Pinkston across the hall. She unties her shoes, slips them off quietly, and lies back on the white nubby bedspread. She should have explained herself better to the Home Health Care agency, should have made that Mrs. Guynn understand that there are two sides to every story. Instead, she'd sat there and allowed the woman to tell her that the agency wouldn't stand for any physical abuse or mistreatment of patients. As if Mrs. Fleet was some sort of monster who kept patients in cages and straitjackets. Mrs. Fleet, who up until the incident with Mr. Bevel was known as one of the most highly respected nurses at Peaceful Glen, a nurse who for twenty-seven years had never asked for anything from her superiors but the right to do her job correctly. At least when they fired her, they'd had the courage to apologize first. "We know how many years of service you've given us, Mrs. Fleet," said the Director of Programming, "and we'll certainly be taking that into account. But we have to be sensitive to public opinion." As if she wasn't. As if she'd locked Mr. Bevel in that closet purely to punish him for stealing her brandy. It wasn't punishment, it was protection. That's why she'd locked him in there. She was only trying to protect him from the shame of his own drunkenness. Of course she would have brought him out and cleaned him up as soon as the son left. What kind of nurse did they think she was? But no, the son wouldn't listen. Neither would the other nurses. She hears Miss Pinkston out in the hall, testing the doorknob. "Go away," she says. There's a pause and then footsteps creeping back across the hall. Mrs. Fleet lies back again and stares at the ceiling. In another month—maybe even less—the poor woman will have forgotten all about Mrs. Fleet. She'll have forgotten her name and her face and which room she slept in and why and what she did and how hard she worked and who she was—everything. Perhaps she's already forgotten. Mrs. Fleet doesn't really care. The truth is, she's tired of elderly people, tired of the long hours and low pay, tired of doing everything right and never being thanked for it, of working too hard for no reason, shoring up their lives just to watch them die anyway. Tired of the whole business. Nobody appreciates how much she gives. No one ever notices. And always someone poking their nose into her business, some ignorant layperson telling her how to do her job. She gets up slowly, pulls her suitcase out from under the bed, and begins to pack. When she's done, she brushes her hair in the mirror. It's a dark brunette color with red highlights, so artful no one would ever guess it's not real. That sheriff hadn't guessed. He was a fool. A young, blushing, handsome fool, just the kind of fool Mrs. Guynn would talk to. *I know you need this job,* he'd said. What a laugh. Mrs. Fleet has never needed a job. She's never needed anything, but everybody has needed her. All her life. Needed and needed and needed. She ties the laces on her shoes, arranges the twelve steel padlocks and keys in a row on the bureau, picks up her suitcase, her purse, and her coat, opens the door, and walks out.

13

God give me grace I ask no more
Contentment is a constant store.

—from an American sampler, 1798

What I didn't expect was how different the motel would feel without Birdie. I didn't realize it at first except in terms of the fact that I could live off his pantry for a couple of months. But when I saw him get wheeled away into Alice's house, everything changed. I couldn't forget the look on his face. I began to think hard then about where I belonged and why. The motel had been my home for twelve winters, and I'd done more than just live there. When Bird was in his cups, I answered the phone, registered guests, handed out keys, and helped with luggage. I shoveled snow, vacuumed rugs, made beds, and cleaned bird crap off the porches. I wasn't asked to do it, and I wasn't paid. I did it because that's where I lived and what Birdie needed me to do. Maybe that's all a home is, just the place where you know what's needed. I knew which toilets ran, which doors stuck, which pipes tended to freeze. I knew how the furnaces worked, where the fuse box was, when to turn on the water heaters, and what direction to point the roof antenna. I knew as much about the motel as Birdie did—maybe more, since I'd slept in every cabin at least once. I knew the place inside out, the same way anybody knows their own home. What did Alice know?

But I didn't want to start World War III with her. I just wanted to get the point across that, in a town as small as Queduro, locals like me don't have that many choices in winter. Also, that we're easy to get along with as long as people are willing to get along with us. Also, that regardless of my financial situation, I could still be helpful. That, more than anything, is why I didn't leave.

I also wanted to see if she could buy her way out of her problems. Most of the time you can—99 percent of the time, if you're rich enough, you can—but when life goes truly haywire, you need someone you can trust, and trust is one thing money can't buy. If Alice had understood that, if she hadn't been so quick to jump to conclusions about me, it would have been a different story. We could've worked something out. I didn't want trouble.

So I decided not to hide anymore. The day after she brought Birdie home from the hospital, I pulled the blanket off my front window so she could see me if she wanted. I parked my Plymouth in front of the motel so it would be in clear view of her house, and then I went in Birdie's office and opened the curtains wide so she could watch me. I turned on the neon Indian and checked Birdie's answering machine and watered his geranium and tidied up, salted the front stoop, and went out to collect the mail. Whatever he might need. Then I went in and sat behind the front desk and worked on my embroidery. I worked until five that night and then closed up the office, turned off the Indian, and went back to my cabin. But I was back at eight sharp in the morning. It took three days of that before she was openly watching me from across the street. I'd notice her at one of her upper windows, staring at the office as if she expected it to explode. She watched all afternoon, and after that I saw her at her windows every day when I came to work. If I waved, she'd narrow her eyes to slits and snag her curtains closed. Still, I waved. I told myself that if she chose not to take it as a friendly gesture, I'd just have to keep doing it until she did.

Then one afternoon two Mormons showed up, asking for a cabin. After I registered them, I gave them Birdie's extra set of keys for the Navajo (which was another thing Alice didn't understand about her brother, that Birdie kept extra keys for everything with a lock on it), and showed them to their cabin. When Alice didn't call me on the phone afterward, I began to feel hopeful. It seemed to me that I was getting through to her, that she'd finally decided to give me a chance. I was so sure of it by the next morning I took a cutting off Bird's best geranium for her. I put it in a clay pot, wrapped a few embroidery threads around one of the stems, and tied on the Mormons' credit card receipt along with a card, *Merry Xmas, from Next Door.* To make sure Birdie's nurse wouldn't take the gift herself, I waited until she left to go shopping in Alice's car. Then I took it over.

Alice was at the upstairs window on the right. When I held up the geranium, she ducked back as if I was going to throw it. When I rang the doorbell, she didn't answer. But I could understand. Alice and I had a lot in common. We were both strong-willed, we were both stubborn, and we were both loners. I set the geranium on the porch, went out to the lawn and called up to the window I'd last seen her at.

"It's a geranium," I called. "You better take it before dark so it doesn't freeze. We haven't had much of a winter yet, huh," I added, "but it's still too cold for geraniums." I waited. "We could be friends, you know." There was no answer and she didn't come back to the window. But I left the geranium anyway.

Then I had a real stroke of luck. On Christmas Eve day, three hunters from Durango showed up at the office, saying their Toyota had broken down out on the highway. They'd managed to drive it into town, but the universal joint was broken and Ruben Johnson would have to order parts. Ruben Johnson was even slower at fixing cars than he was at plowing roads. The hunters might not be able to leave for weeks. I looked them over, watched the way they talked and moved their hands and held their wallets, and after we chatted about hunting in the valley and where they could buy liquor and a good meal, I told them they could have the Apache for sixty a night. Sixty was double what Birdie charged, but I wanted to impress Alice. I wanted her to realize what a person like myself could do for her and Birdie. "Sixty," I said. "Pay in cash and we'll call it Christmas, no tax." They took it.

In this way, Alice found an envelope in her mailbox every night for the next two weeks with her name on it and sixty dollars inside. I could picture her opening each one, shaking her head as the money spilled out. I could see her weakening slowly but surely and finally giving in, admitting that she'd been wrong, I'd opened her eyes, she couldn't sell the motel. I could see Birdie behind his desk next spring, choking back tears, trying to tell me how grateful he was. I couldn't see any way that it wouldn't turn out right for all of us.

Meanwhile I kept working on my embroidery. I was still behind and there was no point in denying it, but I was beginning to think I'd have enough work done by spring to make a showing. Plus I'd started in on the big magpie Birdie had drawn. It was coming even better than I could have hoped, especially after I mixed a few blue and red threads into the black feathers to give them that glimmery look. Set against the bright gold silk, so cocksure and bold, that magpie wouldn't be just another piece of needlework but more like the god of magpies, like if you asked it the meaning of life, it could shiver up its feathers, croak out a burp, and give you the answer. It was only half finished, but it was the best thing I'd done. It made my smaller pieces look about as artistic as old bumper stickers—which was all right with me as long as it convinced the Commerce Committee that I still deserved a booth.

But then one day while I was changing sheets in the Apache, it hit me that the Committee didn't even know I was still in town. As far as they were concerned, I was on welfare and food stamps in Madrillas and probably never coming back. They might have already given my booth to someone else. I went back to my cabin, folded the magpie-on-silk piece into my workbag, dressed in my good skirt, fixed some dinner for the dog so he wouldn't worry, and, since my car needed to be started to keep the battery young, I drove down to the bar.

I was right. As soon as I walked in, the bar felt as if all the air had gotten sucked out. Nobody looked up from their work, nobody said hello, people stitching at the tables frozen there like they'd been stuffed with wax. I hung up my coat and strolled toward Dick Sweeny, who was sitting at a table in the middle of the room with his son, Billy, and Hank and Barby Wellston. The way the back of Dick's neck reddened as I got close, the way his spine stiffened, I didn't have to ask. He'd given my booth away and he didn't know how he was going to get it back. It's not my fault, he was thinking. Still, there I was without a booth. What could he say? I plopped my bag next to his elbow and unlatched it—"How you guys doing? Mind if I join you for a few stitches?"—making sure Dick got a glimpse of my magpie piece while I leaned to the next table and borrowed a chair. When I turned around with it, he goggled a little, swallowed hard, and then gathered up his workbag, said he had to go, yanked Billy from the table, and asked Astra if he could use her phone. I signaled hello to her and began laying out my yarns and needles. *Every embroiderer over the age of eighteen shall have a booth made available when needed,* that was the Committee's guarantee to us Quedurans. I was only there to remind them of it. Also to remind them that I was no quitter. I smiled across the table at Hank and Barby Wellston, who were sewing so fiercely they could've played tunes on their thread, and then reached in my bag for my scissors.

That was the same night I drove home and found that Alice had fixed a padlock on the outside of the office door. I took a deep breath and walked around to the courtyard. The hunters were gone, vanished, nothing, and their cabin door was padlocked too. And worse, so was mine. A big steel link and padlock. No eviction notices, no warnings. Not even a message.

But worst of all, the dog. When I whistled for him, thinking she'd tried to run him off with the hunters, I saw him peeking over the edge of the windowsill inside the Ute. She'd padlocked him inside. She'd padlocked my dog and everything I owned inside the cabin. That was the last straw. That was what did it. She wasn't ever going to turn human.

I marched back out to the street.

"You can't do this," I yelled at her house. "You hear me over there? You can't lock me out of my home without a warning." Then I got in my car, revved it up till it was belching black smoke, and roared down the alley to my cabin's parking space. I locked it and went around behind my cabin, pushed open the bathroom window, threw in my workbag, and crawled in after it. I jammed the window shut with a kitchen knife, jammed the front door with the table, and retaped the blanket over the front window. She'd turned off the heat and electricity, but I had plenty of clothes for warmth. I had a box of storm candles and a sleeping bag. At night I could haul water up from the river in town. *I'm a lot more pigheaded than you are,* I told the cabin. *Ten days' notice. Three days, minimum.* It was reassuring out loud, and when I said it a second time it was true, and eventually I stopped shivering.

14

Is there ambition in my heart
Search gracious God and see
or do I act a haughty part
Lord I appeal to the.

—from an American sampler, 1789

Nothing happened. By morning I was pacing around in the dark, feeling wired and fighting with myself, wishing it hadn't gone this far and wishing I'd thought it through a little better, wishing I had some light to see by, a better parka, a bigger food stash and a toilet that flushed, wishing a hundred things at once but most of all wishing she'd make her move. She had to do something. She couldn't just ignore me, not anymore, not if I was waiting. That's what I thought all day and most of the next night until I finally fell asleep.

By the third night, sleep was out of the question. Every time I closed my eyes, I thought someone was at the door trying to slip the key into the padlock. I'd hear whispering or footsteps outside, and before I could believe I was making it up, I'd have to go to the window and peel back the blanket to look. I put my pillow over my head, but that was worse, as if there was someone already in the cabin, bending over me in the dark, waiting for me to throw off the pillow and see. When I couldn't take it anymore, I got out three storm candles, lit them, dripped wax onto a pie pan, fixed them there, and started packing. I packed everything I could find in bags and put the bags in the bathroom under the window. Then I got in bed with the dog and stared at the candles. If I hadn't heard from her by the time the last flame went out, I'd swallow my pride and take everything I owned out the back window. Maybe over to Eli's, see if he could give me a bed for the night, or maybe to Astra's.

When I woke up, I was in a sweat with my hands held out in front of me and my feet already on the floor. The candles were out, and from the light at the edge of the blanket, it was morning. The dog was sitting by the refrigerator, waiting for me to open it and produce something for breakfast. I looked down at my parka and felt bad then, felt how close I'd come to losing my nerve, but as I fell back I heard a car. I propped on my elbows to listen and then jumped for the window and reached it just in time to see the taillights of a white Chevy disappear around the front of the office. I wasn't sure for a moment, but then I heard the squawk of a radio, and it was like Christmas. Alice had panicked and called in the cavalry. It was a stupid move on her part, the first truly ignorant move she'd made. I felt my way in the dark to the bathroom, pulling off clothes as I went, and pawed through the bags for my best skirt and sweater. I put them on and braided my hair and then moved all the bags out to the front room and went to the window and peeked around the blanket again.

It took about forever, but Frank finally came into the courtyard. He was in uniform, and he paused next to the office, looking down at the key he was holding and then out in the direction of his squad car, as if he'd just rather leave. I let the blanket drop over the window and got myself ready. Frank had the sort of easy good-natured looks that, together with his cop uniform, fooled most people into thinking they knew everything about him when they knew nothing at all. But me, I knew. We'd grown up together, Frank and I. Except for his two years in Panama, we'd been around each other nearly every day. Maybe we'd taken different roads, but I'd known him all my life. He was my best friend in Queduro and I was his. I wanted to shout that through the door, wanted him to know I knew that before he opened my cabin. I felt my way to the bathroom and pulled myself up to my full height in the mirror. I straightened my sweater and the front of my skirt, and when I thought I had the right expression on my face, I felt my way back to the front room, put on my parka, and pushed the table away from the door.

I waited until I heard his boots coming down the sidewalk and then picked up three of the bags and my car keys. I closed my eyes and took a breath all the way to the bottom of me, and when I heard the click of the key in the padlock and his voice—"Rose? It's me, Frank"—I came barreling out with both arms full, shoving one bag at him and starting for my car with the others.

"So what were you doing over there anyway, having breakfast with her?"

He didn't answer, which made me sorry I'd said it. When I looked back, he was watching the dog, who'd slithered out the door and onto his back at Frank's feet, wagging all over like he needed forgiveness. "Who's this?" asked Frank, in that quiet way of his, crouching to rub the dog's crooked ear. I told him the dog didn't have a name, and he straightened up and we crossed over to my car. He stood behind me while I opened the tailgate and loaded the back. I could feel Alice watching—somehow it felt as if the whole town were watching—but I didn't care, God, yes, the queen of the tribes of exile, as if it was nothing to me, as if I cared nothing at all, me with my mouth stitched shut and my eyes like thorns, daring anyone, anyone at all, to snicker or try out an opinion or so much as think about getting in my way. The dog jumped in without me telling him to. I ignored the bag Frank was holding and went to my cabin for more. He stayed where he was, looking out at the street.

But inside the cabin, I began to shake. By the light from the door, I had to make sure I had everything and at the same time keep my skirt from getting dirty and hold my breath against the pee stink coming from the toilet. I had to collect everything I hadn't been able to find in the dark and shove it in bags, and I had to do it before Frank decided to come ask if I wanted help. I couldn't stand the idea of him leaning in the door, seeing how I'd been living for the last four days. Each time I got another load ready, I shook out the tension and smoothed back my hair, waiting to feel myself again before I stepped out the door.

But on the last trip I was rushing anyway, and when I tried to fit my Indian-head lamp in the car, the edge of it caught the tailgate, jolting me backward. I tried again, and when it caught a second time, almost as if Alice herself had grabbed it, my mind went blank and I rammed it in, and one of the wooden feathers on the headdress snapped off and flew behind me, hitting the metal gutter on my cabin with a *dink*. I stood still then, clutching the lamp and seeing myself slamming it back and forth inside the car until all the windows broke; but besides being the only piece of Bob's work I still owned, it was my only piece of furniture. So I let go of it, straightened slowly out of the car, and walked over to the cabin to get the broken feather—only, when I bent over for it, the bag I was holding began to tip sideways, and when I grabbed for it, the canned soups I'd taken from Birdie's pantry began to fall out of the bag and roll off down the parking space. A dozen cans, all directions. It felt as if I'd pulled the pin on a grenade for the silence that fell over my ears then. I turned to look at the dog, who was watching from inside the car.

"What're you staring at?" I shouted. "You don't even like soup." I glared until he disappeared below the seat and then scooped the cans back in the bag, picked up the feather, squared my shoulders, and aimed for the car. But by then my head was roaring, and all I could picture was Alice watching from across the street, glitter-eyed and grinning, toting up my crimes, quiet as a spider.

So as soon as I had everything tucked in the car, I turned toward her house and sang out, "I sure am glad you're getting me out of here, Frank. The way this place is run, *I can see why that old woman lost her hair!*"

Yelling felt good, almost as good as being let out of the cabin. I patted Frank on the arm to keep him from worrying about it too much and started pawing through my box in the back to make sure I had everything.

"All I can say is, if you've got any bright ideas, I hope it doesn't have anything to do with rich people. I hate rich people. I just decided."

"You should be glad she's rich. Anybody else in town would've evicted you weeks ago."

I felt a rush of relief that he was still talking to me. "I just hope my car starts. The battery's as sensitive as a newborn baby." I got in, slid the key in the ignition, looked over at the dog curled up on the passenger seat, and then looked out through the windshield and turned the key, aware of Frank beside the door, aware suddenly that the paper bag he was still holding was probably the one that contained Birdie's Kama Sutra embroideries. And as if that wasn't enough, just as the engine started to growl, I spotted Alice. She'd come out of her house and crept into the far corner of the courtyard for a better view. She was wearing her pink quilted parka and standing next to the hedge at the back of the office, and as I watched she stepped behind the hedge. She'd forgotten her wig again, the top of her head showing just above the hedge like a half-blown dandelion puff.

"Come on, sweetheart. You can do it." I leaned forward, pumping the gas pedal. "One more time. Sing to me."

"Rose. We've got to talk—"

"Ah. There she goes. You see? Every time I have my doubts about this car, she comes through with flying colors." I let the engine idle, swung my legs out, and slipped past Frank. "There's not much room up front. You'd better put that bag in the back." When he didn't move, I went to the tailgate myself, waving away the exhaust fumes. "Anywhere in here's fine. Just be careful of my Indian-head lamp." I left him and went back to the passenger side, but Frank didn't move. He was just standing there, watching me. Frank had a lot going for him, but whenever he wore that uniform, he reminded me of the kind of man I pitied, the kind who'd been loyal to all the wrong things in his life and been puzzled ever since. Maybe it was the way he looked in uniform, never quite comfortable, as if he'd borrowed it from someone else, someone a half size smaller and fond of starch. Or maybe it was the way he sometimes looked at me with those dark eyes of his, almost as if he was ready to apologize for what he'd become. Maybe it was the fact that he'd cut himself shaving again. I don't know. Sometimes I had the feeling he was just too much to deal with. I took out my purse and pretended to look for something in it while I turned my back to Alice.

"Why don't you go ahead and bawl me out, Frank. It'll make you feel better. Come on. Tell me what a jerk I am. Tell me you've never seen me do such a stupid thing in my whole life. You think I can't take it?" I turned to him and held out my hands for the bag he was holding.

"Why didn't you tell me about this, Rose?"

"Because it was none of your business. Give the bag here."

"Well, it is now, isn't it."

I gave up on the bag—he'd never look in it without my permission anyway—and glared over at the hedge. Then I went back to the driver's side and switched off the engine.

"Hey! Alice! I'm getting evicted! I don't want you to miss anything."

The dandelion puff quivered as if I'd shot at it. I turned back to Frank. "Is this going to take us all day?"

He sighed and pulled on his cap. "She's not just evicting you. She wants to press charges."

"For what?"

"You want the list?"

"Let me guess. Trespassing?" I looked up at him and snorted. "That's a laugh. I'm running the motel for her and she tries to charge me with trespassing." I started to lean in the Plymouth and then backed out again. "I mean, like that is crap. What'd you tell her? You didn't say you would." I slammed the door. "Now you listen to me, Frank. I've done my best to get along with her, but I've had it. You know what I did for that woman? I collected over nine hundred dollars in rent for her in two weeks. Does that sound like trespassing to you? Plus I cleaned up the courtyard, all the cigarette butts and wrappers out of the weeds. I even scraped dog shit off the sidewalk for her. And what do I get? Do I get a single word of thanks?" When Frank started answering, I cut him off. I wanted to stop but I couldn't. "I know my rights. I was born in this country, and if she doesn't think I know my rights, she's crazy." I stepped past him and called to the hedge. "The law says I have the right to an official notice of eviction. *Official*, lady. That's the law." I popped my jaw, crooked free the muscles in my neck, and turned back. "She ought to at least know the law if she's going to be running this place."

His face had gone quiet. "You didn't ask her permission to take over," he said. "She didn't know what you were doing. And when she locked your cabin, you broke in."

"I didn't break in anything. Is that what she said? All I did was use the back window."

"Jesus, Rose. What the hell are you doing?" The way he said it threw me off, his eyes full of sadness. "You broke the law. In fact, Alice thinks—"

"Oh, I know what Alice thinks. I've been sitting in that cabin for four days knowing what Alice thinks. I don't need to know her opinion of it." I opened the car, sat on the seat, and took my brush out of one of the bags. "None of this would have happened if she hadn't been such an asshole." I looked in the mirror and then turned and pointed the hairbrush at him. "What else was I supposed to do, Frank? She locked my whole life in that cabin. Even the dog. And my car keys. How was I supposed to leave without my car keys?"

His mouth was beginning to look sewn on. "So you climbed in the window to get your keys and the dog. So why were you still there four days later?"

"Because I couldn't find the damn keys in the dark, that's why." I turned from him to unbraid my hair in the mirror. "Besides, I wanted an apology. You try running a motel by yourself and living in a cabin the size of a shoe box. You try it with no electricity or water. You see what it's like."

"All right, Rose."

"No, it's not all right. I wanted an explanation. If she wanted me out, I wanted a little damn courtesy. What's so bad about that?"

His eyes were so sad they hurt to look at. I turned back to the mirror and brushed hard.

"So maybe it wasn't much of a plan. Maybe it was a lousy plan. It was just the only plan I had." I watched my eyes in the mirror, feeling my ribs getting tight. "But I guess you can't understand that, can you? I mean, you obviously made the right choices with your life, you with your Silver Star for bravery and your little picket-fence house and your little wife, Angela. You don't have to worry about your future anymore, do you? Lucky for you, Frank." I dropped the brush and started braiding. "You'd have ended up as broke as I am if you'd had to stick to embroidery."

"Alice told you to leave, Rose. You were told, fair and square."

"Oh, is that what you call it when somebody collects over nine hundred dollars in rent and then slaps a padlock on your home?" I grabbed a rubber band off the gearshift and started winding it around the end of my braid. "And here I thought she was just plain senile. I was worried sick."

"Rose, this isn't funny."

"I couldn't agree with you more." And all at once it was true, so that I was afraid I was going to bawl. I snapped the rubber band hard into place. "You have a rotten job, my friend, you know that? Out of all the big ideas you've had since we were kids, this cop thing has got to be the worst." I got out, slammed my brush into the top of the paper bag he was holding for me, and went around to the other side of the car. "Screw Alice. Screw this whole thing. Let's just go."

"I've got something to say first." His voice was too quiet, almost spooky.

"Good," I said. "We stand here much longer, and Alice'll catch her death." I turned toward the office. "Hey, Alice! Frank has an announcement. You might want to get your tape recorder ready so you can play back the highlights for that nurse you hired. Alice? You *are* eavesdropping on us over there, aren't you?"

A frightened birdlike face poked from the side of the hedge, one hand holding her coat closed at the throat. "It seems to me a person in your position has no right to tell me what I am or am not doing," she called. "And for your information, I have heard too much about you in the past to want to hear more now." She stepped out straight-spined from behind the hedge, yanked her coat free of a branch and then disappeared around the side of the office.

Frank sighed. "You shouldn't have done that, Rose."

"Why not? What's wrong with her anyway? Hiding behind bushes."

"She's scared. She doesn't know what you're doing here."

"Well, that's not my fault. I tried to be friendly. I can't help it if she hates people."

Frank didn't answer. I went to the passenger side, opened the door, and cranked the window for the dog. "So how's Birdie? Have you talked to him?"

"I've seen him." He looked over at Alice's house and sighed heavily. "He's all right, I guess. His nurse left, though. A few days ago."

"You're kidding." I shut the car door. "Why?"

"I suppose the job didn't suit her."

"*Pfft*. That woman looked like she could lead the marines. Birdie's probably grateful she left. He probably had to chase her out." I looked toward Alice's house. "So who's over there looking after him now?"

"We're still working on it."

I turned and stared at him. "You mean he's alone over there?"

"Rose, this isn't your problem."

"And why isn't it? You think I'm too busy with my own life?" I came around the car. "He's my friend, Frank. He's in a wheelchair, he can't talk, and now he's stuck with a seventy-year-old crackpot taking care of him." I looked toward the house. "What if something happens? What if he falls out of bed? What if she forgets to get him to the bathroom?" I looked at Frank. "She's a drinker, you know. Last time I talked to her, she wasn't even making sense."

He sighed. "She's not a drinker. I'll drop by when I can, keep an eye on things until we can find another nurse. And she can call Doc Mutz if she needs to."

"At least get a good-looking nurse this time. One with a sense of humor. That's what Birdie needs."

"Okay."

I looked back at Alice's house. "Can you imagine? Stuck in that wheelchair with her in charge?"

He was rubbing at the back of his neck. "Rose. I need you to listen a minute."

"Just promise you won't let anything happen."

"I promise."

"And make sure he keeps eating. Check her refrigerator to see if he's got chocolate bars and stuff. And where the hell are his friends? I haven't seen hardly anybody but you dropping by over there. Tell his damn friends to get off their asses. I don't care how busy they are, they ought to know better than to let him get stuck like this."

"We're not here to talk about Birdie."

"He trusts you, you know. He's always trusted you. You can't just forget that."

"I know."

"Just because he's old and crabby and you got more important things to do."

"All right. I promise. Will you shut up a minute?"

I went back around the car, opened the door, and told the dog to get in back. When he just wagged the end of his tail at me like I was telling a joke, I picked him up and shoved him hard and then leaned over to feel under the front seat for my sunglasses. "So talk if you want," I called. "Did you see my sunglasses? I'm not sure if I packed them or not."

"I'm thinking it's time you tried someplace new, Rose."

I looked down at my hand on the seat, holding me up, white at the fingertips from the pressure, and then backed out of the car.

"Excuse me, Frank. What do you think we're doing here? Packing the car just so I can take a drive around the block and come back in time for lunch?"

"I mean another town."

I barked out a laugh. "*This* is my town. I live here. I've always lived here."

He was looking over his shoulder toward the street. "I was reading in the paper the other day that things are really opening up down in Albuquerque. Last time I was there, I noticed it myself. They have a lot more housing there than they do here. More jobs. More government programs. Food stamps." He turned and his eyes were flat. "It can't last long, but right now, Rose, the roads are clear. The pass would be easy. You could get yourself to Albuquerque in less than a day if you put your mind to it."

I had the feeling he was talking to someone else. I turned and looked behind me, and then I propped my elbows on the roof of the car and shaded my eyes.

"Albuquerque?"

"You could file for unemployment down there. Angela's dad runs a program out of his church for people in transition. You could get in touch with him: Kenny McComb. He could probably steer you toward a job. And if things went okay, maybe next spring you could enroll in the college down there."

"What are you, some kind of career counselor? I don't want to go to college."

He raised his eyebrows. "But I remember you used to—"

"I know what I used to tell you, Frank. I used to tell you a lot of things. I have a bad habit of doing that when I'm in bed with someone, so how about you just step out of my life and we get on with it?"

We stood still then, holding our breaths and looking out at the street. Sometimes I was not even sure why we were still friends. When we could breathe again, he came around to my side of the car.

"I can tide you over a little. Not a lot this time, but enough to help you get down there anyway. Here."

While he made a production out of getting out his billfold, I turned away and looked down through the trees at the yellow light at the bottom of the hill, blinking for nobody. I'd been in Queduro longer than that light. I'd been in Queduro all my life. I took the money without counting it and folded my arms to keep my hands from shaking.

"So what's the deal? You're paying me to leave town?"

He shifted my bag to his other arm. "I'm just trying to help."

I nodded hard and looked away from him, up at the trees. Ancient cottonwoods like mother elephants, sighing on their great scabby feet, interlocking their branches together over our heads. I'd always liked cottonwoods. I liked them even now. I was thinking this and thinking that I wouldn't think right now about anything else. But I could feel it bunching up inside me, starting to grab at the edge of my mouth.

"You think I haven't tried to come up with a better solution," he said. "Is that it?" I felt him sag against the Plymouth. "You know how small this town is, Rose. What do you suppose they're talking about down at the Magpie right now? They're not talking about needlework or who's screwing who. They're talking about you getting evicted. And even if I could find you another place to live, what are you going to live on? Teresa's ready to close down your credit at the store. I figure the only thing you've got left right now is your car, and from what I hear, there's plenty of people who are willing to see it towed the minute you try to park anyplace where they can call it an eyesore." He stopped and reached up to pull off his cap, a pink line across the bone of his forehead. "You've got people in this town pissed off at you, Rose," he said. "People you think of as friends. They say they're tired of dealing with your situation every winter. They say they don't want to think about it anymore. That's what they told me. You see what I'm saying?"

So I saw it. He was thinking like everybody else, that this was it for Rose Devonic. "My 'situation'? What's that supposed to mean, mister?" and I grabbed the paper sack from him, but he held on and the paper tore, Kama Sutra embroidery spilling everywhere.

Frank's mouth fell open.

"If it's any of your business, they belong to Birdie," I said. "He's been working on them every winter. I'm just keeping them safe until he's better."

"This is *Birdie's* work?"

"And he doesn't need the whole world to know, either. Help me get them up before they get dirty."

I knelt, grabbed some of the protective tissue, twitched clean a piece of embroidery, smoothed it on my knee, layered tissue over it, and held it down while I chose another piece. After a moment, Frank crouched next to me and started doing the same thing, our heads nearly touching.

We didn't look at each other and didn't talk, but as it often happens when men and women do handwork together, the silence between us began to thicken and then suddenly there were all kinds of things going on in it. Things we hadn't said to each other in years, maybe ever. I kept working and so did he and neither one of us said anything, but I felt my cheeks begin to burn as if we were looking right into each other. He was trying to stack the pieces on his knee as quickly as I was, trying not to look at their beauty, but then I felt him slowing down and stopping and I knew he was staring down at his knee, at his hand holding the tissue over Birdie's work, seeing his own life raveling out. He wanted to raise his head and look at me and say it; he was thinking about it hard, I knew it as if he was whispering it in my ear. But I didn't look at him, and after a moment he made a sound in the back of his throat and stood. That's when I could look at him again. The circles under his eyes were as dark as bruises.

"We've been friends a long time, Rose," he said, taking a long breath, "but that doesn't mean squat to them. If you want to survive, you have to get out of here. I just don't see any other way."

The whole time I'd been stuck in that cabin, I'd been thinking pretty much the same thing, but I was so mad at him for announcing it right then and in public that I could see stars. What did he think he was, the town crier? Frank might have been true to his duties, but when it came to a woman's pride, he was a fool.

So I patted him on the arm and told him to buck up. "And don't worry so much, pal. You're very convincing as a cop." Then I tucked Birdie's embroideries under some clothes in the back where the dog wouldn't lie on them and got in behind the wheel and started the car, and with Frank following on foot, I pulled out into the alley and drove out to the street. There was no snow, everything the color of frozen iron. I parked at the curb, got out, slammed the door, and went up the front walk to Alice's porch.

"Knock, knock!" I banged on her picture window. "I know you're in there, Alice." There was no answer, but I saw the curtain move. I pulled the frozen geranium out of its pot by the roots and then went to my car, honked good-bye to Birdie, waved the geranium at Frank, who looked like he was trying to think of another way to say no, and laid rubber all the way down the hill to the intersection, which fortunately was clear since I don't have good brakes. It was probably one of my better exits. When I looked in the rearview, Frank was standing out in the street, and Alice coming down her front steps to join him. He had his cap off and he was rubbing his wrist against his forehead. I knew what he was doing. He was either deciding to pretend he'd expected me to do that, or he was going to tell Alice that it didn't matter because he'd pay my bill and I was leaving anyway.

I wasn't the only native-born person left in Queduro who'd had to sleep in a car to make ends meet. Plenty of us had done it, including my friend Eli when Maria had kicked him out. And Ruben Johnson, when he had to make the payment on his crane or lose it. Al Mello was collecting cans to help pay for his linsey-woolsey, and I knew for a fact that Hattie Rodriguez was going to marry Tommy Steelhead only because she couldn't afford not to. And there was poor old Eufanio Johnson, who'd gotten banned from the sales booths forever just because sometimes in summer he liked to take out his teeth and leave his pants home before he went out to talk to tourists. When your own neighbors could turn on each other in the name of making money and nobody willing to say it was wrong, how could you call it home anymore?

But Albuquerque? Frank was out of his gourd. Albuquerque was a city. Who would I have known there? Who would care? A woman with a dog, some embroidery, and no place to live? I'd have ended up on the streets.

Because Frank was so wrong, I took the highway north instead of south, holding the geranium out the window until all the petals blew off. Then I spread Frank's money on the seat. A hundred and seventeen bucks. Not enough to hold me and the dog more than a week, but just enough to get his wife's attention next time she went to the bank. I scowled and felt in the glove box for a lighter. The first time I saw Angela, I was walking back to town from the booths and she and Frank were coming behind me in his truck, and as I turned to wave I saw she was going at him about something, leaning in on him, all the muscles of her face working. Though I only saw it for a moment before they passed me, it looked way worse than just a woman yelling at a man. It looked like a sickness. I could feel the chill of it right through the windshield. That's when I knew what he was dealing with was worse than anything I could imagine. I was still glad he hadn't offered me a ride. I shook my head and scooped his money into my purse. For a lousy hundred bucks and some change, he'd be sweating the end of a short leash hoping she wouldn't find out. If she did, he'd probably be lucky to come away with his skin on.

The dog gave a heavy sigh and laid his head on my shoulder, looking out at the road ahead of us. "Be glad you picked me instead of him," I said. "Angela's a nutcase."

I lit my first cigarette in four days and sucked the smoke in deep. It was beginning to occur to me that I was not quite on the road yet—but where was I going? I took another puff. "What if I told you Durango?" I said it as if Frank were in the car listening, and I said it for myself too. I said it over and over, first one way and then another, and all the time I was looking ahead at the road, at the place on the mountain where it slid out of view around the next bend. I was feeling a little dizzy, but it would be all right. It was just the cigarette and the fresh air. It was just four days of being stuck in a box and now all this bright sunlight and fresh air. When the dizziness didn't go away, I took my foot off the gas and pulled over to the side, way over, way off to the side where it was safe, and turned off the car. I put my forehead down on the wheel, closed my eyes, and waited, gasping for air.

Most of the time I could remember my life before the accident and my life afterward, and if I had to talk about it I could tell either side without a blink. As long as I jumped from the before to the after, I didn't have any trouble. But on the highway the middle of it always came back, and as soon as I closed my eyes it was worse. The family in the car, heading for Denver and night coming on, Bob and me in the front seat belting out Christmas carols at the top of our lungs while my mother sat in the back with Kyle, giggling and leaning forward to bat us on the back of our heads now and then when we went off key. How happy were we at that moment? How sure were we of living forever? And then that screech sound as six hundred pounds of carved wood scraped the roof of the Plymouth over our heads and the *thwap* of the rope slapping my window as Bob slammed on the brakes and my mother shrieked and we fishtailed and then stopped next to the guardrail on a sharp curve at the edge of the view. And then the four of us sitting there, stopped for those last few seconds together as if to say good-bye before time would start moving forward again, moving us from the before to the after, all of us together and looking at each other and silent and then turning to look out the rear window where our Indian was still bouncing, light as a rubber-tipped pencil, end over end on the frozen pavement before rolling to a stop in the middle of the highway.

When Bob leapt out of the car, I reached for the door handle on my side. My mother's hand swatted the air behind me, I felt it and the panic in her voice when she told me not to get out, felt the gray frozen air of that coming night in my lungs as I ran along the guardrail through the icy weeds. Our Indian was face down on the pavement and Bob bent over him, his face purple and straining, trying to roll him off the highway. A pair of headlights came around the corner, honked, swerved on the ice, and went on. The next one did the same. Bob paced back and forth along the shoulder of the pavement, running his hands through his hair, trying to figure it out, staring at me on the other side of the highway as if we'd never met. I remember looking back at my mother, standing next to the Plymouth holding Kyle, her red hair scribbling against a sky of lead. She was calling at us to get off the road, Bob should leave the Indian, the road was too icy, the cars wouldn't see us, and what we were doing was stupid, and suddenly a feeling came to me at the sight of her standing so sharply outlined against the sky that she was right. But when the semi came around the corner and slammed into the Indian, catching him under its fender and dragging him in a shriek and spark of brakes before spitting him out, it was my mother and Kyle who got hit, the Indian snapping out from under the semi to smack them both over the guardrail like a pair of rag dolls before hitting the guardrail itself and bouncing back in slow motion to dive headfirst into the windshield of a pale blue Chrysler, which tapped Bob as he was trying to cross the highway and then skidded over to the guardrail and stopped, releasing the Indian again, one last time, one last joyful leap over the edge after my mother and Kyle. And after that, the silence and the wind clicking the icy weeds and the sound of the semi backing up and me looking at the place against the sky where my mother and Kyle and the Indian had gone. How long I stood there or when Frank and his dad pulled up or what they said, I don't know. That wasn't a part of the memory.

I opened my eyes and I could breathe. The blue Chrysler had been Florie Pinkston Snow on her way to San Luis to visit a friend. She died instantly without even knowing what hit her, and so did my baby brother, or so they said. My mother probably took longer because she landed in a snowbank down in the ravine, but she was dead too by the time the rescue people finally got to her. As for my uncle, he lasted all the way to the hospital and died that night in surgery.

And me, I came out without a scratch. After the funerals, I went to live with Mr. and Mrs. Doby and Frank for a while, and when they got tired of that I went to stay with Birdie so I could learn embroidery, and then I went to work for myself. Nobody could call me a quitter. I was a Devonic, not a Bean. It was just another story. A leads to B leads to C, and if you could follow the thread of it all the way through, it was over. Everybody has stories, all kinds of stories. Good and bad. That's how you learned to take it. It was part of you, and if you took what you needed from it, if you didn't run from it, in the end it made you stronger.

It was cold enough in the car to see my breath, but I was sweating all down my back. I was sure I could get to Durango before dark. The weather was bitter cold, but Frank was right, the road was amazingly dry, not a single patch of snow left on it and no cars or trucks to slow me down. No one out on the highway but me. Not my mother, not my uncle, not Kyle, not our Indian. I lifted my head, nodding hard, and then I sat for a time not thinking anything at all, and then I started up the car again.

Part II

15

Work, work, work,
Seam and gusset and band,
Band, gusset and seam
Till over the buttons I fall asleep
And sew them on in a dream.

—Thomas Hood, "The Song
of the Shirt"

Frank sat at the table, looking at his mashed potatoes and listening to his wife in the next room. He had meant to follow her but he hadn't been able to, and now he would have to sit there; he would have to wait it out, so waitful and quiet that she would come back in the kitchen and ask him what the hell he was doing, and then he would push back his chair, look her quietly in the eye, and tell her he wanted a divorce. This is the way Frank sinned: in secret and to himself, squeezing it and pumping it until sometimes his mind was so filled and black with it that there was nothing he could do but sit still and almost without breathing and wait for it to ebb back down so he could talk like a man to his wife again. He looked down at his shirt, covered in gravy, the crease of his gut showing through the wetness, and then at the back of his left wrist from where she had gotten him with the meat fork. When he tightened his fist, the blood pooled but did not spill over. He was sorry for that. He wanted to see the two puncture wounds spurting blood, enough to make him leap from the table roaring, kicking the casserole dish on the floor out of the way. The calendar on the wall shivered as she went through the highboy in the next room, jerking drawers open and slapping them shut. Had she used the knife, it would have changed everything; they could have become two different people in an instant. He had thought she was going to, in fact he had been almost certain of it when she leaned over the table and he saw her eyes and the way she held the knife to carve the brisket, the muscles around her mouth rising up under her skin as if she were strung together with cord. But instead she had stabbed him in the wrist with the meat fork. The meat fork! She'd staggered back with her hands held out, expecting and afraid of his rage, but when she saw he was waiting, that he was not surprised she had tried to hurt him, only that she had not tried to hurt him more, it had sent her reeling off through the house, holding her head and screaming *you fucking bastard!* Frank squeezed his eyes shut. He should have told her right then he wanted a divorce. He should have chased her through the house and held her down and shoved the evidence in her face. But instead he had let it go; he had sat there like an idiot, as calmly as if nothing had happened yet, and now, as far as she was concerned, nothing had, and all she wanted was the Xanax.

He wondered how long he'd been sitting there. It seemed to him a very long time. He unstrapped his watch and laid it face down on the table without looking at it. He had learned this in the military, that looking at the time when you needed sleep was almost as lethal as closing your eyes. At work, he always took off his watch. Maybe he wasn't always sure if he was conscious or not, but as long as he didn't start wondering how much more of his shift he had to stay awake through, he could keep his eyes open. Plus he had coffee and cigarettes and the anticipation of that first call and what he would do about it and if he would do it right. Even when he'd been up all night with Angela, he rarely thought about sleep at work. But at home it was another thing. Sometimes when he walked in the house, it seemed to him that Angela had sprayed the rooms with some kind of opiate. He could fall asleep with the TV blasting sirens and gunshots. He could nod out over meals or even with Angela screaming at him from the next room. There were times when it was such an unnatural, violent fall into sleep—one minute awake and the next out cold—that he wondered if he was getting sick. It drove Angela crazy, the way his body could betray them so suddenly, throwing him backward, downward, telling him to stop thinking, stop moving, telling him to sleep. He had tried to convince her that it was the stress of his job, but she didn't buy it and, in truth, neither did he. He liked being a cop. He didn't want to quit that. He wanted to quit his marriage. He wanted to quit it tonight. On the other hand, if he let go right now, he could fall asleep in about half a minute. But he was not going to. He was going to stay awake this time, all night if he had to, and when she decided to talk to him again, he would say it: I want a divorce. He was going to say it, and because he had never said it before, it would change everything between them. That was the crazy part. Angela threatened him with divorce all the time, screamed it in his face, and it never got them anywhere—in fact, nowadays he didn't even flinch when she used it against him—but all he had to do was whisper it once. She knew it, he knew it, and it made them both frantic. As if they were playing with a loaded gun, only every time she pulled the trigger, the bullets were blanks.

After it was over, he would sleep. He would not try to make it better between them because that would be pointless, even cruel. He would simply grab some clothes and drive off somewhere where he could sleep. Up to the overlook, maybe, park facing east so the sun would wake him for work. He would drive up there and close the window, turn off the radio, lean back against the seat, close his eyes, and let himself go, like easing slowly into a hot bath, he thought, the quiet echoey tiles, water dripping somewhere. . . . There was a crash in the living room and he snapped back with a start, staring at his hands. He lifted them to his face and then put them, palms down, on either side of his plate and pushed to his feet. He could not sleep yet, but he could not sit still anymore, either. He would have to do something.

Through the doorway he could see her in the living room, her back to him, her blond hair sliding sideways out of its bun as she crouched on the rag rug to pull out the tapes under the cabinet. Despite the season, she was wearing cutoffs and one of his sleeveless undershirts, and he watched the quick, lean movements of the muscles across the bones of her upper back and under her arms, where the shirt fell forward to show a shadow of rib and breast, her skin the color of dark honey, tupelo honey maybe, everywhere like that except for the startlingly chalk-white upside-down question mark of her instep when she pitched forward to reach deeper into the cabinet. She was twenty-seven, four years younger than he, and even when she was not trying to be beautiful, she was. More so, in fact. Sometimes he'd come home early in the summer and find her in the back yard adjusting her suntan goggles, groping for her water bottle or her lotions or the radio, curling her toes under the plastic weave of the lounge chair as if to grip against the heat, everything about her so fierce and solitary, so disconnected from the world. He would stand at the window and watch her struggling until her body began to give itself over to the heat, her feet relaxing their hold on the chair, her neck and belly softening, the muscles of her face going slack, hands falling away. Sometimes it only lasted for a few moments before she thought of something else she needed, but other times she would surrender herself to it utterly, and he would find himself saying the word aloud to the living room. Angela. At times like that, he could not believe such a beautiful woman, such a mystery, was his wife, Angela, asleep in their back yard.

He picked up the brisket, put it on a plate, and cleaned the juices off the floor with a sponge. The dinner that had made it to the table, he wrapped in foil and put in the refrigerator. Behind him, a sob and a curse, the clatter of tapes as she kicked them aside in her hurry to try somewhere else. He lifted the pile of dirty dishes out of the sink, opened the drain, turned on the water, and held his wrist under the faucet, watching the blood thin and run into the palm of his hand and between his fingers. When the water ran clear, he wiped down the sink with the sponge, replugged the drain, and turned on the hot tap. Under his reflection in the window, all the neighborhood porch lights were off now, the houses and back yards invisible in the dark. He felt as if he were out there looking in, seeing the silhouette of a man in a brightly lit kitchen too late at night, waiting for the sink to fill.

As he restacked dishes, he could hear her out in the front hall, going through the coat closet, cuss words leaking under her breath. Where had she learned those words? What part of her did they come from? A year ago, she hadn't been able to say so much as damn without clapping her hand over her mouth. Now she could barely turn it off.

But he, too, had changed. He couldn't deny it. When she'd first met him, he'd been a quiet, gun-shy ex-soldier who'd suddenly found himself not only burying the father he'd thought of as indestructible but being hounded by the Committee in Queduro to fill his father's shoes. Who else in Queduro, they'd cried, could call himself the son of a great sheriff? Who showed the strength of character that he did, the clean record, the quick mind, the generous heart? Who had fought for his country down there in Panama and returned with a Silver Star for bravery? Taking care of people was in Frank's blood. A family tradition. A sacred calling. Why couldn't he understand that?

So Frank, understanding only that the choice was not his to make, had dropped his plans to go to college on the GI bill and ended up in Albuquerque at the annual sheriff's convention. He was hoping to run into one of his father's cronies there who could reassure him about his future, but, more important, he was hoping to learn enough law enforcement to at least delay the acute embarrassment he felt every time someone referred to him as *sheriff*. He arrived at the hotel early the first day, name tag already on, fiddling with his pen, anxious to get started—but not ten minutes into the start of the first Q and A panel discussion on crime prevention techniques, he felt his throat constricting, and on the excuse that he needed to find a water fountain, he sidled past the other sheriffs and left the hotel by a side door. It was a Saturday in August, the traffic sporadic, dry desert heat blaring off the buildings. As he followed the sidewalk from one block to the next, he was thinking of something his father had once said—that as long as he could stay on the square with himself he could accomplish anything—and then he was thinking about Rose saying she couldn't love him anymore; and then he was thinking about what he'd been like as a kid and what his life would be like from here on out if he did what he was supposed to do; and almost without knowing it he wound up sitting in a vinyl booth in an empty sports bar on Central Avenue with a drink in his hand. He was sweating from the walk and his tongue was swollen dry and he was trying to remember the last time he'd been this scared. Panama City, he thought, those early morning patrols through the El Chorillo district, when the streets felt too quiet and the crumbling tinderbox buildings too dark and he'd been certain that the itching at the base of his neck was not just sweat trickling from the inner band of his helmet but someone watching him through the sights of a rifle. But what was scaring him now? An empty fern bar in the middle of the day with a scotch in his hand and a giant TV in the corner pounding out the sounds of a football game? He felt a loneliness closing over him, a loneliness he had no wish to examine, the kind of loneliness that felt as big and permanent as death—and then out of nowhere, a blonde in a pale blue T-shirt and shorts slid into his booth. Not even smiling hello, just glancing around the corner of the booth as she gathered up her hair in a knot at the back of her head, and then leaned forward to call over the roar of the TV, "Buy me a drink?" He was so disoriented, he thought she was someone from the convention whom he was supposed to know. She was picking at a pack of Marlboros, trying to open it, a startlingly pretty girl under her makeup, pale eyes, tawny smooth skin, and a full valentine pout, but her hands were shaking, and though she met his eyes directly, almost angrily, before looking toward the door again, everything about her seemed somehow slapped together. She looked as frightened as he was, and as he realized this, she reached out, sank her manicured nails into his wrist to hold him there, and leaned forward until her lips brushed the edge of his ear: *Don't ask.*

Remembering it now, he grimaced. *Don't ask.* She'd only been trying to warn him, but at the time, he'd felt a heady rush at the sound of those two words in his ear—a sudden sureness that in some mysterious way this girl not only understood the loneliness he was facing but was giving him permission to step out of his own skin and kick it away, to stop trying to figure out who he was and how he fit together and where he belonged. *Don't ask*. He hadn't. His time with her that weekend, and in the weekends to follow, had nothing to do with words. They always met at the bar in the booth under the blaring noise of a televised sporting event, and after a drink, or sometimes a row of drinks, he'd pay the bill, she'd meet him by the door, and they'd drive in his truck around the corner to a motel. The sex was rough, sometimes awkward, and always hungry—on the floor, against the wall, in the shower, on the sink—often violent enough to leave scrapes and bruises on both of them. Each time he told himself this was the last time, he wouldn't call her again, it was wrong to keep sleeping with a woman he didn't like and wasn't even sure he could trust, it was better to be alone. But then the weekend would loom, and if he couldn't find enough work to stay busy, he'd wander his house, his life stretching out before him in an endless series of loops, Monday to Friday, Monday to Friday, until he couldn't stand the quiet, until nothing felt safe and the house full of danger again and him sweating all down his back and dialing the number she'd given him. She wouldn't say where she lived, where she'd come from, how she'd been raised, or why she kept agreeing to meet him. Did she have a husband? A family? He didn't know. The only thing she ever asked about him was how he made his money, and when he told her, she laughed for a good five minutes, effectively corking any desire he had of telling her more. *Don't ask*. So he hadn't asked anything, not until one day while pushing her hard up against the bathroom wall and holding her there by the hair at the back of her head, half because she'd bitten him on the cheek and seemed interested in doing it again and half because he was getting close and wanted her to be still when he came, he asked her if she needed to be married. He had no idea why it came out or even if that was what he meant to say. He expected her either to laugh or hit him for saying such a stupid thing, but instead she'd gone soft in his arms, allowed him to come, and then pushed him out of her way and gone into the bedroom to light a cigarette. "Maybe you're right," she said, sitting at the edge of the bed, her arms over her breasts as if to hide them and crossing her legs twice, hard at the knee and again at the ankle. "Maybe being married to a cop is the answer." And that was that. The end of any truth between them, if there'd ever been any to begin with. But hadn't she tried to warn him? *Don't ask.* He'd just been too slow figuring out why.

If she didn't find the Xanax soon, she would come back in the kitchen, tight and chattering and trying to apologize, begging him to call Doc Mutz again and then accusing, and they'd start again. If it got bad she'd try to get his gun out of the car, lock herself in the bathroom, and threaten suicide. Twice in the last year she'd tried that. If she tried it now, he would bust down the door and slap her. He would slap the hell out of her. He would black both her eyes or break her jaw. Frank felt as if he were sleepwalking.

But when he opened the sink cabinet to get the dish soap and saw the small plastic vial of pills next to the silver polish, it was as if another version of himself were in the room, pointing at him and laughing. If he told her where they were, she'd be grateful and the whole thing would end, she'd rush to the bathroom and then rush back and beg him to forgive this night and all the other nights like it, and it would be easy, she'd be eager and willing for comfort, and if he asked for it they would end up fucking in the bedroom. On the other hand, if he didn't tell her, this night would go on and he didn't know how it would end. What did he want? What did either of them want? He straightened slowly with the bottle of Joy in his hand and squirted some into the water. Maybe she wouldn't remember where she'd hidden her pills until she remembered why. He turned off the faucet and began to wash the dishes. When had she taken them last, three days ago? A week? This morning? She was in the living room now, going through his desk for the second time, pushing his papers to the floor. He could only imagine the terror of it, alone in the house while he was at work, telling herself she was going clean, starting fresh, a new leaf, praying for it, trembling all over while she took the pills from room to room, trying to decide where to put them because she was never going to need them again, never going to be that kind of person, she was going to be Angela, just normal, beautiful Angela from Albuquerque. How many times had she been through it, five? Ten? More? He did not want to think about it. He rinsed a cereal bowl, put it in the rack, and took another.

But he *was* thinking about it, so hard that in the instant he was aware that the living room had suddenly gone silent and her mind was circling back to him and that she was going to come into the kitchen, he panicked, letting go of the dish, his thoughts racing around like monkeys. He had no idea how he'd say it, no idea of how she'd take it. But she'd have to take it, straight for once she'd take it, take it like he did, divorce. He began to wipe clumsily at the gravy on the front of his shirt. Yes, he'd say it and he'd mean it, and by God she'd know it as well as he did, the word like napalm, taking everything, sane and insane, good, bad, and indifferent up with it. It was the only way; they'd tried everything else; they could not go on like this, not like this; it had to be said. And what a relief it would be to get it out finally and have it over with, his old life back, his friends, another chance. His mind began to slow down and then to loosen and focus again.

"Oh, baby."

She slipped around him from behind, holding on to his shirt, her body small and bony against his back. He put his hands deep into the hot, soapy water. "You always know where things are. Come on, sweet. I only want one. Then you throw them all away. That was what I should have done. I know that now. Just one. Everybody takes one now and then. You've taken one before." He could feel her teeth chattering against his back. "It's so bad, honey. You can't know. I'm really sick this time. I'm about to break."

He rinsed another dish and put it in the rack. "Ange, I didn't hide them. You did."

"I know, but I can't remember," she whined into his back. "Sweetheart? I need them. I mean it this time, honest. *Please?*" and then she took a long, ragged breath and howled into his shirt. It was a terrible sound, like some kind of animal with its foot caught in a trap. He looked down and saw her fingers, digging into his chest. "Stop it," he said, over the howl, and at once the howl stopped. She pressed her face against his armpit as if she meant to push in under his arm. He squeezed his eyes shut.

"Let go of me, Angela." He raised his voice. "Let me go."

She let go. He looked out at the dark in the window as he spoke.

"I used to think that if we could just stick together, we could make a home for each other. I don't think that anymore, Angela. I don't want you to suffer anymore, but I'm tired to death of feeling guilty about you not willing to get help. In fact I don't think I can do it anymore."

He stopped then, waiting for the crash, hoping it was coming, knowing he was asking for it this time. It reminded him of driving drunk down a mountain road at night without headlights, exhilarated and weeping. He could say it now, he could say anything.

But when he turned, almost at once his heart slowed down. She was an arm's length away, and her pupils so small he could not make them out in the blue. She was sweating and shivering at the same time, her skin almost transparent, her lips cracked dry, gray lines of mascara down her cheeks. The last time he'd seen her this ill, he'd spent a good eight hours talking her into trying the drug rehab program in Santa Fe, and the next morning, when he was ready to take her there, she hadn't remembered a word of the conversation. He turned to the sink and gripped the edge.

"So? Go ahead." Her voice like a razor. "Come on. What is this, some kind of new home therapy?"

"I'm just tired. I've got to be to work at seven."

"Oh. I see. He's got to be to work at seven. How thoughtless of his wicked little harpy wife to bother him at a time like this."

"I'm not saying that. I'm saying I'm not interested in arguing now."

"You're not saying that. You're always saying one thing when you're saying another. What are you saying? Look at me."

He looked at her. "I'm saying it's too late."

She made her mouth small and folded her arms over her chest, her hands trembling visibly from the effort of holding still. "Too late for what?" When he didn't answer, she cried, "Always the gentleman, aren't you? Always pulling your punches." Then her whole face twisted and she leaned into his face and shrieked, *Too fucking late for what?*"

"I can't talk to you when you're like this."

"Oh my God." She moaned, rolling her eyes. "Can't you get it through your head I don't need your fucking talk? I've had enough of that, and look what it's done. You understand that? My *pills*. What'd you do with them?"

"I didn't do anything with them. You did."

"But you know where they are, don't you? I can tell you know. You just don't want to tell me."

"It's not that. I just want—"

"You just want me down on my knees, that's what you want. You want me to beg for help so you can play Big Daddy Savior again." She took a step forward. "That's why you married me, isn't it? Because you're so good? Isn't that why you do everything you do? So you can make everybody else feel like shit?" She waved him off and went into the living room.

"Angela," he called.

"No." He heard her in the living room, going through the china cabinet.

After a moment, he put the copper pan on the counter to scrub the blackened food off, a dot of soapsuds sliding slowly along the metal strip holding down the Formica. He scrubbed hard. Where was Rose now? Three weeks since he'd evicted her from the motel and still nothing. And then he yawned suddenly and for several minutes, over and over again, and when he stopped yawning, it occurred to him that there was no point in trying to outwit Angela's panic. Maybe she was right. Maybe he didn't understand. Maybe he was just too tired to play the bad guy for her anymore. He opened the cabinet under the sink, took out the bottle of Xanax, and put it on the phone table where she'd find it. Then he turned back to the sink, and without looking at himself in the window he finished the last of the dishes.

16

Teach me the measure of my days
Thou maker of my frame.
I would survey life's narrow space
And learn how frail I am.

—from an American sampler, 1808

Four hours later he woke himself before the alarm went off and took a shower. He did not think about Angela until he tiptoed into the bedroom to get clothes and found the bed empty. She was asleep on the couch in the living room, curled tightly under his mother's throw rug with a pillow over her face. Only the white bones of her knees showed, and the gold storm of her hair draped over the end of the couch. Her prescription bottle was not in sight. He covered her with a blanket from the closet and dressed in the bedroom. Although he was sure she was out cold, he crept through the living room in his stocking feet, collecting boots, cap, gloves, coat, and gun belt on the way out and taking care not to let the door click too loudly behind him.

The sun was already peeking over Red Mountain at the snowcapped houses on the opposite ridge, but down in the valley, the air was still gray and bitter cold, the snowy streets wide and empty, the windows without curtains or shades, black. This was the easiest time of day to imagine Queduro as a frontier mining town. Maybe the mud had been turned to pavement, boardwalks to sidewalks, and hitching posts to parking meters, but most of the buildings along Hemming still had their false fronts and tall windows and narrow doors, and in the dead half-light of dawn—if you ignored some of the more obvious changes, like the double-wides for sale on Modoc Hill and the Texaco and the Committee's blinking yellow traffic light and their neon Indian up at the Ten Tribes (which hadn't been on since Rose's departure), not to mention their new plastic outdoor benches and trash bins and tourist information center—if you could ignore all that, it could have been 1836 again, and as day wore on the streets would fill with barking dogs and horses and women in long dresses and hard-rock miners with hand-pulled tool carts. It pleased Frank to imagine it, though sometimes, for no reason he knew of, it made him melancholy afterward.

He stopped for coffee at the Texaco, and as he got back in his car he waved to Ruben Johnson, who was coming out of his garage and heading toward him with a plastic travel mug, and then he drove to his office and parked, gathering up his coffee, radio, and gun. He looked up and saw the moon lingering at the edge of the snow on Pisby Mountain, where miners had once swarmed like ants and found nothing, a white smear of frosting on a curtain of crystalline blue. Down the block, Teresa Steelhead was out in her apron, sweeping the snow off the sidewalk in front of her store. "It's always us early birds, isn't it?" she called, her voice echoing clear and pretty as a bell against the storefronts. Frank waved back and let himself in the office.

He clocked in by feel, switched on the overhead light, and groaned. Silas seemed to think the best way to convince Frank that he was doing a good job was to leave the desk looking like a tornado had hit during his shift. Frank had tried to talk his dispatcher, Emily Moralez, into some housekeeping, but apparently she didn't feel the Committee paid her enough for that. He hung up his coat, closed the file drawers, unplugged the coffeemaker, threw away a half-eaten taco and several doodles of cars he found under the folders on his desk, and then sat with the message book, pulling the wastebasket next to his chair.

Some messages were for him and some weren't. He sipped his coffee and looked for news of Rose, a phone message at least, but still nothing. An APB out for Sam Krieger in Taos County, another complaint about Eddie Walk shooting off his gun behind the cafe, several memos from Ruben Johnson warning Frank that the squad car needed an oil change, a fender-bender report that Silas had taken the night before, and another 10-24 message from Alice Pinkston.

Frank shook his head. He had to get a new nurse in there. She was doing all right as far as her brother's welfare was concerned—surprisingly all right, considering how neurotic she sometimes acted—but the power of her loneliness was growing. He could hear it in her voice, see it in the elaborate jewelry and makeup she put on for his visits, in the look on her face every time he got up to leave. The last time he'd gotten a 10-24 from her, she'd opened the door in tears and all but fallen into his arms, some long confusing story about a trip to Africa she'd been planning before Bird's stroke, an hour at least before he discovered that what she needed was help opening a bureau drawer that was stuck. That was what all her calls for help amounted to: a dead lightbulb, a door that creaked, a stray dog that might be rabid, a blown fuse. He tried to be patient, tried to remember that at her age, her willingness to look after her brother by herself was nothing short of heroic, but each time she called he groaned at the thought of spending more time with her. Yet she kept calling him for "emergencies," and it was always him she wanted. When he tried to send Silas up there, she refused to even unlock her door. "I want Frank Doby," she'd call through the crack. It was a big joke with Silas. Hubba, hubba, Frank. Wait till your wife finds out. Frank had told Alice she couldn't keep calling for help just because she was lonely, but her response had been drastic. *"Lonely,"* she cried, her blue eyes blazing up like a pair of propane torches, *"lonely?"* and then storming into her house, slapping the door shut behind her.

But her loneliness was not the only thing that bothered him. Although she looked healthy and sounded perfectly normal when talking about her brother or her childhood or how she'd worked as a nurse in Africa, she regularly lost the thread of the conversation and had to start over. She had always loved showing off her Eldorado but he had not seen it out of her garage since Mrs. Fleet's disappearance. She no longer left her house at all, save to step out on her porch, and when she did, she sometimes forgot her wig. He'd also noticed she'd been looking even skinnier than normal, she often blamed her confusion on a lack of sleep, and she was increasingly obsessed about robbers who might break into her house. He'd asked Doc Mutz to stop by her house for a visit to see what he thought, but Mutz had come away unconcerned. "She does seem a little more eccentric than usual," he said, "but I wouldn't take it too seriously. I prescribed a mild sedative and told her to eat more, get more rest. That should help. I know, I know," he said, patting Frank's arm. "She's probably calling you twice a day to talk, am I right? But we can't exactly prescribe medications for selfish behavior, now, can we, son?" Frank had blushed with shame. Was that why he kept thinking something was wrong with her, because he didn't like her? The fact that Birdie seemed all right—always shaved and clean and in his wheelchair for Frank's visits, always with a plastic cup of water and medicine and some kind of food within reach—all of that denied Frank's worries about Alice's deteriorating mental condition. But how could you tell what was going on from a ten-minute visit with an old man who couldn't talk? The whole thing depressed him mightily. He sighed and threw her message in the OUT bin. He'd get it over with early so he wouldn't have to dwell on it all day. And he'd call Mrs. Guynn at the agency in Madrillas again, put some pressure on about getting another nurse.

He went to the filing cabinet and got out an accident form, went back to his desk, rolled it into his typewriter, and took another sip of coffee. After studying Silas's notes on the fender-bender, he began to type.

At 9 A.M. when Emily showed up with her embroidery bag to take over the dispatch radio, Frank went out to his squad car. He liked cruising during the morning shift. He drove up Hemming to the dormant school site, crossed over at Gobelin, cruised Soutache, then turned on Filoselle and cruised Tambour, doing a visual check of side streets and alleys.

For weeks, now, he'd been expecting to find Rose's rusted-out Plymouth parked somewhere, or at least her new address mailed to someone so they could know where she was. He drove up Flax Hill and pulled into Alice's driveway. As he got out he glanced across the street at the motel. The snows that had held back all through January had finally come, but there were no footprints or tracks over there. Maybe she'd taken his advice about trying Albuquerque. He just couldn't quite believe it. He was sorry he hadn't given her more money. He was sorry the whole thing had happened.

He reached in the car, took his sheriff's cap from the dash, and pulled it on. Angela knew him as a cop and a name that, once spoken, opened the doors for her at the pharmacy over in Madrillas—but what the rest of his life was about seemed to bore her, tire her out, piss her off. Rose, though, had known him most of his life and, in a deeper way, known him for what he was and for what he was not, and she had liked him for it anyway.

He climbed Alice's front steps. "Miss Pinkston? It's me."

The house with its spindly railing and fancy trimwork and narrow windows reminded him of a gingerbread house, only sad. When the door didn't open, he rang the bell. Then he went back down the steps into the yard. Sometimes she watched from upstairs to make sure it was him before she came down to unlock the door. "Miss Pinkston," he called up. "It's Frank Doby."

The front door moved just enough to allow a small white hand to reach out past the screened door.

"Is that you, Frank Doby?"

"It's me." He came back up on the porch, already tired.

But instead of inviting him in, she was peeping around the edge of the door, her hand holding the wrinkle of her throat. With a start he saw she not only had forgotten her wig, she hadn't put on any makeup.

"How are you, Miss Pinkston?" When she didn't answer, he said, "You called my office. Is everything okay?"

"Yes. Why are you here?"

"Because you called my office."

She turned away from the door and then looked out again, squinting hard at him. "I did?"

"Yes, ma'am. You told my deputy you were having some kind of trouble." But he was already wondering if he'd read the date on the message. It was not like her to be so unprepared for him. Maybe he'd picked up a message from two days ago. Or maybe Silas had made up the message as a joke. Alice was peering at him from behind the door as if he might unsnap his gun. He was suddenly sure that Silas would think this was funny. He aimed his gaze away from her and then reached up slowly and took off his sheriff's cap.

"I'll be on my way if everything's okay." He hesitated. "Everything *is* okay, isn't it, Miss Pinkston?"

She craned out the door, and he saw that she was still in her nightgown. She looked at his squad car, then down the street. Tipping a bald eyebrow at him, she hissed, *"I'm occupied."*

"Oh. I'll be going then. Sorry." In spite of himself, he blushed. "Say hello to your brother."

He walked quickly to his squad car. After checking the date on Silas's message, he backed out the driveway. When he glanced at Alice's house, he saw her at one of the second-story windows, peeking out from behind a blue curtain. He picked up the mike and called Emily. "I'm taking the squad car over to Ruben's to get the oil changed. Any calls?"

"Negative. What's the update on the hill?"

He thought her voice was laughing, and that made him even madder. "Let's put it this way. You can tell Silas the next time he pulls a stunt like this, he's fired."

"You want me to contact him now?"

"No. Just leave him a message. He'll know what I'm talking about."

"Okay, boss. Ten-four. Over and out. Ta-ta." She squawked the radio twice.

By the time Ruben had finished changing the oil on the car, however, Frank was beginning to wonder. Ruben was Silas's ex-brother-in-law, a short gorilla-shaped man who blushed easily, worked sixteen-hour days, slept in his garage with his engines, and never seemed to get anything finished. Ruben was convinced Silas would never make up a false call as a prank.

"No, Frank. Silas may not be much of a deputy, but he wouldn't fool around like that when he's on duty." Ruben leaned over the engine to unscrew the wing nut on the air filter. "You know how Alice Pinkston gets," he went on. "Always tizzed out with emergencies, and half the time she don't even remember what for. Her mind's coming loose, that's what I hear. She probably just forgot who you were or something. Whoa." He'd lifted the cover off the air filter. "Look at this, Frank." He whistled low under his breath and held up the air filter. "Look at what you done here to this."

"Looks pretty grimy."

"Grimy ain't it, Frank. Ex-military man like yourself oughta know better than to let the Committee's patrol car go six thousand without an oil change."

"Think we need a new filter?"

"I would." He shrugged. "But everybody's different. I can just blow it out if you want to save a few bucks. It'd be your choice." He bulged his eyes. "It wouldn't be mine, though. Not for this engine and what she's got to do for you."

"Good. Why don't you just give me a new filter, Ruben."

Ruben nodded, sighing with relief, went to a wall of boxes containing air filters, and opened one. Frank watched as he placed it inside the casing.

"That's better," he said, using a rag to wipe the dust off the casing, inside and out. "Makes me sick to see an engine nice as this one get so dirty. You should see the engine on my LiftAll. She was sitting all winter because the damn torque converter burned out, but she's still clean enough to eat off of."

The LiftAll crane was the one topic of conversation Ruben lived for, his heart wide open, always ready to explain to anyone interested enough to ask. He had purchased it at a government auction in Albuquerque three years back, hoping it would allow him to quit the garage business once and for all, but because of what it had cost him so far in repairs, he was more in debt than ever.

"I stuck with her all winter," he continued, "checking her fluids and hoses, painting the body, revamping the transmission—you know, inside out, the works. Goddamn, though, it pisses me off. She would've paid for herself twice over already if that fuck of a torque converter hadn't gone out." He sighed and leaned under the hood of the squad car to set the filter back in place. "An engine has to get the kid-glove treatment, or it'll never perform when you need it to. I say it over and over and nobody listens. I don't know why. And come over here," he said, wiping his hands on his rag. "Take a look at the oil I pulled out."

Ruben loved to show customers how they'd failed their vehicles. He took a penlight out of his overalls and shined it on a coffee can of black liquid down in the pit.

"See that there?"

Frank squatted down to look. "Wow."

"Yeah, wow. That's yours." He went down in the pit for the can and brought it back up. "Engine oil ought to be the color of thin honey. But you see there?" he said happily, dipping one finger in and holding it up. "It's like mud. Like pure mud."

"Yeah, it is. Ruben, you honestly believe that Silas wouldn't make up a false call for me?"

Ruben dropped his shoulders in pure exasperation.

"It's just that I can't make it out," Frank added. "Alice seemed to have no idea I was coming this time. She acted scared half to death to see me there, and then she tells me—" He stopped. He was watching Ruben wipe his hands, finger by finger, on his rag while he squinted narrowly at the car.

"Ruben. You were over at my office last night when her call came in, weren't you."

"Well." Ruben sighed. "Could be maybe I was."

"What were you doing there?"

"Talkin' mostly." He gave a delicate shrug.

"Goddammit. Silas had you bring him a six-pack."

Ruben scratched one sideburn thoughtfully, a sound like metal against metal.

"Silas was on duty last night, Ruben. I'm supposed to fire him for that shit. Don't you know that?"

Ruben looked at him in surprise. "Well, of course I do, Frank. Why the heck do you think I didn't tell you to begin with?"

Frank groaned.

"Hell, Frank. I heard him take that call. I could hear her voice clear across the room, saying she needed you to come over as soon as you got in. Silas didn't make that one up. I was there. That call come in."

He drove to the cafe, ordered toast and coffee from Linda, and then went in the kitchen to talk to Eddie Walk about the shooting complaint.

Eddie was a nervous sandy-haired entrepreneur who wore gold chain necklaces and a digital watch. He'd moved to Queduro five years ago, thinking he'd make a killing in the restaurant business, but he was always complaining about Quedurans being cheap. He thought it wouldn't be good for business to have Frank in his kitchen, so he took off his chef's cap and they went out back. Eddie stood at one corner of the Dumpster, pointing with his spatula, while Frank stood at the other.

"Now, right over there," said Eddie, pointing, "is where Linda put the meat loaf from last Sunday's special. Monday, *boom!* it's gone. Same with the turkey I had to throw out last week. Every scrap in there has been gone through. That's why I was keeping my eye out. And last night, when I was closing up, I heard something out here again."

"And?"

Eddie's eyes narrowed, he smiled, and his voice dropped. "A god-damned bear was in here, Frank."

Frank leaned away from the warm, furry smell of the Dumpster. "What kind of bear do you think, Ed?"

"What?"

"Black bear? Brown bear? Grizz?"

"How do I know? It was pitch dark."

"So you shot at it anyway?"

Eddie nodded excitedly. "And then it took off through a hole in that fence over there. I might've winged it, though. Couldn't tell."

"So you hear something and you come out and shoot at it, only you're not sure what you hit?"

Eddie looked up at Frank, his eyes going mean. "I have a right to protect my property."

Frank went over to look at the hole in the fence. The snow had been worn down and packed hard, speckled with bits of trash from the Dumpster. There were boot prints of all sizes going in all directions, but no signs of blood. Frank squatted and took out a cigarette. In the army, he'd known people like Eddie, people so afraid of appearing weak you couldn't even look at them without them drawing their guns. It was a virus, that kind of fear. It could spread through a whole country overnight. It could make people do anything. He straightened, lit his cigarette, and went back to Eddie.

"It was a bear," said Eddie. "I heard it."

"Mm-hmm." Frank took a hit of smoke. "I hear that Paul Two Trouts's kids play in the alley at night sometimes. You ever notice kids playing back here?"

"Nope."

"Well, I've heard they do. And I know Al Mello cuts through here at night on his way home from the Magpie. Lots of people probably do."

"That's their problem. This is my property, this is my Dumpster, and whatever I shot at, it was trespassing." His eyes were getting hard. "Besides, I said it was a bear, didn't I?"

"Yes, you did." Frank looked away in disgust. "How about I call the Fish and Game? I'll see if they have a bear trap they can spare for a few days."

"It better be big. This thing was goddamn big."

"I'll ask for the big size. How's that?"

"All right. But I don't want anything that's going to scare off business."

Frank took a pull off his cigarette. "Seems to me there's not much can scare business faster than a man willing to shoot at whatever he can't see."

Eddie's eyes narrowed to slits. "For goddamnmit. I said it was a bear."

"So you did, Ed. I'm going to go in now to have my breakfast before it gets cold." He flicked his cigarette in the alley. "But Ed? I just want you to know. If I get one more complaint about you discharging your gun in the middle of town, you're going to have a lot more to worry about than who's eating your garbage. You know what I'm saying?"

He did not get halfway through breakfast. Partly it was because people like Eddie Walk always gave him indigestion, but mostly because he was thinking about Alice. He had a bad feeling about her. For all the times he'd blasted up there in a sweat and found nothing, this time he hadn't stayed long enough. Maybe Bird had had another stroke. Maybe he'd fallen out of bed or died during the night, and Alice was either in shock or too mixed up to know what to do next. Maybe she was afraid of being accused of negligence. Whatever it was, something was going on. He was sure of it. He couldn't believe he'd left without even asking to have a look around. He pushed away his plate, paid his bill, and went back out to his car.

"Any calls today, Em?"

Her voice clicked in. "No. Just the ten-twenty-four that Silas received last night."

"I'm going up there again. I want you on standby. Don't go out for coffee, and stay off the phone till you hear from me."

"For Pete's sake, don't I always?"

"You do." Frank slid the mike onto its hook and did a hard U-turn for Flax Hill.

17

Except this posey from a Friend
Whose Love will never end.

—from an American sampler, 1819

The door opened before he could knock. Her face a plate of makeup this time, her gray wig dented at each temple with a red barrette that matched her lipstick.

"So *there* you are."

"Miss Pinkston, may I come in?"

"Not to see Birdie. He's taking his nap." She was smiling, coyly wrapping her necklace around her fingers. "You may, however, have tea with me if you wish."

"I'd like to see Bird first." He waited, passing his hand over his mouth. "Look. Why don't you put on the tea while I go check on your brother?"

"Oh. Well. If you put it that way—"

In two steps, he was inside and moving up the stairway. Behind him he heard her giggle. He opened the door slowly to Birdie's bedroom, ready for anything, ready for the worst . . . and found it empty. The bed was made, the closet door closed, the television on with no sound. He felt the hair rise along the back of his neck and realized how frightened he was. He stepped out into the hallway.

"Miss Pinkston," he called. "Where's your brother?"

He could hear her running water in the kitchen. He started down the stairs and then stopped. The chair lift platform was at the top of the stairs, so Bird had to be somewhere on the second floor. He turned and looked at the hallway. There were four other doors, all of them closed.

He opened the one to the left. A small, stuffy, tidy bedroom, probably the room where Mrs. Fleet had stayed. The wallpaper dainty and pale, the furniture dark and old-fashioned, the bed covered by a rich white damask spread like his mother had always wanted. He stepped into the room to check the closet, then decided, no, if she'd put her brother in there he'd see wheelchair tracks, footprints at the very least, across the lime-colored plush of the rug. He closed the door and took three steps down the hall, his body alert, listening for Alice on the stairwell. The next door opened to a white-tiled bathroom. The door to the right of that a linen closet. He closed it, went to the fourth door, held his breath, and opened it.

Birdie was not there, but everything else was. Two chests of drawers spilling out clothes, filing cabinets, an unmade bed in the corner, a card table with a jigsaw puzzle pushed out of the way to accommodate a pile of laundry, a typewriter, a makeup mirror with lights around it, cosmetics and perfumes, a large oak desk, another card table with a pile of silverware and boxes of laundry soap, two floor-to-ceiling bookcases, a stack of dinner plates under a hand towel on the chair, a sea of Kleenexes and sections of newspaper apparently laid out to cover the floor. The shades were drawn and the air was thick and warm, a musty acrid smell mixed under the stench of Pine-Sol. He understood at once that this was where Alice slept.

"Sheriff? Your tea's ready."

He closed the door quietly and stepped to the stairwell. "Where's your brother, Miss Pinkston?"

She was standing at the bottom of the stairs balancing a teacup in her hand. "You mean he's gone? You can't find him?" She started up the stairs and then tapped her forehead. "Oh, how silly. He's probably rolled himself into the corner behind the door. Did you look?"

Frank stepped into Birdie's room and looked behind the door. He leaned back out into the hall.

"Okay, Miss Pinkston. You go sit in the parlor. I'll be down in a minute."

He stepped back into the bedroom and closed the door, let out his breath, and sank down on the bed, covering his face with his hands.

"Jesus, man. You scared the shit out of me. I thought you were dead."

He heard a low moan. When he looked up, Birdie lolled his head from one side to the other, rolled his eyes up into his head, and let out a grunt. Frank studied him a moment and then sniffed the air and stood. He peered at Birdie and then went closer, bent, and sniffed again.

"What the hell," he whispered. "You've been drinking."

The sound that came out of the old man's mouth was somewhere between a croak and a chuckle. Frank turned and looked around the room. The ivy-patterned wallpaper above the white wainscot, the white lace curtains, the bed with its embroidered comforter neatly folded, the table with food, the jars and bottles of medicine on the bureau, the television, the picture of his parents on the wall. There was no sign of bourbon anywhere, just the smell. Frank caught his own reflection in the mirror behind the television and started. His face looked gray and sunken, his eyes red. He sat on the bed.

"I'm not saying it's wrong. I just thought you'd quit. I mean, I always thought your sister was kind of against you boozing." Birdie jerked his head up, tucked it hard to his chest, and let out a roar, an enormous spill of noise, a wild sound, more animal than human. Frank jumped to his feet to stop it.

"Okay, okay, okay, I'll never tell her, I swear! You can trust me, okay? Okay?"

When he was sure Birdie wasn't going to yell again, he backed up to the bed and sat.

"I had no idea you could do that."

The old man's mouth dropped open, and then his head fell back as if his neck had snapped.

"You could roar the walls right off this house." Frank looked around the room and then back at Birdie. "It's a relief to know."

Birdie made a sound that could have meant anything. The right side of his face was masklike, and his right hand was loose in his lap. Frank sat with his elbows on his knees, waiting, and then looked down, studying at his feet. He needed to call Emily off standby, get downstairs to Alice, and go outside to close the door of the squad car, which he was almost sure he had left open. He did not feel like leaving yet. It occurred to him that he rarely got the chance to be quiet with someone else in the room, and that he didn't mind being quiet with Birdie. Also that he was changing his mind about how much the old man understood.

"Did you know I evicted Rose last month? Your sister somehow managed to fix a padlock on the door of the Ute and Rose was inside with a dog. I guess she used the back window. I told her she had to leave."

Birdie was slouched to one side, one pale eye at half-mast. Frank looked down at his hands, shaking his head.

"I wish now I hadn't. She took off with everything she owned. Hell if I can figure out where she went, though." He looked down at his feet and chuckled. "You should have seen her. Pissed as hell. You know how she gets." He went to the window, leaning one elbow on the edge to look out. "I don't understand it. How can somebody who grew up here end up homeless? How can folks like you and your sister end up living alone? Where is everybody, Bird?"

The staircase out in the hallway creaked. "Birdie? You're not going to keep him to yourself all day, are you?"

Birdie's mouth had fallen to one side, and he moaned from it, a thin drooling sound. Frank ran his hands through his hair. "I got to get back to work anyway." He went to the door, leaned over, and put his hand on the old man's papery wrist. "Glad you're still with us, you old fart. You figure out how to let me know what kind of booze you drink, and I'll make sure you get it."

When Birdie didn't say anything, he closed the door and started downstairs.

Alice had set up her tea service. She was waiting behind it on the couch, her dress smoothed over her knees, her ankles crossed. "*There* you are," she cried.

"Yes, ma'am."

"What can I get? Coffee? Tea? Water?"

"Tea's fine." Frank made himself sit beside her. "You remember making a call to my office last night?"

"A call. . . ." Her eyes fluttered, as if thumbing through her mind for the memory.

"Yeah. You talked to my deputy and said it was urgent. You remember?"

Her face blazed up. "Of course I remember. What do you think I am, senile?"

"I didn't mean to imply that."

She stared at him blankly and then leaned in as if conspiring. "Let's have tea first, shall we? Then we'll have our conversation."

"I can't stay long. I'm on duty."

But there was no stopping her, hands fluttering over the cups, the sugar bowl, the cream, the plate of cookies, the teapot, checking to make sure each thing was there. Frank looked around the room. Everything in it looked expensive, old, and fragile. Along the west wall was a bookshelf lined floor to ceiling with glass figurines. He thought of Angela and what she could do to a bookshelf like that when she was sick. He accepted a cup and saucer and cleared his throat.

"What I wanted to talk to you about—"

She held up a finger. "Not until you accept a sweet. And call me Alice. I don't think anybody would mind, do you?"

He accepted something that looked like a sugar puck cracked with age. "No, I expect not."

"Now. Do we have everything?" With her hands stretched in front of her, she studied the tea service. "All right." She clapped her hands once and then turned to Frank with great intensity. "Do you think you'll need another cookie? Or not?"

He looked at the one in his hand. "One is fine. I want to ask about the call, though."

"Oh my yes," she said, clapping her chest dramatically. "Of course you do. I can't tell you how frightening it was. I could barely talk. I was a wreck, an absolute, utter wreck." She stopped.

"Alice?"

"Ohhh," she moaned, closing her eyes and rocking back. "I know how you young people think these days. I know how you'd like to put us all behind bars. Cram us into some warehouse for old people where you can't hear us crying. Don't think I don't know about that." She leaned forward, her chin quivering. "The least a woman of my age can ask for is protection. That's the least you can give me. Don't you think?"

"Are you worried about intruders again?"

She widened her eyes and nodded.

"What kind of intruders?"

She pointed to the back window. Frank turned and looked.

"You mean out in the back yard."

She nodded.

"You want me to go look?"

She nodded again, silently imploring, and then shutting her eyes. But when he stood, her eyes snapped open. "But you only just got here. You haven't even touched your sweet. It's from Phoenix."

"Alice, I—"

"Sit down before I get a crick in my neck."

"All right." He sat. "I'm going to say something, Alice—"

"Is this going to be a lecture about Birdie's wheelchair? Because I ordered him an electric one. Just as Mrs. Fleet suggested. I ordered the most expensive kind. He'll be flying around in no time under his own power. A touch of a button, they told me. It'll be here any day."

"Good. Alice, I want to talk about something else, though, and I don't want you to interrupt me until I'm—"

"I won't. I swear."

"Good. Now, the thing is—"

"You young people work too hard, you know. I just want you to enjoy yourselves. That's what my life is about, making people feel at home.

That's why my brother and I . . ." Her voice trailed off. "Did you hear something?"

"No, I don't think so."

"I thought I heard a horn. Maybe someone's coming to the motel. We could certainly use the money."

Despite the heat in the room, a shiver went through him. He looked grimly at his tea. "It's February, Miss Pinkston. The pass is closed most of the time these days. I don't think you're going to get a buyer until spring."

Her eyes were very still and blue. "Well," she said, slowly looking down to rearrange her skirt. "That's certainly a shame, isn't it."

He decided to go with it. "I agree. You need someone to keep you company until winter's over, don't you think?"

Her hand flew to her throat. "But when are they coming?"

"No," he said. "I mean it wouldn't hurt if you asked someone to move in here with you for a while. Until we can find another nurse for your brother. You have that extra room upstairs."

"But why on earth would I want to do that? That's Mrs. Fleet's room. If I give it away, she'll be furious. You don't understand how she gets. I couldn't let someone else sleep there. But what are you saying?" Her voice was growing thick with confusion. "Birdie and I are all right, aren't we?"

He steeled himself. "I don't know, Miss Pinkston. I'm worried. Having a friend here might be the best way to—"

"Just a minute." She stood up, walked to the other side of the room, and peeked around the curtain at the motel. Then she turned, wringing her hands, and came back toward the couch. When her eyes lifted to meet his, she flinched backward and stopped, her mouth dropping open.

"What in the *world* are you doing here?"

"You asked me to come."

"I did?"

"Last night. You called my office."

"And you've been sitting here ever since?"

He stood, balancing his teacup. "You need somebody with you, Alice. Somebody besides your brother. And besides me. How about your nieces?

Do you know how to reach them? You remember the girls, don't you—
Jessie and Andy, Florie's twins? What if you call them up to see if one of
them can come visit for a while?"

Whatever he had said, it was wrong. Without another word, she marched
out of the room. He heard the sound of the lift rising up the stairs, and
then a door banged.

He looked down at the china cup in his hand, so thin he could see the
shadows of his fingers through it. It was filled with water instead of tea.
Not even hot water.

He took everything back into the kitchen for her. On the counter was a
pile of tea bags. He bit the inside of his cheek and turned to the sink. It
was a deep old-fashioned sink, dry and clean, so clean he doubted she'd
been using it. But what did that mean? Nothing. He was being narrow-
minded. She could use her sink to store gin if she wanted, so long as
she was still looking after her brother properly. She was, wasn't she? He
looked over his shoulder to make sure she wasn't there watching him and
then turned to the refrigerator and opened it. It held two boxes of the
awful chocolate cookies she gave him and a can of Pine-Sol, but he
also saw yogurt and cheese and meat and milk and leftovers that looked
perfectly reasonable. In the freezer, frozen vegetables, and in the crisper
drawer, a bag of carrots and some Butterfinger chocolate bars. He began
to feel better. He eased the door shut, listened, and then stepped to the
nearest cupboard. Inside was a plate with food crusted on it, but also
several bottles of vitamins, canned soups, a loaf of bread, and pasta. He
opened all the cupboards and shut them again. Most of them were organized in perfectly normal ways.

He shook his head. She might be forgetful now, but how could he possibly judge her for it? She was doing fine. She was taking care of an old
man in a wheelchair all by herself, wasn't she? Just how sick could she be?
And that's when he turned to look out the window to her back yard and
saw, wedged in among the snowcapped bushes behind her garage where
no one could spot it from the street, Rose Devonic's Plymouth.

18

Delight in Learning Soon doth Bring
a child to learn the Hardest Thing.

—from an American sampler, 1797

Of course I knew it was dangerous to come back. Everybody in Queduro knew my car, and if anyone spotted it, even if I was only idling on a side street for a few minutes, they'd climb all over Frank. They'd say he hadn't done his job right. He'd probably have to arrest me or something. I knew this, and Frank knew it too, which is why I got off the main road to town as soon as I could and took the old mining road up to the overlook instead.

Because I needed to think. Trips take planning. Too many things can go wrong. What if I went north and then realized I should've gone south? What if I got all the way to Durango and then remembered someone back in Queduro who could take me in? That was the worst thought, that I might end up too far away to come back. I needed to focus. I needed to turn off the car and be still. It's impossible driving everything you own in the world around in a station wagon you're not sure is going to live much longer. By the time I'd remembered the overlook, I could hardly breathe.

The overlook was perched high on the west ridge above the homes, a flattened-out tailings pile. The road ended at an old mine-shaft building, a black rusted thing made of tin wrapped in barbed wire and faded NO TRES-PASSING signs. A popular place for teenagers in summer, a place where they could drink, throw rocks, and fool around with each other—viewing the overlook, we used to call it—but hardly anybody went up there in winter. I pulled behind the shaft building and turned off the motor and, after a minute, opened the door. When I told the dog to get out, he looked as if I was planning to dump him, so I left the door open.

It was a good place to stop, the sun out full strength, the ground mostly dry and warm, some big rocks to sit on, and nobody around. There was a chuckle behind me and I nearly jumped out of my skin, but it was only a magpie on top of the mine shaft, wagging its tail to keep its balance. "Get lost," I said, "scram." But of course, it wouldn't. Magpies never do. I went to the edge of the tailings and looked down. I could see the whole valley, from the wooden truss bridge at the south end to the Ten Tribes at the north, and all the buildings and trailers in between, the newest ones scattered like toys along the upper foothills, and the older ones lining the streets below, and then the oldest buildings of all, the shops and stores that made up the downtown along Hemming Street, many of them with their stone backsides cantilevered out over the Queduro River, which had served in the old days as the town sewer. I pulled myself onto the same boulder Frank and I had once used as a meeting place and rolled another cigarette. The rock under me was warm as flesh. Almost warm enough for me to take off my parka. I lit the cigarette, looked around, and then settled down tailor-style to study Queduro while I smoked.

I ended up studying the house on Tambour. It was a brown house with a red tar-paper roof, a yellow porch, and the garage out back where we'd carved and painted the Indians. After the accident, the bank had repossessed it and put it on the market, and after five years it had finally sold to Manny Pinella as a fixer-upper. Now his son Jack lived there. I smoked and thought about Jack as a possibility. We weren't exactly close—the previous summer, I'd smashed his hand in the Dumpster lid to get him to understand that—but if I asked him right, he'd give me a place to stay. I wondered more about the house, about what it would feel like to live there again. I couldn't remember that much about it, good or bad, but I sometimes dreamed about the little piece of cracked sidewalk out front. In my dream, it was full of fish—big, heavy, gray fish sliding over each other as they passed the front yard.

I lay back on the rock and stared up at the blue sky. Getting thrown out of the motel was bad, but it wasn't the end of the world. I could still make a decision, get in my car, and drive off to a new life. Birdie couldn't. He was stuck in a wheelchair with his sister at the helm, maybe stuck now for the rest of his life. I rolled onto one elbow and looked down at her house. It was off to the right, like a white face tucked in under the trees. All the windows at the back were dark, but I could picture him there, looking up the hill at me. You think *you've* got it rough? he'd cry. I lay back again. He was right. From here on out, what he'd have to deal with, I couldn't even begin to face.

The dog jumped up beside me on the rock, and I felt as if we lay there a long time, his head on my hip and my hand on his head and me looking up, maybe even drifting off, but when I opened my eyes the sun was still high. I sat up and went back to the car. The focus I needed had come on so surely I could have thrown a rock at it. I wasn't going anywhere. Queduro was my home. Frank knew I wasn't going to buy that crap about needing a new life in a new town. I still had my old life in *this* town. Maybe it wasn't a perfect life, maybe it was sometimes a lousy life, but that didn't mean I should dump it like it was worth nothing. Let go of where you belong and who you belong with, and you're lost. Frank understood that. He understood it more than anyone. I was in Queduro and Queduro was in me. I said it out loud, and like an answer a breeze came up over the lip of the overlook just then and rattled through the dead grass behind me: *yesss*. Even the dog looked up. Had Frank been there, he'd have heard it himself.

I got out my brush, my workbag, and a couple of flannel shirts and carried them over to the mine shaft. There was a livestock trough on the south side, left over from the sheepherding days, and though the bottom of it was lined with a green slime that grew year round, the water was clear as glass. I stripped to the waist, unbraided my hair, gripped the edge of the tank, took a breath, leaned over, waited to be sure I'd do it, and then dunked.

The cold was like being slapped with a metal plate. I came up not even knowing where I was, staggering back and grabbing for air. In the old days, Frank and I had done this together; in fact, somewhere I had a photograph of him as he pulled free of the water, his mouth twisting open, the cords of his neck hard as wire, the water like a rooster's comb as he threw back his head. I wrapped one shirt around my hair and got dressed in the other and, still shaking, dug through my workbag for the mirror I used to transpose embroidery patterns. I wedged it under a piece of loose tin on the building, so I could see my reflection, and then brushed my hair flat and got out my canvas shears.

My uncle liked cutting hair. Sometimes my mother cried when she saw the haircuts he gave me and Kyle, but I never minded them. Bob used to say a new haircut was a new lease on life, and he was right. Short hair would be like a statement, something honest and capable. I pulled a wing of hair from behind my ear, slid the shears in around it, and cut.

I didn't hear the car until it was too late to do anything but jump behind the shaft building. The engine sounded too heavy for Frank's patrol car, and sure enough a green Ford truck rumbled up over the lip of the tailings pile and made a circle around my car before stopping. I let out my breath. It was Eli Sanchez, one of the few people in town I could trust, a bear of a man with a big sad plainspoken heart. Before he'd gotten married to Maria, we'd spent time together, but he was too old for me and he knew it, and it was a relief for us both when I'd told him we were better off as friends. I stepped from behind the building and watched him climb out of his truck, cluck at the dog, and walk over to my car. When he bent to look in the back, I called over.

"What're you doing here, Eli?"

He turned and broke into a grin. "Thought I might find you up here."

"Did Frank send you?"

"You're not planning to stab me with those, are you?"

I looked down at the shears. "If you're here to give me a lecture, I might."

"Nope." He went to the back of his truck and lifted out a six-pack of Bud. "I thought you might be thirsty." He brought the beer over and pulled one loose for me.

"Later, maybe." I stepped back to the mirror.

"You're cutting your hair?"

"It looks like it."

I studied what I'd done so far and then lifted the shears. Eli bent over to pick a clump of hair off the ground. "There ought to be a law against red-haired women cutting their hair. In my opinion, anyway. I remember when your mom first cut hers."

"She always had short hair."

"Not when she first came to town. It grew just like yours, too. Had the same weight to it or something. Used to make my heart skid around just looking at it."

I glanced at him. "I don't remember you dating my mother."

"I didn't. She was already with your dad. And after he took off, she didn't seem interested. Besides, she was like you, too scary to date."

"Now there's a compliment."

"You know what I mean." He put the beer on the ground, popped one for himself, and leaned with a sigh against the building. "That your dog there, Rose?"

I looked over. "The way he follows me around, he's more like a guilty conscience. You want him?"

"Not if he's yours."

"He's not mine."

"Ah."

"He's not. I haven't even named him."

He laughed. "When are you going to get tired of being so tough?"

While I went back to my haircut, he stared out at the view.

"You know what I think? I think ever since this town started selling the embroidery tradition, we've been falling apart. It's like we have nothing holding us together anymore. You know that grandson of Tom Perkins, the one who was supposed to come out here last winter to help move Tom into the rest home? He sold Tom's house. Sold his own inheritance without hardly looking at it. And you know what the people who bought it are planning? They're going to paint the outside yellow with lavender trim and turn it into a bed-and-breakfast for tourists. The Happy Embroiderer Inn. And a slate roof. You know how much a slate roof costs? Going to make my house look like old shit." He slid down the building onto his heels.

I didn't answer. Eli could complain all he wanted, he still owned a place to live and it was going up in value every day.

"Rose, if you're trying to figure out a place to live, I got an idea."

I looked down at him. He was still looking at the view, stroking his chin with the twist of my hair. "No, thanks, Eli. Besides, you're married. I'll be all right." I looked back in the mirror. "I got an idea of my own anyway."

"Like what?"

I cut a chunk of hair loose, looked at it, and dropped it. "I'm going to go talk to Jack Pinella, see if we can't work a deal."

I could feel him staring at me. "A deal with Pinella?"

"I don't see why not. He has two bedrooms, a living room, a kitchen, and a basement. Not to mention the room my mother used to sew in. I could stay there easy."

"Stop it, Rose. Guys like Jack Pinella don't give a shit. Haven't you noticed the way he watches women in the bar? He's not going to want your money."

"That's good, because I don't have money to give. I'll be his housekeeper. Or his cook. Maybe he'll need help finishing his embroideries for spring."

Eli snorted and turned angrily to the view, his face dark. "Does Frank know?"

"What's he got to do with it?"

Eli looked away in disgust and drank half a beer before he came up again. "He'd never want to see you do this, Rose. Never."

"Then he shouldn't look. Get off it, Eli. Life isn't a fairy tale. Frank's got his own problems to deal with these days. Or haven't you noticed?"

Instead of answering, Eli shook his head in disgust and slugged the last of his beer.

"Okay, Eli, pretend you're Frank. You got everything, right? Looks, brains, great parents, a nice home, top grades, a Silver Star from the army—and not only that, as soon as you get back from the war, you've got everybody begging you to be the new sheriff. And what about that old girlfriend of yours from high school, what about her? Why, nobody even talks to her anymore. She's so broke she can't afford a decent dress, so in debt she can't get a cup of coffee at the cafe, so pathetic she can't even keep her canvas work clean. Now, if you were Frank, just how long do you think you'd want to hang around someone like that?"

"You know what you're doing? You're talking self-pity."

"I'm talking survival. Frank was Queduro's blue-ribbon best. If I hadn't bowed out gracefully, they'd have lynched me."

"You're just like your mama, you know that?"

I turned back to the mirror. "I don't know why you came all the way up here to find me, but I wish you'd go home. I've got to concentrate."

He crushed the beer can in his fist and threw it hard at the back of his truck. "You've never made me ashamed of knowing you, Rose, and I don't think I'm going to let you start."

"Oh, really?" I craned my eyebrows at him. "And who are you?"

"Your friend. Maybe the only friend you got left anymore. Plus I'm twenty years older than you. So I'm going to tell you something, and I expect you to listen." He stood, snapped another beer out of the six-pack, and pointed it at me. "You ought to try Alice Pinkston again."

I laughed and turned back to the mirror. "Alice is the one who had me evicted today, pal."

"I know." He popped the beer. "But what if it wasn't all her idea?"

I lowered the shears. "What do you mean?"

"What if somebody on the Commerce Committee called her? What if they told her you were hiding out in the motel and you were dangerous?"

I stared at him. "They told Alice I was dangerous?"

"I can't say for sure, but I wouldn't put it past them."

"Why?"

"Because you *are* dangerous, Rose. You're supposed to be the local charity case, the one with no home, no family, no future, no friends—and yet there you are, taking over the motel for Bird when he gets sick and calling yourself a trade embroiderer, demanding a sales booth just like everybody else. They can't stand the uppitiness of it."

My throat felt raw. "What are you saying?"

"They're betting you'll be gone by spring. They're betting you're gone right now."

I swallowed and turned away, yanking the nest of old hair out of my brush. "They may not like me much, but she's the one who locked me out."

"Maybe so. But do you think at her age she can screw a padlock hasp onto a door by herself? I don't."

"Not just one padlock. Three."

"I know. I also know this. When Ruben Johnson came into the hardware store last Friday, he bought the three padlock hasps I had on the shelf and told me to order more. When I asked what he needed so many hasps for, he flinched like I'd grabbed him by the ear. Said he didn't know, he was just running some errands for the Committee."

"You mean for Dick Sweeny?"

"I'd say so."

"Ruben works for Dick?"

"Ruben will work for anybody right now if it means he'll be able to afford a new torque converter for his crane."

"But why would Dick suddenly buddy up to Alice Pinkston? Wasn't he just campaigning against her on account of her driving?"

"Yeah, well. Dick's always got several different irons in the fire. Seems he's begun to realize that Alice may be making every effort to look normal, but something's not quite right there anymore, mentally speaking. And information like that tends to interest assholes like Dick. Truth is, I feel sorry for her. I think she's so scared lately, she'll do just about anything anyone tells her to do in order to get them to leave her alone."

"How come you know all this?"

"Frank, mostly. He's been visiting her every day since last week when Birdie's nurse ran off. He needs someone in there right away, but he knows nobody's going to want to move to Queduro this time of year. And Alice hasn't got any friends to help her out in the meantime. Nobody even likes her. They never have." He shrugged and took another drink. "All I know is, she forgets more than she remembers nowadays and she's probably feeling pretty lonely, especially with nobody to talk to but a brother who can't answer. Why not try being a little nicer to her?"

"I've been nice to her."

"So try it with a little less push. You can do that, can't you? I remember when Willy got sick last summer, how you kept dropping by to visit. You were sweet with him, Rose. He always felt better after you came."

Willy was Eli's son, a soft, split-grinned, slobbering mongoloid kid who liked to call himself the Goofball. The product of a brief affair with a tourist named Belinda from Oregon, Willy had been raised by his dad, going to work with him every day at his booth in summer until Eli crushed his hand and got forced into early retirement. Willy had loved crowds, though, so he went on packing his little sack lunches and catching rides out to the booths every summer until his twenty-eighth year when—to the secret relief of many embroiderers, who felt his enthusiasm scared away tourists—he caught a cold that turned to pneumonia in less than a month, and killed him.

"All I did," I said, "was come over a few times to watch TV with him."

"Yeah, but you had a way of talking with him. Of being with him. I always appreciated that." He took a long hit of beer before he went on. "The point is, if nobody steps up to bat for Alice and Birdie soon, they're both going to be in deep shit."

"She doesn't like me."

"Maybe she can learn. And you've always had a way with Birdie. Even when you were a kid. Everybody knows that. Even Alice knows that."

"Believe me, Eli. If I had to be stuck in a wheelchair with some nut like her looking after me, I'd be yelling my head off."

"Just my point. You understand him." He handed me his beer. "It's worth a try. If you just disappear, what's the Bird going to think?"

"He's going to be grateful, that's what." But I didn't really believe it. I took a sip. Blue shadows in the valley were creeping up toward the edge of the tailings pile. I looked over at Eli. "If I go try to talk to her, can you keep your mouth shut about it?"

"I'd do that. Sure."

"You can't tell Frank. He can't afford to know right now. I can't afford it, either. Especially if you're wrong."

"Tell you what. I promise to keep Frank busy if you promise to stay away from Jack Pinella."

"You think he's that bad?"

"Jack's like a bear sniffing for food. You can go over there looking like Woody Woodpecker if you want, but it's not going to make a bit of difference to him."

I took a drink of beer and felt my hair at the back. "It's a bad haircut?"

"Yeah, but it's still not going to stop him. I shouldn't have to tell you that. Remember when you had to mash his fingers with the lid of the Dumpster to get away?"

"How'd you know about that?"

"Everybody knows." He hitched his pants. "I guess I better get back to the bar, before my wife starts looking for me." He started toward his truck.

"Don't forget your beers."

"You keep them. I can buy more. Besides, if I get fat, you young girls won't lust after me anymore."

I went over and kissed him on the cheek. "I'll lust after you, Eli."

He laughed; then his eyes got sad. "If there was any way I could give you a bed at my house, Rose, I would. That's what I wanted to do."

"I know. You got your marriage to think about."

"If I'm wrong and Alice won't let you in? I'll get you over to Madrillas myself. The road's clear and dry for now, but that'll change soon enough and I know you hate driving that pass in winter. Frank and me, we'll get you over."

"Okay. But don't tell anybody I'm here now. Especially Frank."

He pushed in the ignition button, turned the key, and pumped on the gas until his truck started. "Be careful."

"I always am."

"I know." He paused, pulled his door shut, and unrolled his window. "That's why you wouldn't marry me."

I lifted my beer. "Consider yourself lucky."

He grinned and started circling my car, his truck jouncing on the chalky gravel. "Saddest day of my life," he called, and then he waved good-bye, rolled up his window, and drove away.

By the time I finished the haircut, the shadows were climbing the ridge behind me and night was coming on fast down in the valley, turning the air gray and cold. I threw the dog a sandwich, made one for myself, and ate it with the car door closed, staring out at the red mat of hair on the ground by the shaft building. It probably wasn't as bad as Eli said. At least it would grow back.

I dug through my bags for my mother's embroidered scarf and tied it around my head. Quedurans never wear embroidery—the last thing you want is to dirty your work before you sell it—but when my mother first quit the tradition, she'd worn the scarf to keep the hair out of her eyes while she helped Bob and me out in the garage. The middle of it was still speckled with yellow from the day I'd dripped varnish on it. I remember the way my uncle's face caved in when he saw what I'd done, the way we waited for her to look up at me on the ladder and explode, the way she untied the scarf and looked at it and laughed instead. "Embroidery," she said, shaking her head. "A piece of nothing with a little thread. Can you believe all the years we bowed down to it?" Then she tossed it at me with another laugh and picked up the spokeshave to finish her half of the log. It was Bob who picked the scarf off the floor of the garage, shook it out, and tucked it in the pocket of my overalls. "The trick isn't to curse your past," he'd whispered. "It's to keep your mind on what you do next."

I put on my bright red lipstick, told the dog to get in—"Wish me luck"—and locked him in the car with a bowl of water. There was a foot trail angling from the tailings pile down into the woods behind Alice's, and I took it, moving slower as I got in under the trees. All the windows at the back of her house had their curtains and shades drawn. I went several hundred yards past her property and then cut off the trail and pushed my way down through the tangle of scrub oak to the street. I could see her kitchen light on, and as I came out onto the pavement I saw her front porch was lit too. I brushed off my coat, readjusted the scarf, and after looking around at the dark woods, trying to think if this was much of an idea or not, I started toward her house.

19

Jesus invites young children near,
Oh, may we straight Obey.
Give us, O Lord, the attentive ear
And teach our hearts to pray.

—from an American sampler, 1803

Birdie was out in her driveway again. I couldn't hardly believe it. He was out in the middle of her driveway in the dark, facing away from her house and wrapped in so many scarves and blankets that the only reason I knew it was him was the gleam of his wheels. I slipped across the street, keeping in the shadows thrown by the wolf pine next to her porch.

"What are you doing out here, Bird?"

He tilted to one side. He had a scarf wrapped around his neck to his nose and a fur hat pulled down over his eyebrows. I stepped carefully out from the shadows, waiting for her front door to slap open. Birdie swung his head around to look at me, and I stepped closer. Why had she left him by himself? I leapt the last few feet across the light thrown from her front porch and crouched in front of him so his chair was between me and the house.

"Listen," I whispered, "I hope you're all right about this because Eli says he thinks maybe she's willing to work a deal with me. I don't want to make anything harder for you, though." I stopped to peek up over his shoulder toward the house. "Shit. I shouldn't be here. This is a bad idea, isn't it? The last thing you need right now is me. I shouldn't have come. Bird? The dog's locked in my car, so I have to go. Don't worry about your embroideries because they're safe. I'll make sure they get back to you somehow. And I took your liquor so she wouldn't find it. And I took some food from your pantry. And a book, I took the book I gave you. I can't think of anything else. There isn't anything else, is there?"

His head rolled back and he made a noise. I looked around and then pulled the scarf off his mouth. He didn't say anything, but when I started to speak he fixed me with his good eye.

"Ay-er." The word slid out of his mouth like a live fish.

"Air? You mean like air, like you're hot?"

"Ay-er."

I looked around for Alice and then back at him. "You do kind of look packed in there."

"*Hay*-er!"

"Okay. If you want air, don't answer."

He didn't answer. I pulled his blanket away and loosened his scarf. He was wearing a parka good enough for Alaska and, when I unzipped that, two ski sweaters and a turtleneck. When I took off his cap, his hair was matted around his ears with sweat. "*Pfooo,*" he said, lifting his chin. I crouched next to his chair.

"At least she's keeping you warm. I've got to go, Birdie. She's going to throw a fit if she comes out and finds me now. It's going to be bad for both of us."

His left hand came out from under the blanket, raised itself in the air as if to check the breeze, and then shot at me, catching my wrist. When I flinched back, he held on. His grip was strong and hard as a hawk's claw.

"Birdie, let go. She might come. Let me go. Come on."

But he wouldn't. He rolled his head until his chin touched his chest and held on and then he made sounds like an old engine trying to start, *rowww,*

rowww, it sounded like. I started to panic. I tried to pry his fingers off my wrist, but he made the noise again, and when his head rolled toward his shoulder I saw his face was wet with tears. That's when it stopped for me. That's when it was over. I felt something hard shiver through me, almost like hunger, and I put my forehead down on his knee, hard and skinny as the handle of a wrench, and I began to cry too.

I didn't hear her coming. When I raised my head, she was already standing there in the driveway, silhouetted by the porch light. I looked around but there was no place to hide. I wiped my face on my sleeve and stood. She was holding some kind of bundle close to her throat. I couldn't see her face, only the black outline of her against light.

"I just stopped to talk to your brother," I said. "He was out here, so I stopped. I didn't mean to scare you. I'll go along now. I'm leaving." I put Birdie's cap back on his head and turned to go.

"You can't just do this to me," she cried.

I turned. "I can't, huh? What about what you've done to me?"

"What?"

"Don't try to pretend. First you locked me out and then you had me evicted. You didn't even have the guts to warn me first."

"Oh, dear," she murmured. "This is bad. This is very, very, very bad."

"You bet your ass it's bad. I was Birdie's friend. I was sending you money. I was trying to help. What kind of person are you?"

"But you can't know what it's like!" she cried. "How am I supposed to do everything by myself? He was getting so upset and then his chair got stuck in the doorway, so I thought if I just, if I just. . . ."

She stopped. She wasn't wearing her wig. Her hair grew straight off her skull, fine as spun silk and thin enough to let light through.

"All right," she cried, "I'll never do it again. I will never, *ever* do it again. It's just that if I put him out in the morning, everyone will stare at him, so I thought if we waited until dark, it might be . . ." She choked back something and stamped her foot. "You have no right to tell them. I'm doing my best. I am. I've been that way all my life."

She was crying. I didn't know what to say. I looked around and back at her. "Tell who?"

"I brought him another blanket. You see? It's not like I don't take care of him." She held out her arms, and I saw she was carrying a blanket.

I looked down at Birdie. His head had rolled forward to his chest, and I couldn't see his face. "You've got him pretty well bundled up as it is, don't you think?"

"Do I?"

I wasn't sure what she wanted. "Yeah. I think you're doing a good job, though."

"You *do*?" she cried. "You think I'm doing a good job?"

"Sure." The night air sifted between us, cold and fresh, and I noticed she was wearing a dress thin enough to see through. So thin I could see the hollows between her thighs.

"Aren't you freezing?"

"Should I be?"

I got a bad feeling then. It was the same feeling I had once as a kid, when I put on a Halloween mask and hid under Kyle's crib as a joke and then realized it wasn't going to be funny at all. Little Kyle had no idea of what a joke was, he was just lying there sucking on his pacifier and patting the plastic rings on his crib, all his defenses down.

I started edging sideways, one step at a time, trying to keep it casual. "I guess I'll get going, then. See you later."

"Don't you think I should take him in?"

"Yeah. If you want." When she didn't move any closer to his chair, I tried again. "Why don't you take him inside."

"But what about the brake? Can't you at least help me with that?"

I looked around the driveway. I took another step back.

"Why are you sidling away like that?" she snapped. "Do you think I like this? Do you think I can do everything around here by myself?"

I looked over at the black shape of the motel and the branches of the cottonwoods above it and the night sky above them before I turned back. "You really don't want me to help you. Believe me, I shouldn't even be here. Hey, Birdie," I called over. "Tell her."

"My brother can't talk," she cried. "He's very ill. He's got to go in. He needs his medication." She stepped to the back of his chair and began to tug at it, trying to pull it backward up the driveway to the house and then trying to push it forward.

I watched her and then I went over, careful to stand with my back to the porch light so she couldn't see my face. "I'll get him in the house if you want," I said, "but just remember, this is your idea, not mine. You go get the door." I took the chair handles from her and bent over Birdie to get the brake. When I looked back, she was at the top of the driveway, holding the back door open for us.

"Right in here, right in here," she called.

I leaned over Birdie's shoulder. "Next time tell her to remember the brake, you bastard. She's going to have a coronary when she realizes who I am."

I pulled him over the threshold into her kitchen and swung him around so he was facing the table, but when I made for the door with my head down, she was already busy locking it, gabbling about how grateful she was, how glad she was to be back in the house, how she'd never let that happen again. On and on. I looked at Birdie and then at the swinging door that led to the rest of her house, wondering if I could make a run for the front door. She was finishing the last lock. I steeled myself for the worst, but when she turned, though she paused to stare at me for a moment with her mouth open and her painted eyebrows knitted together, nothing happened. Her stare just shifted to the counter behind me and to Birdie and then she went to him, clucking, and zipped his parka closed.

"You've got to stay warm," she cried. "That's the rule for being a good nurse: Keep the patient warm. Let me think now, where did I put that hot-water bottle?" She tucked the blanket in around him, turned in a slow circle, looking at the kitchen, and ended up staring at me.

"Do you know?"

"Me?"

She hurried to the door to the living room, pushed it open, pausing there for a second to flutter her fingers against her mouth, then disappeared around the edge. Birdie was watching me, his head trembling on its stem, his good eye sharp as steel, the other a dull blue. I eased sideways into the chair next to him.

"Let me get this straight," I whispered. "She doesn't remember who I am? She thinks I'm somebody else?"

"Ah-yer," he groaned.

I pulled away the blanket and unzipped his parka as far as the belt that was keeping him in the chair. His left hand came out and grabbed my arm in the death grip again, but I heard her coming down the stairs and pried loose from him, staggering back.

She was holding a hot-water bottle. "I can't get the capper off," she cried, "but I will." When she sat next to Bird and started pulling on the stopper, he groaned and rolled his head back, closing his eyes. "Now don't start that with me," she said. "We can't let you to catch a bug."

I studied her from the side. Her mouth was cracked at the corner, and from the size of her neck rising out the back of her sweater, it seemed to me she'd lost a lot of weight. She'd always been skinny, but now she looked as if she was made of chicken bones and tissue paper. Her hair looked as if a bomb had gone off in it. When she put the bottle between her knees and tried pulling at it, her face squeezed tight, I stepped around her so she could see me.

"Do you know who I am? Or not."

She opened her eyes. She looked at Birdie and back at me. "Did we go to school together?"

"Here." I grabbed the bottle and unscrewed the cap. When I held it out, she stood, shaking her head, and then folded her arms tightly and disappeared around the corner of the swinging door into the living room.

I looked over at Birdie. "Am I supposed to go along with this," I whispered, "or is she going to remember later?"

He wagged his head back.

"What are you still doing here?"

I turned and found her inches away, her mouth pulling at the corners like she was chafing against a bit. "Give me my hot-water bottle," she hissed. "You're spying on us, aren't you? You'll have the whole town talking about us soon. I know why you're here. How dare you! Go away. Go home. Shoo!"

"I'm leaving."

But when I reached for the chain on the back door, she took a fistful of my parka and yanked me back. "Not that way. You think I'm some kind of idiot? This way."

She pulled me through the living room, heading for the front door, her fingers working my sleeve, but as soon as we got to the front hallway, she suddenly stopped and let go. She was standing rigid, her eyes welling up, gripping her sweater closed at the throat.

"I know what you're thinking, but you're wrong. You can tell them that."

"Tell who?"

Tears started spilling off the hard pink rims of her eyes. She stepped back into the living room, her chin high and quivery, and placed her hands on the wooden edge of a knickknack cabinet.

"You may come back when my brother is feeling better, but now it is late and he's had enough visitors. In fact, it is very late. I think it's high time you went home to your own family. Good night."

She reached to the wall, turned out the lights, crossed the living room to the kitchen, and swung the door closed.

I waited, but she didn't come back. Except for the slit of light under the door to the kitchen, the place was pitch dark. I edged over to the wall and felt along it out into the front hallway. I found a light switch there, the old-fashioned kind with a button, and when I pushed it a small pink-glass chandelier clicked on overhead. There was a metal wheelchair lift on a silver rail at the foot of the dark stairwell, but everything else in the hallway looked old and dark. I turned to the front door and opened it. Then I stopped and turned toward the stairs. I tried to think about what Birdie would say, what he would want me to do. I thought about a lot of things, including my career as an embroiderer and what would happen to it, and then I shut the door and switched off the light. I could hear her out in the kitchen, talking to Birdie, her voice rising and falling. I put out my hands and groped around the lift and felt my way up through the dark, trying not to creak the stairs.

20

Tis true twas long ere I began to seek to live forever
But now I run as fast I can, tis better late than never.

—from an American sampler, c.1830

The murmur of a woman's voice, far away, no words, just sounds. I was on the floor under one of the eaves in her attic, blocked in by steamer trunks, with a raccoon coat for a blanket that smelled of dust and cedar. I craned up to see how late it was, but through the little round window all I saw was gray sky. I wondered how the dog was doing in the car. I lay back, not wanting to think about it.

The attic was cold enough to show my breath and full of furniture, picture frames, garment bags, luggage, rolled-up rugs, and cardboard boxes. So much stuff. I hadn't been able to find the light switch last night, and I saw how lucky I was that I hadn't broken my neck. I pushed off the raccoon coat, retied my scarf, and crawled over a steamer trunk. As I stood, the raccoon coat snagged the paw of a blue and white cat, and I caught the thing just before it hit the floor. A life-size porcelain cat puffed over its haunches with a sort of screw-you grin, at least I thought so, but as I slid it back into place I realized that the top half was a lid that came off. As quietly as I could, I set the bottom half on the floor and lifted my skirt. Maybe Bob's idea to make wooden Indians was crazy, but he wasn't any crazier than whoever thought up the idea of a china-cat chamber pot.

Alice's voice was going steady downstairs. After a little exploring, I found a floor vent behind some boxes of hangers, and after I moved those, her voice was much louder. When I opened the vent and put my head down next to it, it was like she was talking through a mouthpiece.

"—so I'm not going to talk to them anymore. It's that simple. They'll just have to call somewhere else for answers. I'm too busy. How can they know what it's like to have a brother who can't even zip his pants? They can't even guess." Water turned on somewhere and then turned off. "Apple, sandwich, juice. Mm-hmm." Then there were footsteps across a hard floor, then nothing. I sat back, breathing into the raccoon fur collar. She'd been talking to herself, and now she was bringing a meal upstairs to Bird. I tiptoed over to the pocket staircase that had gotten me into the attic and crouched down next to it to listen. A low hum started—the wheelchair lift, I thought—grew in size, then stopped. I heard footsteps, a door creaked, more footsteps that went away. I moved across the attic until I thought I was over Birdie's room, and underneath a rolled-up rug was another vent. When I opened it, I not only heard her steps crossing the wooden floor of his bedroom, I could see a corner of his bed through the grate and then part of the tray as she set it down. A melted cheese sandwich, two apples, milk. The tray went away. My stomach growled. I could smell the toast. Birdie started moaning.

"Now, we won't put up with nonsense. I'm the nurse now, and I've made a nice cheese sandwich. I'll put on the television while you eat, shall I? Then we'll have every bite inside that tummy of yours before you even know it. Ready?" I bit the edge of my teeth. I'd heard the same kind of baby talk when I'd first lost my family, all kinds of people reminding me every single day that the game was over, my goose was cooked, I might just as well give up, I'd never make it without their help. That was what baby talk was about: power. She went on.

"First bite now. Too big? Fine, I'll cut it. I've cut it once already, but if you insist, I don't mind. I know how sensitive your teeth are. There. Here you go. . . . Now, Birdie, don't do that. You have to eat. Come on. Try again. We don't want people to start thinking I don't feed you enough, do we?" Then Birdie let out a roar like a lion and there was a crash. I saw an apple roll under the bed.

After that, faint sounds from the television but nothing else. It was so quiet, I almost thought she'd gone back down to the kitchen. I was thinking about food, about eating. She started talking again.

"I don't have to be here, you know. I could put you in a nursing home and go back to Phoenix. They'd help me, too. They told me so. They told me to put you away for your own good. Do you hear me?"

Birdie didn't answer.

After a time, she said, "I wish Florie were here." She said it with no temper in her voice, the same way a person might say that they wished they had a better TV program to watch. Then the sound of the TV went away and I heard her collecting dishes. A moment later, the lift hummed its way back downstairs.

Birdie? You there?"

I waited.

"I'm up in the attic. I'm talking through the vent. Look at the ceiling near the foot of your bed. Say something if you hear me."

Instead, his chair rolled into view. I was looking at the snowy top of his head, and then it rolled back and he stared up, his mouth wide open, the right side of his face blank as a slab of gray wood.

"Aaffaw."

"Yeah? Well, I didn't leave. Sorry if you're mad. What the hell was that crack about putting you in a nursing home?"

He gave a long answer, but it sounded like somebody talking underwater. I didn't get a word. When he finished, he groaned and shook his head in disgust.

"Don't worry," I said. "Frank won't let her do it. Neither will Eli. She's just trying to piss you off."

He didn't say anything.

"Birdie?" I whispered. "I don't think I can keep fooling her, do you?"

His head swung, and he glared up at me with his ruined face. Maybe he was angry with me, or maybe he was amazed. Maybe he was only wondering why it had taken me so long to figure it out. The right side of his face was so different now, I just couldn't tell what he was thinking.

I closed my eyes and put my head down, resting my lips against the grate, tasting the soft attic dust there. I lifted my head a few inches. "I'll tell Frank you need help, okay? I'll tell him he has to do something about her. But that's all I can do. Okay?"

But he didn't have time to answer because the lift was coming back up to the second floor. I watched him fumble for his wheels trying to get himself back to where she'd left him, but since he only had one hand that worked, all he could do was roll himself back into view a moment later, facing the opposite direction. She was coming up the lift humming "Here Comes the Bride," and when she opened the door she cried, "Lunchtime!"

An hour later, after a terrible fight, she finally gave up trying to feed him and took him downstairs on the lift. I swapped the raccoon coat for my parka, opened the pocket stairway, and went down into his room. There was half a sandwich on the bureau and I wolfed it, groaning for the relief of food, while I studied myself in the mirror. With the scarf on, I did look different. On the other hand, whoever Alice had thought I was last night, she'd probably see the truth in daylight.

Then Birdie started yelling downstairs. Above his yelling was Alice's sharp voice, *no, no, no!* I felt for the keys to my car and stepped out into the hall. Distracting her so I could get away, I thought. Either that or telling me to hurry up and go get help. He was making awful noises, screeches, banging, and wails, even howls. I started fast down the stairs, my chest knotted tight. Halfway, when the noises suddenly coming from the kitchen stopped, I stopped too, gripping the banister.

"Ooh-hoo. Hello?" Her voice grew suddenly louder as she came out the door of the kitchen. "Is someone here?"

And then she was coming across the living room. I sucked in my breath and started down. "What a *great* house," I cried. "I've always *adored* it. I wonder where Alice is."

My face got hot with the shame of it. I didn't know what I was supposed to be, or what I was even trying for. I whipped off my parka and balled it up under one arm. As I got to the bottom of the stairs, she peered cautiously around the wall separating the hallway from the living room.

"Why, hello!" I burst out. "I was *just* looking for you."

"You were?"

And then Birdie let out a howl, and at the same time there was the sound of a chair falling over. Alice winced, looked over her shoulder, and then back at me, her eyes very blue and wide.

"You better get that," I said, "don't you think?"

She swallowed hard. "Get what?"

Then Birdie started crying. I could hear him crying, and I didn't care who I was supposed to be. I pushed by her into the dining room and realized that I couldn't get through to the kitchen. I turned and passed her and tore through the living room.

"Wait," she cried. "My brother!"

I turned to her. "He's in there alone. He needs something. Don't you understand?"

"Of course I understand."

"For God's sake, then," and I pushed through the swinging door.

He had a bib around his neck and his good arm was strapped under the belt of his wheelchair so he couldn't move it. He was moaning and tears were rolling down his face and he was covered in tomato soup, everything dripping and spattered, his chin and the table and the floor, clear over to the counter on the other side of the kitchen. I almost couldn't breathe when I saw him. I spun around to Alice, nearly knocking into her. "What the hell are you doing? You just fed him, didn't you?"

She was wringing her hands and shaking her head.

"You don't feed *anybody* like this, you hear me? Especially not him. If he's not hungry, he doesn't have to eat." I dropped my coat on the kitchen chair, stepped to Birdie, and snapped loose the seat belt. "And he doesn't have to be tied down like this. You keep his hands free. All right?" I turned to her, saw she'd turned away. "All right?"

"Yes." Her voice small as a mouse.

"Shit, you don't even know who I am, do you." I picked up the chair Birdie had kicked over, set it hard on its legs, and sat. "Screw this. Who am I trying to kid? This isn't right. You can't be left alone with this. Bird, tell her. Stop moaning like that and tell her she's—"

"*Quiet!*"

She was holding her fists against her ears. "Do you know what it's like for me? Do you have any idea? I don't know what's wrong with every-thing. I don't *know*."

"Well, I sure as hell do." But when she clapped her fists harder against her ears, I felt all the air go out of me. "Okay. I'm sorry. It scared me seeing him tied up with soup all over him. I didn't mean to hurt your feelings."

She'd begun to pace, still holding her ears. "This is not right. This is not right at all."

"Look, slow down. You're doing okay. I didn't mean to scare you. I was just worried about Birdie." I slid the scarf off my hair. "I'm not used to seeing him so helpless like this—"

"*Rowww,*" roared Birdie, making us both jump.

"It's just a haircut, Bird," I said. "It's not like I can't grow it back." But when I turned, Alice's face had fallen open and she was blinking hard as if to hold it there.

"You remember who I am now?"

"My God," she said. "I didn't know it was you. What are you doing here?"

"I don't know." I gathered up my coat. "Just be nice to your brother. Please."

I got as far as the back door before she caught my sweater. I tried to duck, I thought she was going to hit me, but she held on, her voice rising up like a little sparrow.

"Florie," she cried. "Florie, forgive me!"

21

Happy is the man that hath a friend
Form'd by the God of nature,
Well may he feel and recommend
Friendship to his creator.

—from an American sampler, 1798

In March, the Committee asked Frank to attend their monthly meeting. When he arrived, though he wasn't late, he could see through the plate-glass window at the front of the Mineral Building that the meeting had formed early and that, along with the usual group of inheritance embroiderers, most of the trade embroiderers were in attendance. He eased open the door and stepped inside, slipping off his wool cap. The room was hot and noisy, much of the crowd near the door still in the process of taking off coats and gloves, settling in chairs, and greeting neighbors.

As he shut the door, he noticed Ruben Johnson standing against the back wall, scowling darkly, biting a fingernail. When he saw Frank, he beamed, sidled over, and stood on tiptoe to whisper at his ear. "You should've found some excuse not to come, Frank. They're out for blood tonight."

"I kind of figured." He glanced down at the small mechanic. "What are you doing here?"

Ruben shrugged. "Betty wanted to come. That guy she's with now, Vic, he didn't want to bring her."

Frank nodded. Betty was Ruben's ex-wife, a shrill, shark-eyed woman who'd been ruling over Ruben's heart and most of his life since the sixth grade. As the two men turned from each other, an argument started at the front of the room between Tommy Steelhead and Vernan Medina, the crowd looking on openmouthed. Before Frank could catch the gist, Dick Sweeny banged his gavel on the table at the front of the room.

"He's here now, folks, so we can start the meeting. Thanks for coming, Frank. There's a chair up here, if you want."

Everyone turned to look at him, their faces washed out from work, eyes small and red. He nodded hello and sat in the nearest chair.

"I'm okay back here, Dick. Thanks."

"Meeting's called to order, then. You want to read the minutes from last month, Peg?"

Peg Trujillo stood, adjusted her dress, cleared her throat, and opened a folder. She was a speed-reader, and in order to keep up with herself she had to skip all commas, periods, and pauses, her voice in a flat-out, let's-just-get-to-the-end-of-this monotone, making her nearly impossible to understand. Ruben tapped Frank on his shoulder and motioned him with a black hand to lean closer. "You ought to stop by to see the crane," he whispered. "Got her painted up like a French whore on Saturday night. Cab, boom, hubs." Frank nodded and started to straighten, but Ruben caught his shoulder and pulled him down again. "I'll be getting that torque converter I told you about pretty soon, so if you have any lifting jobs, just let me know. And tell other people." Frank nodded, noticing a tiny scrap of paper tangled in the curly black hair at the top of Ruben's head. Ruben was not only plowing roads nearly every night to help pay off his crane, he'd also doubled his normal workload at the garage by offering oil-and-lube discounts—and from the haggard, hollowed-out look on his face, he was probably still moonlighting for Dick Sweeny as well. Frank made a thumbs-up sign. After Ruben burst into a grin and did the same back, they shook hands and Frank moved forward to sit in the nearest chair.

Peg droned on. The embroiderers who weren't bent over their work or whispering to each other were flexing their fingers as if playing invisible keyboards in their laps, cracking their knuckles on the backs of their necks or their knees, their workbags tucked under their chairs. Frank suspected that nobody was listening to Peg, only waiting for her to finish. When she did, Dick banged the gavel.

"First order of business. I asked the sheriff to come tonight so we can tell him our concerns regarding the situation up on Flax Hill. Anybody want to start?"

"Wait a minute." Vivian Archuletta stood. "I think first we should ask Frank what he thinks. He's the one who's up there all the time." She turned to find Frank at the back of the room. "You know more than we do, Frank."

"All right, sheriff," said Dick. "Floor's yours. Why don't you come on up front where we can see you."

Frank stayed where he was. "What can I help you with?"

Dick's eyes glanced meaningfully at someone in the front row before he answered. "We're not trying to interrogate anybody, Frank. We just want to know your opinion of Alice Pinkston. She's been taking care of her brother without a nurse now for two months. How's she doing?"

Frank cleared his throat. "I'm not sure I understand, Dick. Don't you know her well enough to go ask how she's doing yourself?"

A murmur floated through the room and then faded. Dick banged his gavel.

"This is a busy time of year for most of us in the embroidery business, Frank. You know that. Now, the thing is, we got some members who think she's doing fine on her own, and some who don't. We just want to know what you think, so we can know how to be good neighbors for her. That's all."

Frank turned his cap in his hands. Coming from Sweeny, the word *neighbors* sounded like a threat. "I think she's fine," he said. "I think they're both fine." He smiled at the members who turned in their seats, and added, "I've always thought neighbors are the people who accept you for what you are."

"I have something to say about that," cried a voice, and Teresa Steelhead stood. "Last month I promised the Committee I'd go visit Miss Pinkston and find out how she's doing, and I just want to say that I offered that because I believe in being Christian to everyone, no matter who they are. But, Frank"—she turned to him, holding out her hands—"I've tried half a dozen times and she just won't let me in. She says she's busy and then I phone her and she says she's busy again and then she doesn't call back. And now there's an answering machine to pick up the calls. How are we supposed to work with that? We all know she's in there, but she won't let us in. Plus, when my grandson delivers her groceries, I always tell him to ask how she's doing. I always tell him to have a look around. You know how sweet Augie can be when he puts his mind to it. But she hasn't even opened the door for a peek since that nurse she hired disappeared. She just shouts through the door to him to unload his wagon on the stoop and then mails me the check. And in my opinion, that's hardly a normal way to act in front of a sweet little ten-year-old who's only trying to deliver your groceries. So no, I don't know anything about how she's doing and I've probably let all of you down, but I don't really see as how it's my fault, either. That's all I have to say." Abruptly, she sat.

"You did fine, Teresa," said a voice from the front.

"Birdie and I used to do a little embroidery together back in the old days," said another voice, which Frank recognized as Duncan Griego's, "so I wouldn't mind stopping by to see him sometimes. But Silas K. told us last meeting that Alice never lets anybody in the door except Frank. So *I* say let Frank do the visiting!"

There was applause. Several people called *amen.* Dick banged his gavel. "All right, everybody. Shut up and let's get to the point. Frank? Here's what it boils down to. We're worried about next summer. Is Birdie going to be able to open his motel, you think?"

Frank coughed into his fist. "I believe Alice hopes to have it sold by then."

The members up front groaned and Dick glared at them to stop.

"Now, that's just our point, Frank. The Committee found out that her property isn't on the market. In fact, when I asked Walt, my new deputy chairman here, to call Alice to ask what she wanted for it, she all but hung up on him. So the question is, if she won't sell it and Birdie can't run it, where do our tourists stay next summer? That motel's all we got."

Frank sucked on his teeth. "Do you want me to tell her to sell the motel to you, Dick?"

"Gosh, no, why do that?" called a voice from the front of the room. "Who cares about tourists anyway, right, Sweeny? Let's just start a funny farm up there."

There was loud laughter. Dick was laughing too, but then he caught Frank's look and lifted his gavel, banging it against the desk for quiet.

"We're not making fun of Miss Pinkston, Frank. We're just worried because we want that motel for our tourists next summer. That's why we bought that neon Indian with our own funds back when it first opened, so our customers could find it easier. Second point: Alice doesn't seem interested in talking about real estate. Third point: Birdie doesn't talk at all. See what I mean?"

"I got something to say." Vernan Medina stood. "My biggest customers stay at that motel. I've got a man-and-wife team from the folk art museum in New York coming out here on vacation as soon as the pass opens. They're worth a good nine thousand to me, maybe more. But if they stay at that motel and she walks around acting nuts, why, I could lose them like that." He paused to snap his fingers. "And another thing I want to mention is—"

Dick cut him off with the gavel. "All right, Vern, we got the idea. Frank, what do you think. You got any suggestions?"

"Suggestions?"

"Like which law we use to put her away," cried Betty Johnson. There was laughter and groans, and Dick hammered the table for order. As the room quieted, Frank spotted Eli Sanchez a few rows ahead and off to the left. As he watched Eli's maimed hand scrub at the thick grayish part of his neck, it occurred to him that Eli somehow knew Rose was in Alice's house, and Eli was the only one in the room besides Frank who did, and they were both thinking the same thing, that Rose could run the motel. In the past few days, though he'd seen more and more obvious signs of where she was and why, he'd gone on pretending not to know anything. He wasn't sure why—something to do with the feeling that he owed her this much, that his silence was a show of respect for who she was and what she was trying to do—but since she hadn't chosen to come to him first, he'd have to go to her. He'd have to explain that he'd known all along where she was living and what she was doing, and then they'd have to figure out some way of explaining all that to other people.

He waited until Dick stopped banging his gavel and then he stood. "I understand you all are worried," he said, "but right now I think the Pinkstons deserve to be left in peace for a while. I also believe we'll be able to figure out the motel problem before long. Thank you, folks. I've learned a lot tonight. I'll let you get on with your meeting."

As he pulled on his hat and stepped to the door, the room broke out in noise.

"You can't just leave, Frank. We haven't even started."

"What's he mean, figure out the motel problem?"

"Does he think we're going to let her run it?"

"He's not going to do anything."

Then a voice from the front of the room: "I still say a one-way trip to the nursing home in Madrillas would solve everything. We all know she's got the dough for it. And that old crab's been working for years without spending a dime. I'll bet he's got plenty packed away in his mattress." Frank felt his stomach churn. He turned to the crowd, searching for the owner of the voice.

"Hey, Abel," he called. "You ever been inside that nursing home in Madrillas?"

Abel Steelhead turned to Frank, his jaw pushed out like a boxer's. "I have."

"And you believe the Pinkstons would be better off there than in their own home?"

"I do."

"Well, then, why don't you just go tell them?"

Abel craned back, waving his hands in disgust. "No thank you. I had to put my own mom away. I'm not going through that bullcrap again. That's a family's responsibility."

"They haven't got any family, you idiot," called somebody from the other side of the room. "That's our whole problem."

"Then let Frank do it." Abel looked back at him. "You're the sheriff. That's your job."

Frank looked down before he answered. "That's not my job, and even if it was, from what I've seen I don't believe it's necessary. In fact, Abel," he added, more quietly, "I think if I listen to you, I could be in a hell of a lot of trouble. Weren't you the one who pulled onto my front lawn last Christmas with a bottle of Everclear and told me to get off your property?"

There was laughter. "Fair enough," called Dick from the front of the room. "But you'll let us know, right, Frank? You'll tell us when it's time to start the legal work so we can get her and her brother the help they need?"

"I'll tell you."

Without looking back, he pulled open the door and stepped outside. After the brightness of the meeting hall, it was very dark. He heard his name called and turned. Ruben was standing in the shadow of the building, hopping from foot to foot, hands tucked in his armpits. "You won't let them get to you," he called quietly, "will you, Frank?" Frank grinned and went on up the block with his chin tucked. It was bitter out. He planned to stop by his office, but when he saw Silas through the front window with his feet propped on the desk, he walked on to the corner and stopped beside the squad car. He fiddled with his keys, looking for the right one, got in, and started the engine. He waited a moment and put it in drive and then realized how angry he was and punched it back into park. He was breathing hard and it was snowing.

22

Give me a House that will never decay
And Garments that never will wear away—
Give me a Friend that never will depart
Give me a Ruler that can rule my heart.

—from an American sampler, 1792

One of the things you learn when you lose your family at a young age is adaptability, but I didn't know anything until I lived with Alice. Most of the time when I came out of the attic she thought I was the plumber, though sometimes I was a tourist looking for the rest room and sometimes I was supposed to be fixing the roof. I was also the porter who'd left her luggage in the car, the gardener who'd tracked mud through her house, and the cook she had to fire for drinking too much. Every so often, she knew it was me or, as she put it, "You're the one my brother likes." The more I got the hang of it, the easier it was on all of us. She might start yelling and ordering me around or telling me to get out, but just by going upstairs and coming back down, I could become a whole new person. I was like a book of pictures. If she didn't like what she saw, we both just turned the page.

The dog was a different matter. From the minute I let her see him, he was Buddy, the dog who'd belonged to her sister's kids. Her ideas of who I was could change by the hour, but the dog was always Buddy, naughty little Buddy who'd jumped out of a car to chase a cat one day and never returned, lost forever—and yet by some miracle, there he was again. "Oh my God!" she cried every time he walked in the room. She carried him around like a pocketbook, cooed at him like a baby, fed him whenever he so much as glanced toward the kitchen, and dared anyone to speak above a whisper while he slept. In her eyes, his only flaw was that he was housebroken. Those were her worst times, times when I regretted having introduced them, the way she'd rush to the window, tapping and calling him through the glass, trying to keep him near the house, trying to make him hurry, pushing me out of the way to get to the next window, all but fainting if she lost sight of him. "How can he *do* this," she'd cry, and then, of course, he'd scratch at the door and she'd run to open it, scream *oh my God!* and there'd be a reunion like nothing Lassie ever dreamed of. It ticked me off a little how much the dog enjoyed it. Sometimes I knew he was staying out longer than he needed to just so she'd fall all over him when he came back. Just so she'd grab him up, rocking and snuggling him, telling him how naughty he was, how she missed him, how she'd never let him get lost again. *Thank heavens you're home, Buddy!* Sometimes he'd look up over her shoulder at me and all but wink.

And Birdie? Considering that she didn't always know who he was, she was doing a pretty good job. Because of her training as a nurse, she knew how to dress him, how to lift him, how to give him a bath and shave him, keep him warm. Her only problem was that she couldn't remember what she'd done last, which is why she might try to bathe him three times a day or fix him lunch every half hour. It made me crazy, but then I realized she got much worse when I yelled at her and much better when I didn't. Besides, Bird wasn't helpless. For years, he'd bottled up spite against his sister, and his stroke had finally popped the cork. Now, when he wanted something, all he had to do was throw a tantrum. Sometimes he did it to get his blood pumping, and sometimes just for his own crabby pleasure. I realized that after the electric-powered wheelchair arrived. He waited until the delivery man left and then turned it around and rammed Alice in the shin to get her to stop talking. When she welled up with tears and hobbled past me to the stairs, he and I had our first real argument since his stroke. Maybe he wasn't using words yet, but he was working on them. When I told him to quit being an old bastard, he not only yelled *bastard!* he chased me to the foot of the stairs where Alice was waiting. He liked that chair all right. With the touch of a finger, he could zip in and out of the kitchen before Alice or I could turn around.

But there was one problem he couldn't solve. One morning, while she was giving me a lecture on how to dress him, just as he should've started crabbing about breakfast or wanting a different shirt, he fell asleep instead. When I shook him, he keeled over sideways and snored at the ceiling. It scared the hell out of me. I asked Alice what she'd given him, but she huffed up, grabbed Buddy, and stormed off to her bedroom to type, which is what she did when she was nervous. I put Birdie to bed and ran around the house looking through cabinets and closets and bureaus for anything that looked like it might be a sleeping pill. Then I went and banged on the door to her room.

"Have you got some pills for Birdie in there?"

"Who wants to know?"

"Open the door and I'll tell you."

She opened it a crack, holding a feather duster under her chin. When she opened the door a little wider, I noticed a knobby bulge in the pocket of her sweater. I looked away from it. She was studying my face.

"Didn't I hire you to do the cooking?"

"Yeah, but I'm supposed to check on the pills too. The ones there in your pocket. That's why I'm here."

She was quiet. Then she drew herself up. "*You* give out pills? Why, you're no more of a nurse than the man in the moon!" She threw back her head. "For your information, I saw better nurses when I was in Africa. They *all* say they're nurses over there, you know. Nurses and actors."

When Birdie finally woke up, it was past eight at night, and I'd calmed down enough to think of a plan. I sat on his bed, lacing my fingers through his to bring him awake, his blue eyes blinking slowly and far away. I helped him eat dinner and then, instead of going back up to the attic, which is what I usually did before dark, I jammed his door with the over-stuffed chair and sat down to wait.

At nine-thirty she came and tried the door. She walked up the hall and then came back and tried it again. She discussed the problem with the dog and tried it again. She went downstairs and came back up to try again. She tried four or five times before she finally gave up. When she went in her bedroom, though, she was too keyed up to sleep, I could hear her mutter-ing, getting into bed, getting back out, opening her door to check the hall-way, trying to remember why she was nervous. It went on until I fell asleep.

When I finally jerked awake it was 3 A.M., and when I listened there was nothing outside Birdie's door. I pulled away the chair, sneaked out into the hall, turned on the light, and opened the attic staircase for an escape route. I could hear snoring behind her door. I went to it and eased it open.

I didn't want to see her asleep, it was like seeing somebody dead, her face yellow and everything sunken in and cracked but the bones, mouth wide open. I looked away. Alice was a tidy woman, but because she was hoarding more and more of what she remembered as familiar in her room, everything there was a tumbled mess—in fact, it was worse than the attic. If she hadn't left her sweater hanging like a white flag on the bedpost clos-est to me, I'd never have seen it without turning on the light. I stepped over two footstools, a stack of paintings, and a pile of laundry to get to it, slipped it free, and took it down to the kitchen.

There were three different pill bottles in the pocket: Valium, something called Warfarin, that he was supposed to get once every other day, and a bottle of aspirin. I poured each one into a reclosable plastic bag and put them down the front of my shirt. Then I went to the cupboard where she kept the vitamins and sorted them into the three vials: vitamin C for the aspirin, E for the Valium, B for the Warfarin. She was still snoring when I hung her sweater back on the bedpost, but as I was leaving she suddenly sat up and said, "Who is it? Buddy?" Yes, it's Buddy, I said and walked out and pulled shut the door and waited. After a moment, her light came on under the door and I heard her get out of bed. I jumped for the attic stairs and pulled them up behind me as she came out in the hall. She stood there, listening, and then I heard her go downstairs to call Frank. I felt bad about tricking her, especially when I heard her crying, but I didn't see how else to do it.

Besides, she loved calling Frank. She called him all the time for anything. When he was in her living room, I didn't exist, Birdie wasn't ill, and she hadn't had anyone to talk to in months. I knew this because I'd be up in the attic with my ear to the vent. Not that I liked to eavesdrop, but how else could I know when he was gone again? Besides, I got lonesome. The only other person to drop by the house was Augie Steelhead, who delivered our groceries, and she wouldn't even invite him in for a cookie. Sometimes at the end of a day of bouncing back and forth between Birdie and Alice and the attic, I just wanted to hear somebody normal. That's why I didn't mind her calling Frank with emergencies.

But listening to Frank through the vent ended up being spooky. He sounded too normal. I'd hear him down there agreeing with everything she said, pretending she made perfect sense, pretending they were both on the same track. "I never thought of it like that," he'd say. So polite and gentle, his voice so soft and deep and full of comfort. I decided it meant he knew I was in the house. He had to know. Frank always knew everything. So why couldn't he say so? Was he waiting for me to say something first? Was he thinking that if he ignored me, I'd leave? Did he care? That's why I never tried to stop Alice from calling him. The more he saw of her, the more he'd understand the situation we were in. That's what I kept telling myself. I was only sorry I couldn't tell it to him.

Finally, one day when he was down in the living room, I heard him say my name. Alice was in the kitchen, so I could tell he wasn't talking to her. He called my name twice—*Rose*—and then Alice came back in the living room.

"Did you say something?"

"I was just saying you've got rows of knickknacks here."

Oh, he was smooth.

I changed into clean clothes, tied on my mother's scarf, and got my coat. When I opened the stairway, he was down in the front hall. I could see his boots and the dog sniffing them and his hand on the door. The dog turned and trotted to the foot of the stairs, wagging. I took a deep breath and started down.

"Hi, Frank."

Alice turned to stare, amazed. "I didn't know *you* were still here." She turned to Frank, cupping her mouth in a stage whisper. "She's been upstairs fixing the roof all day, but she's not very good at it."

"I expect not." Frank's dark eyes held mine, but they wouldn't talk to me, not even a little. "I better get going now, Miss Pinkston. I'll see you later."

"Call me Alice. We've known each other forever, haven't we? Good-bye, then." She held out her hand until he shook it, then turned to me and snatched her hand back. "Not *you*."

"The roof's fine," I said, "but I'll have to come back later to make sure."

"As you like." With a sniff, she lifted her chin and marched to the kitchen.

Frank opened the door and I stepped out with the dog. Frank followed, and before I could stop him he'd shut the door, the dead bolt clicking shut.

"Good work," I whispered. "You locked us out."

"I expect if you got in once, you'll be able to get in again."

I don't know why I found that funny. Maybe it was because we were whispering for no real reason, maybe just because I was glad to see him face-to-face. It took effort not to giggle, and then I couldn't help it. Frank shook his head, but he started in too. It felt good. When we stopped, it was still all right. Then I asked how long he'd known.

"I noticed your car in the back yard about a month ago. You been staying up in her attic?"

"Yeah." I pulled on my parka. "I'm sorry. I *was* going to leave."

"I'm glad you didn't."

Then it felt awkward again, as it always did when we hadn't seen each other in a long time. He leaned down to pat the dog while I zipped my coat. There was a foot of snow around the Ten Tribes office across the street and the trees arched overhead, bare and black as iron bars. It looked as if nobody had lived there in years.

"Sometimes I'm the roofer," I said, "and sometimes she thinks I'm the cook or the porter who's forgot her luggage. If I don't wear the scarf, she thinks I'm her sister. It's kind of creepy, being mistaken for a dead woman. That's why I keep it on." I was talking too much.

"She thinks you're Florie?"

"She thinks I'm dead Florie. I guess it's because I cut my hair." I pulled off the scarf to show him. "What do you think?"

"Ah. So you did."

"I'll take that as a compliment." I tied the scarf back on. "I think even if I hadn't cut it, though, she wouldn't be able to remember me. She's coming unfixed, Frank. You can't believe how fast. Every day it seems like she's worse."

"I know." He looked down the hill toward town. "I think everybody knows. That's why I needed to talk to you." He turned to me, and I saw how old his eyes looked. "The Committee met last night. They were discussing what to do about her and Birdie."

"Like it's their business. None of them visit, you know. Bird could be dead for all they care. And Alice, all they do is call up and ask questions to get her confused so they can gossip the next day about how crazy she is. You know what they did last week? Teresa calls in the dead of night, and when I get on the downstairs extension, she's saying, 'Aren't you scared of being alone, Alice? What if somebody broke in and robbed you and Birdie?' Of course Alice spends the rest of the night walking around the house with her padlocks, trying to fix them on all the doors and windows. She thought the whole front yard was full of robbers. She wouldn't even go out to the mailbox the next morning. I got the answering machine out of Birdie's office for her. I figured it was the only way to stop people from scaring her out of whatever wits she has left."

"It's not going to stop them for long. Dick Sweeny called me this morning." Frank turned to the view. "He says that as soon as the pass reopens, the social service people in Madrillas are willing to send someone out to give Alice a competency test."

"They can save themselves the trip. She can't pass any test."

"If she can't," he continued, "the state has a legal responsibility to step in." He turned to look at me. "Depending on how she's diagnosed, Rose, she'll either end up in the state hospital in Albuquerque or the nursing home over in Madrillas. Birdie too, unless we find him another nurse."

I didn't know what to say. I looked out at the dog sitting in the snow with his back to the house. I looked at the motel and back at Frank.

"Birdie's lived here his whole life. And Alice has money. Doesn't that count?"

"Not if they can't take care of themselves."

"So tell the Committee I'm here. Tell them I'm looking after things."

He shook his head. "If I tell them you've been in Alice's home for the past two and a half months, who's going to believe you were here for the right reasons?"

"But I was. Honest to God, Frank. I wouldn't have stayed if she didn't need me."

"I know, but she doesn't remember you."

"So?"

"So everybody else does. They remember you were the one she didn't like. You were the one she locked out of the motel. If you've been living in her house since then, it's only more proof she's not making competent decisions anymore."

I stepped to the railing, shivering under my coat. Frank came up beside me and we stared at the town. "You want to know why this is happening?" he said. "Because the Committee wants to buy the Ten Tribes, but Alice apparently changed her mind about selling it. That's why they're so interested in her welfare all of a sudden."

For the second time, I felt my mouth drop. "The motel isn't for sale?" When Frank nodded, I grabbed his sleeve. "Oh, man, wait until Birdie hears." I let go of his coat and turned to the house. "This is going to make him so happy."

"It's not making the Committee so happy, though. They're afraid if they don't deal with Alice's problems now, she's going to try to run the motel by herself next season."

"I'll run it then," I said, turning to him. "I know how to talk to tourists. I know the motel front to back. And Birdie would approve."

"Yeah." Frank nodded. "That's what *I* was thinking at first, too. But if you do that, who's going to take care of Birdie and Alice?"

"You have an idea?"

"Maybe. Suppose a rumor got started that you might be showing up in town soon, and you might need extra work to tide you over. Wouldn't it be sly of the Committee to send you up here to talk to Alice about a job? After all, they don't have the time or the inclination to deal with her and her brother, and maybe she's just loony enough these days to take you on. And if she did, that would mean they wouldn't have to worry about giving you back your old sales booth. In fact, if they could somehow talk you into dropping embroidery and moving in with the old folks before the season starts, they could tie up a lot of loose ends in one nice neat knot. They'd have a motel ready for tourists, no more guilt about you or the Pinkstons, and it wouldn't cost them a dime."

"The trick is to make the Committee think it's *their* idea."

"That's right. I think I can do that."

"But if I look after Alice, what about the motel?"

"Eli. He said if you're willing to take over Alice full time and make sure he gets a paycheck from her now and then, he'd be interested in running the motel and helping with Bird. Bird would be all right with that, don't you think?"

"Jesus. You've got this all worked out. I guess I should be grateful, huh?"

He gave me a stiff look and turned away. "I'm not offering you charity. It's just the only way I can think to keep them from tearing apart whatever kind of home life Birdie and Alice have left. But if you want to go on hiding in that attic every time the doorbell rings, fine. It's only going to last until somebody else finds out, and then everybody's ass will be cooked, including mine."

"Frank, wait. I meant that I am grateful. Just for myself. I mean it."

His shoulders relaxed and I saw he believed me. I also saw how tired he was, how many hours this had kept him awake.

"I think Birdie's getting better lately," I said. "Have you noticed?"

"Some." He squinted at the view. "You think the liquor's good for him?"

"He's not as sad. I don't give him much and I don't mix it with his pills. Plus I can understand him better when he's a little loose. And you should see him when he gets ticked off. He's like a razorback hog with that new chair. Chases Alice and me all over."

"Good."

"He understands everything. He was the one who told me there was booze hidden in her house. He talks fine when he's forced to it. Mostly fine. He might even be able to run the motel by himself next spring."

"I hope so."

"That reminds me. What happened to the tree he cut down? Is it still lying over there behind the office?"

Frank shrugged. "I was planning to haul it away after you left, but it was already gone. Somebody must have figured it for free firewood."

"Good. I'll tell Birdie. It's one less thing he'll have to cope with next spring."

We looked away from each other.

"I guess I better get back inside," I said.

"Yeah, I better go too." At the bottom of the steps, he turned. "You need anything, Rose? Food or anything?"

What I needed was for him to stay. I shook my head. "You should see how we live. Alice gets three bags of groceries every week. Half of it goes bad. I'm eating like the hogs of Sheba. I bet I eat better than you do now."

"Good. What about cigarettes? You want me to pick some up for you?"

"I kind of quit. She thinks the house is on fire every time I light up. I haven't actually thought about tobacco at all." Then I added, "But thanks, anyway."

He shrugged and looked out toward his car. "You been able to get any embroidery done?"

"I don't know. One big piece on yellow silk, it's almost finished. Birdie helped me with it. It's turning out pretty well."

He nodded, tapping the bottom of the banister as if he were testing to make sure it was in the ground. "If you need anything, I'll stop by as often as I can."

"I know."

He walked to his car, stopped, tapped the hood with his knuckle, and came back to the porch. "One last thing."

"What."

"If you call my office, be careful about talking to Silas."

"I know."

"A lot of folks feel guilty for turning their backs on the situation up here. If something bad happens, the first thing they'll want to do is to find somebody to blame. I'm the most likely target so far, but you'd be even better."

"I know."

"I know you know." He tapped the bottom step and then squinted out at the town. "My dad once said this town works like a piece of embroidery: pull the wrong stitch and the whole piece puckers up. The trick, he used to say, was to turn the piece over and study how the threads were tied together at the back. That way you wouldn't risk cutting the wrong knot and maybe ruining the whole piece." He turned back to me. "I'm thinking that's how I need to handle this," he said. "I need to start thinking in terms of embroidery. Does that sound crazy?"

"No. I always liked your dad."

"He was a great cop, I know that. I wish I was half as good as him."

"You are, Frank. And don't worry. Nothing's going to happen."

After he left, all I had to do was knock on the window and hold up the dog. *"Oh my God!"* she cried, and we were in. She took the dog to the stairs and sat, rocking him baby-style, his eyes rolling to white while she kissed under his chin.

"Oh, Buddy, darling, never get lost, please. Please. Swear on the Bible you won't get lost."

"You want lunch?"

"Aren't you happy enough here?" she cried. "Don't we give you everything? What would my favorite nieces say if I lost you again? Why, they'd never speak to me!"

I leaned on the banister. It was something about the dog, about the way she was kissing him, smothering him with it, the way he was lapping it up, loving every minute. I was angry. "How come you call them your favorite nieces?" I said. "You haven't seen them for thirteen years."

She looked up, amazed. "I haven't?"

"Not that I know of. You sent them away to two different schools back east. What do you call them, finishing schools? Finished them off, all right. They couldn't even come home for Christmas, you sent them so far away." When she tried to look bewildered, I shook my head in disgust. "Come on, Alice. The twins who were planning to grow up with their dad, only you made other plans? Jessie and Andy? Florie's kids? Ring a bell?"

"Oh, oh. That awful man." She narrowed her eyes and pointed. " 'Children are gifts,' I told him. 'Gifts from God, Ben Snow.' And you know what he did? He laughed. Laughed like a wolf. Oh my God, that's right. I'd nearly forgotten." She began rocking, a white look on her face. I cocked my head to watch.

"So that's your excuse for splitting them up? Ben Snow laughs at you, so you decide he doesn't deserve to have kids?"

She jerked back to look at me. "How dare you! Didn't you know him?"

"No. But I used to see him sometimes. Outside the laundromat with a bottle and a workbag full of embroidery, crying about his losses. According to what Birdie told me, he never did truly recover after his kids left. Couldn't get his work done, couldn't pay off debts, couldn't afford friends. And then of course—as you've probably so conveniently forgotten—he parked his Mazda in his garage, plugged up the cracks, turned on the motor, and that was that. That was what taking his kids away did for him."

She shivered away. "I had my own God to answer to. Those poor little lambs. They weren't safe. I was desperate."

"Alice?" I leaned over the banister so she'd look me in the eyes. "I don't buy the angel-of-mercy bit. You didn't really need to save your nieces from anybody, did you?"

"I beg your pardon—"

"You just wanted to play God. You wanted a little excitement in your life and maybe a little revenge too, especially since your sister had ended up with two kids and a husband and you didn't. Isn't that why you decided that Ben Snow was a pervert?"

She reared back. "It is *not*."

"What if I started the same kind of rumor about you? What if I said, 'It seems like Alice probably has sex with her brother'? How'd you like that?"

Her guttered mouth dropped open. "What in the *world*—"

"Because I could, you know. I could drop one juicy little suggestion in the right ear and make everything you and Birdie ever felt for each other look like smut. That's how it works. Matter of fact, they tried it on my uncle. You remember Bob Devonic? There was a time when half the town would've guaranteed you that he was diddling me and my brother. And you know why, Alice? Because my uncle was different. Because when it comes to love, most people don't even want to see the real thing, not when all they have left of their own families is just a lot of hunger and duty and suffering. So they start talking. Why would a man want to take care of kids that weren't even his own? Why did he spend so much time with us out in that little garage? And how come I never got married? And how can I love his memory when everybody else blames him for the accident that wiped out my family? Oh, it's a sure case of child molesting, all right.

"And you know what, Alice? That kind of story doesn't die. It's there forever; it's like a layer of dust in the weave, so that every new stitch you pull into place comes out looking dirty. That's what really gets to me, you know, people like Doc Mutz and Teresa Steelhead. They're still trying to convince me that the one person who loved me and took care of me and made me proud of who I was and taught me how to hope for something better—that he was bad and evil and dangerous for me. Don't you see how unfair and crazy that is, Alice?"

I had to stop to catch my breath. She was giving me a long look.

"Forget it," I said. "I don't know why I'm telling you anyway. You don't even remember Bob."

"Bob? Bob had red hair, a blue denim shirt, an extremely loud voice, and an aggravating way of strutting down Tambour every morning shouting *hello!* as loudly as possible to everyone he met." She paused, as if listening. "He was also a very thorough repair man."

I blinked. "You remember that?"

Instead of answering, she turned her eyes to the door. "He offered to fix my refrigerator once. I remember because when he rang the doorbell, he had an enormous toolbox under one arm and a baby under the other. It was a beautiful baby, a tiny thing with big brown eyes. He put it on the floor next to his knees while he worked."

I'd come back to the banister. "You mean Kyle."

"Yes . . . I think the name was Kyle." But I could see the memory was skipping. She tried again. "I think so. I invited him for lunch, but he wouldn't stay. He just wanted his money. He never did come back. Maybe he was involved with another woman."

I leaned forward. "*You* liked Bob?"

"What's so shocking about that? I was young then. He was a bit too short and perhaps a little too talkative for my taste, but certainly a very eligible bachelor. I thought he liked me too. . . ." Her voice trailed off, and she looked at me sharply. "He was no child mobster. You have my word on that."

"You mean molester."

"That's what I said." She clucked to herself. "He was nothing like that horrible Ben Snow."

I groaned and sagged on the banister. "But that's my point, Alice. You start a rumor that Ben Snow is a pervert and you ruin his whole life. Isn't it possible that he was a good father but you didn't understand why? And even if *you* hated him, can't you see that his kids needed him?" I paused, because she looked as if she might faint. "Look, can't you at least admit he was human?"

Her whole face was shaking. She pushed the dog off her lap and stood up, groping for the banister. "I saw what I saw," she cried. *"I saw!"* She stared at me, as if to see what I was going to do about it, and then covered her mouth and fled to the living room.

I sighed and leaned against the wall. Maybe she *had* seen something. Or maybe she'd cut me off because she knew she was wrong. Or maybe she'd suddenly realized that she didn't know what the real story of Ben Snow was. Whatever the case, I could see she felt it right to the bone. I pushed off the wall and followed her into the living room. She was standing behind the curtain with one hand over her eyes and the other over her mouth.

"Okay, Alice, don't cry. I shouldn't blame you like that. For all I know, you did the right thing for those kids. I just get touchy about rumors, that's all. I'm sorry. Honest."

After a long moment, she turned, tears tracing her wrinkles. "If you're so sorry, where's Buddy?"

When I called him, she snatched him up, glaring at me. "This is *their* dog," she hissed, "and *I'm* the one who takes care of him."

I went in the kitchen, looked down at a pink shoe she was storing in the sink, and went back out to the living room.

"Any chance you remember where your nieces are now, Alice?"

"No." She leaned to peek around the edge of the curtain, and the dog blinked over her shoulder at me. "They may be coming to visit, though."

"Don't they ever call here?" I waited. "Maybe you have an address book where we might find their address. A telephone number somewhere?" I waited. "Alice? Are you listening?"

"Why can't you see the price of my life?" When she turned, her face was twisted with fury. "I forget, all right? I forget because none of it is something I was supposed to remember." And then she lost the thread, I could see it happen, and when she fought to get it back, she found nothing. "Well?" she blurted out finally. "Isn't it high time you fixed the roof?"

23

By mid-March the snows had begun to taper off, and as soon as the pass reopened, Angela packed up the flowered suitcase she'd come with and disappeared. In a note Frank found taped to the mirror, she said she'd caught a bus to Denver to go to a friend's funeral and she'd return in two weeks. She didn't mention the friend's name or leave a number, and he waited a week before admitting to himself that she had no friend in Denver, no funeral to go to, and no intention of coming back. She'd only wanted a head start.

It was a strange feeling to be alone in the house again. In the year and a half since their marriage, he'd encouraged her to do over the house and given her money for it, but nothing had changed. It was almost as if she'd never been there—the same furniture, the same rugs, the same dishwasher and toaster, even the same pictures he'd known since childhood. Yet somehow none of it felt familiar anymore. The couch, for instance. How many times had he done his homework on it, opened Christmas presents on it, napped and read books on it? His mother making it into a bed for him back in grade school, when he had the chicken pox, and the Sunday afternoons spent sitting on it with his father to watch football. Not to mention all the nights his mother had waited up for his father to come home, sitting under a cone of light at the end of it, her blanket over her legs, her magazines on her lap, her radio on. Under the last reupholstery job, there was a stain from where he'd spilled a glass of red wine at her wake. That couch had been in his family longer than he had, a whole history mashed and pressed and spilled into its cushions, and yet somehow when he looked at it now, all he could think was that was probably just something else about him that Angela had hated. He sat on it to look through his address book for her parents' number in Albuquerque.

He'd met the McCombs only once, a small, cherry-faced, aim-to-please sort of couple who'd introduced themselves as Mom and Dad, held hands through most of the civil wedding ceremony, and left immediately afterward without saying good-bye or even asking for his phone number. Angela had referred to them as the Hansel and Gretel from Hell, the bitterness in her voice almost choking her. Still, they were her parents. They had a right to know. He dialed the number and waited. Somewhat to his relief, Angela's mom answered.

"Hi, Helen. This is Frank Doby." He waited. "Your son-in-law. Angela's husband?"

"Oh, yes, of course!" she cried. "How silly of me! Wait a minute, I'll go get Dad."

Angela never talked about her childhood, but Frank had always pictured it with air-conditioning, venetian blinds, peach-colored carpets, silence, maybe a doorbell that played, and plastic covers on the lampshades and floors. Like a mortuary, he suddenly realized. Flowered wallpaper and floral air fresheners, a soft humming sound under the floor.

"So how you doing, son? Got any spring weather up there yet?"

"Hey, Kenny." He tried for the word Dad, but it did not come. "I hope this isn't too early in the morning to call."

"Couldn't be better," Helen piped up. "Could it, Dad?"

"Go ahead, son. Talk away. You know how much we like you. What's on your mind?"

"I was just wondering. Angela left here a week ago saying she was on her way to Denver, and I haven't heard from her since. I was wondering if you knew anything."

On the end of the line, there was a stunned silence and then a click.

"You still there?"

"I'm here," said Kenny. "My wife——" He hesitated. "Helen doesn't like this kind of news."

"I'm sorry. Angela hasn't called there, has she?"

"No. That's not unusual, though. We don't know much about Angela's private life. She likes it that way."

"Well. I just want to tell you that I don't think she's coming back here. She took everything she came with."

He expected Kenny's concern and grief, questions, and offers of advice and consolation. Maybe even anger. Instead there was a heavy pause on the line. Kenny cleared his throat.

"I'm going to ask you something, and I don't mind honesty. Did you kick her out?"

"No. She just left."

"All right." He sounded as if he was steeling himself. "So what'd she take? Furniture? Money? Your car?"

"No, Kenny. I just thought you should know she's gone."

Another silence.

"I guess you think Helen and I are pretty shoddy parents."

"No, sir. I don't think that."

"Because we tried, Frank, let me tell you. All the best schools, the nicest clothes, trips, cars, dresses, anything she wanted. We even agreed to send her to cooking school in California a few years ago, and believe me, *that's* money. And you know what she did for us in return? She came here while my wife and I were on vacation in Honolulu and cleaned us out. I don't mean just money. Every stick of furniture, every curtain, every appliance, every rug, every piece of clothing. She hired movers, you understand? The andirons, the deed to the house, the photo albums. She even took all the covers off the light fixtures. And what did she decide to leave us? A fork. One lousy plastic fork, Frank. That was her idea of humor. So don't come crying to us with your problems. We've been through it, Helen and I. Angela took everything we had. We were getting ready to retire until she decided to drop by for a visit."

He was wheezing a little. Frank didn't know what to say.

"Was she on medication then, Kenny?"

"You mean drugs? How should I know? Fred Tiersol said she was. According to him, she was taking everything she could get her hands on, legal or otherwise. 'Course, we didn't believe him. Back then, we still refused to believe anything they said about our daughter. Not Angela, no way. No, we decided to blame our fourteen-year-old, Teddy, for what she'd done. We took him down the police station and told him to confess or we'd disown him right there on the spot. That did wonders for our relationship with him, believe me. Then we went around to the pawnshops trying to find our things. That's how we discovered the truth. They gave us her description right down to the minute."

"Did you ever confront her?"

"Hell, no. My wife and I may be gullible, but we're not complete fools." There was a pause. "Are you telling me she didn't take *anything*?"

"I don't know," said Frank. "I haven't really thought about it."

"Well, if I were you, I'd lock my doors. If she's on one of her rampages, she'll be back when she needs more money. And she won't just take what you give her, she'll take everything. Helen and I don't think of her as our child anymore. We can't afford to. We offered our love for her up to God and He took it, that's how we see it now. Helen, honey, you want to add something?"

Frank heard crying in the background. Kenny came back on.

"You're a good kid, Frank. We thought so the day we met you. Too good for something like this. Good luck." And the line went dead.

He lay back on the couch, staring at the snow falling in heavy flakes outside the front window. Andirons? Light fixture covers? The only reason would be to cause a reaction. That was what Angela had always needed, more than she needed drugs or money. She needed a reaction.

That's why she'd left his house intact, he was sure of it. Why steal from someone who wouldn't notice what was missing and wouldn't care if it was? He *wouldn't* care, would he? He looked around the living room, trying to think, and ended up staring at the desk. Some things he'd care about. His father's badge, for instance. If it was missing, he didn't want to know, but if he didn't go over there and check, he wouldn't be able to sleep.

He ran his hands through his hair and hauled himself off the couch. The desk was a heavy old-fashioned piece that had belonged to his grandparents, a rolltop that still opened and closed with a smooth, satisfyingly quiet movement. With one finger he pulled open the little drawer above the pigeonholes on the right, and his heart sank. How could she have known that out of everything he had in this house, a whole lifetime of memories, this one little piece of metal would be something he would miss? He hadn't told her how much it meant to him. He hadn't even shown it to her. The way she'd so easily dismissed her own past had made him hesitant to tell her anything about his own. He'd tried once, but talking about his parents felt too much like he was bragging, parading his good luck, shoving it in her face. After their marriage, he'd hidden that part of himself away, never quite sure whether he was protecting her or his own memories.

Then he thought of something else he didn't want to lose. He closed his eyes and then opened them and turned to look up at the top shelf of the bookcase. Of course he was right. The photo of his father and Rose and himself on the front steps of the house in the spring of '84 was gone.

24

Remember man thou art but dust
From Earth thou came to Earth thou must.

—from an American sampler, 1756

I didn't realize the situation, how heavy the weight of it was getting. I knew I was feeling crazy sometimes from being around Alice so much, not enough sleep, nothing else to think about and nowhere to go, and Birdie so hard to talk to. Sometimes, when she wouldn't leave me alone, I'd feel the tiredness building up and pushing me down and I'd yell at her to be quiet and, if she wouldn't, I'd crawl up into the attic and close the stairway with the rope tucked inside so she couldn't open it. Birdie would be growling at me through the vent in his bedroom and she'd be wandering around downstairs all confused and not able to remember why. But I just couldn't care. "She's *your* sister," I'd tell Bird. Sometimes I'd look in the mirror up in the attic and think that out of all the people Alice thought I was, I wasn't anybody. Just as much of a ghost as the rest of my family. Sometimes I'd break things up in the attic just to feel them break, and sometimes, for no reason, I'd start crying and hating my life for what it was supposed to have been and what it wasn't and what I was ending up with instead.

But after I found out that Frank was counting on me, everything was easier. Maybe that's all there really is to happiness, not money or a big house or friends or even love, just knowing somebody out there is counting on you. The very next morning, I got up early and made scrambled eggs, bacon, and biscuits for everybody. When Alice came down and found breakfast made and me and Bird already eating, she flew into high gear, wringing her hands and throwing fierce glares at us, a dozen trips to the door to check the lock, a dozen trips to the stove to sigh over the pan I'd used, to wonder whether she should let it soak or not, to ask when I was leaving. I would've ended up in a yelling match with her before, but now everything came clear. I wasn't what pissed her off. It was her memory. It was the fact that every time she tried to grab on to something familiar, it came apart like a crust of sand sifting through her fingers. All she had left to depend on anymore were the daily habits she'd practiced all her life—and what had I done? I'd decided to get up early and cook breakfast. With a wave of the spatula, I'd thrown her off everything about mornings that she knew as familiar. When I looked at it that way, her actions made perfect sense. She was only trying to hold on to what she had left of her life and make it enough. She was no different from any of us.

Still, I had things to do. After breakfast, I handed her the dog for comfort and cleaned the kitchen. Then I took out the vacuum and started on the living room. I hadn't had a home to clean since I was a kid, and it was a fine thing. I went from one end to the other and then upstairs. From here on out, if anybody came to visit, they'd think Alice was born with a broom in her hand. She was on my heels the whole time, unplugging the vacuum when I wanted it on, plugging it in when I was finished, ordering me to do this or forget that, chattering and nervous, and, after her, Birdie, leaning sideways in his chair to watch. When I was done cleaning, I changed the beds and then went through the house again, collecting laundry. It was everywhere, including under the sofa and along the windowsills behind the curtains and behind the refrigerator. "So," Alice sniffed as I piled everything in the front hall, "I see you're stealing clothes now. Fine."

"I'm going across the street to the motel to do laundry. I'll be right back."

She laughed bitterly. "You expect me to believe that?"

"Yeah." I snapped open a trash bag and started filling it with clothes. She stood in front of me, rocking the dog.

"How can I possibly believe you?" she burst out. "If you were doing laundry, you'd do it here."

I stopped stuffing the bag. "You have a washing machine?"

"Well, I'm rich, aren't I?" She stopped, her face dropping in horror. "You don't mean to say somebody sneaked in the basement and stole my brand-new washer and dryer?"

She was right. Under a bedspread in her basement, in the corner under the stairs next to an old-fashioned metal laundry sink, I found a washer and dryer with the price tags still on. I dropped the bag of laundry and flipped open the washer. Inside was a box of soap and some books.

"Excuse me," she called from the top of the stairs, "but if you're looking for money, you certainly won't find it down there."

"I'll be right up." I pulled the books out of the washer. One was called *When Half Is Whole*. Another one was titled *Stroke: A Practical Guide Towards Recovery*. I filled the washing machine with laundry, poured in some soap, figured out the dials, and headed upstairs with the books. "We're going to school, Alice."

Back when I was sent to stay with the Dobys after the accident, I read every book they owned. Frank's dad said it was a sign of intelligence, but he was wrong. Reading was a way to erase memory, not improve it. I could finish a book and not have a clue what it was about. I could read something twice in a row and not even remember the title. Following the words, that's what I liked, watching them come and go, word by word, line by line, page by page. It was like counting backward into a trance. The first winter I lived with Birdie, I got through the *Book of Knowledge*, A through Z, in four and a half months, and when it was over I walked away without knowing a single new thing. Since then, so as not to end up with the kind of eyestrain that ruins an embroiderer's future, I'd taught myself to stay away from books with small print that took more than an hour to read; but now, with winter almost over and no embroidery to show for it except the yellow silk magpie, which I'd already decided to give to Birdie on his birthday, I just couldn't see as how my career on the needle mattered that much. I took the books up to Birdie's room, planning to read them all.

But my housekeeping had boiled up Alice's nerves and she kept interrupting, trying to find the thread that would lead her back to what was familiar by asking what time it was or when I was going to leave or why I hadn't fixed the roof yet or did I need lunch. Over and over. I tried handing her a book, but she couldn't seem to fix on the idea. I put on the radio, and she kept thinking it was someone singing. Then Birdie needed to get on the john, and while I was in with him, Alice heard the washing machine buzzer in the basement and decided that somebody had rung the doorbell, and then Birdie wanted his shot of brandy in milk and Alice was piling clothes in the hall, trying to decide what to take and how many porters we'd need, and it went on like that pretty much straight through until I had to make dinner.

Finally, at ten-thirty that night, Birdie was in bed snoring and Alice was calm enough to sit in front of the TV with the dog on her lap to hold her there. I got some paper and a pen and settled in the kitchen. I'd decided to do it right, to stop at the bottom of every page, look up to think, and then write something about it. It was the only way I could read without missing the whole point. I listened for noises in the house and then opened the first book about strokes.

But trying to read slowly when you haven't had time to read is like holding back hunger. It's like having a meal in front of you and knowing you should be polite and use a fork, when all you really want to do is lean over and shovel it in with both hands. But as I went along, I realized I wasn't reading just anything. I was reading about Birdie and what he was going through and what he'd survived. I was reading what I should have already known, all the information I should have gotten ages back, before Birdie ever got home from the hospital. By the third chapter I wanted to go wake him up and tell him so. I hadn't done anything right. I hadn't even tried. When I read that he wasn't able to move his dead hand because he couldn't know where it was unless he looked at it, I covered my face. What had I been thinking, that this was a game? That Birdie would get well just because I loved him? I started a list: a full-length mirror in his room, the side bar up on the right side of his bed so he wouldn't worry about falling out, the radio to listen to, ways to make him do exercises. I'd bring the fan down from the attic so he could feel a breeze, I'd read to him to keep his mind busy. The more I wrote, the more I wanted to slam down the book and do the whole list at once, right then. Somehow make up for my ignorance, for all the time I'd wasted, for all the help I hadn't given him. I felt as tight as a coiled spring. It was like the letters Frank had written from Panama. Instead of sending them, he'd brought them all home afterward and told me to read them, so I had, and I'd written an answer to every one so I'd never forget them, and then burned everything, all of it, all in one night. The difference, of course, was that Frank's letters had been about things that couldn't be fixed, a relationship nobody could save. Birdie, on the other hand, had a chance. According to this book, a good chance. I flexed my hand, stared up at the clock over the stove without seeing it, and went back to reading.

Books couldn't solve everything, of course. I made him a beanbag, for instance, just like they said to buy, but when I told Birdie to squeeze it, he glared at me as if I'd lost my mind. When I put up the bar on his bed so he wouldn't fall out at night, he banged on it until I put it down, and when I propped the full-length mirror in his bedroom, he turned his chair to the wall, tears leaking down the gutters of his face. But he was dead set on learning how to talk again. He made me read those chapters of the book aloud twice, and though he groaned with despair when I came to the part about using a mirror, he eventually locked himself in the bathroom with a screwdriver to get his shaving mirror off the wall. When he couldn't do it alone, he came out in a rage, ran over my foot, and wheeled himself into Alice's bedroom. He backed out a minute later with a rouge compact in his lap, and after a lot of growling and groaning and chasing me with his chair, he got me to understand that he needed me to fix the compact with a piece of embroidery thread so he could wear it around his neck. It worked, too. Watching his mouth in the mirror, he could make words slide out, sometimes whole sentences. Most of what he said was rude, especially when he was frustrated, but it was a relief to see that even if his body didn't work right yet, at least his personality was still normal. And once I realized that the more ticked off he got, the more he had to say about it, our speech lessons got interesting.

"If you want your bourbon and milk," I'd say, "you're going to have to say something nice about me. Go ahead. I have lots of nice qualities. Pick one and then say it so I understand."

"Yawrr tarch me!" he'd yell at his mirror.

"I starch you? What are you, laundry?"

"Yawrr tarching me!"

"Yes, I'm teaching you, and aren't you the cheerful young man. Now watch me say it and then look in the mirror and say it yourself. I'm teaching you."

"Naw!" he'd yell, and then he'd twist his face all kinds of ways at the mirror. "Tar . . . tawr . . . tawr . . ."

"Tired? How can you be tired if all you do is sit there?"

"Tawrsher," he'd snarl, "tawrsher."

"Tar shirt?" And then I'd pretend to yawn. That would drive it out of him.

"Taw-chur! Tow-shur! *Torture!*"

He'd fall back in his chair and we'd grin at each other. He was coming right along.

But during that month, as Birdie worked to get better, Alice only got worse. She wanted to help her brother, but her own needs drove her too hard. Thieves were everywhere, she couldn't find her pocketbook, I'd stolen the luggage, someone was at the door, her brother wasn't breathing;

she still had to pack for the trip, take my temperature, fire the cook. One night as I was falling asleep, I heard an engine start up and I got down to the garage just in time to keep her from leaving for Africa with the dog and a pink vinyl suitcase full of pasta. Nothing else, just pasta. When I caught her leaving twice more, I stole her car keys and hid them in my pillowcase. Then I realized she wasn't sleeping at night anymore, and I decided I had to move out of the attic and take the bedroom next to hers. It wasn't something I wanted, not by a long shot, not with her wandering around like a ghost in her nightgown worrying about danger, coming in to whisper me awake, three, four, sometimes even five times a night, her face leaning over me, sick with terror. But what else could I do? I'd hear her on the phone after midnight, sobbing to Frank that we'd been robbed, and when I'd run downstairs and grab the receiver from her to tell him to forget it, no one would be there. The second time she tried this trick, I was mad enough to tell her so. She wailed and sank down on the edge of her suitcase. "*He's* been robbed too?" That was the night, after I took her up to her room, tucked her in with the dog and her suitcase, that I unplugged the phone and took the cord to my room. When I woke up the next morning and felt her car keys under my head and the phone cord twisted around my foot under the sheets, it seemed as if we were both going crazy, that in another few months we'd have everything in the house divided in half and hoarded in our bedrooms. On the other hand, it was the only way I could get enough sleep.

Frank helped as much as he could. He called Teresa's store to change our grocery orders, he bought Birdie's liquor and refilled his prescriptions, and after studying a pile of bills Alice had stuffed in the back of her desk, he came down from her study with a line of checks for her to sign and then drove around town delivering them. When I mentioned that Birdie's heat lamp had died, he borrowed a heating lamp from the beauty shop. I gave him Alice's extra key so he could let himself in and out. Most of his visits he spent downstairs, letting her fret and flirt and make him tea, which gave me time with Birdie. Some days I was so busy, I never even called hello to him, but I was always grateful for his visits. Alice trusted him all the way, no matter who she thought he was, and on the days when she was wound up about robbers and me catching cold and whether or not Birdie needed his pills, the sound of Frank letting himself in the back door was a gift to us all.

One night after a long sermon from Bird about underwear that I never quite understood, I went down to make dinner and found Alice sitting on the couch with the dog on her lap, her eyes closed, and her mouth open. Frank was standing behind her, brushing her hair. Not her wig, her real hair, little yellow-white wisps, like leavings from the barber's floor gathered up and glued together. He didn't speak, and neither did I. I sat in the Queen Anne, kicked off my shoes, and leaned back. It was almost dark in the room.

"She sure trusts you," I said.

Her eyes shot open. "Didn't I fire you yet?"

"Yeah, but I'm still here." I pointed to Frank. "So's he."

She twisted around. "Who are you?" she demanded.

"I'm Frank Doby," he said.

She turned back. "Why are we in the dark? Did the porters steal my fuses again?"

"No." I leaned over and turned on the lamp. "You know what Birdie did today, Frank? I was getting him out of his bath and he goes, 'Where's my goddamn dinner anyway?' It came smooth as silk, not even using the mirror, every word."

"You're doing a good job, Rose."

"Birdie's the one doing it."

"You'd better check the fuse box," said Alice. "I wouldn't put it past those porters to steal every fuse I own."

"Porters don't steal fuses," I said. "And see the light? It's on."

"But what if it goes off?"

"Then we send Buddy to the store for more."

"You'll do no such thing! My dog is not to leave this house!"

"Say, Alice," said Frank, in an easy quiet voice. "Would you like your hair brushed?"

She looked at him in astonishment. "Aren't you Frank Doby?"

"Yes, I am."

"Well, then, fine." She faced forward again, readjusted Buddy on her lap, and closed her eyes. "I don't mind having my hair brushed," she murmured. "It's like driving with the top down, don't you think?"

"I do."

I watched him brush her hair. He was very careful.

"She'd never have let you do that a month ago," I said.

He shrugged. "A month ago I'd never have thought to offer."

I watched him brush her hair for a while and then said, "You know what she's been doing lately, Frank? Putting me to bed."

He nodded. "She told me."

"Every night she comes to me now. 'Isn't it bedtime for little chickens?' she says. Tucks me in, kisses me on the nose. In a weird kind of way, I'm getting to like it. If she'd stick to doing it only once a night, I'd probably like it a lot more."

I closed my eyes. Birdie wanted dinner, but I just wanted to sit another few minutes. Alice couldn't make it through a single night anymore without waking me at least once. When I didn't wake up fast enough to answer her questions, she'd go to work on Birdie. I wondered if Frank would consider spending a night or two in the house so I could catch up on sleep, and then I remembered that he couldn't because he was married. Nothing would stop her. I felt myself falling, jerked back, and opened my eyes. Alice had slipped back against the couch, her face slack as if she'd died, her breath coming out in little snores.

"The other night while she was doing the bedtime thing," I whispered, "just as she leaned over to say good night, she had one of those memory flashbacks. 'You're not my daughter,' she said. So I told her I was there because of Birdie. She thought that was all right, but then she goes suddenly quiet and says, 'It's not working, is it? Pretty soon everything's going to start falling apart.' 'No it's not,' I say, and she goes, 'Yes, it is.' She was so sure, so clear on it. It was spooky. Made me wonder if she wasn't seeing into the future for a minute. You think that's possible?"

"Could be. Since she's able to time-travel backward so easily these days, maybe she knows how to go forward, too." He shrugged. "Though maybe what she remembers of the past just sounds like the future sometimes."

"That's even scarier."

"For some people."

He was still brushing her hair, each stroke taking up less and less hair, lighter and lighter.

"You want dinner, Frank?"

"You're too tired to cook."

"We're all tired," I said. "You just keep her busy, will you?"

He nodded. "Nothing fancy."

I pushed to my feet, went into the kitchen, and closed the door.

I don't know why it's nice cooking for a man, but it is. I cooked burgers with Bermuda onions, red potatoes, and peas. We usually ate off TV trays in Bird's room, but I got out a blue-and-white checkered tablecloth instead and set the table. Birdie needed a Tupperware bowl and a plastic cup, which kind of ruined the effect, but I used Alice's silver and china on the rest of the table and put an orange candle in the center.

When dinner was ready, Alice was spread lengthwise on the sofa with a throw rug tucked around her, her head resting on her wig and Buddy curled up behind her knees. Frank was over by the knickknack shelf, holding one of the glass birds to the light. I pointed upstairs for him to go get Birdie. After he left, I pushed back my mother's embroidery scarf, stole Alice's hairbrush, and hurried back to the kitchen to use the glass door on the toaster oven as a mirror. I brushed hard. The haircut was getting better, but a cowlick I'd never known about stood straight up like a firecracker. I glanced at the table behind me and then back to the toaster oven, and then I just stopped.

A linen tablecloth? A meal by candlelight? Frank would be polite about it, but he'd never come back. All he wanted was dinner. I blew out the candle and hid it under the sink, but as I started to grab the china plates off the table, I saw him leaning in the door.

"Smells good."

I placed the china back on the table, my face hot. "Where's Birdie?"

"He's as asleep as Alice. Should I wake him?"

"We had a long night last night. Alice was busy as hell. Better let him sleep."

I served the burgers and told him to sit.

Frank and I had eaten together plenty of times: at the Magpie, at town picnics and embroidery fairs, at holidays and weddings and funerals, and sometimes out at the booths, too. Not to mention all the meals we'd shared as kids: at school, on the playground, on the bus, in cars, at the overlook, at his parents' house, at my mother's house, a few times on top of Red Mountain. But in the quiet of Alice's kitchen, with me serving on fancy china and him the guest of honor, it was a nightmare. I had nothing to say. It was a joke even trying, the whole thing a big fat joke, and when he not only tried to pretend it wasn't, but bit into his burger and moaned how good it was, I started to get angry. When he took another bite and made the same noise, I banged down my knife.

"It's just food. Why make such a big deal about it?"

"Because I'm hungry. And it's good food."

"Of course, it's good. You think I'd poison you?"

He swallowed and then laughed. "If you wanted to poison me right now, Rose, you'd probably have to get in line." He sighed and looked down at his burger and then grinned again. "God, you remember the first time you came to live at my parents' house, when your mom was having your baby brother? You remember those dinners? And playing Parcheesi afterward? Remember how we used to laugh? My dad used to say he'd never met a kid that could make him laugh like you could."

I felt all the cold drain away and then a quick, hard heat rushing into its place. "Your dad never said that."

"He did. He said it all the time. So did my mom."

I couldn't help myself. "Really?"

"Yeah. You remember." He lifted his burger again. "I'm sorry they're not here now."

"It's just as well. There's nothing to laugh at now."

"Sure, there is."

"What?"

"Your haircut."

"Bastard."

We laughed.

"No, I like it, Rose. Honest. It's different but I like it."

"Stop."

"Okay. I'm just glad to be here eating dinner. That's all."

That was the thing about Frank—just when you least expected it, he could slap his feelings so hard on the table, it made your eyes water. He took another bite and so did I. Then he pushed back his chair.

"What do you think about a beer?" he said. "I've got a six-pack out in my car."

While he was gone, I had another bite. It *was* good, crisp and juicy. But as I watched myself in the toaster oven, squeezed sideways, happily chewing away, it occurred to me that I'd been had. Frank was such a perfect bullshitter, such a crowd pleaser, such a liar. By the time he came back with the beers, everything inside me was stone. I watched him open the refrigerator and crouch to fit them inside.

"You must think I'm an idiot."

"What?" He glanced over his shoulder.

"I'm supposed to believe that line about your parents? About how much they liked having me around?"

"Why wouldn't they?"

I snorted. "Well, for one thing, they tossed me out like two bits' worth of dirty rags after my family died."

Frank straightened, holding a beer in each hand. "What are you taking about? After your family died, you lived with us."

"And for how long? A month? Wow. Your folks sure gave it the old college try, didn't they?"

He came to the table and sat. "But you're remembering it wrong. You didn't want to stay. You told everybody. *You* were the one who wanted to leave."

"Yeah, sure." I dropped back against my chair. "I'm sixteen years old with no family, no home, no future, and instead of choosing a nice little picket-fence home with a normal mom and dad like yours, I'd rather go live in an empty motel with an old hermit I don't even know who hates kids? Somehow that's hard to believe, don't you think?"

"Maybe it's hard to believe, but it's what happened. You said you didn't want to stay. *You* made the choice. You said our house was too crowded and you didn't like sleeping in the attic, and you didn't want to sleep on the couch. Rose. You think I wouldn't remember something like that? My parents didn't want you to leave. Hell, they were talking with a lawyer in Madrillas about legally adopting you."

I sat very still, watching him open the beers. Was that how it went? In those days, my mind had tended to fall away sometimes—not like daydreaming but something scarier, like a cloud coming in the room, getting thicker and thicker until I couldn't hear or see anything and didn't know what was going on anymore. Sometimes it only lasted a few minutes, but sometimes I lost whole scenes, even whole days. It had happened a lot while I'd lived with the Dobys. I closed my eyes, trying to think. I could remember a radio playing opera in the kitchen and me on the couch pretending to read and watching Frank and his mom set the table. Frank's dad used a cane, and I could remember staring at the words in my book because of shyness as he walked by, and how he grabbed my toe to wag it hello and then went to the table and kissed Mrs. Doby and sat next to her while Frank finished setting the table. And then some time passed and there I was, taking my bag from Frank and following Birdie Pinkston across the courtyard at the motel, not only suddenly freed from the problems of being an unwanted house guest but, for the first time in my life, holding a key to my very own home, a little log cabin named the Ute.

"Even if I did say I wanted to leave," I tried, "your parents didn't exactly bar the door, did they?"

"How could they? You said you wanted to be an embroiderer. Nobody in my family could teach you that." Frank put a Heineken in front of me and leaned back to drink from his own. "My parents sure argued about it, though. My mom said you didn't know what you were doing, and my dad said you'd had too many people telling you that. He said if you had a plan,

we shouldn't try to talk you out of it just because we didn't understand it."
He picked up his burger. "I don't think he was happy about it, though."

I swallowed hard and looked at my plate. "Were you?"

"Me?" He grimaced and shook his head. "I was just being a teenager. I
didn't know how to handle your family being dead. I couldn't even think
about it. All I could focus on was the idea that if you moved out of our
house, you and I might be able to . . . you know. Be the same as we were
before the accident. That seemed to me to be the answer to everything.
That's why the more my parents talked about adopting you, the less I liked
the idea. I didn't want to have to start thinking of you as just my sister."
He sighed, shook his head again, and bit into his burger. "Eat, Rose. This
is good."

But I couldn't. One of the things he didn't know was that even if his
parents had adopted me, I'd never have been just his sister. On the night I
lost my mother, my uncle, and Kyle, I was eight weeks' pregnant, and
when I realized I was the only one to survive the accident—the only one
out of five people to walk away from that night without so much as a
scratch—I knew the reason. I'd been saved so Frank and I could have the
baby. Or Frank and I were going to have the baby so I could be saved.
Either way, it didn't matter. I'd found out why I was still alive. As long as
I had that baby in me, I was safe. I was all but bulletproof. That's why I
didn't want to stay on with Frank's parents, because I didn't need a family
for safety and love and protection anymore, I had all that inside me.
Stronger than family, stronger than love and fate and death. I was stronger
than death. That's why I even went ahead and named the baby. Ray, I
called him—because he'd made me like an X ray, like a ray of light shining straight and sure from who I'd been to who I'd be, from the way life
was to the way life was supposed to work—and that's why I decided to
learn embroidery, too, because when they told me I couldn't make it as an
embroiderer, I knew suddenly I could and had to prove it; and after a
month of searching for a teacher and being turned down by every inheritance embroiderer in town, still so sure of myself and still waiting to tell
Frank why, I ended up at the Ten Tribes taking lessons from a crabby-
assed old bachelor too lovestruck by my dead mother to turn me out,

where one day shortly after I'd arrived, I put away my embroidery and marched out to my little cabin, my little home in the woods, and locked the door and crawled into bed and woke up in the middle of that night to find a pool of blood under the blankets. Almost as if my little ray of light and surety, my last little Ray, had known enough to wait for a place of his own and just enough privacy before he'd let the floodgate open to swim out, at last, into the world.

I watched Frank finish and then lean back to put his plate on the floor for the dog. I was glad he didn't know. It would've made everything between us that much harder for him to get over. Besides, as soon as I'd realized I was having a miscarriage, I'd known that it wasn't a baby named Ray coming out. It wasn't even a baby. It was just the last part of me to survive the accident. Or maybe just the little bloody leftover chunk of what I had believed in after the accident. Whatever it was, by the time it came out, I could see it had nothing to do with anything I wanted to remember.

"You want another beer, Frank?"

"Maybe." He lifted my beer. "You haven't touched yours. And you're not eating. You okay?"

"Have another beer," I said.

"Okay. I've only got a half day to work tomorrow. I will."

The way he pushed up from the table, set his plate on the sink, and swung open the refrigerator to lean inside, everything about him so different from me, so easy and graceful. I got up and took my own plate to the sink.

"You can use the phone in the hall to call home, Frank."

"Hmm?"

"If you need to call, to tell your wife where you are or something. Isn't she going to worry?"

He didn't answer. When I turned, he was still leaning on the refrigerator door, looking into the fridge, the dog wiggling all around his heels. He closed the refrigerator and turned. His eyes looked black against his skin, almost like holes. He looked past me at the window as if somebody had tapped on it. Then back at me. "Did I put that bottle opener somewhere?"

I found it next to the sink. "Here." When he came closer, I reached for his beer and opened it for him. When I handed it back, he started to thank me.

"That's all right," I said, because, after all, we'd been friends our whole lives. I lifted my bottle to his, and after a moment we clicked and drank.

After the dishes, we opened two more beers and sat talking about nothing important until midnight. After he left, I went upstairs, looked in on Birdie, and then, though I needed the sleep, I ran myself a bath. I felt good, better than I had in a long time. It's nice to pretend that you can fix the world and everyone in it, but sometimes it's nice to pretend you don't know a damn thing—or care much, either. Sometimes it's the only way to shut up your brain for a few hours so you can think with it later. I dozed off twice in the hot water and then dragged myself to bed and fell asleep without even knowing I would.

Later that night, I was in a dream about a river when Alice came into my room. I tried to put the pillow over my head but she tugged it away. I pulled the blanket over my head and when she couldn't pull it off, she sat next to me. I could feel her bony weight on the mattress by my hip. She was bawling and talking about robbers and the porters and being a nurse in Africa. She kept grabbing my shoulder and whispering at me through the blanket. Finally, she gave up, tucked me in, and left.

25

Adam and Eve in paradise
that was their pedigree.
They had a grant never to die,
wold they obedient be.

—from an American sampler, 1745

He didn't like to cook for himself, but he'd been avoiding going to Eddie Walk's for meals. Sooner or later they'd all know he was alone—most of them probably suspected as much already—but the difference between a married man and an abandoned husband was a threshold he felt uneasy about crossing. Too many people seemed too eager to help. Emily Moralez, for instance. When she found out he was coming into the office late at night to catch up on work, she told her mother and they brought by a picnic basket for him: roast beef, mashed potatoes, gravy, bread, hard-boiled eggs, apple pie, and four beers, obviously prepared to pump his losses to the surface. He thanked them, said he'd have to eat it later, and went back to typing. They looked at each other, incredulous.

"You can't just starve yourself to death," said Emily's mother. "Can't you stop for even a few minutes?"

"I can, Mrs. Moralez, and I want to, but then I still have the work in the morning." He grinned at the two women and went back to typing.

"Well, if I was your wife," tried Emily, "I sure wouldn't like you working late so many nights. I'd be worried about your health. I might even get suspicious."

"Better never marry a sheriff, then," said Frank.

They left shaking their heads. They were on his side, that was what bothered him. They'd blackballed Angela from the start. Maybe because she was from the city and beautiful and unwilling to attend their parties, or maybe only because he'd married her without telling them in advance. He didn't know why they'd decided to dislike her, but they had. Even the men. The way they'd greeted her when she was with him, the way they'd kept their eyes turned away while she talked, the way they watched her when she turned her back, the way they asked after her—or not. They had imagined problems in the marriage from the very beginning and been waiting ever since to help him solve them. As soon as they found out she was gone, that she'd turned out to be exactly the woman they'd predicted, they'd never forget it. They'd be worse than ever in their opinions about good and bad, about what was needed and who was right and how much they understood of the world. The thought of how smug they would be made Frank tired.

The irony, of course, was that out of all the people who had disliked Angela, Rose was the most honest about it, and yet he felt she was the only one who would understand why Angela had left. Possibly the only one who'd be able to forgive her for it. He'd been planning to tell her; last night, sitting with her at Alice's house, he'd come within a breath of it. He was sorry now that he had not. Rose might not like Angela, but she'd never judge her the way the others would, and she'd feel no pity for Frank. She'd simply take the information of Angela's disappearance the way she took everything Frank told her, as just something else that was true.

As he reached his office door, he could hear the phone ringing. He undid the lock, let himself in, and glanced at the clock as he answered. It was 6:30 A.M.

"Can you talk?"

"Rose." He pulled off his wool cap and laid it on the desk. "Yeah, I can talk. You're up early. I was just thinking of—"

"Hush, Frank. I need you to do something."

He heard it then, a shakiness, a tightness of something reined in hard under her voice. "Are you okay?"

"I need information about one of Birdie's medicines. It's called War-farin. Alice gave him some last night. At least I think so. I keep it in a plas-tic bag in the back of my bureau, but this morning the bag was out on his nightstand. I don't know how much she gave him. I don't even know what this means."

"Spell it for me." She did, and he wrote it down. "How's he look now?"

"Fine. He's just pissed off at me for sleeping through it. And he's scared." He heard her suck in her breath. "She tried to wake me up, Frank, but I wouldn't. I thought it was just like all the other nights. I told her to go away. I didn't realize she'd found the pills. I never thought she'd go looking through my bureau, honest."

He shoved open a drawer for the Madrillas phone book. "Get him dressed in case we need to get him to the hospital. I'll call you right back."

"He's sitting by the front door ready to go. He's scared. Hurry, Frank."

He dialed the number of the poison control center in Madrillas and gave the woman who answered the name of the drug. "He's in his late six-ties, had a stroke about four months back that left him paralyzed on his right side. I don't know how much of the Warfarin stuff he got. It hap-pened sometime last night. After midnight," he added.

"Stay on the line, please."

Music came on. While he waited, pen poised above the paper, he stared out the window. It had rained during the night, maybe snowed at higher altitudes. The pass would be lousy with ice. Maybe closed. He shut his eyes. If he'd let Rose go to bed early, she might have woken up before Alice got to the pills. He'd seen how tired she was and he'd ignored it. All he'd thought about was wanting to sit in that kitchen and drink beer and talk. All he'd done was think about himself. The music stopped and a voice came on.

"Warfarin—that's accented on the first syllable—is an anticoagulant used to prevent strokes. Side effects include headaches, vomiting, bloody stools, severe hemorrhaging. Has he shown any of those symptoms?"

"I don't think so."

"And you say you're over in Queduro?"

"I'm the sheriff."

"Then I'll tell you that you're dealing with a serious situation. Warfarin can be fatal in higher-than-prescribed doses—in fact, it's more commonly used as rat poison. Tell his family to get him to the hospital ASAP and have him put under observation."

She sounded almost bored. Frank thanked her and dialed Alice's number. On the sixth ring, Alice picked up.

"Alice, this is Frank Doby. Can I—"

"Do we know each other?"

"Yes, we do. Can I speak to Rose a minute?"

There was a deep silence. "You should check the directory next time, young man. I'm far too busy for nonsense. Good-bye."

She hung up. He cursed, banged down the phone, and grabbed his keys off the desk.

Her front door was unlocked but Birdie wasn't in the hall. Frank heard the radio upstairs and, when he called, Rose answered.

"It's okay, Frank. We're all up here."

At the top of the stairs, he saw Alice in her room packing a pink suitcase and singing to herself. He looked in Birdie's room and found Rose on the bed reading aloud and Birdie in his chair across from her, listening. When she looked up, Frank saw how bad it had been for her—her shirt buttoned wrong, her mouth tight with exhaustion, dark rings under her eyes—but she grinned crookedly. "I shouldn't have bothered you. I tried to call you back, but you were already gone."

"What happened?"

"I panicked, is all. Alice said she'd given him pills, and Birdie said he'd woken up in the middle of the night chewing on pills, and when he and I saw the bag of Warfarin pills on his nightstand, we both just assumed . . . It's my fault, Frank. When I finally got my head on straight and asked her what she'd given him, she showed me the vial of vitamin C pills in her pocket. If he did swallow anything, all he got was an overdose of C. I'm sure of it."

Frank looked at Birdie. "How do you feel?"

The old man rolled back his head. "Ah feeahawl fiah."

"You see? He feels fine."

"I don't know, Rose. The poison control people said to bring him to the hospital. If she took the Warfarin pills out of your bureau, isn't there a chance she gave him a few of them too?"

"I thought about that, but let me show you something." She swung her feet off the bed. "Al," she called. "You want to come in here a minute?"

Alice stepped around the door, folding a sweater she was holding. "I hope you're packing." She sniffed. "We've got to leave soon now."

"Frank needs one of the Warfarin pills. You know where they are?"

"Well, of course I do. What do you think I am, an idiot?" She looked at Birdie, then back at Rose. "I should give him one now?"

"No, not Birdie. This guy here." Rose put her hand on Frank's arm for a moment and then let go.

Alice looked doubtful. "He doesn't look sick. I saw people in Africa far sicker than that."

"I know. Better just give him one Warfarin pill."

She turned away, reached into her sweater, and came out with a bottle. She read the label, unscrewed the cap, tipped a pill into her palm, and screwed the lid back on.

"Keep track," she whispered to Frank, gesturing toward Rose. "These Warfarins are very expensive pills, and unfortunately she's still addicted."

Frank turned the pill over and looked at Rose. She was holding out a plastic-capped cup of water with a straw.

"Vitamin C. She gave me some too."

"Will you stop calling them vitamin C?" snapped Alice. "I'm the primary caretaker here. It's right on the label what it is."

"You're right. Go ahead, Frank."

Frank put the pill in his mouth and took a hit of water.

"I don't mean to lose my temper," said Alice breezily, "but you know how it is when you're busy. We're about to leave for a long trip. I'm doing all the work." She rolled up the sweater she was holding, tucked it under her arm like a football, and marched back to her room.

"She thinks she has the Warfarin," said Rose. "When I asked her what was in the plastic bag, she had no idea. She didn't even remember touching that bag. When I asked if she'd fed any of them to Birdie, she got mad as hell. She said she'd never give out pills that weren't labeled."

"The bag with the Warfarin wasn't open?"

"No, and it's hidden now where she'll never find it. If I just relax and think the way she thinks, she does kind of make sense. I mean, she *was* a nurse once. Anyhow, I'm sorry I didn't think of that before I called you."

"I'm just glad everything's okay. This is my fault, Rose. I shouldn't have stayed so late last night. You were dead tired to begin with. No wonder she couldn't wake you."

"I invited you to stay. I did that, not you."

They stared at each other for a moment, and he nodded. "All right. I'd better get back to work."

"Fray!" brayed Birdie. He turned his chair, his head swinging back. "Fray alow . . . alow . . . alowwn."

"He wants to talk to you alone." Rose leaned over, picked the compact mirror off the old man's chest, and held it up to his face. "Say it to him right, Bird. Say it or I don't leave."

Birdie glared at her and batted the mirror away. "Gat ridda har."

"Very nice. You hear that, Frank? When the old crab gets mad, he speaks as clear as Abe Lincoln at Gettysburg." She slid the compact into Birdie's breast pocket and went to the door. "And Frank? If he tries to run you over with his chair, get on the bed. That drives him nuts." She walked out, shutting the door.

Frank looked at Birdie. His chin was wet and one side of his face looked as lifeless as a wall, but his good eye was round and clear.

"Yaw. Ssit."

Frank took over Rose's place on the bed. "You want to talk?"

"Doe tay . . . do no lay toy. . . ." He sighed in a vast despair and then slapped his pocket for the compact, opened it, and lifted it to his face. "Don't. Layt. Them. Take. Hat."

"Take what?"

"Awl . . . Alizzz."

Frank hesitated. "You're worried about Alice?"

Bird banged the mirror on the arm of his chair. "No. Narzing. Hoe-em."

Frank swallowed. "You don't want her in a nursing home."

"No. Noo."

"All right. I'm glad to know that." He looked down at his hands and spoke carefully. "The thing is, Bird, if you know what you want for Alice and how you want it done, you probably ought to have a will drawn up. I can help you find a lawyer and see that whatever you decide is carried out, but you have to do the legal part alone." He looked up. "You understand why, don't you? If I help too much, people might think it wasn't your decision. They might decide you'd been coerced. Especially if you're planning to ask Rose to live here. Is that what you're planning?"

Bird's face twisted into a bright knot. He lifted his hand to push spittle off his cheek and then leaned forward as far as the belt of his wheelchair would let him. "Get me a loyal," he snarled.

Frank studied his face. "You mean a lawyer?"

Without taking his eyes off Frank, the old man fumbled for his wheelchair controls, found them, and backed up. "Rose," he bellowed. He let his head fall back, and his good eye blinked at the ceiling. "Make. Frayk. Lunch."

When Frank returned to the office, he thumbed through the files until he found his notes on the two hunters he'd helped dig out of a snowbank up on the pass back in October. He'd clipped their business cards to his report and, just as he'd remembered, one of them was a probate lawyer, a speed-talker by the name of Max Westerman. He took off his coat and placed the call. If this worked out, Rose would have a decent place to live from now on, and a job. A hard job, yes, but a job with a future waiting at the end of it, maybe the first chance at a real future she'd had since before her uncle's death.

Westerman himself answered, which Frank took as a good sign. As soon as he began to explain the situation, the lawyer interrupted in a voice so rapid it seemed to cost money.

"Any chance this Birdie Pinkston is related to a woman named Alice Pinkston?"

When Frank said they were brother and sister, Westerman barked out a quick laugh. "Miss Pinkston's my client. Was, anyway. I used to change her will for her at least once a month. Mr. Max, she calls me. We had a falling out over some property I thought she wanted me to sell for her. I always liked that old gal, though. She reminds me of my mother. What's up?"

He'd spoken so fast it took Frank a moment to realize he was supposed to answer. He started to explain that Bird was in a wheelchair and Alice was having memory problems, and almost immediately Westerman cut in.

"Thought so. Presenile dementia, right? She been diagnosed yet?"

"No, we have one doctor in Queduro, but I don't think he even—"

"Any relatives?"

"A couple nieces, but nobody's been able to locate—"

"And this Devonic woman, Rose: she's not related?"

Frank started to explain that the connection was there regardless of whether it was by blood or not, but the lawyer jumped in over him. "I can handle Mr. Pinkston's situation, no problem. It's not a bad idea to draw up a general power of attorney for Miss Pinkston as well, in the event that her condition worsens. Then all she has to do is sign it."

"Mr. Westerman, I—"

"Call me Max."

"Max. I don't know how Alice is going to react—"

"No, no, we're old buddies. Tell you the truth, I knew something was coming down the warpath last time I talked with her. If she's as bad as you say and her brother can't cover for her anymore, we'd better jump on it."

"All right. I'm also wondering if I could talk you into—"

"Making a house call? Sure, if somebody pays me travel time. I love driving that Jeep. The wife says I spend too much time in the office anyway. Let me just look at my schedule—"

A muzak version of "Let It Be" cut him off, but in less than three bars, he was back.

"Queduro's tiny, right? I should be able to find your office and we'll go meet the Pinkstons together? Okay, how about the seventh at noon?"

The seventh was two weeks away, but Frank agreed. He tried to add that Westerman should make sure the pass was still open before he left, but he'd already hung up.

Frank took a moment to recover. It was not just the speed of the conversation but the fact that he'd stumbled on Alice's lawyer without even trying. It was a piece of luck that could save days, possibly weeks of research when the time came. He started to dial Alice's number, but then changed his mind halfway through and hung up. Rose needed to hear about Birdie's plans from Birdie, not him. She'd probably unplugged the phone to keep Alice from making calls anyway. He'd drop by tomorrow after work. Maybe he'd bring them dinner. He looked at the files, pushed them to one side, and started a grocery list.

26

Awake, Arise, Behold. Thou hast
thy life; a leaf, thy breath, a blast.

—from an American sampler, 1756

That night after dinner, Birdie started thumping on the wall upstairs. When I asked Alice to go check on him, she took her pocketbook and put on her raincoat. She was gone a long time. When she came back, her raincoat was gone and she was wearing one of Birdie's cardigans. She went to the refrigerator, put in her pocketbook, and took out Frank's last Heineken. I turned off the water and listened. Bird was still banging on the wall.

"What's he need, Alice?"

"He needs to wash his mouth out with soap, that's what he needs." She put the beer in the cupboard and started looking in the other cupboards, shaking her head and circling the room, her mouth working. "Now we're going to have to hide everything," she said. "I personally think it's hopeless. I won't even talk to him anymore."

"He was asleep a few minutes ago." I dried my hands on the dish towel and went to the doorway to listen. The noises had stopped. I turned back to Alice. "That's funny."

She pulled a long face. "You may think this is funny, but I don't. He's barfing everywhere."

"What?"

"You heard me. Or isn't that the word you people use?"

I ran through the living room and up the stairs. She'd jammed a bath towel against the bottom of his door. When I yanked it away and pushed open the door, my heart stopped. Birdie was lying on his side in the bed, his one good eye like a marble of blue glass, his lopsided mouth open, his sheets and pillows covered in blood.

There are two kinds of nightmares. One is the kind that starts in a peaceful, happy dreamland where you don't suspect anything wrong can ever happen, and then suddenly it's jumped to another world. The other kind is like sitting down to watch a movie you've paid for, you know it's a thriller as soon as it starts, you can hear the dark music and you know something awful is about to happen, something evil, and all you can do is hold your breath and tell yourself it's not real and wait for it to end.

That's how it went that night. As soon as it started and for as bad as it got, I knew that I'd expected all along that something like this was coming. I remember thinking that all I had to do was keep my head and do the next thing and the next until it was over, but it seemed to me that the more I did the worse it got. I had him on the john in the bathroom, with his good arm hooked around my neck, I had his pajama bottoms down around his ankles and the water running, but when I tried to take off his pajama top he yanked me to his shoulder as if to say something in my ear and began to shit a dark red liquid. Then he was talking again, trying to thank me for something, and I kept telling him to shut up and that he was all right and yelling through the door for Alice to call Frank, and then I leaned sideways for another towel and he rolled forward like a bag of sand into my belly, coughing a foam of bright red down my jeans and onto the white tile. I held his head until he stopped, calling to him to answer me, his wet hair like shredded white silk, and then I staggered through the doorway with him to the bed and laid him on his side, telling Alice to watch him, and stumbling past her downstairs, seeing the phone cord wasn't there and pushing by her again, ripping the blankets off my bed to grab the cord, pushing by her again and downstairs in the hall on my knees, jamming the cord into its sockets, and dialing Frank. I remember the smell of dust and floor polish and my fingernails digging into the bottom of the banister, whispering into the phone for Frank to answer and then pulling the telephone book off the table for the ambulance in Madrillas and calling that number and as a voice finally answered and I realized Birdie wasn't crying anymore, I looked up through the banister to see Alice crouched at the top of the stairs with her eyes squeezed shut, clutching her pink suitcase and peeping like a baby bird. That's when I knew it was over, that calling for an ambulance was as useless as waiting for Frank to realize we were in trouble, that the waiting was over, that we were lost.

27

The eye findeth
The heart chooseth
The hand bindeth
And death looseth.

—from an American
sampler, 1802

At midnight, Frank wound the clock on the mantel and then turned off the lamp beside the couch and sat again, listening to the ticking in the dark. The clock had belonged to his grandmother and then to his mother, but since her death he'd only occasionally remembered to keep it wound. When Angela first moved in, she'd told him not to bother. All that ticking and chiming, she said; it got on her nerves when she was alone, gave her the creeps, like she was in a mausoleum with all the doors and windows bricked up. He had thought she was being unkind—the clock's ticking, with its slow gulping hour gong, was for him as much a part of the house as he was—but now that he was trying to get used to being alone again, he wasn't sure he liked it either. He wondered if he was missing Angela, if that was why he'd taken to staying late at the office and sleeping on the couch instead of in his bed. He expected to miss her and he thought about her often, but only in terms of where she was and if she was all right. Not if she was coming back. Maybe he was in denial. Listening to the clock, he did not think so. He was unhappy that he had failed her and lonesome for someone to explain it to, but he was relieved the marriage was over. He knew it because every time the phone rang, he could feel his heart bang with the fear that it would be her, telling him she'd straightened out, that she was all right again, that he had to take her back. He looked down at the pale oblong phone on the coffee table. Which was worse, waiting for the call and hoping it wouldn't come or hiding from it and knowing it would? He reached behind his head and switched on the CD player to block out the sound of the clock. *La Bohème,* his mother's music. He cranked it up high and laid his elbow over his face, breathing in the faint smell of motor oil on his sweater. Then he sighed, reached over, and plugged the phone back in. It was ringing before he even lay back.

"Hey, boss, it's Silas. You still awake?"

He turned down the radio. "What's up?"

"I don't know yet, but something funny's going on. About two hours ago I was closing up for the night and a call came in from someone crying and asking where you went and then hanging up without saying who she was. My guess is, it's old lady Pinkston."

Frank sat up. "Two *hours* ago?"

"It wasn't like I didn't try to get hold of you. Your wife must have unplugged your phone or something. But that's not all. A few minutes ago, I started hearing something—thought it was somebody's alarm from next door or something—getting louder and louder, and then what do I see screaming full blast past the office? An ambulance. All the way from Madrillas, can you believe it? I'm surprised you didn't hear them. I tried to flag them down before they went up the hill to Miss Pinkston's, but they didn't see me."

"They're up there now?"

"Yeah, I'm on my way up to explain things to them, but I thought you'd want to know what's going on first."

"Good man. You stay where you are."

"But Frank, I'm the one who—"

"I need a deputy by the phone in case we've got an emergency. You understand?"

He hung up and was halfway out the door before the phone started ringing again. He ran and grabbed it, begging for Rose's voice at the other end.

"This is Astra at the bar, Frank, and we want to know what the hell's going on up at the Pinkston place. Did she finally crack or something?"

"I don't know, Astra, but she doesn't need the whole town on her front lawn waiting to find out. Can you please tell everybody to just sit tight until I find out what's happening?"

"I would if I could, but they're gone. Eli tried to stop them, but it was no good. They're not about to sit around waiting for someone else to tell them what's going on when there's an ambulance in town."

"Is Eli there now?"

"Eli? He gave up and went home."

"Thanks." Frank hung up, and the phone started ringing again. He moaned and grabbed it from its cradle.

"It's me, Frank."

"Christ, Rose. Are you okay?"

"Yeah, I'm okay. I'm just really tired. I don't know if I've ever been this tired." Her voice was steady enough, but her breath was jagged. He hadn't heard her cry since they were kids. "I probably shouldn't have even called you," she said.

"No, Rose. You were right to call. Where are you?"

"You know what I've been thinking about? What I said about your mom and dad. I was crazy about your folks, you know. I used to watch them before you got up in the morning, the way she'd come out in that pink bathrobe to make coffee, the way he'd take his cup from her and they'd sit at the corner of the table, watching the dawn come up over Red Mountain, whispering so they wouldn't wake me. They were the family I wanted to have if I couldn't have my own. I used to lie awake at night praying they were going to adopt me. You didn't know that, did you?"

"I—no, I didn't."

"You remember that day you and your dad drove me over to the motel to live with Birdie? We went in the squad car, remember? And I was sitting up front with your dad, and we were almost there when he said to me, 'Rose? I want you to remember that the world will stand aside for someone who knows where he's going.' You remember him saying that?"

"I do," he said, though he was not sure if he did or not. The thing he remembered most clearly from that day was that when his father had told him to get her suitcase out of the trunk, she'd grabbed it from him and waited for him and his father to get back in the squad car before she went inside.

"Well, Frank, I'm still trying to believe that," she said. "I'm trying real hard to believe it right now. I've got one more shot at this, and I'm going to take it."

"What's happened, Rose?"

"I'm taking her with me. You know as well as I do she hasn't got any friends left in this town. Maybe she never did. Birdie would want me to look after her, and I'll find a way to do it. I promise. Just give us a few days' head start."

"Wait, Rose. You can't. Alice is too sick to travel. Where can you go?"

"Just remember they trust you, Frank. They've always trusted you. Tell them you don't know anything. They'll believe you. Tell them if they throw Birdie a nice funeral and let us go, they can have the motel and the house and everything else. Tell them Alice said so. Good-bye, Frank. Take care of yourself."

As he came over the top of Flax Hill, he saw lights shining from every window of Alice's house. The ambulance had pulled into the driveway and so had several cars, including Silas's Camaro. People from the bar stood in groups on her lawn and her front steps, many still holding beers. He parked across the street, got out, and headed toward them, slow at first and then faster, seeing them turn to watch him come. He chose the first face he recognized in the dark, Tommy Steelhead.

"I'm going to need you to help everybody move their cars, Tommy, so the ambulance can get out. I need everybody out of the way. Can you do that for me?"

"Sure, Frank, but what's going on? Silas K. said he'd tell us, but he hasn't come out yet. Is something wrong in there?"

"Well, of course something's wrong, Tommy," said a voice, as Frank hurried up the steps. "Why else would she call the ambulance?"

"Silas K. says Alice won't even remember she called that ambulance," called someone else. "Is that true, Frank?"

"If you ask me, it'd save a lot of grief later to take both of them to the state hospital tonight. That's where they belong."

"My dad's saner than she is, and he's in the state hospital."

Frank tried the door and then knocked and called Silas. The upper half of Silas's face appeared briefly at the half-moon window at the top of the door, and then the lock clicked open. "Jesus, Frank, get in here," he cried with a happy grin. "All hell must of broke loose upstairs. You won't believe what's going on."

Frank stepped inside, shut the door, looked to make sure no one was in the hallway, and then gripped Silas by his fur lapel and shoved him hard to the wall. "Did I ask you to wait at the office, deputy?"

"But I was the one who saw the ambulance, Frank. Besides, I knew it'd take you a minute or two to get here and I was worried about the EMTs. What if they couldn't get in or something?"

"The question is, what if they can't get out?"

"What?"

"The ambulance. Not only did you park directly behind it, you let everybody else park behind it. Meaning they can't get out now, deputy. Emergency traffic control. Ever hear of it?" As he leaned into Silas close enough to smell the soap he used, Silas's eyes widened in disbelief. Frank knew better than to do it this way—Silas had spent most of his childhood dodging a father who was known for smacking his kids around—but he didn't care anymore.

"When I come out of this house, I want to see those cars moved to the other side of the street, and I want to see you in your Camaro sitting at the bottom of that hill keeping the rest of this town from coming up here. And if I don't see that, Silas? If I see you standing around out there with that fucking crowd, talking about what you don't understand? I'm not only going to fire your ass, I'm going to arrest you for blocking an emergency transport vehicle and interfering with the law. You hear me?"

"I hear you. Let me go, will you?" But as soon as Frank let go, Silas's eyes instantly relaxed. "You can't talk to me like that. If it wasn't for me, you wouldn't have even known there was an emergency."

"Thank you. Are you leaving now?"

"Yeah." He sulked. "I'm leaving." He straightened his bomber jacket, a navy silk thing with a black fur collar and a deputy's patch on the shoulder that he'd bought with his own money. He opened the door, stepped out, and then leaned in again. "But say, Frank? Don't you think it's kind of late to worry about that ambulance? Like I was trying to tell you, all they're doing is waiting for the coroner. That old man's dead as a doornail—all right, all right, don't get sore again." He held up his hand. "I'm going."

Frank locked the door behind him, listened for voices, and then took the stairs. He knocked on Birdie's door and stuck his head in. A bright orange medic kit lay open on Bird's wheelchair, a backboard on the floor, three men in parkas and white uniforms standing around Birdie's bed. He was surprised how young they were.

"I'm Frank Doby. Mind if I come in?"

The freckled man at the foot of the bed narrowed his pale eyes to slits. "I told that jackass deputy downstairs I don't want anyone coming up here."

"I'm the sheriff."

"Oh." The man blushed, darting a look at his friends. "Come on in." He came forward to shake Frank's hand. "I'm Tom Patters, EMT-P and team coordinator. These are my EMT-As."

"Thanks for coming. Mind if I take a look?" Frank moved around him and went to the bed. He'd taught himself not to be squeamish, and he was not now. He simply looked and then breathed out slowly and turned to focus on the freckled EMT-P. He was like a kid trying to play a grown-up.

"Whoever called this in shouldn't have bothered us with it. He's been dead quite a few hours. No point even moving him off the bed."

Frank nodded. The other two EMTs shifted quietly in front of him, like basketball players, he thought, gathered in the locker room after a disappointing game. "What do you think he died of?"

"Massive internal bleeding," said the freckled EMT-P behind him. "That's what causes all those black-and-blue marks you see there around the face and throat. Probably from some kind of anticoagulant overdose: Heparin, Warfarin, Dextrin, something like that. Maybe just aspirin, if he took enough. Hard to say till they do the autopsy. We notified the hospital and they're sending a medical examiner first thing in the morning. So if you're willing to sign off for the body, I guess we'll get going."

He came forward, picked a clipboard off the two points of Birdie's knees, and handed it to Frank. Frank signed his name without looking and handed it back.

"I thank you for coming."

"Kind of a waste of time, sheriff. Whoever was here with him before we got here not only watched him go, they washed him, dressed him, shaved him, put his teeth back in, and left a note downstairs for us about where to find him. Plus they had time to clean up. This kind of internal hemorrhaging, there should be blood everywhere. I mean everywhere. You should have seen the one we found over in Manassa last month. This room should have been a mess."

"Yeah," agreed one of the EMT-As, a chunky man who'd probably once played football. "The only blood we found anywhere was on that winding-sheet."

His boss turned. "The what?"

"The winding-sheet. You know, Tom. The grave cloth." The chunky EMT-A went to the wastebasket, reached in, and came out with a thin wad of yellow material, which he opened carefully and held by its corners. Frank saw at once that it was the yellow silk piece Rose had mentioned, with a large black-and-white magpie embroidered in the center, most of it stained dark brown. "When we first got here," the EMT-A went on, "the old man was laid out under this, fine as a funeral, only his orifices were still leaking blood. That's how come it got spoiled. You want us to throw it away or put it back over him?"

Frank considered. "I think it can be thrown away. Thanks for asking, though."

"I told you so," said the other EMT-A.

"Can I see the note you guys found?"

The freckled man stiffened. "You didn't see it downstairs?" He turned to his EMT-As. "Where the hell's that note? That's evidence. I told you guys not to pick it up, didn't I?"

"I didn't." The thinner EMT-A pulled back the corners of his mouth in apology. "Honest to God, Tom, I didn't touch it."

Tom turned to the other EMT-A who ducked away, saying, "You were the one picked it up, Tom."

Tom shoved his hands hard in his pockets, jingling change. "What is this? You two think I'd be dumb enough to move evidence?"

The two EMT-As looked at each other. Then the chunky one said, "We're not saying that, Tom. We're just saying—"

"Hold on," said Frank. "My deputy probably has it."

The freckled kid turned, his face relieved. "Well, that takes care of that. We better head over that pass, boys. Get the bag and the straps. Gary, you drive."

"Sheriff?" said the chunky EMT-A. "I was looking through the other rooms while we were waiting and I think you—"

"Gary," groaned the freckled kid. "How many times do I have to tell you? The man can do his job without you telling him how." He turned to Frank, shaking his head. "I keep trying to tell these guys they're paramedics, not private eyes, but they just won't listen." He turned to them, his voice suddenly sharp. "Let's go, guys. Chop-chop."

Frank watched them pull off their latex gloves, zip their parkas, and fold their gear slowly back into the medic bag. He guessed that the two EMT-As were used to being bullied and had learned nothing from it so far but a resentment for their supervisor and an unwillingness to do anything until they were yelled at for doing it wrong. He regretted jumping so hard on Silas. He'd been right to correct him, but he'd gone about it wrong.

Silas was the kind who would always be hungrier for power than for learning to do things right. Humiliating him and pushing him around like a dumb animal was exactly the kind of encouragement he needed to stay that way. These boys were proof of that. He followed them downstairs to the door, thinking that after he chased off the crowd outside, he'd sit Silas down and tell him what he'd done right instead of everything he'd done wrong. He'd encourage him to do better. It was the only way Silas would learn.

But he didn't have to disperse the crowd. Silas had done it—in fact, there was nobody at all waiting in the front yard or the street. Maybe believing in Silas was all it took. Frank said good night to the EMTs, watched them back out of the driveway, and when their taillights had blinked out on the edge of the hill he went over to Alice's garage and cupped his hand to the window.

Sure enough, her Cadillac was gone. In its place, sitting next to an empty ripped-apart hot-dog package and looking as guilty as a car thief, was the little black-and-white dog, Buddy. When Frank raised the door, the animal crawled forward on his belly, the pencil-thin tail spanking the floor in supplication, every inch of him shivering and prepared for the worst. Frank picked him up and, after reassuring him a moment, carried him out to the squad car. He settled him in the back and then opened the driver's door and picked up his mike. From where he stood, he could see Silas's Camaro idling at the bottom of the hill.

"Good job on crowd disbursement, Silas. You can go home now."

"You don't want me to wait down here no more?"

Frank could hear the sulk in his voice. "No," he answered. "Thanks. Call it a night."

"I'm coming up there first. Out."

Frank put the radio back and stepped to the other side of the street. Instead of turning around, Silas roared up the hill in reverse. As he arrived, Frank leaned to the window, but even before it opened, he knew Silas had been drinking. He bit down hard to keep from saying it.

"I just wanted you to know," said Silas, "I been sitting in my car down there for at least a half hour now with no heat."

"You better get on home, then. You closed up the office, right?"

"You think I can't do anything, don't you?"

"No. You let the EMTs in, you cleared the cars out of here, and you took care of crowd control. That's what we needed. I'm sorry I lost my temper and shoved you. That wasn't right."

Silas's face went blank, trying to take it in. He was very drunk. "Well, God *damn* it"—hitting the steering wheel—"why'd you have to get so mad at me, Frank? I'm not a fool."

"No, you're not. You *are* kind of high right now, though."

"No, I'm not. I'm too damn cold to be high." He stared out the window. "Besides. You can't fire me for drinking. This is my private vehicle and I was supposed to get off at ten-thirty." As if to prove it, he reached under his seat and brought out a fifth. "You want some?"

"No, thanks. You go on home and get some sleep. I'll see you at the office tomorrow. We'll talk then."

But as he stepped back on the curb, Silas swatted at him. "Wait a minute," he said. "Wait just a fucking minute, Frank. I got something for you. Two things. Come here."

Frank stepped to the car again, took the piece of paper from Silas, and held it up to the light. Inside were two words: *He's upstairs.* Rose's handwriting. He folded it and put it in his pocket.

"Good job, Silas. I was looking for that."

"Want to know who wrote it, boss? I know who. And you know why? Because I also found this."

He pointed over his shoulder. Frank got his penlight out of his coat and turned it on, aiming the beam at the back seat of the Camaro.

"It's Rose Devonic's Indian lamp. I know because I saw it stuffed in her car last September when she left everything she owned parked behind the laundromat. And guess where it was this time? In the bedroom up there. Right across the hall from where that poor old man died." He leaned back and took a drink from the bottle, smacking his lips.

"Mind if I take it?"

"Help yourself. That's why I stored it in my car, 'cause I knew you'd want it."

"Thanks." He opened the back door and, with some difficulty, managed to wiggle out the enormous Indian head.

"So I was thinking," Silas continued, "while I was waiting for you at the bottom of the hill, how you don't never hardly mention Rose Devonic anymore. What became of her anyway? And then I was thinking how you're always coming up here by yourself looking after poor old Miss Pinkston and her brother. All winter now you've been doing it, being the good Samaritan that you are. And you're always telling me to mind the office, aren't you? Yep. You are always telling me to just shut up and mind the office." He took another drink. "So I was thinking, I mean, what do *you* think this town would say if they found out their sheriff was letting his ex-girlfriend sponge off a pair of helpless old gray-haired farts who couldn't think straight? Whee-oo. I bet there'd be a stink, don't you? Especially seeing as how one of them's dead now of what looks like unnatural causes, and the other one's disappeared." He looked up, grinning, his teeth stained. "What do you think, Frank?"

"Silas." Frank looked up at the night sky, shaking his head. "Listen to me."

"No, I don't think so. You been telling me to listen to you for a long, long time, boss, and I don't think that's going to work anymore. You want to be an accomplice to a murder and a possible kidnapping, go right ahead. Be my guest. Not me. No, sir. I'll pass this time." He slugged hard from the drink and then looked up, and his voice cracked with emotion. "I believed in you, Frank. I thought they were right, that you were the real hero or something and I was just your fucking nigger. I didn't even mind all those times you treated me like I wasn't fit to talk to. You with your Silver Star. Shit. There wasn't even a war going on when you got that fucking star. What'd you do to earn that thing?"

"It's not important. What I—"

"No, I want to fucking know. How'd you earn it?"

Frank felt his gut tightening. "A man was shot by a sniper. I dragged him into an alley."

"Alley, huh? Then what? You performed open heart surgery right there with your bayonet and saved his life?" Silas guffawed, drank again, and then hurled the bottle with sudden force at the sidewalk, glass exploding at Frank's feet. "I want to know why you treat me like shit!" he cried. "That's what I want to know. I may not be a big war hero like you are, but I don't deserve to be brushed off so easy."

"Go home, Silas."

He started to walk up Alice's front walk, but Silas laid on his horn, a sudden sharp cry in the dark.

"Your wife doesn't give a shit about you!" he bawled. "She told me so. You didn't know that, did you? You were too busy up here with your girlfriend to know Angie and me had talks. Lots of talks. I'll bet if I went over there right now and gave her five bucks to leave you, she would. You hear me, Frank?"

He turned. "You might as well save yourself the trip."

Silas started to go on and then stopped. "What's that?"

"She's already gone. She's been gone two weeks now. Anything else you need to know?"

When Silas didn't answer, he went in Alice's house and closed the door.

Part III

28

This to my friends when I am gone
I leave for them to look upon
Remember that I wrought the same
For underneath you find my name.

—from an American sampler, 1805

I couldn't remember leaving that night. I tried, but it was like describing photographs I'd heard about but never seen. I was a little worried about it. It's one thing to shut out memories on purpose, knowing they'll wait outside until you're ready to let them in—but when you open the door and they're not there anymore, you get nervous. If I'd learned anything from Alice, though, I'd learned not to panic about lost memories. You can spend half your life trying to shut them out and the other half trying to keep them with you, and either way they make their own plans. The best thing to do is to keep your mind on the road ahead. That's how it was that night. I cleaned up the blood and packed our bags and wrote the note and called the ambulance and got Alice in the car and said good-bye to Frank from the phone outside Ruben's garage, and then I drove over the pass without even knowing it. If someone told me afterward that I'd been holding a knife in my teeth, I would've believed it. But if anyone ever needs to hear my side of it, I don't have one. As far as I can tell, I wasn't even there that night.

But I do remember one scene right in the very middle of it, when I was sitting across from Birdie with the piece of embroidery in my lap. I knew I had to go get Alice and make her help me put everything in the car, but instead I just kept sitting there fingering the yellow silk and trying to decide whether to leave it with Birdie. Embroidery may be just a lot of stitches to some people, it may be a hobby or a tradition, a form of work or entertainment or slavery or even death, but that night I saw that all my years on the needle were coming down to one last thin thread of a dream that was about to break, and all I knew was that I had to sit still and wait for it to happen. When it did, I tied off the threads where I'd last worked and then shook out the material so it floated down over him. Then I held his face through it and told him I loved him and that we'd be safe. When I let go, wherever I'd touched, big red flowers bloomed in the yellow silk. That was the last part of that night I remembered.

Then I was parked beside a red-and-white gas station outside of Albu-querque. I'd been aware for a while that I needed to pee and get food, but it was the quiet after I turned off the engine that did it. I walked to the front of the car, undid my jeans, and squatted on the pavement, holding on to a chain-link fence. On the other side was a field of short brown weeds. The sun was coming up and some kind of a bird started to sing, its voice clean and fresh enough to break your heart. I could have been anyone, anywhere in the world. I looked down and saw my pee running under my shoe, and I squatted there, watching it, until I heard a truck pull in. When it went to the far side of the station, I stood and buttoned my pants. The truck engine quit, a truck door slammed, and a teenage boy with a thin ponytail and sunglasses came around the corner jangling keys. "I over-slept," he called. "Don't tell my dad." I watched him fiddle at the lock and open the door. "Come on in if you're coming," he called. When the lights went on inside the station, I went closer. It was a convenience store with

fluorescent lights and aisles lined with plastic packages of food and supplies. When I opened the door a buzzer went off that jumped me out of
my skin.

"Nice morning, huh? Aren't you hot in that coat?"

He was hidden somewhere in the store, under all those packages of
food as bright as toys.

"If you need gas, the pump's on."

I turned down the aisle. Under the fluorescent lights, the linoleum floor
felt like it was floating. I found orange juice and four packages of Little
Debbies, a box of raisins, a loaf of bread. Peanut butter, a jar of honey in
the shape of a bee. Then I saw something move in the corner and spotted
the top half of him behind a counter camouflaged by candy and cigarettes.
I went and set the groceries down. He had flat brown hair and dull skin,
but everything else about him was sharp and narrow. When he took off
his sunglasses, his eyes were as narrow as coin slots. Under the right one
was a birthmark like a little brown button you were supposed to press. I
looked down and saw TEXAS taped to the counter, right there in front of
me like it was possible. At least it was a start. When I looked up, the boy
had taken off his coat and moved behind a pillar of Frito bags. I heard a
bell and watched him take a wad of bills out of his pocket and count it
quickly into the drawer.

"Can I have one of these maps of Texas?"

"Hold on. My dad goes nuts if I don't set up the register before he gets
here." I watched him bang paper cylinders against the edge of the drawer
and spill in the change. His fingers were waxy-looking and quick. "All
right," he said, pushing the drawer shut, snapping open a paper bag, and
sliding a map into it. "That all you need?" I watched his hands, as they put
the food in the bag and clicked the buttons on the cash register. He could
have been an embroiderer.

"How much gas you want?"

"Okay."

"No, lady, how much gas?"

"Oh." My heart fell straight down, like when you jerk out of a dream.
"You need money?"

He cocked his head and smiled, showing a row of small sharp-looking teeth. "You ought to get some coffee."

"Money." I felt inside my coat pockets—I was only pretending to look—but it was there. Money. I separated one of the bills by feel and pulled it out. A fifty. I put it carefully on the counter. This was how Alice must feel, I thought. Every day something new, something amazing, every moment a fresh new world.

The boy groaned. "You got anything smaller?"

But I couldn't answer, because I'd just remembered putting her in the car. I covered my face and saw it in the dark, saw me doing it; she'd been with me and I hadn't seen her since. I turned and rushed out the glass door.

But she was there. She'd been there all along, curled in the back seat with her suitcase of pasta and the embroidered quilt. I pressed my forehead against the cold metal top of the Eldorado until I'd caught my breath, and then I leaned in and took my purse off the front seat. I was shaking. When I closed the door, her eyebrows puckered together in warning, but she didn't wake up.

I left the gas station with two cups of coffee to keep me awake, but as the sun got higher, my eyes began to feel like they were full of sand. By noon I knew I had to stop. I pulled off an exit that said Socorro—small, I thought, with a school and a park in the middle of town and everybody off at work—but instead I found myself driving along a strip of fast-food joints, car showrooms, and motels, and when I tried a side road to get away from that, I ended up surrounded by empty lots scraped down to dirt. It didn't seem safe to park without knowing what was private property, so I turned and went back toward the fast-food strip and pulled into a church of red bricks. It had a parking lot on three sides and a magnetized sign out front: EVERY FRIEND IS OUR FRIEND. No one was there. I parked in the back, turned off the car, and looked in the rearview. Alice had pushed away the quilt, but she was still out cold, her mouth open. I pulled off my shoes, cracked the window, made a pillow with my sweater, and lay down with my coat over me. The Cadillac had white leather seats, roomy enough to stretch out on like a bed. Way better than my Plymouth. Thinking of my station wagon reminded me that I'd driven over the pass last night. Or maybe I hadn't, maybe this was a dream. When I was little I used to have dreams about driving with Bob, but all that stopped after the accident.

I drew up my knees, looking out the windows above me. The church looked more like a bank than a church. Maybe it was a bank. Maybe the cross on top and the sign out front was an insider's joke. On the other side of the seat, Alice was snoring like a motor. I didn't think I'd sleep with all that noise and the sun glaring through the windshield, but as soon as I closed my eyes and pulled my coat over my head, I was gone.

29

One look of mercy from thy eye
One whisper of thy voice.

—from an American sampler, 1760

It was 5 A.M. and Frank lay full-dressed on his bed with the phone in his lap. Over the last hour, the dog had found the courage to make his way across the living room and through the doorway, and now, having inched his way up on the bed when he thought Frank wasn't watching, he was getting close enough to rest lightly on Frank's shoulder. Like a predator at work, Frank thought, as the animal—apparently having conquered whatever it was he feared most—let out a sigh of relief, slapped his tail twice against the bed, and fell asleep, breathing short warm shoots of air at the underside of Frank's chin. It made Frank smile to himself and feel sad, too. Somewhere in the dog's past, he'd been beaten for crimes no more serious than this, trying to find a safe place to fall sleep. He took the edge of the dog's ear between his thumb and forefinger and massaged the silkiness of it.

He was staring at Rose's Indian-head lamp out on the table in the living room. Thirteen years she'd kept it with her, moving it from one tumbledown place to the next, wiggling it in and out of her Plymouth and maneuvering it in and out of doorways: her uncle's work, the one carving of his she still owned, was openly proud of—and she'd left it behind. He could understand her leaving behind her embroidery, and Buddy too—the need to travel light, the need for one less worry, the belief that the dog would be better off with someone else, even the possibility that she'd forgotten him until it was too late to go back. There were all kinds of logical reasons that could help soften the blow of that loss. But the lamp? It was a beautiful piece: the face handsome, even heroic, the muscles of the mouth ready to speak, the eyes dark and watchful. For all the mockery and derision that her uncle faced during his lifetime, no one had ever doubted his skill with a chisel. Even the texture, the shadow of age under the skin— and that war bonnet, a whole separate world of its own, like a great rumpled bird of paradise spreading feathers to dry. Rose liked to say that she only kept the lamp to do embroidery by, but how could anyone believe that? Looking at it, you didn't have to wonder what her uncle's ideas had been worth, only why the town had not listened to them.

Frank closed his eyes. Two days after the last funeral, his father had taken him back to that curve on the highway. They'd stood without speaking, looking at the skid marks, at the glass still glittering in the gravel along the shoulder of the road where Florie Pinkston Snow had died, at the stain where Bob had gone down, and then at the other side of the highway and the view beyond. Frank had stood with locked knees, hating his father for bringing him back here so soon, for thinking he was strong enough to take it. When he saw his father pull a chain saw, pry bars, and ropes out of the trunk of their car, he'd wanted to run away. Run anywhere, run as hard as he could, run until his heart burst. Instead, he'd wiped his face and walked over to where his father waited next to the buckled guardrail.

"I don't want people remembering this place any longer than they have to," Frank senior said. "Rose's uncle should be remembered for what he did right. Not for this. Especially if she decides to stay in Queduro." He turned to Frank. "You're welcome to help if you want. If you don't, you can stay up here and pass the tools down to me by rope. It's your choice."

They'd tied the ropes to the guardrail and let themselves down the side of the cliff, and then, together, they pried the gigantic Indian out from between the rocks and the bloody snow where Mrs. Devonic had lain and sawed it into six pieces. They buried the pieces under the loose scree at the base of the cliff—all except the head, that immense carved face with its crown of red, gold, and blue feathers, all broken, cracked, and chipped, but still such an undeniable thing that they decided instead to haul it out of view from the road up above and set it on a flat boulder next to the river, looking downstream. It was a sight Frank would never forget, that gray stone with the huge head on it, mysterious and beautiful as a god. Rose never asked to see it. Though he'd tried several times to talk her into going up there, she hadn't wanted to hear about it. She was satisfied to remember her uncle with one of his smaller carvings, one she could turn into a lamp and carry around with her and call useful. Frank grinned at himself in the dark. All these years he'd thought they'd saved the Indian head for Rose? They'd saved it for themselves.

He looked at the clock, lifted the phone, and called Eli.

"Maria?"

"No, Eli, it's Frank. I'm sorry to call so early."

"I wasn't really asleep. Is this about Maria?"

"It's about Rose." Frank hesitated. "I need to ask a favor. You know that ambulance that went to the Pinkstons' last night?"

"How could I not know? There was a free-for-all at the Magpie when that thing screamed past the window, everybody betting on who it was coming to pick up. I went home." Eli paused. "You don't mean it was for real."

Frank explained how Rose had called him and what the EMTs had said. There was a silence afterward, both men listening.

"I'm glad he wasn't alone when he died," said Eli.

"So am I."

"But if Rose and Alice are gone now . . . what's that mean legally?"

Frank sighed. "If the medical examiner declares it an unnatural death, it could be serious. Depending on Alice's mental competency at the time of the death, Rose could be charged with either kidnapping or accomplice to murder."

"Shit."

"I got two things I need right now, Eli. One is, the coroner's going to show up at the Pinkstons' house in a couple hours and somebody has to be there to let him in and show him where Birdie is. Could you do that?"

"Sure I can."

"Thanks. The other thing is, I need your opinion."

"About Rose?"

"Yeah. Which direction you think she's heading?"

"You probably know more than I do. I don't know." Frank heard him lighting a cigarette. "Where do *you* think?"

"I want to hear you say it first."

"Well, if I was Rose . . ."—there was a pause—"my first inclination would be Carlos Jaramillo up in Durango. He's earning money now, he's single again, and he's always had a thing for Rose." Eli was quiet a moment. "On the other hand, Carlos never had much heart. He'd want to take Rose in, no problem, but I doubt he'd like the idea of Alice joining the party."

"I agree."

"So maybe Rose is heading to Phoenix first, to drop Alice off at that condo she owns, and then she'll go to Durango."

"You think?"

"I don't know. Ditching Alice in the middle of a city doesn't sound much like Rose."

"I agree."

There was a long pause.

"Shit. I know where she's going, Frank. Last fall she told me that Harmon Waters was building a house on his ranch for his grandfather. She said any man willing to do something like that for his grandfather was someone worth believing in. In fact, I remember thinking that Waters's money didn't impress her half as much as how he was trying to keep his family together. You know how she gets about family."

Frank nodded, pressing his eyelids with his fingers, seeing lights flash in the dark. "She and Harmon might have had a falling-out, though," he said. "Isn't that why she came back alone last fall?"

"Maybe she just decided to come back. We don't really know what happened between them, do we? And that Harmon has real money. He could afford to take on both Rose and Alice, and he probably would, too. Probably without a lot of questions."

Frank took his hand away to let his eyes refocus. "I think you're right."

"I remember Rose saying he worked for the phone company in Austin. I could call directory assistance and get the number."

"Thanks. I already got it."

"You figured this out already, did you?"

"Yeah, but I needed to hear your opinion before I could convince myself. I thank you, Eli." He swung his legs off the bed. "If Silas shows up to talk with the coroner, that's fine, but tell him to drop by my house afterward, will you? I'll leave the door open."

He hung up and set the phone back on the nightstand. The dog opened his eyes just enough to check and then shut them again. Frank rolled him onto the pillow and sat up, staring at his feet and then cradling his face in his hands. He could picture Rose driving east in the Eldorado, both hands on the wheel, her jaw set in that iron way she had when her mind was made up. She'd tell him to butt out. She'd tell him to handle Birdie's funeral, leave her alone, and take care of his own life. And what was his own life? He raised his head and looked at the bedroom. An empty house? A wife who'd never return, a job he didn't want, and a town full of people he didn't understand? The only thing with any power to hold him in this place was memory. Memories of growing up, of his father and mother, of what he had believed in, of Rose. He'd been surviving on memories for years.

He went over to the bureau and took out his badge. He'd tried to convince himself that he didn't need to wear it because everyone knew who he was, but in truth he hadn't had the confidence for it. He didn't believe in the power of law and order, not the way his father had. He believed in the power of memory. No wonder Angela, who'd tried so hard to erase her past, had been so miserable with him. No wonder he'd been inept as a sheriff. He went into the living room and dropped the badge on the coffee table next to his gun, the keys to his office, the note to Silas with money for Bird's funeral, and then, after a last look around the room that had at one time or another contained everyone he'd ever loved and everything he'd ever believed about himself and who he was, he called the dog, picked up his suitcase, and walked out to his truck.

30

Learning do but try to love
And then surely you will improve.

—from an American sampler, 1806

I woke up staring at the dashboard, knowing I'd overslept. When I sat up, I saw that the sun had moved behind the church, dusk was already coming on, and then my heart squeezed shut on the memory again and I whirled, expecting to find her gone. She was sitting up, grumpy and flat-faced, her eyes blue enough to fall into and full of blame.

"I've been waiting for you," she said.

"Shit." I dropped back against the seat. "Don't do that."

"Do what?"

"Make me think you're gone."

"Why are we here?"

"I drove us here."

"Well, you've got us in a fine mess. Where's my Buddy?"

I took the orange juice out of the bag and opened it. "Want some juice?"

"No, I don't want juice. He ran off with that cat, did he?"

"He did." I took a hit off the orange juice and handed it to her. "You want some?"

She looked as if she was going to cry.

"He's not lost, Al, he's just busy. You know how dogs get. We're okay, though. We're fine. Forget it. Just sit back and enjoy the ride."

She gave me a shocked look, settled her suitcase against her belly, and turned away. "The ride to where?" she muttered. "We're already lost. Totally, utterly, hopelessly lost. I'm not going to listen to you."

I glared at her and then recapped the juice and started the car. Sometimes she sounded more like a fortuneteller than an old woman with no memory. I pulled out to the street. I felt as if I'd dropped out of the world and then been yanked back, days lost in sleep, maybe years. I crept half a block and pulled into an empty parking lot in front of the American Family Steak House. There were two cars parked at the side. I had no idea how this was going to work.

"We need to eat before it gets dark," I said. "And you need the bathroom."

"I do not."

"Well, I do," I said, "and I'm the driver." I got out and opened her door. "You can bring the suitcase if you want."

She leaned forward to peer at the building. "I don't know this place. I've never been here in my life."

I felt a small hard place inside me getting harder. "What if Buddy's in there?" I said. "What if he's waiting for you?"

"Then he should come out." But she sounded uncertain, and her face changed and she gasped, clapping her hand to her heart. "Don't *tell* me they'd try to keep him against his will!"

"Only one way to find out." I helped her out of the car, smoothed her hair, took her coat off her, and led her inside by the strap attached to her suitcase.

There was a long orange Formica counter and a row of booths at the windows. When a waitress leaned out of the kitchen and told us to sit wherever, Alice flared up and turned to leave, but I caught her wrist and led her into the bathroom, to the handicapped stall at the end. She looked at me in astonishment when I opened the door.

"Buddy's in *here?*"

I led her in.

"Look, you've even got a bar to hold on to while you pee."

"This isn't my bathroom. I don't even remember this place."

"It doesn't matter," I said. "Bathrooms aren't places you have to remember."

I shut her in, went in the next stall, and peed, hoping she'd get the message. There was silence. When I leaned over, I saw her feet pointing toward the toilet. She was wearing a pair of blue sneakers, and from the blister she had going on her heel, I should've reminded her to wear socks.

"Alice," I called, "sit down and pee. You hear me?"

Her voice came back in a whimper. "Is anybody watching?"

"It's just us girls. Lock the stall door if you want."

As soon as it came out, I knew I shouldn't have said it. Her feet turned and there was a click. Then they turned back toward the john.

"You can do it, Alice. Pull down your underpants and sit."

I heard her doing it. "I still don't think this is right," she said. She peed hard, stopping now and then and starting again. "I wish I knew why we were here," she went on. "This isn't a very clean bathroom. I'll have to talk to the guide."

"Me too." I buttoned my pants, flushed the john, and stepped out. I washed my hands and dried them on a paper towel while I stared at the mirror, asking myself what I thought I was doing. Under the fluorescent light, I looked like some kind of maniac, my face washed out, my hair standing straight on end. When I looked under the stall, her feet were in the same place.

"Alice? Come out now."

"I don't like other people's bathrooms. I want to be in my own bathroom."

"You need help getting the door unlocked?"

"No."

But she did. In the end, I had to crawl underneath the door into her stall.

Though the place was empty, we took a booth at the back next to the window. She wouldn't let go of her suitcase and scowled at the blinds on the window, but when she opened the menu, she sucked in her breath, suddenly happy. "So, we're finally on our way, are we?"

"You could look at it that way."

"My Lord. It took just about forever, didn't it?" She bent over the menu, murmuring as she read, studying the pictures as ferociously as if each one held the meaning of life. The waitress crossed the empty room toward us, flipping her hair like a mane.

"Meat loaf and coffee." I looked at Alice. "You know what you want?"

"I beg your pardon. I haven't been reading for nothing." She turned to the waitress. "I'd like a steak, medium rare, orange juice, a salad, and some rolls."

The waitress snapped her gum. "Dressing?"

Alice's jaw dropped. She looked at me and back at the waitress.

"Italian's fine." I handed the menus to the waitress.

Alice narrowed her eyes to watch the waitress leave. When the kitchen door closed, she leaned over the table to me. "I am sorry, but that woman is *not* Italian."

"I didn't say she was."

"You did. And she's not. She's not even swarthy."

I decided to change the subject. "What'd you pack in your suitcase?"

"Things for the safari. Have you paid the bill yet, or should we just leave?"

"First she brings the food and we eat. Then we pay the bill. Then we leave."

"Oh, everything's just so *complicated*, isn't it?"

She sighed, tapped her fist on her cheek, and looked dismally around the room.

"Isn't this just *marvelous*, though?" she cried suddenly. "Two bums like us on the road? No more wheelchairs, no more doors to lock, nobody holding us down anymore, no more humming noises from that horrible neon Indian. Oh, he used to keep me awake! Such a happy life, such wonderful freedom!"

"Okay, Alice, Jesus. Cool down a little." I looked around to see who was listening. "You don't have to get so enthusiastic about it."

"But I'm so *glad* to leave that place, aren't you? I don't care if I never go back there again. And isn't it nice to know that all our best friends helped us get here?"

She waited for an answer and then gave a high, shrill laugh with her head thrown back so her fillings caught the light. It went right down my spine, and I was glad when she stopped. She looked both directions and then leaned forward over the table.

"So, where to first?"

"What do you mean?"

"Kenya? Tanzania? If they've got a war in whatever that country is that starts with an E, we don't want to go there. We've seen enough blood for one lifetime, haven't we? I'm sick to death of blood, blood, blood, and poor Birdie, he doesn't even—"

"All right, all right." I speared back my hair with both hands and looked toward the door to the kitchen. "I thought we'd try Texas first, okay? I have a friend there. You'll like him."

"Texas?" She looked doubtful. "I don't think I know anyone in Texas."

"You will. His name's Harmon." I drummed on the table, willing the waitress to show up with food. "Harmon Waters. He's got a grandfather about your age."

She shook her head, pursing her lips when she leaned forward. "But what about Africa? You said that's where we were going. Stop that tapping."

I stopped drumming. "When did I say that?"

"Last night. When you handed me the pudding. You said we were leaving for Africa first thing in the morning."

I stared at her. "You remember the pudding?"

She tucked her chin. "Do I remember the pudding." She looked around the room and then leaned forward, cupping both hands to her mouth. "That pudding had sleeping pills in it," she whispered. "I could taste them."

I didn't know what to say. I took her wrists and held them, the skin under my thumbs pale blue as fine china. "Listen to me, Alice. You were a wreck. I was afraid you were going to get sick or hurt yourself. I had to calm you down so I could think straight. That's the only reason I did it. Okay?"

I checked around the edge of the booth to see if the waitress was coming.

"The other thing, Alice, is that now that we're on the road, you've got to keep it together until we get to Harmon's. We don't want to talk to the wrong people, we don't want to look funny. We've got to fit in. We've got to act normal. You understand?"

"I understand perfectly. You're ashamed of me."

"Okay. Yeah. That's kind of it. That's good enough."

"My brother was ashamed of me too. He thought I was an ugly old maid. He was absolutely ashamed of introducing me to his friends in Queduro."

I took a drink of water before I answered. "Yeah?"

"He called me a neurotic old bag once," she went on. "I heard him say it. Of course, after Florie died, I was all he had. That's why I never married, because my little brother always had so many needs he could never admit to. Poor Birdie. Always fighting his heart." She sighed and unfolded her napkin. "Fortunately, I still look very nice in a swimsuit. Size eight. Most women my age can't say that. When I'm in my yellow swimsuit in Phoenix, the men just stare and stare."

When our food came, she was still talking about Phoenix. She talked about it the whole meal. It was as if a little box in her head opened and thirty years' worth of memory fell out. I kept waving at the waitress for more coffee. I was shaking from the caffeine and tired at the same time.

"Hey, Alice. Eat something. You're hungry, aren't you?"

"Not after that meal. I'm stuffed."

"You haven't eaten anything."

"I haven't?" She looked down at her plate. "Isn't this somebody else's?"

"I'll go pay the bill." I went to find the waitress.

Thank God!" she brayed, rushing to the Eldorado. "I thought they'd stolen my car, too!" But when I unlocked the passenger door, she balked, gripping her suitcase to her. "You don't actually expect me to sit *there*," she snapped. "That's not where I belong. Just who is in charge here?"

I groaned and looked over my shoulder at the restaurant. The waitress and a cook were at the window, watching. "Remember what I said about fitting in, Alice? Let's just quiet down and get in the car."

"You sound like James Cagney, ordering people around like that."

I raised my hands in surrender and held out the key. I'd let her get us out of the parking lot and then, if I had to, I'd take over the wheel by force.

But, instead, she stepped to the back door. When I opened it, she sniffed, handed me the suitcase, and folded herself in the car. "Trying to put me in steerage. The nerve." She looked up and took back her suitcase. "You may close my door."

I slammed it and went around to the driver's side. The waitress was pointing to us. "Wave to the nice people," I said between my teeth, as we pulled out. Alice raised her chin and, haughty as a parade queen, lifted her hand to the waitress in a farewell salute.

The drive was awful. She kept thinking she had to call someone before we could leave the country, and I didn't know how to talk her out of it. We made four stops at four different phones. Each time, as soon as she got out, she couldn't remember who she wanted to call, and she needed the number, and then she couldn't figure out why we were there, and then I couldn't get her back in the car. She was like a rubber band stretching tighter and tighter with every mile we drove. I wanted to call Harmon, but every time I tried, she'd storm off in a sulk and I'd have to run after her.

After our fourth stop, I started thinking about Birdie's Valium, wondering if I'd thrown the bag of it in the trunk with our clothes or not. I didn't want to drug her again, but I couldn't see how I was going to make it to Austin without losing my mind if I didn't.

But after three more stops she finally got tired of phone calls, and at midnight, right after she fell asleep, we finally crossed into Texas. I rolled my back against the seat and flexed my hands. The car was a dream to drive. I hadn't even realized I was driving before, but now it felt good. The least little tap on the gas and the thing jumped to obey. I pushed it up to seventy-five and thought how good a cigarette would taste. I'd get a pack of Winstons when I stopped to call Harmon. No, Camel Lights. Camel Lights was Harmon's brand. He'd be flattered that I remembered.

"Harmon," I whispered to the road, testing to see what kind of feeling came with it. I wasn't worried about him taking me back. I'd left without telling him, taken his snow boots, and charged a phone call to Birdie on his card, but he'd get over it. Harmon was the kind of man who could get over anything for the sake of a woman. The only reason we'd split up was because I'd gotten homesick. I'd been fine all the way to Albuquerque—laughing and drinking and smoking and hopping around the car and telling stories and being all excited about Texas—but as soon as we'd gotten on the far side of Albuquerque, my brain had started drumming worst-case scenarios. What if we crashed and he died? What if he didn't really have a place to live, or what if he dumped me before we got there, or disappeared, or one of his ex-wives came back to him, and what if the weather was bad and the pass was closed by then, how would I get home?

But his tweed cap, that was what finished me off. That stupid tweed golf cap he'd worn the whole time he'd been in Queduro, and then in his car and in the bars and gas stations and restaurants, and then, when we finally got to the motel in Lubbock that first night, he'd worn it to bed. That's when I decided I wasn't going another mile with him. What was the big problem with showing me he was bald? Did he think I'd scream? Did he think I'd faint? Did he think I'd never notice if he wore his little tweed cap to bed every night for the rest of his life? I hated that kind of fear.

But I shook my head. I'd been dead wrong to make that cap such a big deal. It was just something else to accept about Harmon and who he was and how he lived in the world. If he wanted to wear a cap to bed for the rest of his life, fine. If it helped him feel safe, why should I care? I could learn to appreciate caps. And I could learn to like Texas, too. Adaptability was one of my strong points.

There was a sharp tap on my shoulder.

"I've driven in the bush a hundred times, but I never drive in it at night. People get lost at night. Or robbed." She paused. "And look at us, driving at night. And you're running away again, too."

"I'm not running away."

"You most certainly are," She waited. "All your life, you've done that."

"You don't know what you're talking about."

"I'll have you know—"

"I don't want to know."

After a while she tapped again. "Do you know where we're going, then?"

"Yes."

"Where?"

"To a safe place. Now go to sleep. Listen to the music. Be quiet." I turned on the radio, found a station full of violins, and drove on. What did she think she was, some kind of soothsayer? I could hear her whispering to herself, and then when we came up on a sign that said five miles to Lubbock, she let out a gasp and grabbed the back of the seat.

"Lubbock!" she cried. "Lubbock's the place where they slaughter the cows."

"I sure like your car," I called back. "We're lucky we have it. What year is it anyway?"

There was no answer. When I looked in the rearview, I saw her clutching her suitcase against her chest, craning up over it to watch the lights of the cars coming toward us.

"We're in big trouble now," she said. "I don't know why I'm here."

"You're here because I asked you to come. And we're not in big trouble."

"Then what about my brother?" she cried. "If you're so smart, why isn't he here?"

I felt a shiver slip down the back of my shirt. I looked down at the buttons on the armrest and pushed the one that locked the doors. "You're doing fine, Alice. Frank says you should buckle your seat belt. Remember? You got your seat belt buckled back there?"

I could see her face working, tightening up, blinking back tears.

"How about some better music?" I slid the dial to an announcer saying he was going to play an old favorite by Willie Nelson. "You like Willie Nelson, Alice? You remember his music, don't you? I do. Come on. Let's sing. Calm down a little and sing with me. Let's see what they play next and we'll sing it together. Ready?"

But of all the songs we could have heard right then, there it was, "Crazy," Willie calling out the lyrics like he was reading the poem on a piece of inheritance embroidery. I started to switch the station, but then I thought, why bother? And as she began to weep, I opened the window wide, stepped on the gas, straight-armed the wheel, and belted out the lyrics at the top of my lungs. Because he was right, wasn't he? What's so sane about loving somebody you'll never be able to save?

31

No Star so bright
As my delight.

—from an American
sampler, 1792

As he drove east, he tried to focus on what would come next, but instead he kept drifting backward, memories he'd all but forgotten coming up out of nowhere, taking him over completely, and sinking back into the dark. The summer his mother had decided to wallpaper the kitchen, for instance—why was it he suddenly remembered how the paste smelled and felt on his hands? The sound of Rose and his mother talking in the bathroom as they soaked the paper, their voices echoing off the porcelain while he waited in the kitchen with the roller in his hand, staring out the window? He remembered a craving for peppermint ice cream that had lasted a whole summer, and for sweet corn the next, and then he remembered his fistfight with Howie Griego in the fourth grade, how frightened he'd been and that hot feeling in the back of his mouth, and how it felt afterward to wiggle his tooth with the tip of his tongue. And the day Mr. Medina came to the back door with a fishhook caught in the flesh behind his ear, his father's hands snapping off the barb with wire cutters and backing out the hook in a quick fresh flow of blood. How long ago was that? He couldn't have been more than six or seven, yet he could remember it perfectly: a gray sky out the kitchen window, the sound of the clock in the living room, the mingle of fish smell and brandy and sweat when Mr. Medina came in, and the way he kept making jokes about how he hated fishing because things like this always happened.

Frank had no idea where these memories were coming from. Were they supposed to mean something? He glanced over at Buddy, who glanced back, and they both turned to the road again. He didn't think so. More likely they were just a tangle of loose ends, the last random threads of whatever had held him all these years to Queduro. He wondered if these kinds of dislocated thoughts were what Alice experienced, this silent sense of free-floating through time. Almost as if a part of him had broken free and disappeared, leaving behind scraps of memory swirling in the dead air like bits of colored paper. It wasn't a bad feeling, not really. He let them come and go as they wished. Sometimes he told them to the dog. Once, thinking back to the night his father came into his room to tell him that his mother had died, he started crying as if he'd only just been told—but a moment later he stopped. He could let it go. The loss would stay, but the pain of it was gone. By the time he stopped in Lubbock for the night, he'd forgotten it entirely.

After dinner, sitting on an apron of concrete outside the glass door to his room with a bottle of beer while the dog investigated a blown field of weeds beyond the motel, he found himself going back to the spring of '87. He'd been told that Panama City was everything a soldier could want— overseas pay, good food, good music, beautiful women, warm weather, beaches—but from the first day he arrived, he'd noticed something terrible in the air as well. It was there in the quiet residential streets of Golf Heights, where mansions hid behind high walls of flowers; in the streets of Curundu, where children and dogs ran out to meet him; and in the dark, twisting, tinderbox alleyways of the El Chorillo slums. Almost like a smell before a storm breaks, he'd thought, or a sound inaudible to humans. Or the lack of a sound. Then he noticed black Mercedeses with smoked windows idling at the edges of public gatherings and marketplaces. He noticed as the summer wore on that the civilian police seemed to be getting more visible and less talkative, a dozen men for each street arrest, always yelling and in a hurry, shoving bystanders away. He noticed that in addition to nightsticks and service revolvers, many of them had new M-16s and AK-47s; and then one day he noticed a group of them had switched from dress uniforms to army fatigues. The next day all of them were wearing fatigues. This is how it happens, he'd thought.

But none of it was real until he noticed the posters. He saw two of them side by side on the wall in the marketplace behind a fruit stand one morning, and then suddenly they were everywhere. *Creamos miedo.* WE CREATE THE FEAR. That's when he realized that power was not about armies and palaces and money, or even machine guns and grenade launchers. It was about the ability to create fear. The rumor of a gleaming black Mercedes idling outside your house each night while you slept—that was what controlled you. It was the whisper of what they were there for and how much they knew and what they could do with their information that could paralyze a family and silence a neighborhood. The little whispers that could not only vaporize opposition but, in the end, bring an entire nation to its knees.

It was getting dark. Buddy came wagging, and Frank put his hand out, moving forward in time to his return from Panama, when he'd heard the first rumors about Rose. She wasn't fitting in, they complained; in fact, in the short time he'd been gone, she'd gone straight from being pitiable to being a public nuisance. She wouldn't go to church, she didn't wear clean clothes or brush her hair, she borrowed money and gave away gifts and napped in public and left her uncle's old junker of a station wagon parked right on Hemming Street like it belonged there. There were rumors she'd offered sex to tourists for money and, with Dick Sweeny losing his wallet, that she might be a pickpocket. Plus she'd shown no interest in marriage yet, or even dating, which made certain rumors about her childhood that much more credible—and despite how it looked, she was still staying alone with the old man up at the Ten Tribes every winter. Frank heard it from the inheritance embroiderers, but he heard it from others too. He heard rumors that stunned and infuriated him, rumors he'd never believe or listen to, no matter who they were about. But he also heard rumors he didn't know how to refute about her irrational moods and public outbursts, her increasing secretiveness and self-imposed isolation. By the time he finally ran into her, he expected to meet a different person.

But she wasn't. She was the same as ever, unpredictable and funny, hard-headed and smart, her laugh clear and clean as ever, her eyes full of life, glad to see him. He'd taken one breath and fallen for her all over again, fallen so hard that if she'd mentioned her two-year-old decision to break up with him—if she'd so much as tried to bring up the subject— he'd have asked her to go out with him again. He'd have begged. As it was, she said nothing about it and, after buying a beer for him at the bar, left to go work on her embroidery. And since he assumed that meant she'd found someone else, he'd let it go. Why? He sighed and looked down, scratching the dog's belly. Because of the rumors about her being too far behind, too unlucky, too damaged, too poor? He'd fought them, denied them, ignored them, hated them—and, yes, he'd listened. That's what towns were all about, neighbors listening to neighbors, people talking to people. That's what held towns together. Rumors. Rose had listened too. That's what had pulled them apart.

He finished his beer, stretched, and went back inside his motel room, hoping to fall asleep early so as to get an early start.

32

When I was young and quite untaught
These letters I with needle wroght
But when Im older and know more
Ill make them better than before.

—from an American sampler, 1808

 It was noon, Austin was on the skyline, and I was so tired I wasn't even sure I was still driving. My plan to stop at a hotel to clean up and call Harmon about our coming had fallen through. Alice was getting worse. For all the bragging she'd done about traveling around the world, now that we were on the road we were just plain lost, lost from anything familiar, and nothing I said was going to change her mind. "I certainly hope we see a boat soon," she kept saying, "because I for one can't even tell which direction we're going anymore, it's so dark out there. Plus, I don't swim." I kept trying to explain that we were crossing Texas, not the Atlantic, but nothing worked, and somewhere just before dawn she saw the sign for San Angelo and flew into a tantrum, trying to open the doors and jabbering about lifeboats for the children.

If I couldn't keep her under control in the car, I couldn't imagine what it would be like trying to keep her quiet in a hotel room. I finally stopped at a gas station, bought a little cup of vanilla pudding with a plastic spoon, and stirred in more Valium. She was so antsed up, she didn't even notice. All she wanted to do was find out where we were and how to get home. I followed her with the pudding as she circled the truck stop, the restaurant, and then a Dumpster, which she seemed to think might have a door to it, and then we went along a pitted side street toward a town until she decided it was the wrong one. Finally she agreed to sit on a stone wall and eat the pudding. Between bites she was crying, hiccuping through her tears that we would never get home, that Florie would never forgive her, that Buddy was gone. As soon as the pudding was finished, though, she lifted her chin bravely, shook my hand good-bye, and set off to find her house again. I threw the empty pudding cup in a bush, took a deep breath, and followed.

It took an hour of walking before she slowed down, and a half hour more before she agreed to go back to the car, but she was snoring before we reached the highway, slumped sideways in the back like a drunk. Watching her in the rearview, I promised I'd never drug her again. I had to get to somewhere fast, though, someplace where she wouldn't have to see so many people she didn't recognize and roads she couldn't remember, buildings that didn't make sense. Harmon would know what to do, he'd have a place where she could stop and calm down, where she wouldn't have to feel like she was lost, where I could tell her we belonged. Otherwise, Valium would be the only answer.

I pulled off the next exit into a 7-Eleven, got a pen and paper from the glove box, and after pinching her hand to make sure that she was asleep, I got out and went over to the bank of phone booths. Each booth had a phone book hanging from a cable and on the front cover of each one was the logo of Harmon's company, same as I'd seen on his business card. It was a good sign. At least it was a start. I looked up the phone company's number, put in a quarter, and after I got the lady to understand that I wanted to visit her business office, not file a complaint, she gave me another number and an address. I wrote it down and turned to the white pages to look up Harmon's home address. There was no Waters listed, not even a Waters, Sr., and that made me feel so seasick for a minute I had to hold on to the edge of the booth—but on the other hand, he said he lived outside of Austin, so maybe he was in another book. Maybe he was unlisted. Since I had his work number, it didn't matter. I picked up the receiver and squinted out at Alice, thinking how I was going to tell him about things and how he'd answer. I did that for a few minutes, rehearsing it one way and another, and then I decided it would be better to hang up and just go get directions to his company instead. Also, more coffee.

The phone company was out past the city limits on the far side of Austin in something called the Lighthouse Industrial Park Complex, which turned out to be four huge black buildings standing around a fresh-paved parking lot full of cars in the middle of nowhere. There was something spooky about it, empty rolling fields for every direction and then these four black high-rises looming up all of a sudden with a kid no older than twenty guarding the whole thing by himself at the front gate. He told me to go to Building Four. I followed a yellow arrow around the cars in the parking lot until I found it, and then I followed the arrow for a place to park. I wasn't sure I'd ever been in a parking lot so full of cars and no people. The sun was bouncing off the fenders and burning everything white, the paving so fresh and black the parking stripes looked as if they glowed in the dark. Maybe it was because I was so flat-out tired, but I felt like I was driving around a parking lot on Mars, like maybe the air would be too thin to breathe or maybe my feet wouldn't touch the ground. Maybe it was because when I backed into a space next to a little white concrete island, the little bushes were being held down by wires.

I scrubbed my face hard with both hands, trying to get some sense back into it, and then got out, leaving the door open so it wouldn't wake Alice, and went to the trunk for a fresh shirt and pants. Since nobody was around, I changed between the cars. I brushed my hair, washed my mouth out with orange juice, rubbed my teeth with my finger, and put on lipstick. Dropping in on Harmon after thirteen hours of driving with no sleep and an old lady drugged in the back seat was not what I'd planned, but he'd have to understand. I'd explain it before I brought him out to meet her. He'd probably get a kick out of it. If nothing else, he'd be impressed by the car. "You got gumption," he'd say. "I like that in a girl." That was Harmon. He liked anything so long as he didn't have to think about it too hard. I unrolled the back windows to give her more air, left the orange juice where she'd see it, and wrote YOU STAY HERE in capital letters on a piece of paper that I folded under her hand and tucked up in her sleeve. "You just get some sleep," I said, "and I'll fix it up with Harmon," and, hoping I was right, I eased the door shut, locked it, and hurried across the lot toward the building where Harmon worked.

The outer glass door gave way to another glass door and inside was an enormous green lobby with a green floor, green couches, and a green circular desk. Even the air was green. It was like stepping inside an aquarium. There was a pale woman, skinny as a bone with black wire glasses, staring at a computer screen. I stood in front of her, but she didn't look up. I leaned over and tapped on the top of her computer.

"I'm here to see Harmon Waters."

I waited.

"Harmon Waters." When she still didn't react, I said louder, "I'm Harmon Waters's sister."

She still didn't move. I couldn't figure it out. I leaned over the desk.

"I'm not here to slit his throat, lady, we just need to talk."

Her hands lifted off the computer keys. "I.D. number?"

I had no idea. "He's a manager. He has a lot of operators working for him."

Her smile was thin. "We have fifty-seven managers and one thousand seven hundred and nine operators in this building. I'll need an I.D. number."

I felt a twitch in the skin under my right eye, and I put my finger on it and turned to the side like I was thinking. When it went away, I turned back. "How about if you just look up his name?"

"My computer doesn't list by name."

"Well, it should."

"It doesn't."

"Then use something that does, why don't you."

Her face hardened and she gave me the fish eye. I felt sorry for her for even trying. I leaned forward and gave it right back until she sighed, blinked, and leaned back in her chair. "Well. I *could* go look in the roster."

"Now we're getting somewhere." I slapped the desk too hard and turned my back to her. I needed to keep hold of myself, keep calm, loosen up a little. Breathe. Beyond the glass doors was a glare of light. It looked sharp enough to cut my eyes. I squeezed them shut, opened them wide, stretched my face to loosen it up, and then turned back to the woman. She'd rolled her chair to the opposite side of the circular desk to look inside a book the size of a sofa cushion. I circled the desk until I was standing in front of her again. She had nails as glossy as the fenders on a car. I read her book upside down, willing his name to be there. It was.

"You see that? I told you he works here."

She gave a pained look, rolled over to her computer, and tapped four keys with the edges of her nails. Her fingers were more at ease with the computer than with the rest of her. She was like an embroiderer that way, her hands with a life all their own.

"Take elevator six in the hallway to your right to the tenth floor, then take the east wing hallway, and it's Ten-thirty-one-A on your right. You'll see his office just inside the door."

I'd taken only one other elevator in my life, the one at Sallye's Dry Goods Store in Madrillas. That one had pink walls, a collapsible metal curtain in front of the doors, a smell like sweat, and a stool for the operator, a bony guy who always nodded hello but never spoke. It crept up to the store's second floor and back down to the sale basement all day long, but it was so slow and creaky that most people preferred the stairs.

Harmon's elevator, on the other hand, was big enough to live in: steel and mirrors with a mush-thick carpet, fourteen floors, and no one at the helm. When I stepped in, I heard music. I pushed ten and the door closed, and the number ten lit up overhead, and the door opened. I pushed the button again, thinking I hadn't gone anywhere. Then I noticed the fake flowers in the space between the two elevators across from mine had disappeared. Also, I heard voices. I leaned out the door and saw a corridor as white as a hospital and a group of fat men in business suits way off at the far end as they let each other through a door. When the door closed after them, it was quiet as death. Everything was white. I felt lightheaded. My uncle had bled to death on a gurney in a hallway like this. I forced myself to step off the elevator and look for where to go next. A little brass sign said EAST WING with an arrow, and I followed that forever until I got to a door with 1031A on it. I opened it wide enough to peek and then slid in.

I was on a metal balcony that extended about twenty feet in front of me and ended at a metal railing and some stairs going down. A big room down below and on the other side, straight across from me as the crow flies, was a metal balcony with two men on it in short-sleeved shirts and ties. They were leaning on the railing, smoking cigarettes elbow to elbow, and if they didn't look up to notice me across the way, it was because there was so much sound between us. A huge hissing sound, a roaring like a waterfall, or a train. Like a bank full of money-changer machines all counting coins at once. I looked around the balcony and then stepped closer to the railing to see over the edge.

It was people, hundreds of them, maybe a thousand, all of them down there in cubicles staring at computer screens, all facing the same direction and talking into little wire mouthpieces. One person typing, one looking at her nails, one scratching his head, one rubbing the back of his leg—all human, all working, but somehow none of them real. They looked like an embroidery, all different bits of colored thread, neat and tidy and stitched into place. I could see they were talking, but I couldn't hear the talk. Not a word. It was just noise, just one gigantic noise of people at work. I could feel it under my ribs. When I plugged my ears, I could feel it on my face. I went back to the hallway door, but it had locked behind me. I turned and saw the only other way out was a door with the name WATERS on it. I couldn't just walk in on him unannounced, I knew that as soon as I saw his name on a brass plate, but I couldn't just stand there thinking about it either. I felt like the noise was pounding against my lungs, like I was going to pass out. I stumbled to the door, pushed it open, and all but fell inside.

His office—white, no windows, a gray carpet, and a black-and-white scribble painting on the wall—must have been as soundproof as a lead-lined coffin, because as soon as the door eased shut it was deadly quiet. My ears rang with it. There was a big desk in the middle with nothing on it but a silver pen, and a small desk in the corner with a computer on it. Also piles of paper, books, coffee cups, and knickknacks. The lady behind the computer had dark red lipstick and a wrinkle like a cut between her eyebrows. She was looking me over hard.

"Are you an operator?"

"How can they survive in that noise? How can they even think?"

"They're on earphones."

"Earphones, sure, but crammed in those little boxes, and nobody to hear you?" I shuddered. "If that's what you call work, good God."

"Are you here to apply for a job?"

"Are you kidding?" She wasn't. I put my hands over my face and pressed hard and then took them away and started over. "I want to talk to Harmon Waters."

"Yes?"

I narrowed my eyes. "I'm a relative."

"A relative," she echoed.

"Yeah," I said, "a relative."

She shrugged. "He's in a meeting. He should be out in a few minutes." She went back to typing. "You may wait if you want."

What I wanted was to sit down somewhere to line up my thoughts again, put them in order the way they were supposed to be. There was a chair in the corner made out of wire, so I went over and sat in that. There was nothing to look at but the secretary. I looked at the door, thought of all that noise on the other side of it, and what it would be like at the end of the day when everybody took off their earphones and left their boxes and streamed out the doors. It would be like watching an embroidery unravel. Maybe they'd just keep talking all the way out to their cars and all the way home. *Wee, wee, wee,* I thought, like that poem about the piggies. I crossed my legs and started swinging the top one. I wasn't hot but I felt sweaty. The clock above the secretary's head said one-thirty. All I wanted to do was leave. The secretary's earphone looked like a piece of black yarn connecting the corner of her mouth to her ear. I judged her to be about forty-five and trying to hide it. I cleared my throat and called over.

"You been working for Harmon long?"

She stopped typing and smiled thinly. "Fifteen years." Then she started again.

"Yeow. That's pretty long. He must be a good guy to work for, huh?"

She kept typing. I crossed my legs the other way, looked around, blew air, and then looked over at the secretary again. Maybe she was listening to something through her earphone. Maybe she wasn't supposed to talk to visitors. I tried to imagine her without the red lipstick and couldn't.

"So how's Harmon's granddad?"

She finished her sentence before she looked up. "Pardon?"

"His grandfather. How's he doing?"

"You'll have to ask Mr. Waters. I don't know about his grandfather."

She went back to work.

"That's funny you don't know about his grandfather," I called. "That's all he ever talked about with me."

When she didn't answer, I walked over to her desk and leaned down so we were eye to eye. I could smell myself. "Can you hear me with that thing in your ear?"

"I most certainly can." She looked shocked.

"How can you work for a guy like Harmon for fifteen years and not know about his grandfather?"

She fixed her mouth back to a smile again. "In this company we have many different jobs. Mr. Waters does his, I do mine. That's the way we do things here."

"Oh." I went to the little chair. Then I went back to her and waited until she stopped typing again.

"It doesn't make any sense, though. Harmon talks all the time to me about his granddad."

She arched an eyebrow. "I'm sure he does." She was still typing.

"Then how come he doesn't talk to you about him? You've been working here fifteen years and you don't know about his family?"

She tapped out a long series on the computer before looking. "Do you really want to know, or are you just trying to piss me off?"

"I want to know."

"All right. Mr. Waters placed his grandfather in the cheapest nursing home I could find out in California and, from what I can tell from the phone calls, he's still alive and Mr. Waters doesn't want me to talk about it. Satisfied?" She went back to typing.

I stared at her hard. "Harmon wouldn't do that. He told me he wouldn't even consider it."

"He not only considered it, honey"—she smiled—"it's done."

I didn't know what to say. "Maybe his grandfather wanted to go?"

She smiled at her computer. "Maybe."

I walked over to the chair and then back to the secretary. "Harmon told me the only person he ever truly loved was his granddad."

"Perhaps that was before Gloria," she murmured. She looked up. "You don't know about Gloria yet, do you? The new wife as of last month. Number four, if I'm keeping a correct count. Now, if you'll excuse me, I have to finish this."

I stood on the sidewalk, confused by the smack of heat in my face when it should have been winter out. I felt like I was about to have a stroke I was so angry, like all the blood inside me was about to boil out my mouth. I started walking as hard as I could. I wound through the cars, hating everything, thinking about the three other buildings around me and how they had just as many people inside them as the one I'd just come out of, and maybe all of them listening to earphones too. I missed the car. I turned and came back the other way. Alice was right, it was like being on the ocean, you could drown if you didn't keep your head up. I walked one way and back and then I was near the door to Harmon's building again. I had to pee but I wanted out of there first. I crossed back and forth looking for the car, mad as hell, hating the goddamn parking lot for being so big and so hot and crowded that I couldn't even find my car. I stood next to a Ford Taurus to pee, hating it all, but as soon as I lowered my pants and crouched, I could feel myself giving way. And how about being stranded with Alice out in the middle of a parking lot in Texas? How about not having a single idea of where to go next or how to get there or what to tell her when she woke up? I pushed it away because it's a waste of time getting pitiful, and when I pulled up my pants, even though I could hardly see anymore, I felt better. I felt like I could find the car anyway, and as soon as I started walking again there it was, right in the middle of the row in front of me.

I stopped to find the keys and wipe my eyes. So I'd made a mistake. We still had the car and we still had money. We could drive somewhere, rent a house or something. We'd do fine. I just had to keep it together, think it out, and not panic. I could do that. I was even giggling a little, because who was crazier anyway? Poor old Alice, whining in the back all night about us going the wrong direction? Or me, deciding just for the hell of it to drive a thousand miles and drug an old lady with sleeping pills so I could ask the favor of a Texan who didn't even have enough faith to take off his hat in bed. Wasn't that rich? I opened the car and climbed in, still giggling and shaking my head, until I craned up in the rearview to see if she was awake. I spun around and stared. The back seat was empty.

I walked around the car, calling. I climbed on top of the car and stood on the roof calling. There were workers' cars in every direction, glistening under the sun, heat waves rising off their hoods. Not a single human being. Nobody to even ask. Wherever she'd gone, I kept thinking, she'd be sleepy and slow. She wouldn't be able to get far before she'd sit down somewhere and go back to sleep. She was probably asleep now, maybe curled up between two cars not a hundred yards away from where I was.

But the longer I stood on the car, turning from one building to the next and yelling *Alice, Alice,* the more I knew what a waste of time it was. All the cars alike, all the buildings, even the little bushes. She'd think she was in some kind of nightmare, the fun house with mirrors, everything familiar gone. I slid off the car and ran for Harmon's building, glancing between cars as I ran, not realizing till I opened the door and saw a red lobby that it was the wrong one. I tripped, caught myself, and started running again, checking between the cars in the other direction, feeling the panic coming on hard and knowing I had to keep it down if I was going to find her. I threw open the outer door of Harmon's building, nearly knocked myself in the face with the inner door, and slapped up against the desk of the bony woman with the black wire glasses.

"Did she come in here? Fuzzy yellowish hair in a blue sweater? Did you see anybody like that?"

The receptionist turned slowly, first her body, then her head, then her eyes, and finally she lifted her hands off the keys. "Excuse me?"

"Yes or no. Did you see anyone come in here?"

"You mean," she asked, "since you left?"

"She's missing. She wasn't supposed to leave the car, but she did. I have to get her back." I hadn't meant to shout it. I put my head down on my arm, and then looked up again. "How about a PA system? You have anything like that? Something that works outside? With a microphone? A bullhorn? Anything?"

The woman was starting to look bewildered. "Would you like me to call security?"

"Yes, security, that's it. Call security."

She turned to the computer, tip-tapped four keys, and lifted the phone receiver. "Shall I tell them you've lost someone?"

"Yes. An emergency. Tell them to hurry. Tell them we need help."

"Mr. Porter?" She turned to the computer screen as if it had called. "This is the front desk of Building Four. I've got a visitor here who says she's lost someone. Female. . . . Yes. . . . I'll find out." She looked up. "How old is the child?"

For a heartbeat, I thought it was somehow in her computer, the list of everything I'd lost. Then I realized and shook my head. "No, lady, this is an old person. You understand? Old. She's lost. I don't know where she's gone."

"All right. Calm down. Let me tell Mr. Porter and he'll get some of his men to find her. Everything will be fine. He's very good."

She was trying to be nice, trying to slow me down, but it was too late. I turned away, put my hand hard to my mouth, and tried to breathe through it, tried to think, but my eyes were filling up again and all I could see was Alice marching off in exactly the wrong direction. I heard the woman hang up the phone.

"I've got to make you understand," I said. I turned to her, trying to keep my voice level. "This person, Alice, she doesn't know what's going on, and it was me who brought her here—so, I mean, I can't just lose her like this. Because the thing is, she needs me, and as a matter of fact"—I stopped, willing my voice to stop seesawing—"I mean, let's be honest here, she's about all I've got left. Can you understand that? You see how it is?"

She answered, but all I heard was the tone of her voice, a soft, gentle tone, the same one all the people at my family's funeral used. It was the sound of pity, the soft insistence on tears so as to allow for the complete and permanent loss of everything. When she came out from behind the desk and touched my arm, I reeled away. I needed to go back to the car, I had to be there when Alice came back, but I couldn't seem to get words out. She led me to one of the couches and told me to sit, and then she came back a moment later and put a paper cup of water in my hand.

"Mr. Porter will be here any minute," she whispered. "You just catch your breath and I'll tell him to hurry again." I tried to tell her, but I couldn't. I couldn't do anything but make awful choking sounds. I took a gasp of air, wiped my face on my sleeve, and made myself drink the water, but all I did was bawl more. I wanted to cover my head and bawl like a baby. I wanted to make up for all the times I hadn't bawled. There was a part of me that kept wanting to say *I'm sorry, this isn't like me at all, there's something wrong with me,* but another part of me knew for the first time

334 • Laura Hendrie

that the game was over. Really over. Everything I'd counted on to hold me in place, everything I'd known as familiar, everyone I'd loved or believed in or tried for. I could give up and let go. In a way it was a relief.

I don't know how long I sat there or when it was that I first felt something brush my foot and then press the top of it. Not hard, just a little weight there. Almost nothing. When I opened my eyes, I thought I was dreaming. It felt like I'd fallen out of the world, like it was true: I'd finally lost hold. I was staring down at a little black-and-white face and it was Buddy, wagging hard with his paw on my foot. Then I looked up and saw Frank.

33

When in love I do commence
May it be with a man of sense
Brisk and arey may he be,
Free from a spirit of jealousy.

—from an American sampler, 1769

He had woken at five, but a flat kept him from leaving before eight, when the garage opened. While he waited for the tire, he paced around the small garage office, staring at the highway and thumbing the magazines. Rose was a good seven hours ahead of him, and though she might've been delayed along the way, what with Alice riding shotgun, she had to be close to Austin by now. If she couldn't talk Harmon Waters into a deal, she'd be gone somewhere else by the time he arrived. And if Harmon did want to take her on? Frank would hand over Buddy, get in his truck, and leave. That would be that. He wondered if Harmon knew she was coming. He doubted it. Rose wasn't the type to warn people before she decided something. He could see her simply walking back into Harmon's life with Alice in tow, and hoping for the best. It made Frank queasy to think of how it might go after that.

But a night of sleep had cleared his head and left him wondering about his own plans on this trip. He couldn't claim to be tracking her as an official duty, not anymore. Nor could he claim she needed help. He hoped to help her, yes, but he had no illusions that she needed him. After all, she'd done everything up to now on her own. She'd done things most people would never have the courage to even think about. So why was he following her? Curiosity? He stood with his hands on his hips, staring at a Penzoil display and listening for the shriek of the air ratchet in the next room. Did he need her to refuse help one last time just so he could finally say good-bye to her with a clean conscience, just so he could know that whatever happened to her, at least he'd tried his best?

But as he turned to the smoke-stained, finger-smeared window, he knew that wasn't true. He was following her because he wanted to see her again. Because he couldn't imagine not seeing her again. And what was more, he didn't even care if it didn't make sense.

He drove hard all morning, and at noon, when he stopped at the edge of Austin for gas, an emaciated teenage girl trying to panhandle told him about a bypass off the interstate that could get him across town to Harmon's phone company in under an hour. Frank repeated her instructions to make sure he had them right and then gave her a twenty, told her to go buy herself a meal, and got back on the interstate. Within a few miles, the route began to splinter into exits on both sides. He was lucky he'd stopped for directions. Had Rose? He saw the sign for the bypass, just as the panhandler had promised, and moved to the exit lane. That led onto a monotonously long strip of car, truck, and farm equipment dealerships, and after ten or fifteen lights, just as he was thinking that taking advice from a half-starved panhandler might have been a mistake, he realized he'd just passed Lighthouse Road, his turn. He blinked hard, telling himself to wake up, and pulled into a used truck dealership, waving *no thanks* to the dealer who started out the door to greet him and pulling back out into traffic.

Lighthouse Road was a fresh black-topped street that led at right angles away from the strip through a bleak neighborhood of low-income tract homes to a four-way stop. From there, the houses gradually gave way to empty dirt lots fluttering with orange survey flags on wooden stakes, and then he was suddenly out in the country again, hills of grass as bright as gold against the blue sky stretching off in either direction. Not a building anywhere. He drove to the top of the next rise and then lifted his foot off the gas and rolled to a stop. This couldn't be right. He must have missed the last turnoff. He cursed at the time he'd wasted, threw his truck in reverse, and backed up on the shoulder to turn around; but as he came perpendicular to the road, he noticed a woman on top of one of the low hills straight ahead. Her back was to him, the wind pulling at her dress and her hand shading her eyes. She seemed to be searching the horizon for something, and though he wasn't aware of knowing why, he stopped what he was doing and waited until she turned toward him. It was Alice.

He backed off the road and got out. The wind was blowing in hot dry gusts. He lifted his hand to wave and crossed the road. He might've missed her completely if he hadn't decided to stop and turn the truck around.

When he stepped into the field, the dirt was like brown face powder, grasshoppers whirring around his feet. Everything about it felt surreal. When he stopped at the base of the hill and looked up, her eyes were the same blue as the sky.

"It's about time you got here," she called. "I've been frantic."

"You okay, Alice?"

"Of course not. I can't find a single thing that's familiar anymore."

"Do I look familiar?"

She looked down at him. "Did we do embroidery together?"

"Kind of." He started up the hill. "Have you seen Rose or Florie," he called, "or anyone like that?"

"Oh, no. Don't start in about her. That damned girl. She stole my dog, you know." She was standing fiercely, chin high to keep it from trembling, tears streaming along the gutters of her face. "As you can see, she's taken my dog and my car *and* my house. I have absolutely nothing."

He'd reached her side. He turned and saw that if he followed the road over the next hill, there was a cluster of dark business buildings. "I'll bet she's over there," he said, offering her his hand. "In fact, she's probably looking for you right now. And your dog is in my truck. Buddy. You want to go see him?"

"That's impossible. Buddy ran away with that cat."

"I guess he came back."

She looked appalled. "That's how you get women in your car, isn't it?"

"I wouldn't invite you unless you wanted to go."

She gave him a wild, panicky look and cried out suddenly, "You can't imagine how *awful* this is! You don't understand what it's like!"

"I do," he said.

She turned rigidly, as if she might start crying, and then banged her fist hard on her thigh, whirled back around, pushed past him, and started down the hill. "We'll just go see who this Buddy person thinks he is."

The guard at the entrance gave them directions, but as they entered the middle of the complex, Frank noticed a security car with a bubble light flashing and, just as he suspected, it led them to the building where Waters was supposed to be. As the security cop got out, Frank pulled up alongside and leaned out the window.

"Any chance you're looking for Alice Pinkston?"

"What the hell's an Alice Pinkston?" A wide, pasty-looking elderly man in a cowboy hat and a mustard-colored jumpsuit covered with embroidered badges turned around. "I'm on a missing persons call. You work here, son?"

"No, but I think I have who you're looking for." Frank swung out of the truck, crossed the pavement to meet the guard, and together they returned to the truck. Alice had fallen asleep with her hands laced over the dog, who was watching Frank, his tail beating nervously against her dress. She was snoring, she was so asleep.

"She's not much at remembering where she belongs these days," said

Frank, lowering his voice so as not to wake her. "She must have gotten turned around. I found her out in the fields over that way."

The guard looked where Frank pointed and then back at Alice. "A few candles short of a cake, huh?" He nodded grimly. "I had a father-in-law last year, same thing."

"I guess it's happening to a lot of folks these days. Anyway, she's okay now. I thank you for your help."

"Help? All I did was drive over here, son. Haven't even talked to whoever reported her missing yet." The guard grinned suddenly, his whole face opening in a wonderful childlike way. "You want to go in with me, find out who filed the report? Just to make sure we got the right person? George can keep an eye on your mother."

It wasn't worth correcting him. "That'd be good."

"George," called the guard, looking over his shoulder to a young man with a terrible complexion in the passenger seat of the security car. "You want to watch this truck, George? Make sure the lady in here don't jump ship again?"

The boy grinned and saluted, an energetic, friendly-looking kid. Frank nodded to him, thinking about his own apprentice with a twang of sadness. Not anger, not even irritation now. Just sadness for who Silas was and what he'd needed from Frank. He ran his hands through his hair as he looked up at the massive black-and-white glass facade; then he reached into the cab, picked Buddy carefully out from under Alice's hands, and followed the security guard inside.

The security guard was a retired military man named Red Porter, and when he realized they didn't know the area or where they were staying, he suggested his sister's motel. "It's close to here, it's cheap, and she don't mind dogs. Plus if you mention my name, you might could get a discount." Frank thanked him and took down the address, glancing toward the rest room where Rose had gone to wash her face. He'd never seen her like that before. Shaking her head and backing away as if he meant to hurt her, as if he were a ghost, her face so twisted and swollen from crying that his first thought was that she'd been physically beaten. If she didn't come out soon, he'd send the receptionist in to check on her. He turned to Red and asked if he could leave his truck in the parking lot overnight.

"No, *no,* son," cried Red, waving him off. "You don't want to do that. They got car thieves circling these lots like vultures. You leave a vehicle sitting out there after dark with an out-of-town license plate, it'll be picked clean inside of fifteen minutes. No, my man George'll park your truck next to the front gate where he'll be working tonight. Just hand him the keys and stand back. He used to be a valet at the Fairmont."

"Good deal." Without looking directly, Frank felt Rose coming out of the bathroom. "We'll be back tomorrow, then, to pick it up." He reached to shake Red's thick pale hand. "Thanks for your help."

Out in the parking lot, he got his bag out of the back, woke Alice, and with some difficulty helped her out of the truck. She was murmuring about her home and leaning heavily against him while he followed Rose across the lot. Rose unlocked the Eldorado and stepped back, holding the dog too tightly against her chest while he settled Alice in the back seat. He popped the trunk and laid his bag on top of a loose pile of women's clothes, seeing in his mind's eye at once what leaving must have been like the night of Birdie's death: the blood, the panic and confusion, the decision to take Alice and leave behind Buddy and her career and everything else she'd ever known. She hadn't spoken a word yet. He didn't even know if she'd seen Harmon. When he asked if she wanted him to drive, she handed him the keys and went to the other side of the car. He watched her stare at the door and then open it and get in. He opened his own side and got in. Alice had already fallen asleep again. The car had a smell to it like warm milk. He adjusted the leg room, checked the rearview, snapped in his seat belt, and looked over at Rose.

"You all right?"

She was holding the dog against her shoulder and staring out at the parking lot. Her face was a blotchy white. He looked at her wrist, crooked over the dog's back at an awkward angle, the way her jaw muscle was working. Maybe she was in shock from thinking Alice was gone. Maybe she didn't know what to say to him about it. She looked as blank-faced as if she'd lost her mind, as if she couldn't actually remember who he was. The thought scared him.

"I'm taking us to a motel so we can all get some sleep," he said. "Rose? I need to know if that's okay."

When she nodded, he put the car into drive and pulled out of the parking space.

The Blue Moon was a white cinder-block building in the shape of a *U*, with the rooms facing a square swimming pool in the center surrounded by a chain-link fence. When Frank asked for three rooms, the woman at the front desk tipped a drawn-in eyebrow toward the car.

"Three rooms for three people. Sounds like an awful lot of room to me. You planning to party tonight?"

"No, ma'am. We just need a block of rooms."

"I don't cater to roughhousing and cars driving in and out all hours. And I don't allow beer kegs on the property anymore, if you're wondering. And there's no air-conditioning. It broke."

"We just want a place to sleep." He paused and then added, "We got your name from Red Porter."

It was as if he'd unlocked her face. "Well, why didn't you say so? For God's sake." She snapped a registration card on the desk. "You work over there in the business park with him or what?"

He picked up a pen. "One of the people I'm with got kind of turned around out there. Red helped us locate her."

The woman craned sideways for another look at the car. "You mean the one sleeping in the back seat?"

"Yeah." He turned to look. "She's pretty tired."

"Memory problems, huh?" The woman clucked in sympathy. "We used to lose my ex-husband's dad all the time. He used to think the Humane Society—that's just around the corner from here—was a POW camp. I can't tell you how many nights we caught him sneaking over there with a pair of wire cutters. Of course, he never found anyone to rescue but dogs, and then he'd just cry and cry. He thought they were eating the prisoners.

It was sheer relief when he finally had his gallbladder operation and couldn't move so fast." She laughed good-naturedly, shaking her head. "I miss him to this day, you know? He made me see everything differently. Tell you what, why don't I put you folks at the back of the courtyard? That way if your mama gets loose again, I'll be able to catch her if you don't. I always wake up when I hear someone sneaking by the office anyway. And especially if I know I got somebody here who thinks like Biggie."

"Biggie?"

The woman patted his arm. "You just need to rest, doll. There's a little shopping center down the block back of here with a grocery store in it if you want to get something to cook for dinner. But look here." She put three wooden blocks on the counter, each with a key attached. "I'm giving you ten, eleven, and twelve, and you make sure to put your mama in eleven. The stove in there doesn't work."

Out in the car, he gave Rose the key to ten. Without looking at him, she got out and walked into the courtyard, the dog looking back over her shoulder. Frank followed in the car and parked in front of the door where Alice would stay. He got out, unlocked her room, and went in.

It was a low-ceilinged pink room, stiflingly hot and smelling of scented disinfectant. There was a kitchenette at the back and a door in the middle that opened onto Rose's room. He unlocked it and leaned in. She was sitting at the edge of the bed with the dog curled against her chest, staring out the door at the car.

"You all right?"

She turned, and for the first time her eyes focused straight on him. "Will you stop asking me that? Yes, I'm all right. I'm fine."

"Good. I'll go get Alice, bring her in."

But when he started to leave, she called him back. "Leave her where she is. She knows the car. All she's going to do is sleep anyway."

"Don't you need sleep too?"

"Not like she does." She gazed back at the door. "I gave her Valium. That's why she can't wake up. I drugged her."

He looked out at the car. "How much?"

"A triple dose." She sounded as if she was in another world. She took a vial of pills from her shirt pocket and tossed it to him. "You might as well know," she added. "I did it once before, too."

He turned the vial over to read the label and let out his breath.

"It's okay, Rose. You don't have to worry about this. This just means a good sleep, that's all."

"Sure, Frank."

"I *am* sure." When she wouldn't look at him, he tossed the vial on the bed next to her. "My wife was taking ten-milligram Valium three times every day when I first met her, sometimes more. Three milligrams of the stuff is nothing. Not even tripled. It's going to be all right."

"How would you know?" She looked at him then, and he noticed the line of sweat on her upper lip and her chin beginning to tremble. "I stole her car, didn't I? Maybe I tried to kill her so she wouldn't talk. That's what they're going to say at the trial, isn't it?" She turned back to the door again. "They're going to say I killed Birdie and stole a car and tried to kill Alice. God."

He stepped into the room and sat on the chair across from her. "So that's why you think I drove all this way? To put you in handcuffs and take you back?"

She turned her face away, her chin jerking hard now. He sighed, leaned back, and wiped his face.

"I'm not here as a cop, Rose. I'm just here, okay?"

She looked at him and looked away, hugging the dog tighter.

"There's a lot you wouldn't believe," he went on, "but it's true. Why don't you sit outside where it's cool while I go get us dinner." He stood. "There's dog food for Buddy in that paper bag I put in the trunk." Then he set the room key on the bureau and left.

He walked quickly, glad to be moving, pulling air in and out of his lungs and moving his legs. One of the delusions he'd been under when he first became a sheriff was that he was going to stay physically active on the job. He'd convinced himself that his father had used the patrol car every day only because of his bum leg, and that he, Frank Jr., could walk where he needed to go and use the car only for emergencies. He even reasoned that the Committee would be happy about saving on gas. Instead, they'd shaken their heads in confusion. Where's that squad car we gave you? they kept asking. Don't you like it? Doesn't it drive right anymore? Your dad, he used it every day. Frank tried to explain and then he tried to ignore them, but they rolled their eyes and then, thinking he was driving a hard bargain, broke down and presented him with a new one. "We just want you happy, son. That's all we want."

But they'd wanted more than that. They'd wanted power. They'd wanted someone to enforce their decisions and legitimize their opinions. Wasn't that what they meant by being a "good" sheriff? Someone willing to give up what he believed? Someone willing to go along with the party line at any cost? He pushed through the glass doors of the store, saw a pile of red plastic baskets by a turnstile, pulled one free, and started down the produce aisle. That's what he'd done with Rose. Maybe he'd protested when the rumors about her grew truly vicious, but the rest of the time he'd gone right along with the party line about her life being nothing more than a tragedy, everything the result of a single moment of chaos she'd had no control over and didn't even want to remember. Telling himself that he could never again see her for who she was but only for what she'd lost. He had done this: he had stopped believing in her. Every time she'd tried to fight her way back to a normal life, every time she'd tried to pull herself up by her bootstraps, he'd been there promoting her as the poor little hapless victim. No wonder she'd told him to get lost. No wonder she felt so unsafe with him now. He lifted a romaine lettuce head out of the bin, shook water from it, and pushed it into a plastic bag. He didn't know how to explain this to her, but he would. Now that he'd found her again, he'd have to explain it all.

34

_____ _____ is my name_
And with my needle I rought the same
And if my skill had been better
I would have mended every letter.

—from an American sampler, c.1630

I was in one of the metal rocking chairs, thinking how orange the sunset was in Texas and how there weren't any customers at this motel, all these parking spaces outside the rooms empty, all these doors with nobody behind them. Everything felt hollow and strange, like I'd been knocked out—that floaty slow-motion feeling when you first open your eyes and maybe you're looking around but you're not really there yet. As he came up, the dog started wiggling and then my arms were empty. I crossed them against me and looked out at the swimming pool. It was like a square of blue had fallen out of the sky, like if I looked up, I'd see a hole overhead that was exactly the same size and shape. I was thinking about this and about the sweat tickling along my hairline, down along my ribs, and behind my knees. It didn't feel that hot out anymore, but the air was so thick. I felt like I was suffocating. I started rocking the chair a little to get a breeze going. It wasn't a rocking chair, more like a nervous bouncing chair, but at least it moved.

"Hey."

He leaned over to pat the dog and then sat in the chair next to mine and put the sack he was holding between his feet.

"I got some stuff for dinner. You like spaghetti?"

"Spaghetti's big with Alice. It's all she ever packs."

"Good. You too, though?"

I shrugged. "Did you know my uncle built a swimming pool before he moved to Queduro?"

"Really?"

I nodded. "Back in Florida. Dug the hole, laid the pipes, gunited the walls, set the coping. I expect he would've built a pool in Queduro if he'd lived longer."

"I believe it." Frank shifted against the metal chair. "He used to scare me a little, the way he could grab onto a problem and then sort of flash all of a sudden on the answer, even with things he didn't really know much about. Remember that time my dad's Ford broke down outside of Madrillas and your uncle told my mom to try tying a cantaloupe to the fuel line to break the vapor lock?"

"I know."

"It worked, too."

I nodded and rocked harder.

"One thing I always wondered," continued Frank, "how come he and my parents didn't get to be better friends."

I shrugged. "I probably bragged about them too much. Bob always listened, but he'd get moody if I went on too long. What he really wanted was just me and Kyle. He just wanted us in his own world so he could shut the rest out."

"He was a great Indian carver, I know that."

"Yes, he was." I stopped rocking and cleared my throat. "I've been sitting here thinking about what you're here for if you're not here to arrest me."

"What'd you decide?"

"That you're here to try to stop me. Only you're trying to be careful."
He looked out at the pool. "Let's go for a swim."

I looked over at him then. "What?"

"I want to get this road dust off and clear my head. Then we can talk."

I stared out at the pool and started rocking hard. "I'm not going swimming."

"Why not?"

"I don't have a suit."

"I know. There was a sporting goods store next to the food market."
When I looked over, he was holding up a dark red woman's bathing suit.
"Think it'll fit?"

I looked back at the pool, shaking my head. "How should I know?
Jesus. I don't buy bathing suits."

"Come on. Get dressed. I'll park the car next to the pool so we can hear
Alice if she wakes up."

Ten minutes later we met at the pool. Frank got in the shallow end, the
price tag still hanging off the elastic of his red trunks. I went around to the
wading pool that led down a few steps into the shallow end and looked at
the water and then over at Frank. I felt wobbly. He went under and pushed
off the wall, and I watched him follow the floor of the pool into the deep
end. The same tawny color he'd been as a kid, and the same shape too,
only larger and deeper-muscled now, glossy and sleek. I looked at my own
body. My breasts were still proud enough, but the rest of me was so
skinny, arms and legs scrawny as bone and skin the color of watery milk.
The bathing suit he'd gotten me was the color of blood. I shook off the
thought that maybe he'd considered this and stepped into the wading
pool. The water felt cold and fresh, much nicer than I expected. I waded
through it to the steps that led into the shallow end; but just as I was about
to slide down into the deeper blue, I realized my mistake, that I couldn't do
this now, not with Frank. I rocked back, lost my balance, grabbed for the
side and sat, my ass nearly missing the edge. I felt ridiculous and stupid,
but I was not going swimming. He could swim all he wanted, but not me. I

tried to look natural where I was, like I'd chosen that place to sit, sweat pouring off me.

He was coming along the bottom of the pool toward me, and when he reached the side I was sitting on, he twisted around and pushed off again. That was Frank, always off in his own world, always testing himself, pushing his limits, everything about him so sure and focused. The same Frank I'd known all my life, the one who lived down the street from me and helped me with homework and argued with me and biked with me and kidded me and swam with me in the quarry; but as he slowed, setting his feet on the bottom to push for the surface, all I knew was that here was a man I didn't know at all, a dark-haired man in a pair of red trunks in a swimming pool in Texas. He broke the surface like an explosion, everything about him big and wide open, gasping for air as he rose out to his waist and then sank back in. I watched him with his back to me, treading water, reaching one hand up to clear his eyes and then turning slowly to look.

"What's wrong?"

I shrugged. "I don't even know if I remember how to swim."

"Of course you do. You used to be a better swimmer than anybody."

When I didn't answer, he laughed. "Come on, Rose. It feels good. It feels good to move."

Then he was waiting, just treading water and waiting, and there it was again, the feeling that I didn't know who he was, that he could've been anyone, a total stranger. It caught my breath. I pulled my feet out of the water and stood, angry and frightened and wanting to tell him off, and instead I walked to the deep end and stepped off. I went straight down, the blood-shocking cold all around me like a promise. I hadn't taken in enough air, but I coiled up and shot off the wall like a torpedo, veering around him to the opposite wall before I came up. I knelt on the bottom and wiped my eyes clear and then looked over my shoulder. He was still watching. When I turned, he was just treading water and watching. He dipped his chin, took a mouthful of water, and pushed it out through his teeth.

"You do still like to swim, then."

"I didn't say I didn't." I turned away, watching my hands, blue-white and long-fingered, gripping the edge. "I like swimming."

"You remember the old quarry?"

I closed my eyes against it but there it was, those hot silent days of August and that green crystal water, our voices bouncing along the stone walls every time we came up, and when we went down under, swooping over the city of granite, dive-bombing the fallen giants, flying around corners and along walls, our lungs crying for air but our control always perfect, our flight effortless, bodies without weight. And afterward, on the warm slabs of rock, spreading our towels side by side as we always had and lying on our backs with our eyes closed, me telling about Bob and the Indians we'd be selling soon, going on about it, talking half to him and half to myself to see how it sounded, just to see if it was real or not, and then that last moment before everything changed, feeling his hand on my wrist and opening my eyes to find him leaning over me.

I dunked under and then came up blowing air and turned. "Not really."

"That's too bad," he said quietly.

I turned to the coping, gripping it with both hands and looking out across the parking lot to the street that led to the highway. Even with my back to him and my eyes open, it was still there, there more than ever, the salty taste of skin and the stone under us and the cool fit of his hand and the whisper of breath against rock, all of that memory there between us again, just by the way he wasn't saying anything. So this is why he's here, I thought. To trot it out one last time, remind me of all the reasons why it still wasn't dead, parade it around a few times, toast it and roast it and maybe even shed a tear or two over it, and then stuff it down my throat, choke me with it, suffocate me with it, bury it in the very deepest part of my stony heart so he'd always know, no matter what happened next, that I wouldn't even be able to draw a breath of air without knowing it was still there.

"I'm getting out," I called. "I'm cold."

"Wait a minute." Then he slid under and started along the bottom, and it was just like a shark coming; I couldn't stand it, I had to get away, get clear of him, wanted to scramble out of the pool and run away. I sucked in air and tightened my jaw hard enough to break it and stayed where I was as he surfaced, not touching me, flicking his hair back and blinking away water. When he reached for the side of the pool, I shrank sideways to give him room. *Now it's coming, now.*

"There's some things you should know," he said, rubbing his eyes with his knuckle. "The first is, my wife disappeared. She's been gone about a month." He took his hand away. "I don't know where she is, but if she comes back, it won't be because she wants to stay with me."

I didn't know what to say. "She's gone?"

He nodded.

"Are you all right?"

"I'm all right."

I looked out across the water. "And that's what you came all this way to tell me?"

"Partly."

When he didn't go on, his eyes burning red with chlorine, I looked out at the pool. "So what's the other part?"

He turned from me, both of us staring across the water. "You know how it is when you're driving?" he said. "How thoughts come up out of nowhere that you don't quite expect and don't hardly remember, but then all at once you do?" I didn't answer. "On my way out here, Rose, one of the things I remembered was a Spanish idiom I learned in Panama back in the days when Noriega was still in power. *Rifa.*" He looked over at me. "You know what *rifa* means?"

I shook my head.

"Yeah, you do. You know more Spanish than I do. Come on."

So sure of himself. "Lottery." I shrugged.

"Yeah, that's the literal meaning. In Panama, though, they translate it as 'lottery time.' It's when everybody knows a change is coming, only it hasn't come yet. It's when everything's still up in the air and anything can happen." I could feel him looking over at me again. "It's when the only thing that makes any sense, Rose, is to do something that doesn't make sense at all."

I didn't like it. The way he was looking, his bright black otter's eyes, beads of water dripping off the ends of his dark hair, the rough of his beard, the blue water lapping at the hollow of his neck. It was like he was waiting for me, trying to make me say something. I ducked under and came up blowing air. "I don't even know what you're talking about," I said. "Are you talking about me or you?"

"I'm talking about both of us."

"Oh, man, that's rich. What'd you do, quit your job?"

"As a matter of fact."

I looked at him, shocked.

"I left things so Silas could take over the badge," he continued. "He probably already has."

"Yeah, right, Frank. You'd quit your job just like that? Walk out on your home, your town, your friends? Everything you've worked for?"

"I would," he said quietly.

I snorted. "And then what? You blow up your future and where to then, Frank?"

He didn't answer. It took me a second to catch my breath, but then I was able to laugh hard. "You'd like to come along with Alice and me, is that it? Head off into the sunset and live off the fat of the land? Christ, Frank. What do you think this is, a vacation? A joy ride, is that what you think?"

"No. This is what I think." He finally turned away then and looked out over the water. "For years now I've watched you trying to fit yourself into what Queduro wants, and all I've seen is them pushing you harder and harder for what you can't give. I think the way they tried to hold down your uncle while he was alive was ignorant, but what they did to you in the name of charity after he died was worse. I also think there's a new kind of greed in that town trying to devour everyone who's not willing to be a part of it. And now, this thing with Bird. They're not going to care what happened. They won't want to hear how he needed you to look after him and how you did. They'll just sew up their own version in living color of who did what to who, so they'll have something to entertain each other with next winter. We both know that. No matter what the truth is, they decide who's got to pay for it."

I turned to him. "You're saying everything backward, aren't you? On the surface, you're saying my best option is to leave, but what you're *really* saying is that if we leave now we'll be letting them win."

"I'm not saying that, Rose."

"Yeah, you are. At least go back for Bird's funeral, right? I mean, how can I leave him to be buried by a bunch of magpies who didn't even care? That's what you're *really* saying. And you know what else? You're implying I'm gutless to run away now. I'm a coward and a fool. A quitter, right?"

"Choosing to quit what doesn't work anymore isn't a mistake."

I growled at him. "And now you're about to tell me my other choice, right? That if I go back there with you, if I do the right thing and give myself up and try to clear my name and hand over Alice, you'll be there to vouch for me. And you will, won't you? You always have in the past. Maybe you'll even put in a good word for me at the trial. That way, I can say you're the same old loyal friend who always tried to help me, and you can say I was a desperate fugitive you finally brought single-handedly to justice. You might even get a medal, Frank. Yeah, that's another choice, isn't it? Matter of fact, now that I've brought it up, it's obviously the only choice worth making, isn't it?"

"That's up to you, Rose."

I couldn't stand his quietness, couldn't stand that nothing was getting to him. I swam out to the middle and then turned, treading water. "All right, Frank. You think I should go back because they don't expect me to go back, right? And it's my town, and I belong there, and heck, I'm not the type of girl to just cut and run, right? I can hear you saying it just like it was pouring out your mouth. But you know what? You're thinking I'm going to fall flat on my face if I try to make a run for it now. You're thinking I'm such a loser I can't survive five minutes without you."

"I know you can survive without me. That's one thing you've made clear right from the beginning."

I turned, went under to feel the water against my face, and came up mad anyway, throwing my hair back. "Very funny, Frank. Ha. Ha. Ha."

"I don't intend it to be funny."

I turned around, treading hard. "Well, fuck you then, okay? Because I think it's hilarious. You think I'm actually going to swallow this crap?"

"It's not crap, Rose."

I started to answer, but I was so mad I got water down the wrong pipe and started choking. I couldn't stop. He caught my wrist and pulled me back to the edge of the pool. I shook him off and grabbed the coping and coughed until my lungs cleared, but then I started crying again, crying at myself for being such a fool, all my life such a fool, all my anger going weepy on me again and for no reason. I turned and put my forehead between my hands, pushing hard into the coping, my breath coming jagged and echoey off the edge of the pool. "I don't believe this shit." I covered my eyes. "Will you at least get out of here so I don't look stupid?"

"You don't look stupid, Rose. You look exhausted. I want you to know——"

"Fuck you. Fuck you and what you want me to know. Don't you understand I don't need to know? I don't need to know anything more about you, understand?" I turned and slapped water in his face, and when he didn't react I rabbit-punched him in the shoulder. "You think life is just so easy, don't you? When something goes wrong, you just say *poof!* and the boo-boo's all better, right? That's how you've always had it, any way you wanted. It's so easy for you to talk about another chance, so easy for you to go out there and get it. You think you can do that for me while you're at it? Pull me out of the gutter, brush the shit off, give me a few bucks, a little pat on the ass for luck, before you walk off and *poof!* I'm the new queen of Egypt? Is that how you think life works?" I turned away again because I couldn't stand the way he was looking at me. I wanted to stop talking, but I couldn't. I closed my eyes and smacked my forehead against the coping. "Well, you're wrong, Frank. It doesn't work like that for people like me. I might look pretty lively to you, I might even still be breathing, but I didn't survive my family leaving me thirteen years ago, and I'm not going to survive you leaving me now. That's what you're say-ing here, isn't it? I'll take you and Alice back to town and then good luck and adios, Rose, I'm off to a new life? Okay. So adios now. Go away. Get lost. I hate quitters like you. Why don't you take your stupid dog and that stupid old lady and your stupid pity and just get out of here. Get out."

Then I was hitting him. I couldn't stop, I wanted to hurt him, sounds coming out of me like a trapped animal, like somebody dying. He let go of the side, trying to block my fists, and we floated out into the middle, both of us treading hard to stay up. He was strong and twice my size, but I was quick, and when I got him square under the jaw he barked in pain, and then I felt his own anger come up and in one move he dunked me and then pinned my arms and then he was shaking me hard and yelling something. When I tried to answer, he dunked me again and then he had me around the neck and started pulling me along, half above water and half under so that I didn't know where the surface was or what was going on. I was crying and choking and coughing up water and trying to hit him, but he had me so that I almost couldn't breathe, and then I felt the bottom of the pool under my foot but he was lifting me up so I couldn't push away and hugging me against him. "Rose," he said. "Please, please, just for once in your goddamn life stop being so bull-headed and listen, will you? I'm trying to tell you. I'm not going to leave. I don't want to leave. Nobody leaves you anymore. You understand?"

He was still talking, and though I couldn't hear the words, I saw Alice pulling herself up to peer at us from the back of the car, her face all disorganized from sleep, her mouth open in a little O, and her hair so soft and fine, thistledown, fine as a newborn's hair, I thought; and I stopped fighting it then and let it come, and it broke over me in a long shudder. I knew, of course, that he was lying, that lots of people I love will have to leave, including Alice. But he was lying for me, lying because he wanted me to believe it, and lying because he wanted to believe it himself, so I cried out for him and grabbed onto him, and when he lowered his head, pressing his mouth to my ear, I felt the warmth of his breath and him whispering to me, telling me he was there.

35

When I am dead and in my grave
And all my bones are rotten,
When this you see, remember me
That I mant be forgotten.

—from an American sampler, 1739

In Madrillas he sold his truck to a used-car salesman, crossed the
street to the bank to cash the check, and walked to Sahd's Army-Navy
Store, which consisted of a Quonset hut with a salvage yard full of bath-
tubs out back surrounded by a fence topped in concertina wire. Inside the
Quonset were long dim-lit rows of wooden bins filled with military mer-
chandise, much of which was pre–World War II, the air full of dust. The
sign over the door said the store belonged to the oldest son, Harry, but it
was still being run by his grandmother, a tiny grim-faced eighty-year-old
built like a box turtle with sharp slow-blinking black eyes and a little stem
of neck you could only see at the back. Mrs. Sahd wore a black wool shawl
and spent her working hours in a red leather chair that was stuck between
the cash register and an old Philco radio. On the rare occasions when she
had to cross the store, she used a walker, stamping polka dots around her

slippered footprints on the dust-softened linoleum tiles. When Frank said good morning, she had to rotate her head sideways to answer.

"Well, look who's here," she said to the floor, her voice a tremulous mew. "I guess the pass to Queduro must be open again, then, is it?"

"Been open for about a month now, Mrs. Sahd. Spring's almost here." He pushed through the knee-high wooden gate and started down the first aisle.

"A mild winter, you say?" she called. "Funny, my grandson kept saying it was a fairly bad winter once it finally got started."

"It was," he called back, "but the highway department has some pretty fancy equipment these days for snow, you know. The pass was only closed for a few days at a time this winter before it opened again. And as long as it's open, all you need is a four-wheel drive or chains."

"Oh, my," she called vaguely. "Isn't that wonderful."

He moved down the aisle and stopped at a pile of army blankets. "You mind if I look through these blankets, Mrs. Sahd?"

"Some of them are in better shape than others. I'll be right there."

"No need." When he saw her making little rocking movements to launch herself, he called louder. "That's all right, Mrs. Sahd. You stay there. I can get it."

"You sure?" she called at the floor. "I don't want a mess back there I'll have to clean up later."

"I'll be careful." When he had two blankets that looked clean and sturdy, he straightened the piles and moved on. There was a bin of tie-downs, but most of them looked worn. He went on to the long glass counter at the back. On the top shelf of the counter, next to an open box of Snickers bars sprinkled with mouse turds, was an engine winch and two pulley hoists covered in a layer of dust so thick he couldn't read the brand names. As he crouched for a better look, he heard the bell over the door and Mrs. Sahd calling to someone else.

"I guess you poor Quedurans are just now digging your way out of the valley for spring, is that right?"

He didn't hear an answer, but when he straightened he saw Ruben

Johnson pushing through the swinging gate into the store. Ever since Ruben had decided to become a crane operator instead of an auto mechanic, he'd been changing: in addition to the bruised-looking bags under his eyes and heavy muscles across his shoulders, he'd developed a nervous flinch to his mouth as if constantly expecting a slap on the head. He'd also gotten his divorce and—perhaps in reaction to that—cultivated a fondness for army fatigues, top to bottom. Frank watched him linger in front of a bin of packaged underwear and then move on to the used army shirts, where he chose one, held it to his chest, squinted at the private's name sewed to the pocket, and then pushed it aside for another. With his short, cannonball-like body, eager-dog eyes, and slow thoughts, there was something likable and sad about Ruben. Frank went down his own aisle until he stood opposite.

When Ruben looked up, he flinched backward. "You're back."

"Didn't mean to scare you."

"Oh, no," cried Ruben, flushing red. "You didn't scare me, Frank. I'm always glad to see you. You surprised me is all. That's all."

"How you doing? Still working hard?"

"Same as always. Can't complain." He swallowed, nodding his head. "Holy cow. I can't believe you're really back."

"I'm back. Say, though, this is a real piece of luck for me, running into you. You're just the man I need."

Ruben flinched again, glancing uneasily toward the door. "I am?"

"Yeah. I heard you were moonlighting for Dick Sweeny last winter. Is that right?"

"I needed a new torque converter for my crane, and Dick was offering cash on the barrel for various jobs." Ruben paused to wipe his mouth with a black hand. "Look, Frank. What he was up to with those padlocks, I didn't ask. I didn't mean to cause any trouble for anyone. I was just doing a job."

"I can understand that."

Ruben looked thrown. "You can?"

"Sure. So did you get your torque converter, then?"

Ruben's face opened with vivid relief at the possibility of an easier and far more interesting subject. "I did, and she's working like a dream now, Frank, you should see. That's why I hitched a ride here this morning, so I could drive her home this afternoon."

"Your crane's here? In Madrillas?"

"It's over in Betty's driveway. I blew another hydraulic last month, and I couldn't afford to drive it back to Queduro, so I just parked it there. That guy Betty's with now, he's been pretty nice about it. Anyway, I'll be in business soon enough now. Did I tell you what I'm going to call myself, Frank? The Get It Up Company."

"You did tell me that. I like it. I guess with all the time and money you've put into that crane, you must be about ready for it to start paying you back, huh?"

"Oh, man. You can't even know——" Ruben's voice went suddenly thick, so that he had to look away, laughing roughly and cracking his knuckles. "I figure once the contractors start hearing about me, I'll have a chance to start catching up. I sure as hell hope so."

"I'll bet you do fine. You still doing odd jobs in the meantime, though?"

Ruben's face fell again. "Some, I guess. Just till I get my bills paid off."

"What kind of work has Sweeny got you on these days?"

"These days?" Ruben had a nervous habit of cracking his knuckles, and he was doing it now, his eyes flicking toward the front door. "I guess I've been doing work for him up at the motel."

"At the Ten Tribes? What kind of work?"

"Painting. Gutters. You know."

"Ah. You must be the one who hauled away the tree." Frank paused. "That's kind of strange, though, don't you think? That Dick's got you bucking up trees and painting buildings on property that isn't his?"

"I wouldn't know about that, I guess."

"Yeah, I wouldn't either."

Ruben looked flustered. "I got bills mounting up, Frank. Big bills. You can't even guess what it costs to get a crane going. Sweeny tells me what he wants, so I do it. I'm just trying to survive. I'm not doing nothing wrong. You ought to be talking to him if you got questions, not me."

"Hold on, Ruben. You don't understand. I've got something heavy that needs moving." He let this sink in a moment before he went on. "I thought I might be able to use a come-along, but I realized as soon as you walked in the door how perfect it'd be if I could just hire you and your crane instead. I'll pay well, Ruben. Cash."

For several seconds, he couldn't seem to figure out what to say and then he burst into a wide grin. "Well, shitfire. What needs lifting? The other day while my ex was at work, you know, I put a couple slings around her boyfriend's trailer and picked it clear off its foundation. And after I set it back down and went inside to check? There was a glass of juice on the coffee table, not so much as a drop spilled."

"Sounds like you can handle this job then, no problem."

But Ruben's grin was already fading. He looked away, wiping the insides of his wrists together. "You know what, though, Frank? I just realized I'm awful goddamn busy. I got a schedule you wouldn't believe. I'd like to help you out, honest to God I would, but maybe I better not. At least not right now. No. Better not. Sorry."

"What's wrong?"

"Nothing," he cried. "Just too much on my plate already." He flushed straight to the collar and blew on his hands again. "Fact is, I should get going instead of goofing off like this." He grinned unhappily and started toward the door. "I'm not saying anything about you, Frank. I've always liked you. I'm just—well, I got this job with Sweeny, like I said. Plus I got to recondition the county's plow for next winter, and business at the garage is going to start picking up any day now that the tourists are coming back, all kinds of cars there I'll probably have to fix. And summer, you know how crazy that gets—"

"Hold on." Frank came down the aisle until they stood opposite each other again. "What if I offer to pay twice what Sweeny's paying? Plus a full tank of gas for the crane. How would that be?"

Ruben looked trapped and miserable. "Goddammit, Frank. What're you doing to me? If I come to work for you, I'll be slitting my own throat."

"What do you mean?"

Ruben's eyes widened in disbelief. "Don't you know? All hell's broke loose. You're not even sheriff anymore. Silas K. took over your job on account of he says you helped to murder Birdie Pinkston and get his sister kidnapped. You're a wanted man. He said so at the funeral last night. I'd be a fool to come work for you."

Frank's heart fell. "Bird's funeral was last night?"

Ruben stopped, uncertain. "Didn't you know?"

"You're the first one from town I've seen. Was it all right?"

"I guess." Ruben sighed. "Considering nobody wanted to cough up money for it except Eli Sanchez, and his wife wouldn't let him."

"But I left five hundred bucks with Silas for Bird's funeral," said Frank. "I left it on my coffee table with a note where he'd find it when he came for my badge."

Ruben gave a delicate shrug. "Maybe Silas thought you were offering to buy his silence."

"Is that what he said?"

"No. He didn't mention any money at all."

"That damn little weasel. I ought to ring his neck. . . ." Frank stopped and refocused on Ruben. "So who ended up paying for the funeral?"

"Sweeny. He's going to reimburse himself off the profits from Ten Tribes this summer."

"Ah. That's why he's got you fixing up the place. He thinks he's earned the deed to it."

Ruben shrugged. "It's work, Frank. When I get work, I don't ask why."

"All right, Ruben, *I'm* offering you work now and better pay than you'll ever make with Sweeny. Plus a chance to get your crane business off the ground. You want that, don't you?"

Ruben looked glum. He stared at his feet and then at the door. "The way my luck's been running lately, Frank, the minute I start working for you, I'll get blackballed by the Committee *and* arrested by my own ex-brother-in-law."

"No, you won't. Silas has a big story to tell and I'm sure he's keeping a lot of people entertained with it, but now that I'm back he's going to have to rethink his version of what happened. He knows it, I know it, and you know it."

Ruben rolled his eyes ominously. "You haven't seen him since he started calling himself a sheriff."

"Well, all we can do is hope, right?"

"Oh, goddammit, Frank, I'm sick of hope." Ruben sighed again. "It's about all I ever do anymore."

"Come on, Ruben. I need a crane operator and a crane. What do you say?"

Ruben pressed his temples with two stubby black fingers. "I'm tired. I got a hell of a headache."

"Tell you what. I'll go make one phone call, and if everything's okay, I'll hire you just for today, pay your fee up front, plus a hundred bucks to show good intent and a tank of gas for the crane. And if you don't want to use your crane for what I have in mind, I'll still pay for your time and you can drive away a free man." Frank took out the money from the sale of his truck and thumbed a hundred-dollar bill off the top. "Interested?"

Ruben let out a troubled sigh. He was.

For tourists heading north, Madrillas is the last chance for fast food, modern gas stations, and clean rest rooms before the mountains take over, and that morning the main avenue was bristling with RVs, campers, trucks, and convertibles with out-of-state plates. Frank and Ruben walked two blocks and turned onto a street draped with weeping willows that ended in the entrance to the trailer park where Ruben's ex-wife, Betty, lived. Frank could spot the boom of the bright yellow crane from several hundred yards away, jutting out from the line of trailers. As they got closer, he saw the words *Get It Up* painted in large flame-red italics along the length of the boom. Also on both cab doors, both bumpers, all four hubs, and the hood.

"Good God, Ruben. You've built yourself a monument."

"Still got to grease the zerks," muttered Ruben, but he was proud. Without waiting to be asked, he started on a full tour of the crane, explaining what worked and what needed work, opening the hood to show the problems he'd run into and the tools he'd used, the parts he'd replaced and the parts he'd decided to trust. Frank began to realize that unless he interrupted, Ruben was likely to pick up a tool and start working on the engine. He held up his hand to stop an explanation about the differential, but Ruben went on, sliding under the truck before Frank could stop him to explain how he'd dealt with the corrosion. Frank looked down at the thin grease-smeared fatigues, the glimpse of pale flesh above work socks that had once been white, and the battered black Keds with broken laces. Not exactly a saint, thought Frank, but there was something both lonesome and honest in the way Ruben believed in work that made his other sins forgettable.

"Ruben," he called, "sounds like the only thing she needs now is a maiden voyage. Am I right?"

The little man slid out from under the truck, peered up at Frank, and then, with a solemn nod, wiped his mouth and got to his feet. "I'll just tell Betty we're leaving, then."

He stashed his creeper on the back of the truck and went to a pale blue house trailer with a flower box of upturned beer bottles hanging off the window. He ran his hand over his hair, climbed the cinder-block steps, knocked softly on the door, and then opened it and leaned in. Frank didn't hear what he said, but he heard Betty's answer: "You think I give a shit what you do with that fucking money-eater? Just get it out of here."

Ruben shut the door as if it might shatter and hurried back to Frank. "All set." He crawled into the cab, his jaw moving as if he were working something out from behind his teeth. When the engine started, it was a gigantic, guttural sound.

"Purring like a cat, ain't she, Frank?" he shouted.

It took Frank a moment to realize that Ruben meant his truck. "Like a cat," he shouted.

Ruben gave a little delighted laugh, shut the door, and unrolled his window. "So where's this job?"

The diesel was very loud. "Let's head toward Queduro." Frank shouted. He went around the cab, swung up inside, and settled himself, arranging the army blankets at his feet and unbuttoning his coat. When he looked over, Ruben was watching dolefully.

"You riding with me then, Frank?"

"Have to!" he shouted. "Sold my truck this morning."

Ruben nodded, turned to the windshield, and turned back. "You going to need a ride home when we're done here, Frank?" he shouted. " 'Cause those back streets in Queduro are hell to maneuver with a vehicle this size. Plus my reverse don't always work."

"Once we're done," shouted Frank, "I'll catch a ride home with Rose."

The name seemed to sink Ruben like a heavy stone. He stared out through the windshield with such a look of dismay that Frank laughed.

"You want to know what's going on, Ruben? I'll tell you if you want."

"No!" Ruben shouted. "I don't want to know. I don't want to be told nothing, I don't hear nothing, I don't want to even talk about it. Don't even look at me funny. Understand?"

Half an hour later, when Frank said to stop along the shoulder of the highway, Ruben didn't ask why. When Frank said they'd need to wait a few minutes, Ruben merely shrugged and looked at the view. It was not until Frank said they were waiting for Rose that Ruben looked as if he might burst into tears.

"I *told* you I don't want to know," he cried. He leaned forward and shut down the engine. "I'm not saying she's a bad person, Frank, but if there's anybody in Queduro who's got worse luck than me, it's her. Plus, she's a fugitive, which means a shitload of trouble whether she's guilty or not. In fact, I seem to be working for *two* fugitives all of a sudden, so goddammit, Frank, if we got to sit here together, I'd just as soon we forget about talking, if that's all right with you."

They unrolled their windows and sat in silence. Ruben bucked forward, squinting into his side mirror. "What the—" He turned, his face twisted in disbelief. "The one stolen car in the whole county that nobody can miss even with their eyes closed, and you're letting her *drive* it?"

Frank looked in the sideview mirror and opened his door. "Do you want to know what's going on, Ruben?"

"No," said Ruben vaguely.

"It might help."

"*No!*"

"Okay. I'll be right back."

He got out, motioned for Rose to park on the inside of the curve up ahead, and then followed on foot, Alice watching him openmouthed through the back window. She and Rose had gone shopping the day before in Albuquerque and they were wearing the results, Alice in a pink square-dancing dress, Rose in a blue wraparound and a pair of oversized sunglasses, her dark red hair shining and arched back like a rooster's tail. He leaned to the window.

"How'd it go?"

Rose shrugged. "We were in and out of that office in five minutes flat. I've never seen anyone talk so fast in my life. I'm still trying to figure out what he said, but I guess it's all settled."

Alice leaned forward from the back seat. "*I* know exactly what he said."

"Good." Frank glanced back at Rose. Her color was high and she was holding the steering wheel as if she expected the car to start bucking, but she seemed all right. He was sorry he couldn't see her eyes to be sure. "That dress looks great on you, Rose," he said. "How do you feel? I mean, about this."

"All right. I don't know. I think all right."

"You still want to do it?"

"Yeah." She pushed her sunglasses back up her nose with one finger, jutted her jaw toward Ruben, and then up at Frank. "You need help over there?"

"No. Ruben's a good man. You can wait here if you want."

"I don't know what I want." She turned to Alice. "You want to get out, Al?"

Alice leaned forward to study the situation, her fingers absently spidering along the silver piping on the skirt of her dress. "I don't think so."

Rose looked up at Frank. "Maybe we'll just sit here for a while."

"Fine." He reached in her window and slipped his hand around her wrist, felt her pulse racing between the thin bones. But she smiled and cocked an eyebrow at him and he knew she was all right. "No matter how everything works out, Rose, this is the best idea you've ever had."

"We'll see. Go help Ruben."

He walked back to the truck. Ruben had one foot propped on the passenger step-up. He was cracking his knuckles, and his forehead was knotted with anger.

"I've had enough bullshit, Frank. I may need money, but I'm no criminal. I got a right to know if I'm about to break the law, don't I?"

"We're not breaking the law, Ruben. I promise."

"Then what're *they* doing here? What are we doing here?"

"Setting the record straight." Frank pointed toward the car. "You see Alice Pinkston over there? That means her car wasn't stolen and she wasn't kidnapped. We're just coming back to Queduro. That's all we're doing. We're coming back and we're going to explain that to Silas and anyone else who's interested."

Ruben's glare diffused while he thought about this. Then he looked up at Frank again. "How come we stopped out here in the middle of no-fucking-where to talk about it, then, Frank? Who're we hiding from?"

"Nobody. Not anymore. In fact, we're standing right out here in broad daylight, aren't we?"

Ruben switched his gaze to the view and started cracking his knuckles again, moving down them methodically as if testing spark plugs, all ten including thumbs. Then he looked up again. "If we're not hiding out here," he said, "what *are* we doing here, Frank?"

Frank nodded and stepped to the guardrail. The mechanic hesitated and then stepped up beside him.

"Rose's Indian is down there. The one she and her uncle carved back in 'eighty-four."

"You mean the big wooden Indian? The one in the accident?" Ruben leaned over the guardrail, his face opening in wonder. "I always wondered where it happened. Yeow." He leaned farther, shading his eyes with one hand. "Long way down, idn't it."

"Yeah, it is."

"I don't see any Indian down there now."

"My dad and I moved it after the funeral. It's over there to the right. Behind that set of rocks."

Ruben grunted thoughtfully and then turned to Frank. "You want me to lift that thing up here with my crane, Frank?"

"That's the idea. Think you can handle it?"

The question seemed to physically expand Ruben around the chest. He leaned sideways to spit over the guardrail and then looked back up at Frank in artless disgust. "I got three hundred foot of cable and a brand-new torque converter. I can lift half a ton straight out horizontal. You're asking me can I handle one lousy wooden Indian?"

"Actually, just the head of the Indian. Maybe two hundred pounds or so. I figure if we wrap it in the blankets I bought, it won't get too banged up on the rocks."

But Ruben was already shaking his head. "Blankets mean slippage. Besides, it's not necessary if the boom's positioned right, and I do that with the push of a button." He hitched his pants. "This thing have any neck and shoulders left to it?"

"We cut it off about here." Frank made a cutting motion along the top of his chest, a ghost slipping through at the end of his finger.

Ruben nodded. "Two slings'll be plenty."

"The thing is," said Frank tentatively, "it's a pretty delicate job. He's wearing a war bonnet that's huge—four, maybe five foot across—and each feather's been separately carved. Some of them are broken, but the ones that aren't—I mean, that's why I thought padding with the blankets might be a good idea." When Ruben gave him a strained look, he added, "Of course, you're the expert here, but maybe we could use a couple more slings than usual? Just to be on the safe side?"

Ruben began to laugh then, a clean belly laugh that echoed back up to them from the ravine. "God in heaven!" he cried. "That thing fell off a car, got dragged by a semi, killed four people, and soared off a two-hundred-foot cliff, and you're worried about it being delicate?"

Frank laughed sheepishly and nodded. "You have to see it, Ruben. Then you'll understand. That's all I can say."

"Okay. You package it up in all the slings you want. Satisfied?"

"Thanks."

Ruben looked back at his crane and then leaned over the guardrail, nodding to himself. "All right. Good. Then what?"

"We'll have to make a couple of stops on the way, but if everything goes according to plan we'll end up at the motel in Queduro."

Ruben's forehead twitched back, and he turned to look up at Frank in astonishment. "You're planning to set that goddamn thing on the roof of the Ten Tribes."

"After we get rid of the Committee's neon Indian that's there now, yeah. Rose and Alice are hoping to open the motel by the end of this week." Frank paused, glancing down with satisfaction at the confusion on the little mechanic's face. "It might take a little more time than that, though, clearing up legalities."

"Legalities," repeated Ruben. He swung his gaze back out at the view. "Jesus Christ, Frank, you just promised me everything here was legal."

"It is. You know what a power of attorney is?" Ruben didn't answer. "Well, I don't either," Frank continued, "but I do know that as of this afternoon, Rose is the only one in town who holds one for Alice, and Alice is still alive. Which means Dick Sweeny's going to have to learn to stick to Committee meetings instead of trying to take over motels that aren't his. And Silas may even have to review a few lessons about honesty and respect." Frank paused, waiting for the anger to drain back out of his voice. "It might help if you want to explain that to them next time you see them. Though if you're uncomfortable about it, I'm sure Rose can do it. She'll probably do it anyway, knowing her. But you know what I think, Ruben?" He rested his hand affectionately on the small man's massive shoulder. "I honestly think that if you can do a good job here, we won't any of us need to explain anything to anybody. All we have to do is get Rose's Indian head up and drive it through town on the back of your truck to the Ten Tribes."

Ruben look dazed. "That's it?"

"That's it. Assuming, of course, we don't get lynched."

"Lynched?"

"Just kidding. Your crane is going to make history. People are going to be watching. They're going to be calling neighbors and gawking out doorways and windows and crowding onto Hemming just to see your crane go by with Rose's Indian. I'll bet every single person in Queduro who's still alive is going to be there."

Ruben chewed his lower lip while he thought. After several long moments, he pointed his chin at the Eldorado. "So if those two are in charge, how come they're not getting out of the car?"

"I don't know." Frank looked over at the car. "Maybe they're talking. Rose has her own way of doing things. You'll find that out." He looked back at Ruben. "So, what do you think? You ready to take over now?"

Ruben was searching Frank's face. "You trust me, Frank? You trust me and my machine?"

"I do."

"All right." He hitched his pants and turned to the view. "I'll send you down the cliff on the end of the cable, then."

"What?"

"I've got a reputation to build. You said so yourself." He went to the back of his crane to unbolt the boom and then went to the cab to turn on the engine, a sudden enormous sound. With a precision that reminded Frank of an enormous mosquito preparing for its first meal, the outriggers floated into position and planted themselves on either side of the truck. Ruben swung out of the cab with the remote control in his hand.

"Ruben," shouted Frank, "maybe it would be better if I scrambled down that cliff my own way."

"Sorry, but no, Frank!" Ruben shouted. "When people hear you rode down that cliff on my cable, they might just think I got a crane worth hiring. Even if you're not a sheriff anymore. It's going to be something else they'll want to hear about anyway. Now step off to the side there while I check to make sure my remote's working right."

You're certainly in a grumpy mood. You're as cross as two sticks."

"No, I'm not. I'm watching."

"Watching what?" She waited. "What are those men doing behind us?"

"You have eyes. Turn around and look yourself." When she wouldn't, I said, "They're figuring out how to get the Indian up. I told you that."

She turned to look. "I don't see any Indian over there."

"It's down below. They're going to bring it up."

"Is that so," she said. "And what's the Indian got to do with me?"

"It's a long story." I glanced at Alice and saw her gathering herself for the next question. "If you don't remember it, it's okay. You're probably better off."

Frank and Ruben were standing where my mother and Kyle had stood. Ruben was fiddling with something in his hand while Frank turned to the guardrail, ran his hand through his hair, and leaned out over the edge. It made my teeth hurt, made me want to push him back. Alice sniffed and turned to face the front of the car again.

"*I* don't want another Indian, and neither does Buddy, thank you very much. As a matter of fact, I was planning to get rid of that nylon one."

"You mean the neon one. I know. We already talked about it."

"We did?" She paused. "Are you sure?"

"I'm sure." I watched Ruben look up, and then the boom started to rise. It rose till it was aiming straight up, like a finger. Ruben and Frank stepped behind the cab where I couldn't see them.

"Well, I'm going to get rid of it anyway," she went on. "It's too much electricity and my brother can't afford it. And it makes that humming noise at night when I'm trying to sleep. I hate that hum. I *hate* that hum. I absolutely—"

"Okay, Alice. That's another reason we're going to take it down. Be quiet a minute, okay?" Ruben had appeared at the side of the cab coiling up handfuls of white ropes and tying them together. He stepped to the guardrail, and with a sickening toss that took my stomach, the loose bundle flew out over the edge and disappeared. I closed my eyes but it was too late.

Alice was talking again.

"What?" I said.

"Are you saying this other Indian isn't going to hum at all?"

"Yeah."

"What's it do then?"

"It's just a message. That's all."

"A message about us?"

I opened my eyes again. "About us coming back."

Frank had stepped over the guardrail and was waiting there against the sky while Ruben lowered the hook at the end of the cable to him. He took it in both hands to guide it lower, stepped on it, and then nodded, and the hook lifted him off the ground and swung him out over the edge. I shut my eyes but it was all right. He wasn't falling. Even when he began to sink a moment later, he wasn't falling. He looked over at me and grinned as he went down, but it was a tight grin. His black hair was moving in the wind. He sank behind the guardrail, and I had a glimpse of his face between the guardrail and the road, and then he was gone. I realized Alice was talking again.

"What?"

"I *said*, what are we coming back for?"

"To prove we don't go so easy."

Ruben was at the guardrail with his hands on his hips. His black hair cut against the iron sky and the rest of him against mountains that rolled like green and white waves, all the way to the horizon, like a picture postcard cut in half by the cable and then fitted back together. I thought about how I'd stopped here in front of this view only once before, but how many times I'd been here in my dreams since.

"Alice? In a way you and I are the family that's left from the accident." I glanced at her. "We both survived it."

"What?"

"We survived."

"Well, of course we survived," she cooed to Buddy who lay splayed on the seat. "Everything survives."

I was watching Ruben. The spool on the crane had stopped moving, and he walked over and shut down the engine. A part of me wanted to get out and go to the edge to look, but the best I could do was lean over to open the passenger window. The air was thin, the way it always is in the high mountains when an engine quits. Somewhere a bird sang three notes and then it was quiet. Too quiet. If Frank was making any noise down in the ravine, I couldn't hear him. Ruben cupped his hand to his mouth and bent over the guardrail to call down into the ravine—*Frank*—his crack showing just above the top of his pants. I shut my eyes, willing him to hear an answer.

"Keep talking, Alice."

"What?"

Ruben lifted his hand again—a remote control, I realized—and the end of the boom above his head began to drop slowly. When it was pointing at the horizon, it stopped.

"Just keep talking," I said. "What do you mean, 'everything survives'?"

"As long as you remember a thing, it can't die. That's why God gave us brains."

"Does that go for remembering people too?"

"Of course. People especially. People can go on forever, as long you remember them. The end of the story, that's where it starts. My mother used to say that all the time."

She sounded pleased with herself. I glanced at her over the top of my sunglasses. Just over her right shoulder, Ruben was cupping his hand to his mouth again and shouting over the guardrail: *What?* I strained for Frank's answer, but instead I heard a car coming. I turned as a red Wagoneer with a canoe strapped to the roof came around the corner. It was hurtling by, a man and woman up front, two kids in the back, all in capless sun visors, turning their heads to the Get It Up as they passed and then disappeared around the next bend. Alice twisted around to glare after them, the edges of her fingers following the edge of Buddy's ear.

"I don't like tourists, I know that."

"You're going to have to like them. We have a motel to run."

"They come out of nowhere," she said to the window. "They look around like they own everything, but they don't. They don't even belong. And they won't remember anything for us. They won't." She turned back angrily, crossing her arms. "If you ask me, they're just a big hole in the world."

"Fine," I said, returning to Ruben out the back window. "What do you want to do then, Alice, turn the motel into a concentration camp? A boy scout camp? A boardinghouse?" I glanced at Alice. "What about a boardinghouse?"

"A what?"

I'd meant it as a joke, but there it was. "It's like a second home for locals. It's like what your brother used to do for me every winter. We offer meals and a cheap place for working people. We stay open year-round." It sounded possible. Without the Committee's neon to pull tourists in off the highway at night in summer, we'd have to do something extra in winter to make ends meet. I looked at Alice. "What do you think about a boarding-house, Alice? You think that would work?"

"I have no idea what you're talking about."

"If we call it a boardinghouse, we won't have to be half so care-ful about you. You could say anything. Fix the roof, change the fuses, put on your coat, clean up your act. Anything. In a motel, you have to play the game the right way so the tourists can come and go without anything personal attached, but in a boardinghouse everybody has to get along together, same as they do at home. I mean, you could be right out in front, giving everybody what-for. You could be the boss. The queen of the Ten Tribes. Would you like that?"

She puffed. "They certainly need to fix the roof. I know that much."

We were quiet, me thinking and watching Ruben. He'd been pacing in front of the guardrail before but now he was just standing, looking down into the ravine. Alice cleared her throat.

"Do you mind if I ask you something personal?"

Ruben jammed his fists suddenly against the small of his back as if to stop a cramp there and leaned over the ravine. He looked up at the boom and went over to the truck. Then the engine started again and the cable started rolling onto the spool.

"What's that?" I said.

"That man this morning. He was Mr. Max, wasn't he?"

"Yeah."

"And the paper he had me sign. That means my memory is failing, isn't it?"

"All it means is I do the remembering for you if you want. That's all it means."

"I know." But she was still looking at me, shaking her head. "I just wish I knew who you were. Why are you here? What do you get out of all this?"

"You'd be surprised." I looked past her shoulder at the view that in some ways, no matter what I did or where I went or who I became, would always hold me and my mother and Kyle and Bob together. Alice was right. What you remembered, survived, and what survived, you would always remember.

Ruben turned suddenly and started waving, and then I realized he wasn't waving, he was pointing with both hands at the ravine below the guardrail.

"Look, Alice," I said, "here it comes," and we both turned to the back window, Alice with her face already going dark, already forgetting why, as the first feathers of Bob's Indian rose slowly into view.